KNIGHTS TEMPLAR

THE LAST
EMIR

by S.J.A. Turney

1st Edition

For Fagi,

Who strives to preserve the vital from

the dangerous

Published in this format 2018 by Victrix Books

Copyright - S.J.A.Turney

First Edition

Also by S. J. A. Turney:

The Damned Emperors
Caligula (2018)
Commodus (Coming 2019)

Tales of the Empire
Interregnum (2009)
Ironroot (2010)
Dark Empress (2011)
Insurgency (2016)
Emperor's Bane (2016)
Invasion (2017)
Jade Empire (2017)

Templar Series
Daughter of War (2018)

The Marius' Mules Series
Marius' Mules I: The Invasion of Gaul (2009)
Marius' Mules II: The Belgae (2010)
Marius' Mules III: Gallia Invicta (2011)
Marius' Mules IV: Conspiracy of Eagles (2012)
Marius' Mules V: Hades Gate (2013)
Marius' Mules VI: Caesar's Vow (2014)
Marius' Mules VII: The Great Revolt (2014)
Marius' Mules VIII: Sons of Taranis (2015)
Marius' Mules IX: Pax Gallica (2016)
Marius' Mules X: Fields of Mars (2017)
Marius' Mules XI: Tides of War (2018)

The Ottoman Cycle
The Thief's Tale (2013)
The Priest's Tale (2013)
The Assassin's Tale (2014)
The Pasha's Tale (2015)

For more information visit
http://www.sjaturney.co.uk/
or http://www.facebook.com/SJATurney
or follow Simon on Twitter
@SJATurney

The Praetorian Series
Praetorian – The Great Game (2015)
Praetorian – The Price of Treason (2015)
Praetorian – Eagles of Dacia (2017)
Praetorian – Lions of Rome (Winter 2018)

The Legion Series (Childrens' books)
Crocodile Legion (2016)
Pirate Legion (2017)

Short story compilations & contributions:
Tales of Ancient Rome vol. 1 - S.J.A. Turney (2011)
Tortured Hearts Vol 2 - Various (2012)
Tortured Hearts Vol 3 - Various (2012)
Temporal Tales - Various (2013)
Historical Tales - Various (2013)
A Year of Ravens (2015)
A Song of War (2016)

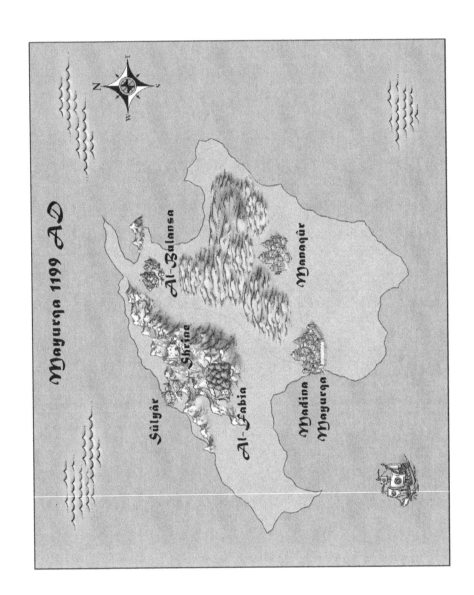

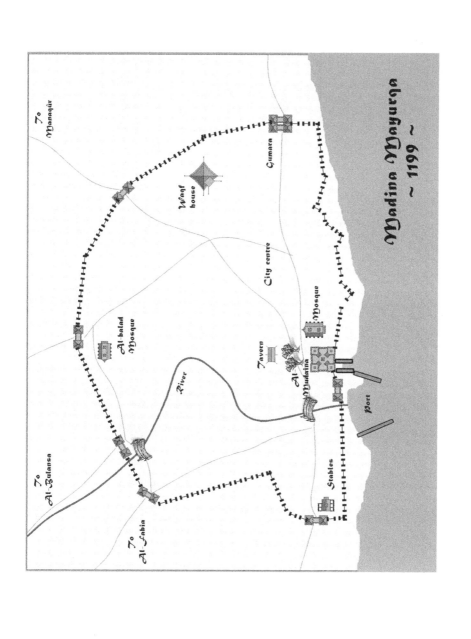

Madina Mayurqa
~ 1199 ~

AL-ARAK – THE PLAIN OF ALARCOS – NORTH OF THE GUADIANA RIVER, CENTRAL SPAIN, THE BORDER BETWEEN THE MOORISH CALIPHATE AND THE CHRISTIAN KINGDOM OF CASTILE

18 JULY 1195

Abu Rāshid Abd al-Azīz ibn al-Ḥasan sat astride his horse, sword gripped tight in mailed fist, eyes narrowed. They had suffered stronger setbacks over the first three hours of the battle than he had ever expected. The Christian knights had charged from the slopes beneath their castle and had smashed into the front lines like some great demon, sending men to heaven in droves, crushing the Berber volunteers and the other mercenary tribes. They had pressed on like an armoured dragon, their cursed cross pennants snapping in the breeze, climbing the lesser slope upon which the command unit of the vizier stood.

Abd al-Azīz had watched with growing hate and the ever-increasing urge to charge as the powerful infantry of Al-Andalus were smashed and put to flight, and his rage had peaked when the great vizier himself fell to a Christian sword. That the Arabs under Yarmun ibn Riyah had begun to flank and enclose those rabid Christians was little consolation as the infidel tore through the ranks of the Faithful like a blade through wool.

His eyes continually raked the ranks of friend and foe alike, as they had done for two days while the army rested for the coming conflict. The bastard was not here, not that Abd al-Azīz had expected him to be. His enemy had disappeared from the world of men, and not even this momentous conflict had drawn him out of hiding.

His irritation and anger reached new heights and he glanced left, along the Almohad line to the Sultan Al-Mansur, who sat with a stoic patience. He almost exploded with pent-up aggression as the flag suddenly dipped, releasing the Almohad lines into the fray. Abd al-Azīz tore his gaze from his sultan and turned it instead upon the enemy.

Despite their lesser numbers, the Christians had struck hard and achieved much, and even now were committing every man they could to press the attack and finish it. The accursed King of Castile himself rode among them, his red and white banner proudly displayed.

Abd al-Azīz's great enemy was not here, but as always had would sate his fury with a sea of Christian blood. He set his eyes upon the figure of the Castilian king and kicked his horse, urging it out ahead of the line. As he rode, he felt the song of the Prophet in his heart and the fiery hatred of his enemy pulsing through his veins.

He was denied the king, for as the Almohad centre flowed like an all-consuming sea of lava into the tired Christians, the knights of one of their cursed orders – Santiago, he thought – pressed to their left to protect the monarch.

Abd al-Azīz hit the Christians three heartbeats before any other warrior, such was his speed and the need to kill. His sword swept this way and that, each strike delivered with care and accuracy, each cut aimed to deliver a death blow or incapacity to horse or rider. Blood splashed across him from both left and right, as his victims fell in agony. He lost sight of all but his enemy, surrounded by them, yet untouched, armoured in Allah's glory.

Briefly, he caught sight of the king once more and, as he turned in an attempt to push that way, he realised that the Knights of Santiago had not just been protecting the king, they had been angling towards the Sultan Al-Mansur, aiming for the heart of the Almohad force. They were struggling, for they were tired, and the Almohads were every bit the match for them, but in a fiery moment he could see one of the knights suddenly find a space opening up, presenting a visible threat to the sultan. In an instant Abd al-Azīz turned his back on the Christian king and raced after the mail-clad knight, his surcoat of white displaying his red cross in the form of a point-down sword.

Other knights of his order hurried across to protect that man, and with that Abd al-Azīz realised that the knight was no ordinary warrior, but the master of the order, a king of his own cursed kingdom. Knights tried to stop this violent Almohad horseman, protecting their master's back as he pressed on to kill the sultan, but they fell like wheat to the blade of Abd al-Azīz. Blood was everywhere now, coating both him and his horse, such that all his garments were now crimson and soaked, even his mail shirt gleaming red. As the last of those priest-knights of the Order of Santiago fell, his neck open like a second mouth and blood spraying up into the air, Abd al-Azīz lifted his sword.

'Allāhu akbar,' he bellowed, holding aloft a blade so coated in gore that blood ran freely down it and engulfed his fist. This was what he was born for: to make the infidel bleed. The master of Santiago was not two horse lengths away from the sultan when Abd al-Azīz's blade, unable to effectively threaten the mail of the knight, sank into his horse's flank.

The knight's steed screamed and danced for a moment in pain, unable to bolt in the press of men. The master of Santiago lost his shield as he fought for control of his beast, trying to keep the wounded horse from bucking. His life was forfeit in that moment as Abd al-Azīz brought his sword around once more, droplets of men's blood flying from it, and struck him levelly in the back of the neck.

The knight's armour prevented the blow from carving through flesh, but the sword struck with immense force and the man's head snapped back in reaction so sharply that it was clear in a trice that his neck was broken. The master jerked and then lolled in his saddle.

Abd al-Azīz met the gaze of Al-Mansur for a moment, in which the sultan recognised the great debt he owed this horseman of his army, but the warrior of Allah had only a passing care for this. His sultan was safe and of no further interest when there were so many Christians left to kill. He turned once more, realising now that the tide had truly turned in just a few short minutes. The army of Castile was all but surrounded, the sultan's forces ascendant.

The day was theirs, but many Christians would yet die before they could reach safety, and Abd al-Azīz vowed to leave as few as possible to flee the field.

Lifting high his gore-coated sword, he vowed a hundred more corpses in the name of Allah and let forth a great roar of fury, then kicked his horse once more and returned to the fray to kill.

ROURELL, IBERIA, THE YEAR OF OUR LORD 1199

Following the dreadful siege that had brought the Templar house of Rourell to ruin and caused the fall of a number of knights, brothers and sisters, the community had slowly begun to rebuild. Over the autumn and winter the structures had been put right once more, the fields brought back to a reasonable state and work begun on the rebuilding of the burned-out shell of the water mill. The tenants who had not fled, both Moor and Christian, had largely returned with a level of chagrin and recomenced their work, and all had begun to settle.

But the fact remained that Rourell, domain of the preceptrix Ermengarda, had never been the most popular or respected of Templar houses, even among their own ranks, thanks to the unorthodox nature of its mistress, and attracting new patrons and brethren proved harder than ever. Despite the need to keep every able-bodied person at work, by late wintertime the preceptrix had accepted Brother Balthesar's proposal, and the two had begun to plan.

Winter turned to spring, and spring slowly gave way to summer, and less than a year into his time with the order, Arnau de Vallbona once more found himself preparing for the unknown…

THE LAST EMIR

CHAPTER ONE

THURSDAY, 3 JUNE 1199

Arnau stood at the rail of the ship, eyes locked on their destination, which was currently little more than a grey smudge, though coming closer with every passing minute. A thrill of excitement ran through him every time he anticipated the task that lay ahead, yet it remained threaded with overtones of fear and nervousness. If ever there were *terra incognita* for a man like Arnau, this was it.

His gaze pulled back from the approaching shoreline, across the white-capped waves and back onto the ship. The vessel, the *Marguerite*, was a single-masted cog out of Perpignan. She was owned by a French trader who had maintained mercantile links with the island through times calm and volatile, carrying goods from northern Christian lands that were hard to acquire there, and returning each time with a hold full of the island's apparently excellent citrus fruit to sell on in the markets of Roussillon. *Marguerite* was an old lady, with the veneer of paint already missing in places and odd boards of slightly different colours where they had been replaced over the years, but the captain assured them that she was still hale and strong. She had certainly weathered the journey well, though it had been far from a difficult voyage anyway.

There were no other passengers, just Arnau and his companion, the grey-bearded knight Brother Balthesar d'Aixere, though those names had not been spoken since before they reached Perpignan. It seemed wrong somehow to Arnau to have been part of the Templar order for so little time thus far and spent so little of that displaying the order's symbols. Following that dreadful siege last year, Arnau had settled into monastic life with gusto, though it had been far from a normal time. Every free moment had been spent not in training or in quiet contemplation, wearing a black robe, but with building works and repairs, and tending the graveyard with care, wearing a drab smock. The young sergeant had perhaps changed a little over that year, become stockier and harder with his labours, become more focused and careful in his day-to-day life, but the greatest revelation of his first year in the order had been that in essence he had changed surprisingly little.

Balthesar, of course, never changed. The old, enigmatic knight had spent much of the winter working away carefully and quietly, recovering from the wound he had taken in the siege, all the while utilising what few moments of time he could find to seeking a way to do more than simply re-mortar the stones of the preceptory.

Balthesar had maintained his stance that to fully rebuild Rourell, and to attract the brothers they needed to make the place viable, they had to find a great draw to bring the preceptory to prominence. With the division between Christian Iberia and the Moorish lands becoming ever more tense and dangerous in the aftermath of the dreadful battle of Alarcos, even sleepy Rourell, far from the frontier with the Moor, felt the pressure to arm and prepare for the coming days. A sacred relic would be sought to bring in much-needed manpower and funds. Balthesar had spent much time in libraries in Tarragona and Lleida, seeking tantalising hints of relics lost to Moorish control in the days of the conquest. It was not until spring that he settled upon the course they would pursue, and it took more than a month to secure the preceptrix's permission, the funds required and all they would need for the mission.

And then, after half a year of wearing the black robe of a Templar sergeant, albeit often overlaid with a beige smock, Arnau was once more garbed in civilian clothes, mounted up and following the old knight out of the preceptory and into the unknown. Balthesar had been unwilling to expound on his plans over the days of preparation, discussing the matter solely with the preceptrix, and it was only on their journey north and east through the Catalan lands that he had gone some way to explaining his ideas and his reasoning for their coming mission.

Holy relics were sought after by all orders and all branches of the Church. Their very presence in a chapel brought pilgrims, esteem and, inevitably, money. A relic could turn a forgotten hamlet into a thriving city of God – had done so in fact, in places such as Santiago, Montserrat and Chartres. Often rifts and disputes would open up between groups over the ownership of the bones of a martyr, and sometimes such disputes resulted in saints having their bones kept in more than one location simultaneously. Sometimes there were even multiple skulls, which baffled Arnau and yet somehow seemed accepted by the Church. Such relics had been kept in the early days of the Christian world, as they were now – the Emperor Constantine's mother was famed for collecting relics and taking them back to Rome. The Order of the Temple itself had brought back from the Holy City some of the most fabled relics in the world, which had, at least in part, been part of the strength that had helped drive the order to prominence. Iberia itself had its fair share of relics.

Then came the Moors, crossing the water from Africa in successive waves of fanatical piety, seeking conquest and control. Their faith did not venerate the same figures, and Christian saints were not accorded appropriate respect under Moorish domination. In their surge across Iberia, the invaders destroyed many relics, and often with great glee. Some were saved by valiant men and carried far to the north where they were kept from heretical hands. Some Moorish lords, though, were more reasonable, and out of respect for what were clearly good men, even if they were Christian, kept relics safe, albeit out of the eye of the public.

These were the subject of Balthesar's researches: relics whose fate was not recorded. Trails that only led part of the way. The choice of relic to pursue had been relatively easy to narrow down. He had swept aside most potential relics for a very simple reason: the vast majority of Moorish Iberia now languished under the violent, strict control of the Almohad caliphate. Most certainly any relics that were found by these zealots would have been destroyed, and hunting for them in their domain would be extraordinarily dangerous anyway.

Balthesar had settled upon the perfect choice, in his opinion. Though the trail was cold, vague and ended abruptly, its location made it a far more attractive proposition than those southern lands of pious hatred. The bones of Saint Stephen, Balthesar claimed, were to be found on the island of Manûrqa. His information was scant, but it seemed that sometime in the fifth century a bishop called Orosius had carried the bones from Africa, bound for Braga in Portugal. According to tantalising sources, the bishop only made it as far as Manûrqa, where he became embroiled in troubles with the local Jewish community and passed from records and, presumably, the living world. One thing was certain: the bones of Saint Stephen, protomartyr, never reached Braga.

To Arnau, it did not sound like much to go on. In fact, it sounded like a complete fool's errand, and while he could not deny the value such relics would have for Rourell, it seemed almost farcical to spend valuable time and effort chasing this tiny trail in the hope of securing one.

Balthesar was of a different opinion. Any time Arnau had voiced his doubt on that ride to Perpignan, during their two weeks there as they secured a ship, and on the voyage from there south, towards Manûrqa, the old knight had simply smiled enigmatically and told his young companion to 'have faith'.

What faith, though, Arnau thought bitterly as he glanced at Balthesar and then down at himself. He was not at all keen on the disguise. It was bad enough wearing the clothes of a common labourer, but to be wearing their Moorish equivalent seemed appalling. Eschewing the colourful and interesting garb worn by the better classes of Moor, Balthesar had plumped for the drab grey *gandura* tunic, with an off-white *burnous* atop it, capped, literally, with a brown hat called a *ghifara*.

Arnau had worried that he would not be able to remember the names of their apparel, but Balthesar had laughed and replied that Arnau was to play mute anyway. Similarly, the old knight had not chosen Moorish names for them. When Arnau had questioned that,

Balthesar had shrugged and told him that sometimes names are best avoided and forgotten. They were dressed to be as forgettable as possible.

Fortunately their Iberian colouring and beards made them look all the more authentic, and Arnau had been rather surprised at how realistic he looked when Balthesar had found a mirror in Perpignan and they had examined their ensembles. In fact, that short time in the port city had been an eye-opener for the young sergeant on a number of levels. The most impressive shock had come when the old knight, garbed as he was in Moorish attire and earning cold glares from many of the Christians in the port, approached the various ship captains, enquiring of anyone bound for the Balearic Islands. He had adopted such a thick Moorish accent for his Spanish that it was hard to understand, and had repeatedly dropped into what sounded like thoroughly authentic Arabic. When Arnau questioned his apparent facility with the enemy tongue, Balthesar had brushed it aside as unimportant, though his seeming familiarity with all things Moorish only added to Arnau's suspicion that Balthesar had chosen to seek the bones of Saint Stephen as much for their location as their intrinsic value.

And here they were now, on board the *Marguerite*, ostensibly poor Moorish workers seeking passage to the islands and closing on Manûrqa at last. The ship's sailors were busy with the sail, and at the stern the two men stood alone at the rail, some distance from any listening ear. Glancing around to make sure, Arnau cleared his throat.

'Is Manûrqa part of Mayūrqa, then?'

The old knight flashed him a hard look. 'You are far too talkative for a mute.'

'I cannot stay silent all the time. I'm keeping my voice low and we're far from anyone listening.'

Balthesar gave him a nod, conceding the point. 'After a fashion, they are one. It is a separate island and always has been, but it is part of the *taifa* and ruled from Madina Mayūrqa.'

Arnau nodded. In the old days, until perhaps half a century ago, the whole of Moorish Iberia – the lands they referred to as Al-

Andalus – had consisted of *taifas*, independent Moorish kingdoms, each ruled by an emir. It had been a good time for the subjects of those lands – at least if the heavy taxation was ignored – who were allowed to worship as they wished, even teach and trade under their Moorish masters. And the fractured nature of the *taifas* had meant the danger to Christian lands in the north had been vastly reduced. But then the Almohads had come from Africa, rolling across the land in a wave of zealous violence, taking the *taifas* and disbanding them, forming one great caliphate ruled from Ishbiliyya, which the Christians called Seville. The *taifas* were all gone now, all consumed by the caliphate before Arnau's birth. All except one: the island *taifa* of Mayūrqa had survived, largely due to its sea-girded isolation.

And it was that very independence, where the tolerant culture of the *taifa* remained, that made the island the perfect target for Balthesar. There were still Christians and Jews on Mayūrqa who were treated as citizens, albeit second-class ones, and not forced into slavery and drudgery like those under Almohad rule.

'How much money do we have?'

The old knight gave him a long-suffering look. 'Are you determined to talk about unimportant irrelevancies all morning?'

Arnau huffed and leaned on the rail once more, arms folded in the drab, itchy clothes, eyes locked on their destination. The island of Manûrqa was becoming much more visible now, coming ever closer. Arnau could not see a port, just a series of jutting headlands, the more prominent crowned with small fortifications.

Tolerant *taifa* culture or not, though, the sight of those walls brought home to Arnau the extreme danger inherent in what they were doing. The Emir of Mayūrqa might be the last of the great independent Moorish lords, but they both needed to remember that this was still a Moorish land, run by sons of Allah and filled with his swords. This place carried inherent dangers for any Christian, let alone members of the Temple in disguise. He could quite imagine those fortifications bristling with angry Moors, each with no love of the order, watching incoming ships for intruders.

He tried to swallow his nerves as they closed on the coast. Finally, as the sail thumped and filled afresh and the vessel began to turn, he realised that two of those headlands flanked a wide inlet and it was for that they were making. His nerves rose as they surged forward and swept between those green promontories and into the sheltered waters beyond. They began to pass Moorish vessels with white lateen sails, and with each one Arnau felt his anxiety rise a notch.

'This is a fool's errand,' he said again. He was sure it was for the first time today, at least.

'Faith, Arnau. Have faith. And button those lips.'

Arnau fell silent and watched as the green slopes of Manûrqa slid past on either side, their destination now finally in view. The town of Mahón lay inland, in the shelter of that inlet on the southern shore. It was a warren of white walls and red tile, a thriving port playing host to numerous vessels, all native.

The ship's captain, well practised at this run, veered towards the port without losing speed and only began to slow as he lined up with a free jetty, shouting commands at the crew, who worked hurriedly in response. The *Marguerite* lost momentum swiftly and finally drifted towards the wooden jetty at an easy pace.

Arnau's eyes danced this way and that, taking it all in with a mix of heady excitement and dreadful nervousness. He noted the town itself behind the port, its alleys and streets narrow and winding, perfect shadowy places for a rabid local to plant a knife in a wandering Christian without attracting unwanted attention. He noted the huge number of Moorish sailors on the ships to either side, all watching the approaching cog with wary interest. He noted the array of armoured figures and the snapping and fluttering flags around the port.

He needed to urinate suddenly. Quite urgently.

He turned, opening his mouth to speak despite having been warned repeatedly not to, but it was Balthesar who spoke first.

'God's bones,' he spat. 'Shit.'

Arnau frowned. 'What?' he whispered. Whatever it was, it had surprised the old knight enough that he had openly spoken Spanish, albeit in a quiet hiss.

'The flags.'

Arnau turned his furrowed brow to the pennants fluttering in soldiers' hands across the port. He could see a variety of banners bearing several designs, none of which were particularly familiar to him, though in fairness most Moorish flags looked quite similar to him. He turned his bafflement on Balthesar, who pointed. 'Flags of Manûrqa and Mayûrqa, flags of thc Ghaniyid dynasty, to which the current emir belongs. But do you not recognise those?'

Arnau's eyes followed the older knight's extended digit. A group of shining, armoured soldiers with brightly coloured clothes stood clustered too far away and hidden by dockside activity to make out much detail. Their banners were all variants of one design: a red background with a black-and-white-checked motif at the centre. It did look very familiar. His eyes widened as memories of a fight by the Ebro flashed through his mind

'Almohads.'

'Quite,' Balthesar said. 'It would appear that we are not the only visitors to Mahón. The Almohad caliphate has no authority within this *taifa*, and they are far from allies. Their presence here is worrying. We must be subtle and circumspect and on no account should you utter another word until we are alone and safely away from that lot.'

Arnau made to reply but stopped at a warning look from his companion. The ship chose that moment to bump against the jetty, and the young sergeant lurched back for a moment, his hands slipping from the rail. He recovered his balance poorly and realised that the mostly Christian crew of the ship were smirking at him. Resisting the urge to show them a very un-Christian gesture, he rejoined Balthesar and waited as the sailors ran out lines and secured the ship. Moments later the boarding ramp was brought out and slid across to the damp boards of the jetty.

Balthesar let go of the rail and turned, gathering up his large canvas bag and slinging it onto his back, Arnau following suit with his own pack, and the two of them made for the ramp. The old man turned as they reached the top of the plank and essayed a short bow to the captain, who stood at the wheel, watching his crew at work.

'*Šukran gazīlan*,' he said with a flourish, then switched to Aragonese Spanish with a thick Moorish accent. 'My thanks for your excellent seamanship. May God keep you safe and fill your sail.'

Playing his best mute idiot role, Arnau simply gave a vacant smile and bowed his head as he followed the old knight. Balthesar thumped down the ramp and onto the jetty and paused there, adjusting his gait and finding his land legs once more. Arnau followed him onto the slick boards and immediately slipped on the wet timber, pirouetting a little and staggering to avoid ending up flat on his backside.

Crewmen of the two nearest ships, both Moorish and Christian, all roared with laughter.

Trying not to blush, Arnau followed Balthesar, who was giving him a flat, unforgiving look, up the jetty and onto the dockside. It was clear that if they wished to move directly into the town, the two men would have to pass close by the groups of soldiers. Behind the dockside was a thriving and busy market, beyond which lay the winding streets up into town, for which Balthesar was clearly making.

As they closed on those groups of armoured figures who stood between the port and the market, Arnau scrutinised them carefully from beneath lowered brows. Several groups of men were wearing green uniforms covered with mail shirts, displaying the various banners of Mayūrqa. The one group of men beneath the Almohad banner, perhaps a score strong, were an entirely different breed. Their clothing was austere black and white, their heads covered with intricate helmets, their faces hidden behind veils of chain. Their leader was the one spot of colour in the group, wearing a red and gold *gandura* with a white *burnous* atop it, his head covered with a red turban, his face open, beard trimmed to a severe point. Somehow his ostentatious apparel made him look all the more worrying amid the drab soldiers.

It took Arnau moments to realise, as his eyes played subtly across them and the other groups, that there was a distinct tension in the air here, which had nothing to do with him or Balthesar. The Almohad soldiers and their master regarded their surroundings with a cold disdain, while the Mayūrqan warriors watched the visitors suspiciously, never letting their gaze wander.

Clearly, while there was no sign of the local guards moving to eject the caliphate's men, they were here under sufferance and were entirely unwelcome. What fresh trouble had the two Templars stepped into here?

Balthesar moved directly between the nearest two groups, keeping his eyes forward, locked on the marketplace, appearing, to all intent and purpose, to be focused on the stalls to the exclusion of all else. Arnau hurried along behind him, face lowered, eyes alert. They passed three stalls and veered off to the left a little. The young sergeant felt a lurch in his stomach as he looked up briefly and spotted three more of the black-and-white-garbed Almohad soldiers moving down through the marketplace, back towards their group. They would pass Arnau and Balthesar in moments.

He almost walked into the older knight as Balthesar stopped suddenly at a stall and bent over it, peering at a selection of blades laid out on a grey cloth. Assuming the brother was avoiding contact with the three warriors, Arnau followed suit once more, turning and looking at the weapons. They were modestly decorated, weapons designed for war rather than court, though Balthesar was paying close attention to one in particular. A straight blade with a gentle taper, its hilt of iron but decorated with silvered flakes and bound in red leather, it was the best on offer. The old knight looked at Arnau for a moment, frowned, then turned back to the table and struck up a conversation in Arabic with the owner.

Arnau, unable to follow any of it, threw a sly glance at the three Almohads as they passed. They each carried a spear, wore a similar sword, and two of them also bore simple crossbows of a very lightweight design. As if Arnau wasn't already heartily sick of crossbows...

He became aware for a moment that he was being gestured at, and realised that Balthesar and the stall owner were talking about him. From the tone of their voices and the looks in their eyes, he suspected that Balthesar had just said something along the lines of 'If I take this one, which one will you give me for the idiot?'

He tried not to look angry, indeed put on his best 'vacant idiot' look, as Balthesar concluded his deal and opened a purse, forking out a worrying share of their meagre funds. A moment later the older man passed him a sword that was far from excellent, but would at least not fall apart when swung. Balthesar himself took the best one and belted it atop his burnous. Suddenly, the simple addition of a blade transformed Balthesar from serf to warrior. It was a subtle change, but a complete one. Arnau did the same. He'd wondered about the wisdom of leaving their own weapons at Rourell, but Balthesar had been adamant that finding a ship willing to bring them here would be considerably easier if they were simple folk and not warriors. At least now they were armed, which was a comfort, with the rabid forces of the Almohad caliphate unexpectedly present.

For a moment, Arnau wondered what Balthesar was up to, for the older knight turned back down the slope a little, almost heading towards the gathering of severe-looking soldiers, but then the man stopped at another stall and began to look at further miscellaneous wares. Perhaps he bought into the notion that to appear least suspicious they should not be seen to be keeping away from the men. If so, then Arnau considered it an idiotic idea, for even the Mayūrqan soldiers were keeping their distance. He saw Balthesar look up from beneath a lowered face twice, and saw something in his eyes that clarified matters. The older knight was getting a closer look at the Almohads for some reason, and his expression suddenly became very hard and stony. Whatever he'd seen he didn't like.

A moment later they were moving again through the crowded market, making up the slope towards those narrow alleys that seemed in Arnau's mind to have gone from dangerous maws that harboured assassins to places of sanctuary and safety.

He hadn't realised until someone shouted how their very posture had changed. As if strapping on the sword had brought out the soldier in him, Balthesar's gait had altered. He was now striding with knightly purpose, Arnau unwittingly doing the same. They were no longer invisible serfs.

'*Qātil wari'a!*' came the call a second time, and this time Arnau realised it was aimed at them, or more specifically at Balthesar. He frowned, looking around for the source of the voice. An old man not far ahead was pointing frantically in their direction and bellowing the phrase.

'*Qātil wari'a!*'

Balthesar suddenly ducked right between two stalls, shaking his head at the old man and holding up his hands in the universal gesture that says 'You have the wrong man.' Clearly he didn't, of course, judging by the urgency now gripping Balthesar as he weaved between stalls, eyes flicking over to the shouting man and back, worriedly, at the Almohads.

They rounded another corner and found their way blocked by a poor stall owner who had suffered some kind of avalanche of large baskets, which seemed to fill the passages in every direction. Arnau knew that something was dreadfully wrong, and the idea that it might be important for him to continue playing the mute idiot seemed suddenly ridiculous.

'What's going on?' he asked.

'Back that way,' Balthesar snapped in Aragonese but still with a thick Arab accent, pointing to a crowded alley between stalls that was at least blessedly free of waist-high baskets. As they turned and became further ensnared in the crowd, Arnau's eyes flitted between those same targets as his companion's.

The man who was still shouting '*Qātil wari'a!*' was on his knees, arms held up. Was that a sign of respect? Veneration? It looked like it, though Arnau knew little of Moorish custom. Whatever the case, while the man was still identifying them loudly, he did not seem likely to load a crossbow and loose it at them. Consequently, Arnau wrote the man off as comparatively unimportant right now, and concentrated instead on the Almohad soldiers. The entire group was now looking their way, and the leader in his colourful garb was pointing at them. *He* did not look to be offering respect and veneration. In fact, his face had gone a rather funny colour. If Arnau had had to put a name to the man's expression, it would probably be 'murderous rage'. What in heaven's name had they got themselves into?

Worryingly that refrain, *Qātil wari'a*, seemed to have spread, and now a number of voices here and there were calling it. Not a chant taken up by a vast sector of the crowd – perhaps three or four voices – but the effect was still nerve-shredding.

'Move,' Balthesar hissed, and pushed Arnau into the crowd, himself elbowing and barging his way through. Arnau risked a glance back once more. The Almohad soldiers were beginning to move towards the market. It seemed very likely that the whole of Mahón was about to explode into riotous, violent activity. His gaze slid this way and that. The Mayūrqan soldiers were moving and shouting too, though their sudden activity seemed to be in response to the Almohads, for they were hurrying towards them. It looked distinctly possible that there was about to be a scuffle between the two armed groups and, while that might not be a good thing, Arnau wouldn't have been unhappy to see it right then.

A moment later they burst from the crowded area into a clear part of the market at the upper edge, close to one of the shaded alleyways. For a moment they were invisible to both groups of soldiers, but then the crowds shifted again slightly, and Arnau could see what was happening. The Almohad lord had reined in his men, who were once more standing in a group, hands on sword hilts, while the local Mayūrqan soldiers bristled and eyed them warily. One of the island's officers was shouting angrily at the visitors, but the Almohad lord was paying him no attention. That man's sharp gaze was on the top of the market, on the two nondescript travellers who had emerged there. Even at this distance, Arnau swore he could feel the heat of the man's hatred emanating from his gaze.

He almost slipped again as a hand grabbed his drab, voluminous tunic and pulled him into the shadows of the alley. They ran.

Three streets up and two across, finally Balthesar came to a halt, leaning against the wall, and Arnau, tired and feeling every breath like a fiery pain through his chest, dropped his hands to his knees, bent over and spat out drool until the need to vomit abated. He looked up with profound respect at Balthesar. Not more than seven or eight months ago the man had looked doomed to end his life as a knight, his arm broken, his leg so badly torn with a sword gash that it wouldn't hold his weight. Yet here the old man was, an autumn, a winter and a spring later, and he could comfortably wield a sword and manage to sprint up a hill with more vigour even than Arnau.

'It truly does appear that we are unable to move in this world without drawing the worst kind of attention, you and I,' sighed the old knight, fingers stroking the hilt of the sword belted at his side as if for reassurance. His Arabic accent had temporarily disappeared, but the street was empty and shaded, and they were about as alone as a man could be in this city.

'What was all that about? Did the Almohads know you? Who was the man on his knees, and *why* was he on his knees? What in the name of the Holy Mother of God is a *Qātil wari'a*?'

Balthesar shook his head. 'All matters for another time. Now we must keep moving.'

'But where? And what is *Qātil wari'a*, since it seems we are it?'

'*Qātil wari'a* means "pious killer" and it's a name long dead that should have stayed buried. And now Abu Rāshid Abd al-Azīz ibn al-Ḥasan, the Lion of Alarcos, has seen us and heard the name. We are now mice in his hawk gaze. Arnau, the past harbours a legion of ghosts. Let us flee this place before we fall prey to them.'

'Where do we go?' Arnau breathed.

'To the Xeuta.'

'The where?'

'It's not a place, it's a people. The Xeuta are all that remains of the ancient colony of Jews that were in this place under the Romans. The last people to see the remains of Saint Stephen, the First Martyr.'

'Oh, well that clears up everything,' grunted Arnau, and turned to hurry off up the hill once more in the wake of the grey-bearded Brother Balthesar.

CHAPTER TWO

THURSDAY, 3 JUNE 1199

Despite the clear fact that the Almohad lord and his men had been waylaid beyond the market under the watchful gaze of the emir's men, Arnau could not shake his nervous feeling as they moved off through the town. He checked every side street carefully as they passed, and continually glanced over his shoulder. There was no sign of this 'Lion of Alarcos' or his men, but that did not stop the young sergeant checking repeatedly.

He made a mental note to ask about this Almohad lord when they next had the opportunity in private. The past of the grey-bearded brother stomping up the street ahead of Arnau was shrouded in mystery, and had been since he first met the man. He was certainly not what the young man had expected a glorious knight of the Temple to be. Yet in the growing catalogue of enigmas that surrounded Balthesar d'Aixere, the identity of the Lion of Alarcos seemed to be rising to the top in terms of priority.

Mahón showed every sign of Moorish city design, its layout based around tribal groupings and religious structures, resulting in a collection of narrow streets separating blocks that were formed of community ties, all with a nod to defensive cohesion, in that much of the city could easily be sealed and held with the minimum of effort. There were no wide thoroughfares such as one might find in the old Roman cities of Tarragona or Barcelona, for example. Arnau was convinced before they had got very far that they were hopelessly lost among the tangle of curving, vertiginous streets. Certainly *he* could not have found his way back to the port even with a map and a guide.

The population of Mahón, naturally overwhelmingly Moorish, largely went about their business completely ignoring the two figures moving through their midst, though one or two noted the swords belted at their sides and gave them a wide berth, eyes narrowed suspiciously. Arnau was careful to keep his hand away from the sword hilt, his face lowered and his mouth firmly shut. Just a poor Moorish mute.

Gradually, though, the town began to change. They passed a grand mosque at the centre, a walled compound, several fountains and smaller civil structures, and then moved out into a more suburban area away from the port. There were subtle differences in the architecture, and only a man who had spent time walking the streets of Barcelona or Tarragona and seeing the shift between neighbourhoods would be able to spot them.

The main difference he noticed as they passed into a distinctly separate region of the city was the level of upkeep. The buildings in this area had an unkempt and shabby feeling about them, presenting only peeling shutters, dirty plaster and blank-faced doors to the street. If this was, as he now felt sure, the area Balthesar had been making for all along, then it differed from other Jewish quarters he had passed through in other cities. Whether you approved of the Jew or not (and Arnau's father had long since drilled into him the fact that the Jew had a legitimate place in Iberian society) it was hard to deny that they kept their tightly packed houses in good order. This place appeared to be different. Whether it was because they were a different kind of Jew, or perhaps that they laboured under the laws and taxes of the Moor, he could not say.

They turned into a street with purpose as though Balthesar had a clear idea of his destination, and ahead Arnau could see a sign on a wall beside a door denoting the presence of a Jewish temple. He had seen such places back in the north, but this had a subtle, almost hidden nature. An old man sat on a stone block close to the temple door, the first person he had seen in this entire quarter.

The old man wore a long, dark blue robe with a white and blue scarf about his shoulders, hanging down the front, and a strange hat that rose to a tall point as though gesturing to God. His face was wrinkled and lined with a century of cares, and his forked beard, though mostly grey, was still long and curled into ringlets.

They came to a halt in front of the man, and Arnau added a new question to his inquisition list as Brother Balthesar immediately opened up a conversation with the Jew in fluent Hebrew. There was a brief exchange, with short and non-committal-sounding answers from the local who then, with Balthesar's aid, rose from the stone and began to pace off down a side street.

The two men followed and as they moved into the narrow alley Balthesar leaned closer to Arnau. 'I have no idea what attitudes to the Jew lurk in that skull of yours, Vallbona, but be sure to be courteous and respectful here. Even if you despise their kind, you will hide it well, for I will not be halted in my search by something so base.'

Arnau made to protest about such an assumption, but Balthesar had turned his back and walked on. In fairness it was a reasonable point to make. Few among the Aragonese nobility would have any time for the Jews, who were largely considered heretical, or even parasitic. It had interested Arnau to discover that the attitudes within the order, a foundation based upon the central tenets of the Christian faith, seemed to be more comfortable with their Jewish and Moorish neighbours than the majority of the secular nobility.

They stopped further down the narrow street and the old man knocked on a bare door and opened it. He entered, beckoning to the two men, and Balthesar and then Arnau both followed him in. It was as he stepped through the door that Arnau realised where he had been mistaken. The exterior of the buildings, facing onto the streets, were drab, dirty, peeling and decaying. But the inside?

The door opened onto a corridor paved with bright, colourful tiles, the walls painted the yellow of a spring meadow. Wall hangings on either side showed scenes from the Jewish scriptures, and Arnau was interested to note that he recognised both scenes from accounts in his own Bible. The differences between these people and his own seemed to shrivel and vanish.

The corridor opened out onto a courtyard that was something of a light well. Three storeys up, the bright daylight shone in and reflected off the white painted walls to make the place light and airy. Pots of flowers hung on the walls and sat in corners, and a small fountain played and burbled in the centre. Three benches sat around the edge. It looked like a small corner of paradise to Arnau and it was with regret that he passed through it and followed the other two through a door and inside once more.

They were led to another room, and the old man introduced Balthesar to the occupants in his own language and then bowed his head and took a seat with the others. Arnau peered around the room. Four more old men sat there dressed in a very similar fashion to the first: long, coloured robes, the scarf with the holy colours, the grey curled beards. They had, however, plumped for small skullcaps rather than the large pointed hats.

Balthesar bowed respectfully and spoke once more in Hebrew. Arnau tried not to look out of place as he stood silent beside the older knight. Finally, the brother seemed to put a question to the men and received a tentative affirmative. He turned to Arnau.

'These men are the Beth Din of Mahón, the men who make rulings in the court of the Jewish population. Two of them speak passable Aragonese Spanish and are willing to voice the words of the Beth Din for us, so that you, too, might be involved in this. Bear in mind, Arnau, that not only are we foreign guests here, but we are also seeking their aid. Politeness costs nothing.'

Feeling peeved again at such an admonition, Arnau stood waiting until Balthesar dropped slowly and with a grunt of discomfort into a crouch. The young sergeant did the same and waited.

'Let me begin by revealing the truth in all matters,' Balthesar said. 'We come in the garb of the Moor, but, as you now clearly realise, we are in truth from the Christian kingdoms on the mainland.'

There was a chorus of nods. The need to switch to the Aragonese tongue alone had made that abundantly clear.

'But we are more than simple Christian travellers. We belong to the Order of the Temple of Solomon, and are here in this guise in order to pass through the Moorish lands without causing undue friction.'

There was a sudden drop in temperature at the revelation, and several faces hardened. The five men leaned closer together and muttered in their native tongue. Finally the rabbi, the man who had brought them here, leaned towards them and spoke forcefully. They all assented gradually with a single nod, and the youngest of the bunch – a man, by Arnau's estimation, old enough to remember Jesus walking – spoke.

'The rabbi reminds us that your order is founded on the principle of saving the poor traveller from peril and takes its very name and heart from our most holy of places. We accept you as friends of the Temple. You may speak freely and without fear of falsehood or betrayal. We would ask the same courtesy.'

'Of course,' Balthesar nodded. 'After all, we are all men of faith.'

Another chorus of nods.

'The rabbi informs us that you seek to unravel the history of Manûrqa, and perhaps our part in it. What is it you seek, Brother of the Temple?'

Balthesar steepled his fingers.

'I seek the bones of one of our saints: Saint Stephen, the first martyr.'

Arnau couldn't say what the look that the five men shared following this statement meant, but it certainly did not appear to be overwhelmingly positive. There was an awkward silence, and eventually, Balthesar filled it once more.

'My research has been limited to certain libraries, and I have found only oblique references and vague hints beyond a few simple stated facts. I understand that Bishop Orosius acquired the bones of Saint Stephen in the Holy Land in the early fifth century and took them to Hippo Regius in Africa. He was then, if I am correct, entrusted with transporting said relics to Palchonius, the Bishop of Braga in Portugal. Things beyond that seem to be a little vague. We are aware that Orosius wrote a history text, but when he did so seems to be a matter of debate. One tale I found said that Orosius came to Manûrqa, realised that the Vandals were ravaging Iberia and turned and went back to Africa, leaving the relics here, and finishing his history back in Hippo Regius. Another story has it that Orosius disappeared on the island after some conflict involving the island's Jewish community, in which I suspect we do not come off as the heroic faithful, and the bones similarly disappear from the record. Whatever the case, it seems that the bones of Saint Stephen never left Manûrqa. It is my quest to secure those relics and return them to Aragon and appropriate veneration. The trail I follow is centuries cold and leads only this far. Since your community is mentioned in one of my sources, you are my single hope in tracing the relics any further. I would greatly appreciate any aid.'

There was another uncomfortable silence, and then another murmured confab between the Jewish elders. Finally, the rabbi began to speak, and the younger man translated it into Aragonese for the guests' benefit.

'The events to which you refer are a dark time in our people's history, and a wicked time in yours. As you say, the story is centuries old, and even a decade sees any tale embellished, so the absolute truth of this perhaps lies only at the core of our telling.'

Balthesar nodded his understanding, and Arnau felt himself starting to get a little excited. The very idea of following this mad quest had been bothering him ever since they left Rourell, but somehow sitting here, in this Jewish house, listening to their elders picking up the fragmentary story, felt like a massive leap forward and a vindication of their journey thus far. Balthesar had been telling him to have faith now for weeks.

'Orosius came here,' the old man said. 'I will not allow him the honour of a title, for to us he is a villain. He came to Mahón bearing one forearm, to the elbow, of Stephen the apostate who angered the Sanhedrin and was stoned to death. The arm, it is said, was kept in a silver case.'

Balthesar flashed Arnau a look full of interest, hope and fascination, and it was difficult not to feel the same.

'It is said that the bone was magical,' the Jew continued. 'In your understanding, it brought miracles to the island. Your Orosius, with the aid of a young priest called Severus, decided that this island would be sacred. The island of Saint Stephen. Whether or not they intended the bone to continue on to the mainland, we are not told. What we do know is that our people were already being shunned and hated by yours. The arrival on the island of this relic fired the blood of your priests and they forced the island's faithful to convert to Christianity. It is said that half a thousand Jews were made to kiss the cross before our temple was burned to the ground.'

Arnau felt sick. No wonder these men had been cagey and cold to begin with. Hardly an auspicious beginning. And yet, somewhere deep down inside, Arnau realised that his soul had latched on to the discovery that the bone of Saint Stephen worked miracles. Had the relic been the cause of half a thousand conversions, and centuries of bitterness had shifted the blame to the man who brought it?

'Orosius left Manûrqa within months of his arrival, and he left it a seething, bitter island of Christians and suppressed, forcibly converted Jews. He returned to Africa, perhaps thinking his relic was better here, where it had shown its power. Severus, it is said, regretted his part in the matter, and wrote an account of it, and for that he is forgiven by our people, but not the vile Orosius.'

Balthesar nodded. 'It may be meaningless to apologise for slights and wrongs perpetrated by our forebears, but in the spirit that all things can change, and that most things must, I offer my regret and apologies on behalf of the Church.'

Arnau nodded his agreement vehemently, and this seemed to please the five men. There was another long silence and Arnau realised, uncomfortably, that this was as far as they were going with the tale.

'Can you tell us of what happened thereafter? To the relic, I mean,' Brother Balthesar urged.

The men shook their heads. 'The relic was placed in the church of Mahón,' the rabbi said finally. 'Beyond that we can say nothing other than there is no longer a church in the city and has not been since the Moors came. Our people returned to the old faith in time, though in smaller numbers, and there are still Christians in the city who owe their history to those forced conversions. Perhaps if there is more to tell, then they can tell it.'

Balthesar straightened and flexed his fingers. 'Thank you for your aid and your honesty. Be assured that if we locate the bone of Saint Stephen, its future holds only good works of which your Beth Din would approve. I have been to Mahón before,' he said, earning a surprised look from Arnau, 'but I was not aware of a Christian presence at the time. Would you be able to direct me to anyone?'

A quarter of an hour later, having profusely thanked the five old men and made their farewells, the two knights were once more stalking through the streets of the city, and despite the lift in his spirits, once more Arnau's gaze raked every alley looking for men with knives.

'I was entirely unaware of a Christian community in the city,' Balthesar said as they walked. 'I was hoping to have learned more from the Xeuta, but perhaps they are passing the torch to the converted here. I am convinced now that there is more to find out. The trail does not stop here. The bone must be somewhere on the island.'

A day ago, Arnau might have disagreed, been scathing even. Somehow that heady half-hour of listening to the tale of ancient days with the old Jews had kindled something, though. Perhaps the faith that the old knight had kept telling him he needed. He realised suddenly that he'd added another question to his growing list to put to the old knight. It was perhaps the least important of them all, but it was the latest.

'When have you been here before?' he asked suddenly.

Balthesar turned a surprised frown upon him. 'I was not born in Rourell, Arnau, though perhaps I was reborn there. I am an old man and I had a full life before I took my vows with the order.'

Arnau nodded his understanding and followed on, privately acknowledging that the old knight's reply was anything but an actual answer to the question.

They moved through the city's outer districts this time, staying away from the central mosque and its busy streets. Finally, with somewhat achy legs, they emerged upon a street that ran along a cliff edge, the water down below and a view of the port off to their right. 'This must be the place,' he said, gesturing to a nondescript shop.

The entire frontage here was given over to commercial premises, and the fishmonger's they stood in front of was flanked by a copper-pot maker's and a bakery. *Loaves and fishes*, thought Arnau with a small, private smile, as the older brother moved towards the shop.

'Good afternoon,' Balthesar said to the shopkeeper in Spanish, then repeated it in Hebrew and Arabic, just in case.

The fishmonger stopped what he was doing, his large, sharp knife sliding back out of the fish's belly, dripping blood. He dropped the point to the table and spun the knife beneath his finger.

'Who are you who looks like a travelling mercenary but speaks with the tongue of the mainlander?'

'My name is Balthesar, and I am seeking representatives of the Christian community here. Might I speak with you?'

The fishmonger gave him a deeply suspicious look. 'Come,' he said, then waved to a woman busy washing fish in the back. 'Maria, I will be back in a few minutes.'

He stepped through a rear door, gesturing for the two visitors to follow. They pursued him into a small room with one high window, furnished with a functional table and two benches. While he sat on one, he gestured to the other, and the two men sat down opposite him. The man, who looked to Arnau like any other poor Moorish shopkeeper, reached across to a platter of food that sat at one end of the table. He forked a slice of pink meat and a piece of buttered bread onto each of two plates and then passed one to each of the visitors.

'Eat,' he instructed, as he poured two cups of wine.

'A test?' Balthesar enquired.

'A confirmation,' the man said in flat tones, and slid a cup to each of them.

With a smile, Balthesar took a hearty bite of the salted pork and washed it down with wine. Arnau did the same and realised with a start that, being in a Moorish land, this was probably the last wine he would taste for some time. He took another pull and savoured the rich red draught.

The man nodded. 'Who are you?'

'I am a pilgrim, travelling with my novice here. We are following an ancient trail, laid down centuries ago. I seek the remains of Saint Stephen, protomartyr. Would you know of anyone who could tell us what happened to the church in Mahón and the relic that lay therein? I would be most grateful.'

The man leaned back and drummed his fingers on the table. 'That is a legend. An ancient tale. Stories for the fireside.'

'And yet I understand that your entire community grew out of the conversions associated with the relic?'

The man's eyes narrowed. 'You are well informed, pilgrim. I can tell you as much as any man in the city about what you seek, though it is not much, and it is, again, from tales told by old men for dozens of generations. How much truth there is in them I cannot say.'

'I would be grateful even for far-fetched tales,' Balthesar smiled.

'The bones were but an arm. I understand that the rest of the body went to Rome.'

Balthesar nodded. 'I had also heard this. An arm is all I seek.'

The man huffed and folded his arms. 'It is said that when the Moors came, the Jews of Manûrqa rejoiced, for they had been oppressed by their Roman overlords, but the Moors offered them relative freedom. They were taxed, like us, but they began to worship again. It is said that the Moors when they came were also accepting of the Church. They would allow us to worship as we had, but certain embittered Jews roused their new lords against the

Christians, remembering the days of their oppression, and the relic was almost destroyed.'

'Almost?'

The man nodded. 'The church was pulled down and our community persecuted for a time. But first the priest of the church, a man we remember as Lucas, took the relic and carried it to safety. It was not in the church when it was destroyed.'

Arnau felt that thrill of excitement again. Perhaps the trail was not as dead as he'd feared.

'Do these old tales reveal where this Father Lucas went?' Balthesar prompted.

'His intended destination is recorded, if not his fate,' the man replied. 'It is told that he took ship to Mayūrqa, perhaps fifty miles west of here. His avowed intent was to seek the place on the islands safest from the Moor. That place would be the ancient fortress of Alaró, which was a Christian bastion and controlled by a rigidly pious man.'

'That makes a great deal of sense,' the old knight replied. 'Strange that this is not recorded in texts I have read, since I know something of Alaró's past.'

The man shook his head. 'The trail ends there, I'm afraid, old man. Father Lucas never reached the fortress. Like Bishop Orosius on his voyage to Braga, the relic never arrived. Perhaps it was cursed in some fashion?'

'It then disappeared somewhere between here and Alaró,' Balthesar said.

'Yes,' the man confirmed. 'Sadly, I believe your search must end there. No one here will know anything further. Centuries have passed under the yoke of the Moor. If the remains of Saint Stephen were not destroyed or hopelessly lost, word would have spread before now.'

The old knight smiled. 'You share a weakness with my young novice here, friend: a lack of faith.' He chuckled as the man's face became hard. 'I do not mean faith in the Lord, but faith in all of his works. I cannot believe I have come this far only to reach a dead end. We shall forge on.'

'But you heard him,' Arnau said. 'The trail ends. We cannot search the whole of two islands and the sea in between in the hope of finding a few bones.'

Balthesar shook his head. 'Faith will take us far, Arnau, but logic will take us further right now. The bone left this island. We can, I think, be certain of that, for if it had not, then its fate would have come down as part of the stories told in this community.'

A point, most certainly, Arnau had to acknowledge. That did not narrow it down a lot, though.

'I think we can rule out a loss at sea also,' the old knight said confidently.

'Really? How?'

'He was a priest, therefore would not have his own boat and almost certainly would not steal one. This means that he would have to have persuaded or paid an islander from Manûrqa to take him across the water. That man must have returned, or his disappearance would similarly be part of the local tales. No, Father Lucas reached Mayūrqa, I am convinced. And if he did so, then we can rule out this island and a watery grave. Our story will pick up across the channel.'

'But where?' demanded Arnau. 'If the maps I've seen are accurate then Mayūrqa is much larger even than this island. We search for a needle in a haystack.'

'Faith, Arnau. And logic.'

The young sergeant sighed. 'Tell me, then.'

'From here, there is only one place the boat might have landed. There is a town there called Al-Bulānsa, and near it an ancient ruin that was a city in the days of the Romans and the Vandals. He would have landed there, and I know the coastline thereabouts. I know also the location of Alaró, which sits atop a peak in the mountains of the north-west. From Al-Bulānsa, Lucas would have been careful and circumspect in his movements. Bear in mind that at that time, the island was still in the early throes of the Moorish invasion. Christian outposts would still be holding out, and I know of several tales of those days, including some concerning Alaró. But Father Lucas would not have risked a direct journey along the island's main road towards the fortress. He would, without a doubt, have run into Moorish soldiers had he done so. A man careful enough to rescue the relic before the Moor came for his church is not the sort of man who would then walk it into the arms of his enemy on an open road.'

'There is a lot of "if" involved in this, to my mind,' Arnau said, his earlier exhilaration at the unfolding tale now beginning to flag.

'Faith, remember,' smiled the older knight. 'Father Lucas, I am certain, landed within a short stretch of coastline on Mayūrqa, and from there took the most circuitous possible route to Alaró to avoid contact with those who would do him harm. The next step in our search lies somewhere along that route. And to discover what path he might have taken from Al-Bulānsa, we must make enquiries there.'

Balthesar stood and stretched. 'I must thank you, my friend, for all your help. I am confident that the arm of Saint Stephen remains somewhere on these islands, waiting to be found by men of faith, and we shall be the ones to do so. We must beg your leave now and seek passage to the next island.'

They made their farewells to the fishmonger and stepped out onto the street again. Once alone, they crossed to the rail and looked down. Arnau's sharp eyes scoured the port off to their right but there was no hope of making out the small group of Almohad soldiers, if they remained there at all.

'We can't go to the port for a ship,' Arnau said quietly. 'That Lion of Alarcos might still be there.'

'Quite,' Balthesar agreed, 'but we are on a trail now and the scent remains strong in my nostrils. We follow in the footsteps of our forebears, and Father Lucas carried the bones from here to Mayūrqa. He would not have done so from the port of Mahón if he were so endangered here. He will have departed from some lesser, hidden location. We must prepare ourselves for a walk, young Vallbona.'

'And a swim?'

'Do not be needlessly facetious. There are villages on the other side of the island, between five and ten miles from here, that face

Mayūrqa across the water. It is almost certain that Father Lucas sailed from one of those villages, and so shall we.'

Arnau sighed. 'I am once more of the growing opinion that this is a fool's errand, Brother.'

The old knight scratched an ear reflectively. 'Do not make me regret bringing you along, Arnau. You must have faith.'

'What is the point of faith in a vague legend?'

Balthesar shot him a dangerous look. 'The whole point of faith, Arnau, is to have it in that which cannot be proven. That which can does not *require* faith. How can you be so unaware of a basic fact of our calling and our duty? Come. We seek a boat to take us to Mayūrqa, and we will not find that in the city. We must away to the far coast, and if we set off now, we might reach it by nightfall.'

The old man stretched once more and shouldered his bag, then began to walk back away from the water and into Mahón, heading west.

Heaving the latest in a long line of sighs, Arnau followed.

CHAPTER THREE

FRIDAY, 4 JUNE 1199

The boat rocked too much to be considered truly comfortable, as far as Arnau was concerned. It was a whole different proposition to the trader's cog that had carried them from Perpignan to the islands. That had been a ship, constructed to hold cargo, weather storms and withstand anything the sea might throw at it. This one, which had a name that Arnau could not pronounce let alone remember, was a small native fishing boat. Twelve feet in length and fat-bellied, it bucked and bobbed even on the low calm waves of the channel, relying on its small, frayed sail.

They had arrived at the west coast of Manûrqa in time to rest for the night, and had secured lodgings and an evening meal of some sort of roasted goat dish in a local inn. It had been one of the dullest nights of Arnau's life, for he had taken on once more the role of the mute, given that every last person they had met once they left Mahón had been Moorish. Consequently, they passed the entire evening in silence. After months of becoming used to the liturgy of the hours in the monastery, with its rigid times of praise and song, an entire evening of complete silence was still peculiar. And the strange tea he had been served had been an inadequate alternative to wine, too.

They had risen early and headed down to the waterfront of the small village. A number of vessels of different styles and sizes were tied up there, from small one-man coracles to this twelve-foot mastodon. As Arnau stood on the shore silently, contemplating the hopelessness of their quest and growing slowly more sullen,

Balthesar had found the fishermen, the hour early enough to catch them before they sailed. He had managed to persuade one to take them across the water to Mayūrqa, in return for appropriate compensation for the loss of two days' fishing.

The journey would take fourteen hours, the fisherman had informed Balthesar, who had indicated as much to Arnau with fingers. Assured of another half day of tedious silence, Arnau had sunk onto the wooden bench in the front of the boat and played the game of 'spot anything to relieve the boredom'.

They had left the island at the unnamed village and struck out a little south of west, making the best of the winds, which seemed to be surprisingly strong in the channel. He had watched the coast retreat gradually, then begun to pay attention to the gulls that wheeled and cried, but soon they were far enough from land that the gulls became fewer and fewer. Once, he saw something huge and grey rushing alongside them, part of its rubbery hide breaking the surface of the water, and he leaped up to shout enthusiastically about it to his fellow knight, remembering at the last moment and clamping his lips shut, pointing frantically instead. By the time Balthesar reached the bench the creature had disappeared, and Arnau settled back down to his tedium.

After perhaps three hours they spotted another vessel. A sleek Moorish trader with a white lateen sail whooshed past them as though being dragged along by some submarine Titan. Had they not been unable to return to the port for fear of meeting the Almohad lord there, they might even now have been on that fast vessel that overtook them in heartbeats and plunged on towards the west. Arnau realised that they were now on the main route from Mahón to the next island, having veered across to join the path.

Still, they had set off much earlier than any trader from the city, and the bulk of the route's users would be far behind. They saw another vessel an hour later, which similarly swept past them, making it feel as though they were standing still. Another, half an hour after that. Arnau kept shooting irritable, accusatory looks at Balthesar whenever a ship passed. They could have been on a fast vessel, he was sure. There had to have been ways to seek passage with merchants, even if they had to go to another city. The old knight's gaze in reply silently but eloquently suggested that Balthesar was more than happy to move at a sedate pace and follow the same path laid down by Father Lucas centuries earlier.

They ate on board at noon, with a merciless sun beating down on the vessel. Needless to say their repast consisted largely of bread and fish purchased in the village before departure, and Arnau concentrated on the bread. The entire boat smelled like a dead fish anyway, and the sight of the fish on Balthesar's platter was far from enticing. Perhaps ten hours after they had left the coast, they caught their first proper sight of Mayūrqa. In truth, Arnau had seen it coming for some time, a dark ribbon that gradually grew as they closed upon it. The young sergeant had felt at last a moment of elation then, thinking that they had crossed much faster than he expected, until they began to turn and he realised that this was only the nearest point of the larger island, not their actual destination. Their voyage was not over yet.

Two more ships passed them within that next hour, both heading off in the other direction, following the southern side of Mayūrqa, while they were now heading north-west. They ran in that direction for several hours more, the rocky slopes of mountainous terrain sliding by. They passed small coves with tiny settlements, and Arnau silently, privately wondered how Balthesar could be so sure that the fleeing priest had not put to shore there. Still, they sailed on. The mountainous coastline gradually gave way to low, flat shores with forest beyond, and then to farmland.

Balthesar chose then to come forward and stand close by. Arnau kept silent still, irritated, wanting to ask so many questions. By his reckoning, that fourteen hours must have already passed, and certainly the light was beginning to dim as the sun settled behind the island now. Up ahead, he could see a high, rocky headland jutting out, the near shores before it occupied by open farmland and a small village by the water. His hope that they would be putting ashore there faded as they turned once more and made to head round the rocky promontory.

He tried to remember what the older brother had told him about the place in the privacy of their room the previous night. The rocky headland jutted out with the ruined ancient city of Pollentia on this side, and the new town for which they were bound on the far one. Yes, they would have to round the headland to follow this nebulous trail upon which Balthesar was fixated.

He watched strange cliffs slide by as they moved out, the lines of strata along the rocks dipping and rising like waves. He studied them with interest as they passed, and was almost disappointed when they reached the seaward end of the cape. It seemed to be shaped a little like a fork, with deep, narrow inlets between the high rocks, and they were heading across them all, making now directly north, when suddenly Balthesar barked out a word that Arnau could not understand but which sounded very much like a curse.

Arnau turned to look at the older brother, and saw Balthesar gesturing to the fisherman to turn urgently, to take the boat into one of those narrow coves in the cape. The boat slewed sharply, and the young sergeant slid from his seat, then rose, more irritated than ever. He would dearly love to say a few things.

As the boat slid into the shelter of the shadowed cove, the sun on the far side of the island, Arnau turned and scanned the sea, trying to identify what it was that Balthesar had seen that had made him change course so unexpectedly. It did not take him long to spot it: another ship was hurtling along in their wake, bouncing lightly from wave to wave with the speed of a sleek courier. It looked not a great deal different to the other ships they had seen on the journey, and Arnau could not understand what it was that had so surprised the old knight, other than perhaps the fact that most other traffic had continued on along the southern coast.

Then it happened.

They disappeared into the shade of the cove and slowed. The vessel that had been on a similar course emerged past the promontory's end and Arnau caught sight of the sail this time. The angle they had been at before had shown him only a very odd oblique view of the sail. Now he saw in all its glory the red square and the black-and-white check pattern at the centre, marking it as an Almohad ship.

The breath caught in his throat and all boredom and irritation dissipated, leaving instead dreadful nervous tension. His eyes swept around the cove. A white sandy beach lay at the far end, beneath a horseshoe of high, grey, rocky slopes scattered with dry-looking bushes. He was fairly sure they were trapped. If the Almohad vessel was intent upon pursuit, then they would be in trouble. The best they could do was land on the beach, but it would be at best a difficult and hair-raising task to climb those slopes beyond.

He turned and glared urgently at Balthesar, desperate to open his mouth. After all, at this point what harm could it do? Answers to that flooded in, unwanted. Perhaps the fisherman was a devout Musulman, who would be horrified to discover he had Christians on his boat? And with the proximity of the Almohad ship...

He bit down on his words, keeping them caged in. Instead, he watched that ship, willing it not to turn. Would they be suspicious of the small fisherman who had veered sharply out of their path, or would that perhaps be the norm for small boats suddenly beset by large, fast ships? The words of the twenty-third Psalm, an ancient beseeching for protection, rose unbidden into his throat and he fought to keep them in. At a moment like this, prayer seemed appropriate, but he could not imagine it being received well by the Moorish fisherman.

Instead he kept his mouth shut, but hummed the words inside his mouth, as silent as he could, a faint murmuration that would not be heard by the others.

The Lord governeth me, and nothing shall fail to me; in the place of pasture there he hath set me. He nourished me on the water of refreshing.

He converted my soul. He led me forth on the paths of rightfulness, for his name.

For why though I shall go in the midst of a shadow of death, I shall not dread evils, for thou art with me. Thy rod and thy staff, those have comforted me.

Thou hast made ready a board in my sight, against they that trouble me. Thou hast made fat mine head with oil, and my cup, that filleth greatly, is full clear.

And thy mercy shall follow me in all the days of my life. And that I dwell in the house of the Lord, into the length of days.

He felt his nerves calm slightly as the Almohad ship surged past without slowing or turning, hurrying on past the promontory. Balthesar turned and began talking to the fisherman in rapid Arabic, and there was a great deal of pointing before they seemed to come to some sort of agreement. Moments later the boat was picking up speed again, heading for the beach.

Arnau's gaze climbed to that high horseshoe of rocky slopes above the beach with a sinking feeling. The sun was setting, and the entire cove was in shadow, particularly the beach and the rocks. The prospect of climbing that in the dark was not an attractive one.

The fisherman reached the beach and the boat grounded with a scrape and a thud, Arnau staggering to stay upright. With a few words of thanks exchanged, Balthesar grasped his kit bag and leaped over the side of the boat, landing thigh-deep in the water. With difficulty, he began to wade ashore, and Arnaud bowed his head as best he could manage to the sailor before following suit, shivering in shock at the cold water as he in turn plunged into it up to his thighs.

By the time he reached the beach, Balthesar had dropped his kit bag on the sand and hurried back in, putting his shoulder against the boat's timbers and heaving. Arnau joined him and together they managed to push the fisherman back out into the water, where he gave them an encouraging call in Arabic, then turned and began to make his way back out to open water.

Once he was sure the man was out of earshot, Arnau spoke, and his voice came out as little more than a dry croak, unused for a day now. By the fourth attempt it began to sound more like words.

'It's getting dark.'

'Yes.'

'Will he be all right? It's a long crossing.'

Balthesar smiled. 'He will make for the nearest village and stay there until morning.'

'Shouldn't we have gone with him?'

'I am taking my lead from the wily Father Lucas.'

'He's been dead for centuries,' grunted Arnau.

'Yes,' the older brother smiled, 'but his example remains. He existed as a Christian in a world where he was constantly at risk, threatened by the Moorish invader. He will have moved via subtle, unseen ways where possible, and we shall do the same for now.'

'I don't want to climb that in the dark,' Arnau said flatly, pointing at the forbidding slope.

'Quite. We shall sleep on the beach tonight and make the climb in the morning.'

The young sergeant sighed. Wonderful. Time to voice the concern that had been bothering him since they veered into this cove. 'Were the Lion of Alarcos and his men aboard that ship, do you think?'

Balthesar paused for a moment, then nodded. 'It is a solid assumption. These islands are still independent, and there should not be an Almohad presence here. Almohads on the islands at all is worrying and unwelcome. Almohads on the islands apparently unopposed is even more troubling. To have seen them in Mahón's port and then aboard a ship here, so close, cannot possibly be a coincidence.'

'They are following us,' Arnau said nervously.

'Utter foolishness, my young friend. How could they possibly be following us? They did not know where we went from the port and we departed Manûrqa from a tiny village on the other side of the island. Also, when we turned into this cove, they carried on blindly. No, we are not in their sights. It is pure ill luck that we happened to be in their vicinity once more.'

'So where are they going if they are not after us?'

Balthesar smiled. 'They are making for the nearest port. Beyond that headland is Al-Bulānsa and its small port suburb. The Almohads will be in the town and in comfortable lodgings by nightfall, while those ships that took the southern coast will not arrive in the capital at Madina until tomorrow. They have chosen a more comfortable, if less urgent, route. It is all logical, my young friend, without being threatening to us.'

It made sense in a very prosaic way, yes, but Arnau's own views on chance did not stretch this far. What if the Xeuta, or even the Christian shopkeeper on the cliff road, had sold them out? What if the Almohads had been so intent on Balthesar, for whatever reason that the old man steadfastly refused to reveal, that they had hunted and trawled the city and found their trail? After all, the two knights were following a much older, much colder trail, and yet *they* were managing.

'Are you going to tell me who he is? The Lion of Alarcos, I mean.'

Balthesar raised an eyebrow. 'Not now, no.' He began to rummage in his kit to find his blankets to lie in.

'Why not? It could be important.'

'Because there is no need, and sometimes the past should stay buried.'

Infuriated at yet more questions and enigmas and Balthesar's flat refusal to explain anything, Arnau wrapped himself in his own blanket and settled down into the soft sand at the top of the beach. He fretted about their situation, their quest, the old knight's secrets and the absurdity of lying on a beach at night, complained in his head a hundred times that he would never get to sleep, and then promptly fell asleep a few moments later.

The young sergeant awoke at dawn to the cries of the gulls, nostrils full of sand and a mouth that tasted like the underside of a shoe, to find Balthesar already laying out bread and fish on his wooden plate.

'Is that the same fish from yesterday?'

'It will still be perfectly edible.'

'It wasn't particularly edible even yesterday,' Arnau said, his stomach confused, gurgling with hunger and yet creasing with disgust at the idea of eating that fish.

In the end he ate an entirely insufficient breakfast of bread and shook the sand off his blankets before packing them once more into his bag. 'What now?' he asked.

'Now,' Balthesar smiled, 'we climb to the top and then make our way along the path to the farms of Alcudia. There, with luck, we can buy horses. From there we make our way to Al-Bulānsa and attempt to locate whatever route Father Lucas took on his fated trip to the fortress of Alaró seven centuries ago.'

He waited for the old knight to eat his fill of fish and loaves, a joke which was beginning to lose its lustre now, and then stumped off in Balthesar's wake across the beach, feet sinking into the soft sand in the footprints of the older man.

The morning sunlight was already filling the cove and illuminating their path, and Arnau's roving gaze brought him no joy. In the dark, the steep slopes had looked daunting, but in the daylight they were far, far worse. Before Arnau could open his mouth to convey his doubts, Balthesar was off and moving. The older knight seemed to select a direction at random and walked forward. Surely this was not feasible? Most of the rocky faces above the beach were actually overhanging, and those that were not were so steep as to be more or less vertical.

Balthesar rounded a small patch of vegetation at the rear edge of the beach, nestled at the base of the rocks, and turned, disappearing. Arnau followed suit, curious despite himself. Behind the bushes was the lower end of a ravine that had seemingly been formed over the ages by erosion and landslides, judging from the state and the shape of it. The older knight was already beginning to clamber up the V-shaped defile with only a little difficulty, damn him. Shale and scree slid beneath his feet and skittered down to Arnau, who stood and looked up.

At least it was possible. Until he'd realised the gulley existed, Arnau really couldn't have seen a way up that did not involve hanging from rocks by his fingertips.

He took a deep breath and began to haul himself up the troublesome slope, feet slipping and skittering, hands constantly out to the rock at one side or another for balance and security. A quarter of an hour later, he finally emerged from the constantly sliding shale and sharp, unforgiving rocks and clambered out onto grass. Parched, brown and vertiginously sloping grass, but grass all the same. The two men paused to get their breath back and then, at Balthesar's signal, moved off once more, clambering up the green slope with heaving breaths.

It took another quarter of an hour to climb the rest of the way, and when they finally passed beneath the branches of trees at the top and into the shade, Arnau collapsed to the ground and sat for some time rubbing the screaming muscles of his shins and calves. It had been little more than half an hour since they had left the beach below, but it felt as though he had been climbing all day.

As he sat, soothing away the aches and concentrating on his feet, Arnau became slowly aware of a low susurration. He turned in surprise to find Brother Balthesar on one knee, sword tip planted in the ground and leaning upon the hilt as he faced the gulley and the bay. He was uttering something quietly, and yet it was achingly familiar. As Arnau realised what it was that the older knight was whispering, he joined the recitation of the sixty-sixth Psalm in time with his brother.

'Ye heathen men bless our God, and make ye heard the voice of his praising.

That hath set my soul to life, and gave not my feet into stirring.

For thou, God, hast proved us; thou hast examined us by fire, as silver is examined.

Thou hast led us into a snare, thou puttest tribulations upon our back

Thou settest men on our heads. We passed by fire and water, and thou hast led us out into refreshing.'

The Psalm wound slowly to a close and Brother Balthesar finally stood. 'A little thanksgiving seemed appropriate and, while the Lord will almost certainly forgive us for our lack of timely devotions to the liturgical canon, it is always well to show devotion when we can, especially when we are most certainly alone and are offending no one.'

Arnau nodded slowly. 'And I presume the fact that you did it on your knees facing Mecca is purest chance?'

Balthesar gave him the blackest of black looks and dug in his pack for yet more bread and more fish that was beginning to look like grease. They rested there for a short while, and then began to move once more.

'You are surprisingly quiet,' Balthesar said as they wandered through the trees, using glimpses of the sun behind them to set a vague westerly course.

'Still getting my breath.'

'It just surprised me, since you seemed unable to keep quiet when required, and now we are alone you're silent as the grave.'

'It's not as though you'll answer my questions, anyway,' Arnau said.

Balthesar gave him an irritating smile. 'My past is my past, young sergeant. I prefer it to stay there, and you prompting me to dig it up all the time is not encouraging me, I can tell you.'

'But if it has bearing on what we're doing? That man, the Lion—'

'Arnau de Vallbona, men join our order for many reasons, and I am certain that you would be surprised to uncover the bleak lives that have driven men to God's service. Men like Ramon and Lütolf did not come to the Lord's service through chance, but through pain and anguish and the need to devote oneself to a source of redemption. A man's past is just that, and will remain so. If I have call to tell you things, then I shall do so. Until then, please respect the privacy of my life in the same way I do yours.'

And that was that. They strode on beneath the trees for some time, clearly moving along a valley, but gradually the gradient began to change, and they started to descend. A dry seasonal stream bed joined them from the left, and they followed it downhill. Finally, Arnau spotted a roof between the trees. They gave the small farmstead a wide berth, dropping onto its rough track further down, past the house. For an hour they followed that rough road, continually descending at a gentle rate and passing occasional farms. Finally, they left the peaks of the promontory and reached flat land.

'That was the Alraas al Sanawbar,' Balthesar said, thumbing over his shoulder, 'the Cape of Pine Trees.'

'Delightful. Where are we heading now?'

'To Alcudia. There we will buy horses for the next leg.'

'You've clearly been here before.'

'I've been *many* places before,' said the old man enigmatically.

Another twenty minutes across flat farmland with occasional farmsteads saw them approaching the first thing they had seen that bore the remotest resemblance to a town.

'This is Alcudia?'

Balthesar nodded. 'It's a village, really. A large farm estate with several other farms attached. But unlike the others we've passed, one of these is a horse breeder, among other things. Come on. And now it's time to slip back into your mute role.'

Arnau threw him another irritated look but stumped on behind, his eyes on his surroundings. The main cluster of buildings of the farm village lay in one small area, around a central circle of dusty ground into which led several local roads. Pens of animals and corrals of horses were visible, the best irrigated land in the area devoted to their pastureland. Stone troughs, formed of coffins from ancient times, stood around filled with drinking water. Half a dozen youths ran around with training ropes and forkfuls of hay.

The more common arable farming that they had seen since they descended from the cape was in evidence too, all well irrigated and tended. It was a testament to Moorish farming abilities how green and well organised it all was. In a way, it reminded him of the excellent farms around Rourell, all run by Moorish subjects.

What struck Arnau most, though, were the ruins of the old city. The farms had been constructed in and around, and from the stone of, an ancient city that remained visible in the form of walls, arches and columns jutting from the ground like sad reminders of its past – stone skeletons reaching to the sky in supplication.

Such ancient remains were far from unknown to Arnau, who had seen similar sights in Tarragona and Barcelona, and other more rural places. Somehow, though, seeing the remains of a lost civilisation, and indeed the very civilisation that given birth to the Church, as little more than fragments being shat on by Moorish animals felt vaguely offensive. He tried not to let it get to him, but it did so, nonetheless.

They made their way to a house, where Balthesar knocked and waited. The door opened to reveal a man who looked more like a raisin in a felt cap and smock than a man, with whom the old brother had a brief exchange in Arabic. When it ended with the usual polite formalities, which Arnau was beginning to recognise, the farmer disappeared inside once more and shut the door. Balthesar gestured at another building, and Arnau followed dutifully.

The same procedure brought forth a very different occupant. This man was better dressed, in brightly coloured clothes, and his skin was a healthy sun-bronzed colour. There was another brief conversation in Arabic, and then the two men strolled out through the door, a dog running along and yapping at the man's legs until he ruffled the hair on its head. The two men continued their discussion as they approached one of the corrals of horses.

When they stopped, Arnau dropped his kit for a moment to take the weight off, and sat on a block of stone that had once carried some great civic inscription. His gaze strayed across the horses in the paddock appreciatively. He had ridden some very good horses in his time, and like most riders he had to grudgingly admit that the horses bred by the Moors were generally superior to those of their northern counterparts. Certainly the beasts in this corral were generally of a high quality.

He wondered which of them would be his, and smiled as he watched a few of the animals cantering around in some strange equine game. It came as no surprise to him, though, when a quarter of an hour later a farmhand arrived leading two of the least impressive beasts on show. In truth, they would still be a vast improvement on walking, but Arnau would not want to take one into battle.

Unlike their horses back at the preceptory, which were large, powerful, muscular beasts bred to carry an armoured man into the chaos and din of war, these were short, stocky ponies that would look more at home pulling a small vehicle. They had tack and harness, but only blankets and no saddles, he noticed.

There was another exchange between Balthesar and the farmer, then the old knight bowed and said '*As-salāmu 'alayka,*' yet again, and mounted with relative ease. The farmhand brought the other beast to Arnau, who clambered up rather inexpertly, since he had never done so without a stirrup in his adult life. With a cheery wave from the farmer, they moved off once more, trotting away along a road that Arnau thought probably headed north.

'Could you not have bought saddles?' Arnau said once they were sufficiently far away to talk unheard.

'The man is a farmer and horse breeder, Arnau, not a leatherworker.'

'Hmm. And why the smallest and shabbiest beasts?'

'My, we are full of complaint, are we not?' Balthesar said archly. 'We do not need warhorses, Brother. There will be no heroic charges into battle here. We are not on Mayūrqa to lead a cavalry charge against the Moor. We are better served with unobtrusive yet hardy beasts. Besides, they cost considerably less than the good horses and we should preserve our coin. We are burning through the purse at an alarming rate.'

'We?'

Another withering look, and Balthesar gestured to the west. 'Do you see that high, dome-like rock?'

Arnau followed the finger and nodded. A grey peak like an upturned bowl rose from the plain, the mountains behind it visible as lines of blue-grey and green.

'Our next destination lies just beyond. The town of Al-Bulānsa. We shall ride north along the shore, and then turn inland. I suspect that it is that stretch of shore where many moons ago Father Lucas landed with the arm of the saint. We shall pick up his trail there once more. The town is perhaps five miles from here. Come.'

He rode off at a trot and Arnau took some time trying to persuade his reluctant pony to move, then had to hurry to catch up.

Another town, another vague clue. More peril, no doubt. Excellent.

CHAPTER FOUR

SATURDAY, 5 JUNE 1199

Al-Bulānsa was not what Arnau had expected. For some reason, it being the town upon which they had been focusing since leaving Mahón, he had assumed it to be some kind of thriving metropolis to rival that busy port city where they had first landed. In fact, this place was a small town, more resembling a village that had assumed ideas above its station than a town at all.

Al-Bulānsa was a collection of white houses and a mosque that spread up the side of a slope, a small walled enclosure at the summit. There were no defensive walls around the town itself, suggesting to Arnau that this place was not ancient, but a more recent foundation of the occupying Moors. If it had no walls, then presumably it had never been under threat of attack.

What he did appreciate about the place as they rode between lush, well-irrigated fields on the flat ground, was how clean and organised it looked. Even from a distance it was possible to tell how well tended the houses and streets were. As they passed from the surrounding agricultural land into the urban area, selecting one of the less winding streets that marched on up the hill into the centre, that impression grew stronger.

Al-Bulānsa had been carefully planned and lovingly built, and clearly its inhabitants took pride in their town. As the two men moved into the heart of the place, they passed from blocks of residential housing clustered around small courtyards and into a mercantile area with bakeries and butchers and all the typical shops of a small town, though all were currently closed or unmanned, likely due to the time of day and the heat.

'Where are we going?' Arnau whispered, close to Balthesar and confident that his voice would go entirely unheard amid the town's ambient noise and the fact that all the ears in this street were inside their houses and stores, out of the midday sun.

Balthesar nodded. 'We make for the souk – the central market. There I can seek information as to any route towards Alaró that does not use the main roads across the island, and I can collect supplies for the journey also.'

'Try not to buy fish this time.'

The older knight rolled his eyes. '*Your* task is to hold the horses at the edge of the souk and wait in silence for me to return with plans and supplies.'

With a sigh, Arnau nodded and fell quiet once more. If only he had at least a smattering of Arabic, then perhaps he might not have had to play the mute. He resolved that when they returned to Rourell, he would spend whatever time he could find in trying to learn the tongue of the infidel. It could only be useful. Perhaps Balthesar would agree to teach him.

The souk came upon them quickly, the street leading to a wide square which radiated other roads. This was bordered to the east by the frontage of a small mosque and *madrasah* religious school up a low flight of steps and, to the north, at the top of the slope, by the walls of the enclosure patrolled by the men of the Emir of Mayūrqa.

Red awnings had been slung across the streets leading up to the square, and also across much of the square itself, tied to surrounding buildings or poles planted in the ground for that very purpose. It looked shady and inviting in the summer heat and, despite the practice of keeping inside during the hottest part of the day, the souk was thriving in the cool shadow of the awnings. Men, women and children manned their stalls or shuffled around between them, purchasing their everyday goods. Likely half the population of surrounding towns and villages were here for the market.

As they reached the edge of the great square they dismounted, and the older knight threw Arnau his reins, wandering across to a fruit stall – all the near ones seemed to sell fruit – and engaging in a brief barter with the owner. A moment later he returned and proffered a large piece of watermelon, which Arnau took with relish. The older man gave a single nod and left him, wandering across into the souk.

Reasoning that Brother Balthesar would be some time making his enquiries and purchases, the young sergeant found a post where three awnings met and tied the reins of both horses to it, testing it first to make sure it was secure. He then looked around and located a large square stone close by that formed the rear of a decorative fountain, and sank onto it gratefully, beginning to tuck into his melon. The cold juicy fruit was a balm in the steaming heat of a Mayūrqan summer day, and he found that despite his ever-present feeling that they were following a pointless quest, and his ongoing enforced silence, he was actually comfortable and currently enjoying himself.

As he ate, he paid attention to the souk and its populace. This was a relatively rural area still, and he was sure that many of the stall owners had come from the local farms with their produce, rather than being merchants from the town who traded in the goods of other providers. The people seemed pleasant and content. All the stalls in this part of the square sold fruit and produce, but he could see the stalls of bakers close by, and in the other direction housewares and rugs. The souk seemed chaotic, a riot of colour and noise, but clearly it was far more organised than it at first appeared.

Lifting his gaze, he scanned the crowd for Brother Balthesar but could see nothing of him, for he was lost in the throng. He would be somewhere in the middle, presumably, for that was the direction in which he had gone. A man wearing a long white robe of light cotton with a simple white skullcap appeared from a road just to Arnau's left and began to move through the heart of the souk. Possibly the *imam* – the Moorish priest – he reasoned from the simplicity of the garb and the fact that the crowd parted respectfully to allow him passage. This suspicion seemed confirmed a few minutes later when the man climbed the three steps up to the mosque and entered the dark aperture in the wall.

Idly, Arnau thought on what was likely about to happen. He knew little of the Moors' religious observances. They had a rigid prayer schedule, he knew, a lot like the liturgy of the hours back home, based upon the time somehow, perhaps the position of the sun. Five times each day, he seemed to remember hearing, they were called to their prayers. He found himself wondering with interest whether it was compulsory. Did everyone have to drop what they were doing and rush to the mosque? Or just stop and pray where they were? Was there some kind of dispensation for those engaged in important tasks? He'd often wondered that about Sundays at home. It was forbidden for the majority of folk to work on the Lord's Day, and yet somehow the Church had managed to make exceptions for priests and for the poor, apparently. He tried to picture this chaotic market grinding to a halt as everyone faced east and said their prayers, and somehow the image was amusing, bringing forth a light chuckle.

A chuckle that died in his throat.

His eyes had risen once more to those steps before the mosque just as a figure emerged from that darkened doorway, but this was no *imam*.

The Lion of Alarcos seemed somehow to dominate the world around him, filling the scene. He virtually radiated power. And menace, though Arnau was perceptive enough to admit that was perhaps only to him. The shock at the sight of the man jolted him and he felt cold suddenly despite the heat.

Why was he shocked, though? On some subconscious level, he'd been at least half expecting it. Balthesar had suggested that the Almohad lord would have spent the previous night here with his men, and yet the two Templars had blithely walked into Al-Bulānsa as though nothing could be amiss.

Jesus, Mary and all the saints, why had they not waited a day or two to allow the Almohads to go on elsewhere about their business? It was not as if their wild goose chase was an affair with a time limit, after all.

Suddenly alert, he focused on the man on the mosque steps. The Almohad lord looked calm, relaxed, his thumbs tucked into his sword belt. What was he up to? What was he doing here? Arnau saw the man nod, once, and turned, scouring the area the man had been facing.

Two of the Almohad soldiers in their severe black-and-white garb stood at the edge of the souk, not a long way from Arnau. With a sinking feeling he looked about again, this time focusing not on the souk and its occupants, but on the periphery and the streets leading off it. Sure enough he spotted three more groups of the monochrome Almohads, including one in the gateway to the fortified enclosure atop the hill, where other local guards in green patrolled the wall top.

While it was still possible, though growing less plausible all the time, that this third encounter was yet another coincidence, it did not escape Arnau's notice that the positioning of the Almohads looked an awful lot like a noose, prepared to tighten, with Balthesar at the centre.

How could they have known, though? How could they have guessed that the two Christians were here? And if they had known enough to follow them across the water, why had they slipped past the fishing boat last night and not simply confronted them then? Logic still suggested this was mere chance, but the likelihood of this sort of thing happening three times suggested otherwise, as did the worrying positioning of the troops.

Arnau began to panic. He had no idea where Balthesar was, other than somewhere in the centre of the souk. He couldn't see the man and, given that the two of them were wearing poor Moorish clothes and so were more than half the market, the chances of spotting him were small.

Should he move? Indecision surged through him. If they *were* tightening a noose on the souk, and they knew Balthesar was there, then every moment now counted. If not, he might be better served staying with the horses so that the older knight could find him easily. But what use would that be if the Templar was grabbed by Almohad soldiers somewhere in the market?

What to do?

Lead us not into temptation, he reminded himself from the oldest of prayers, forcing himself to calm down and not leap into trouble. *But deliver us from evil*, he added, which suggested perhaps he should do something about the growing danger.

His decision fell into place a moment later as he saw the Lion of Alarcos drop a hand to rest on his sword's pommel. It could so easily be an innocent gesture. It could also be a signal. To his left, two Almohad soldiers began to move forward into the souk.

So be it, he finished the prayer in traditional form and, ignoring the horses, who were beginning to become bored and restless tethered to a post with no water or grass, he cast the melon rind into a gutter and moved off into the crowded market. His hand fell to his sword hilt, drawing looks of concern and disapproval from several of those calm citizens he passed.

Having lost his vantage point on the stone at the edge of the souk, he was now effectively blind to the danger. He could no longer see that noose of black-and-white-clad soldiers, who might very well be closing in even now. He caught occasional glimpses of their lord, still standing on the steps at the mosque and surveying the market with interest.

His panic rose. He could feel it now, in his blood and his bones. They were in danger. Grave danger. He had to find Balthesar and get him out of here. Clearly it was the old knight that had drawn the Almohad lord's eye back in Mahón, not Arnau, but that was immaterial. The sergeant had to help his brother out of danger.

He moved into the area of carpet sellers, reasoning that Balthesar would be looking for a merchant rather than a local fruit farmer or the like. If he wanted to learn of less-used paths around the island, that information would more likely come from those who visited the market from other areas.

He realised he was moving a little fast, almost jostling people out of the way now. His worry over Balthesar rose continually, and he was now leaving a few angry market folk in his wake. But he had no time for niceties. He spotted those two black-and-white-clad men who had moved in from the left. They were walking through the market with purpose.

Arnau began to move even faster. The noose was clearly tightening. Somewhere in here the knight was in trouble, and probably didn't even know it yet. Past more stalls now, raising angry shouts. Someone rattled something off at him in Arabic, trying to bar his way, and he ducked past the big man and into the stalls of the leather workers, noting in passing one with saddles. No time to stop and peruse now, though. His eyes were scanning each and every figure, trying to spot Balthesar.

In fact, he found his fellow knight entirely by chance. Rounding a stall, he was looking off to his left when he walked straight into Brother Balthesar, who was hunched over a table of scrolls, each in graceful Arabic script and decorated with beautiful designs.

Arnau swore momentarily and stepped back.

'Balthesar!'

'Quiet, you idiot.'

'No, this is important. The Lion of Alarcos—'

'Is standing on the steps. Yes. Thank you, Vallbona.'

He rose, throwing his bag over his shoulder with difficulty in the press.

'The horses,' Arnau said, pointing in entirely the wrong direction. Balthesar began to move.

'Do you never follow instructions?' the older man demanded angrily as they shoved their way through the market.

'But they are here. The Almohads. They—'

'They had no idea where I was, even if they were looking for me, which I doubt. I was just another customer bent over a stall. I would have been near impossible to find if a young man who's going to get a wallop later hadn't pushed through the crowd, leaving a very noticeable wake, and drawn attention to me.'

Arnau felt his heart lurch. It was true. That was exactly what he'd done. He had very clearly pinpointed Balthesar's position and even identified him by name. He felt sick. Perhaps the Almohads *had* been here entirely coincidentally, but now they would know.

His wild eyes scanned his surroundings as they moved, and he was dismayed to see the Almohad lord on the steps was now very animated, pointing and waving. His men would be attempting to converge on them.

'What do we do?'

'We run, you fool.'

Ducking around stalls and keeping low, Balthesar moved up the gentle incline, keeping to the areas of the souk where the stalls were slightly taller and more densely packed with goods, providing better cover. They rounded a leatherworker's stall and Balthesar was suddenly gone, disappearing sharply to their left. Arnau started, for his attention had been on their surroundings and he'd not been prepared for the change in route. His heart pounded as he caught sight of one of the Almohad soldiers up ahead, with only half a dozen people blocking the way. The man roared something furious and gestured to some unseen friend before barging ordinary folk out of the way in an effort to reach Arnau.

Feeling his panic rising, he pushed between two stalls where the older knight had passed moments earlier, and then felt his nerves rise yet another notch as he realised he had lost sight of the old man. Had he gone left or right? He could see no sign of him, and though he paused for a moment, he could hear nothing of Balthesar. The pursuing Almohad was all too close, and without time to think clearly, Arnau turned left and pushed on.

Alone now, and in a rising state of alarm, he dodged between stalls as fast as he could, trying not to barge people out of the way or fall over anything. After three more stalls, he realised that he was descending the slight slope and cursed himself, remembering that the old man had been climbing. He'd turned the wrong way after all. He paused by an ironmonger's stall and tried to get his bearings, but at that moment a black-and-white figure suddenly emerged from between two stalls. The Almohad seemed almost as surprised as Arnau, and, sword gripped in hand, opened his mouth to shout something. Instinctively, Arnau's own hand jerked out, sweeping a large, black skillet from the stall and smashing it into the mailed face of the zealot warrior. He had probably done the man no real harm, thanks to the armoured veil, but the blow was a shock and knocked the man back, silencing him and sending him falling into a pile of pans. Arnau ran once more.

Now he concentrated as best he could on the gradient, making sure he climbed as he ran. Two stalls further on, he turned a corner and almost yelped with relief at the sight of Balthesar peering left and right irritably. As the old man caught sight of Arnau, he beckoned and ran on. Arnau followed at speed, and moments later they burst from the crowd at the edge of the souk, surprisingly close to the horses. The two men ran over and pulled themselves up, untying the reins. From a mounted position, they could now see black-and-white-clad soldiers moving towards them. Some were dangerously close. Others, at the edge of the market, were grasping the reins of their own horses.

Balthesar tied his bag to the saddle and began to push through the crowd to a side street, the worried young sergeant right behind him.

'Where can we hide?'

'We can't, you idiot. You just showed the whole of Al-Bulānsa that we speak Aragonese Spanish. That sort of identifies us as a likely enemy. Word will be spreading faster than we can ride. There will be nowhere to hide in the town within minutes. We have to leave, and fast.'

Chastened and red-faced with shame, Arnau kicked his own horse into speed and raced off after the older brother, who had cleared the press of people and was now hurtling off up a side street that curved north and east, climbing the slope.

'Where are we going?' shouted Arnau.

'Into the mountains,' the older brother bellowed back.

They crested the hill and Arnau could see now that the street straightened as it descended. Most of the town was built on the hill's southern slope, and this northern descent was shorter. After perhaps two dozen houses, it petered out into green fields again, with an extensive olive grove on the edge. His sharp eyes picked out a defile that was almost certainly a river or stream running along the edge of town and an ancient arched bridge that carried this road across it. His heart rose into his throat as he realised that the bridge was not unattended. Two soldiers in green – local men, seemingly, like the ones he'd seen on the walls at the summit – stood to one side of the bridge, spears in hand, looking bored.

'I'm sorry.'

Balthesar threw him a withering look that made his cheeks burn hotter. 'Later,' was all the older man said.

Peril, though, was following them that day, for as Arnau began to feel that perhaps they were almost safe, two mounted figures in black and white emerged from a side street ahead of them.

'What now?' gasped Arnau.

'We have no choice. We're trapped. Go back and we're entering the noose you created for us. We have to cross the bridge, even if we have to kill those horsemen to do it. With luck the guards at the bridge have not heard about us yet.'

It appeared that *kill the horsemen* was precisely what they would have to do. The two Almohad warriors spotted their quarry and, realising that they had ensnared them, roared victorious-sounding cries, then ripped their blades free of their scabbards and put heel to flank, charging towards the two Templars.

Arnau had time, as he drew his own sword, to register the shock of the two local guards at the bridge. They were arguing urgently and dithering, perhaps unsure whether to intervene or to remain at their assigned place by the bridge.

Beside Arnau, Balthesar also drew his blade. 'Keep your mouth shut,' he commanded, 'if we are to get out of Al-Bulānsa alive.'

Then, as the four riders converged, swords brandished, Balthesar suddenly whooped loudly and let loose a cry that Arnau had never thought he would hear from the lips of a Templar.

'*Allāhu akbar!*'

Arnau stared at the man, but still the old brother bellowed the Arabic refrain as he swept his sword around, whooping. Then Arnau had to concentrate on his own troubles. The man coming for him wore a fine mail shirt and an elaborate helmet with a pointed spike, and neck guards and a veil of chain that hid all but his eyes. He had no shield, but held his sword in his right hand and clutched the reins with his left, much the same as Arnau.

This would be difficult, the young sergeant knew, for the man was well armoured, while Arnau wore none. He would have to be clever to land a solid blow on the Almohad, whereas any strike by the enemy that landed would likely end the fight.

Give me, O Lord, a steadfast heart, which no unworthy affection may drag downwards; give me an unconquered heart, which no tribulation can wear out; give me an upright heart, which no unworthy purpose may tempt aside. Amen.

The two men met even as Arnau ended the prayer, a shortened form of one by Saint Thomas Aquinas that had been a favourite of the knights at Rourell.

Arnau's saving grace, he reflected as they clashed, was that the man he faced was perhaps overconfident, assured of his superiority in both skill and equipment. His horse was bigger and more powerful than Arnau's diminutive nag, he was armoured and strong. Arnau appeared little more than a ragged beggar with a sword.

But while they might be the 'Poor Knights of Christ', the men of the Temple were no beggars.

The Almohad warrior sliced with his sword almost nonchalantly, as if expecting to simply behead this ragged infidel with his first blow. Arnau ducked the swing, feeling the sword sweep out mere inches above his head. In answer to the attack, he swung with his own blade, a backslash that could have been devastating in other circumstances. While the Moor's strike had missed Arnau entirely, his blow slammed into the man's back. It lacked a great deal of strength, of course, since the mail shirt and the sword were not meeting head on, and the armour would rob the strike of much of its effectiveness, but it would certainly hurt. Most of all, though, it might unsettle the bastard.

Arnau hauled on his reins. For a brief moment he considered riding on, making for the bridge, but two things stopped him. Firstly, the two green-clad men of the emir's forces had moved onto the narrow bridge to block it, having perhaps decided that prudence was the better part of valour. Secondly, Balthesar had not made to escape, but had turned and was moving for a second encounter with his own opponent.

Arnau spun to see that the Almohad had done the same. This time when they met there was no speed to the clash, and their swords met in the air with a metallic clang and a grating noise as blade slid down blade.

What was it Lütolf had taught him? Quiet calm and mastery, maintaining his mental peace with prayer. But there simply wasn't time. This was the heat of battle, not some duel.

The swords flicked apart from another clash

Arnau tried to force himself to calm. Concentration and serenity might be hard to come by in the press of a brutal fight, but despite everything, as he pictured the moves he had practised time and again in the dusty ground around Rourell, the words of Colossians 3:15 flowed through him.

And the peace of Christ enjoy in your hearts, in which ye be called in one body, and be ye kind.

With barely a breath of exertion, his sword as he turned met that of the other rider, knocking it aside. Peace and serenity, though, could only take a man so far, as the apostle Matthew knew...

Do not ye deem that I came to send peace into earth. I came not to send peace, but the sword.

His counter-attack was brutal, and clearly surprised the Almohad, who dodged and parried the first four blows and took the fifth across his mailed shoulder. The man cried out, but his shout of pain changed quickly into one of anger, and he came back with his sword sweeping this way and that like a scythe seeking a crop. Arnau found himself in trouble once more and, as the Almohad pulled back to strike hard, Arnau slammed into him. It had been a calculated move to throw the man off balance, but it almost went horribly wrong. The Moor remained safely in his saddle, his feet anchored in his stirrups, while Arnau, having no such support, almost went backwards off his horse.

Recovering badly, he instinctively jerked the reins, pulling his steed away to buy himself time to straighten and prepare once more. Unfortunately, the Moor was not about to grant him the peace to do so, and danced his own horse close again, hacking down with his blade. With no protection and no shield, Arnau was left with no option but to throw up his own blade to block his opponent's. The two weapons met with such force that the shock ran up Arnau's arm to the shoulder and he felt his wrist go numb. Still, he managed somehow to deflect the blow and tried valiantly to counter-attack with his weakening arm. His blow landed, miraculously, but once more was turned aside by the fine mail shirt of the Almohad, which hung down, forming a divided skirt to the knee.

This was ridiculous. He was fighting a losing battle. He could barely get in a blow and when he did he couldn't cause any damage with it. Moreover, this street was not over-wide, and with each loss of ground he was getting closer to the house walls that would enclose him.

It was with a heavy heart that he silently acknowledged the only path open to him. He positioned himself as best he could to encourage another horizontal sweep of the sword, rather than a chop against which he could only parry. He was rewarded with just that, the Almohad pulling back his blade and thrumming it through the air.

Arnau threw himself forward over his pony's neck. He was already lower, thanks to the relative heights of the horses, and his retaliation was simple. Leaning forward, he drove his blade into the enemy horse's throat, ripping it open as he pulled the blade back.

He hated doing that. Horses were such noble creatures. The lifeblood of this particular noble creature came out in a deluge that

soaked the road before them. The horse did not run in panic. It did
not rear, eyes rolling. It had suffered catastrophic damage, and all
it did was fold up and topple. The Almohad fell away, and Arnau
had just a moment to note the wide-eyed panic in the only part of
the man's face not hidden by the chain veil. Then he was gone.

Arnau straightened in his saddle and watched as the horse fell
to the road, jerking and thrashing. The Almohad stood no chance.
He'd had no time, and there was no room. He disappeared beneath
the horse with a crunch of bone and when he next appeared he was
shrieking, his leg and pelvis flattened and misshapen, blood
pouring from half a dozen places.

Arnau heaved in a breath. It was no heroic victory, but at least
it *was* a victory. He looked up to see Balthesar despatch the other
rider with a deft flick of his blade. The second Almohad lurched
back in his saddle, sword falling from dying fingers as his horse
trotted off up the street, carrying the swaying body.

'Say nothing,' hissed the older Templar as he pulled close for a
moment.

A commotion drew their attention, and they turned to look
back up the street whence they had come. The Lion of Alarcos sat
astride his mount at the crest of the hill, half a dozen men around
him.

Behind Arnau, the two men of the emir's force started shouting
angrily. The young Templar felt a moment of panic, but Balthesar
threw him that warning glance once more and as they turned,
Arnau realised the two green-clad guards were, in fact, shouting at
the Almohads up the street, and not the two shabby men before
them.

Balthesar led the way and reined in just before the bridge,
bowing respectfully to the guards. Arnau glanced back. The
Almohads were not pursuing them down the street, and the horse
that carried the dead warrior was now milling about somewhere in
the middle.

'As-salāmu 'alayka,' the old knight said to the two guards in
greeting, and then rattled out a stream of Arabic that baffled
Arnau, yet sounded apologetic, contrite, and a little bit sad.

Whatever he said seemed to satisfy the emir's men, and the two guards stepped aside and waved them on across the bridge. Arnau turned as they crossed that narrow high arch. The Almohad lord and his men were still at the top of the street, and had not moved. Somehow there was more menace in that than there would be had he been racing after them and bellowing. It was somehow proprietorial, as though the two knights were trespassing on the man's land and he would round them up and punish them in his own good time. The thought sent a shiver through Arnau.

They crossed the bridge and made for a narrow trail through the olive grove. As they passed the nearest trees first the Almohads, then the town, and finally the bridge were all lost from sight. Walking the beasts along between the ancient gnarled trunks in the sizzling noon sun, Arnau took a deep breath.

'I apologise, Brother. That was foolish.'

Balthesar nodded. 'That it was.' He seemed to un-tense and relax. 'In the end no harm came of it, and we are moving once more. All will be as it shall be, for God's plan is unknowable, but it is all.'

'I hope you're right. How did we get out of that? At the very least I expected to be arrested by the emir's men.'

Balthesar shrugged. 'I told them we were travellers from Egypt. It explains any slight quirk in my accent, and also means that we belong to a different branch of Islam to the Almohads. I planted a faint suggestion that our presence offended the fanatical Almohad.'

'How do you *know* all these things?'

'I told you before, Arnau, I was not *born* a Templar.'

'I'm starting to wonder if you were born a Moor.'

Balthesar chuckled. 'Not quite. All right. It would seem that our path is somehow intertwined with that of Abd al-Azīz back there. If we are to work together effectively, perhaps it is time I told you a few things. We have a long and fairly solitary journey ahead of us now.'

'And perhaps you could teach me a little Arabic? It could be very useful.'

Balthesar nodded. 'Perhaps. One thing I did learn before you ran into the market screaming my name and elbowing innocent shoppers was our route onwards.'

Arnau felt his face flush again at the reminder of his impetuous actions.

'It seems that there is a lesser-used path,' Balthesar went on, 'that crosses the entire range of hills and mountains in the north of the island. It should take between two and three days to traverse, for it is apparently high, narrow and quite difficult in places, but will eventually bring us within a few miles of the fortress of Alaró. It is also a trail that has been used since ancient times, by traders and mountain folk. Given those facts, I am almost certain that it is the very path that Father Lucas took with the relic. And if that is the case then it is somewhere on that road, in the next few days, that we will reach the place where the bone stopped.'

To Arnau's mind that was still a little feeble as plans went, but it was more than he'd expected at least, and it would be good to move to somewhere a little secluded. He would be able to talk openly.

'Unfortunately,' the older knight added, 'you attracted the enemy before I could properly resupply. We have melon and fresh bread, but no meat. Until we find a village or farm, we're back on the salted fish.'

Arnau's grimace said it all.

CHAPTER FIVE

SATURDAY, 5 JUNE 1199

The lesser-known rural road of which Balthesar had learned spent its first three or four miles winding up a wide, cultivated vale of fields and olive groves, the sides of the valley gradually rising higher and higher with each pace of the horses. Arnau might have been lulled into a false sense of security over the ease of the route ahead, had those rising hills not presaged harder terrain in the coming hours and days.

As they passed along the dirt road, the only other sign of life occasional farm workers visible in the distance tending to their crops, Balthesar remained irritatingly silent, though Arnau quickly realised the old knight was marshalling his thoughts on events of long ago, of which he had probably rarely spoken. Indeed, he was probably sifting through his life story and selecting only the parts that were pertinent to their current situation, and which were not overwhelmingly private.

They were beginning to climb at the end of the flat land, the road snaking up the side of the valley and becoming more difficult with each minute when Brother Balthesar finally began.

'I have said more than once that I was not born a Templar,' the old warrior said simply. 'None of us were, not even you. And one day, when you are grey-bearded and accompanied on some journey by a plucky youth with more hunger for glory than sense, you will end up relating the tale of Sister Titborga, the villainous Don della Cadeneta, and your strange arrival at the house of Rourell. For even at your tender age your story is already full of dark deeds and mystery. Can you even begin to imagine what men like Brother Ramon and myself have been through in our long years?'

He coughed and peered up ahead at the rising track which stretched ahead as a grey line in a mostly grey landscape. 'Like this road, my own journey has had its ups and downs and has not been the easiest of paths. I will not delve too much into my youth, for I see no need. Suffice it to say that I was brought up as a Christian in a true Christian household, but that my family paid their extortionate taxes to a Moorish lord, for I was born in the south of the peninsula. As a young man I lived among Moors, and I came to see them as a simple fact of life, rather than an enemy overlord. When my father decided that I needed to learn a trade, I studied as a carpenter with a Moorish craftsman, and if I say so myself I had some talent in that area. When I tired of that life, and my parents had joined the host in heaven above, I took what money I had accrued, bought a cheap sword and sought out a teacher.'

'You were not a knight? You were a carpenter?' Arnau said, surprised, though more than once over the winter he had seen Balthesar turn his hand to some matter of woodworking in the repairs to the preceptory, so he should have suspected something of the sort.

'*Jesus* was but a simple carpenter, Arnau de Vallbona,' the old knight reminded him. 'Let us not show undue pomposity.'

'It wasn't meant to sound arrogant. I was just… surprised.'

'Yes, well. Anyway, I found a good trainer. He was old, and unusually cheap, but he had good skills, and he put me firmly on my path. By the time I ended a year with him, I was a competent swordsman.'

'But why choose the sword, if carpentry was what you knew?'

The older brother threw him an irritated look. 'Are you planning on interrupting constantly?' His gaze strayed across the hills and peaks ahead, and he settled back into his story. 'I knew there was good money to be made with the sword. There was endless trouble with bandits, and the local emir preferred to pay mercenaries to deal with his problems than waste good men. And so I joined one of the bands of hunters. For five years I did nothing but track and kill bandits. If a man needs practice at war, I heartily recommend such a path. It is a solid way to learn, as long as you can stay alive.'

He breathed deeply in the pause that followed, and Arnau could see something – pain? – in the old man's eyes.

'One day my band was on the trail of a dozen black-skins from across the water in Moorland who had been terrorising certain villages. There were a score of us, and we were experienced, so we had little fear of this particular group. We were, in fact, *over*confident. We tracked them to a group of caves high in the hills near a gorge, clustered around an old, rock-carved ruin. We had split into four groups of five. I only knew things had gone wrong when we closed on the ruin from the heights above – we were the group given the difficult and slow route around behind the enemy camp, climbing rocks much of the time.'

A shadow of grief passed across his face. 'I watched with my companions from the high rock as our captain was led out into the open ground with his hands bound behind his head, along with his own four men in a similar state. Our intelligence had been wrong. There were not a dozen of them, but at least three times that number, and they had had men in position all around the valley watching the approaches. As we watched, the other two groups of hunters were gradually brought in until fifteen warriors were lined up. We five had somehow escaped their notice, perhaps because we had come by such a difficult route.'

He fell silent. There was a difficult pause, and finally he sighed. 'I watched all fifteen of my friends pushed from a cliff to fall, screaming, to their doom. It is a scene that replays behind my eyes on all bad nights, even after all these years. And I think I must stop the tale there for now.'

The silence reigned supreme then for more than an hour, Balthesar unwilling to speak further, and Arnau too respectful to push for it, though he itched to hear more. The terrain became more and more difficult now, with the grassy plain having long gone, and the scrub-covered green and grey slopes now giving way to sharp, bare rock all around. Underfoot, the path was dusty and uneven, a slope fell away vertiginously to the left, and high forbidding peaks rose to the right.

Finally, as they struggled on, Balthesar cleared his throat. 'Soon, I fear, we will need to dismount and lead the horses. They will be suffering, even this small hardy breed.'

'What happened?' Arnau said bluntly, tense from holding back his curiosity for so long and interpreting the broken silence as a signal to continue.

'Sorry?'

'The bandits. You escaped?'

'Clearly. It was a narrow thing, though,' the old man admitted, and now his words flowed like a stream once more. 'One of those men with me slipped and cried out, drawing the bandits' attention. Next thing we knew, dozens of desert savages from beyond even the lands of the Moors were scrambling after us up the rocks, shouting and pointing. The rest of my companions panicked. Looking back on it, I don't think I was any less panicked than the others, but while they let the terror grip and guide them, I managed to think through it, for I knew that if I didn't do something, we were all dead. I took charge. There were boulders up there aplenty, because of the poor terrain, and with a lot of desperate kicking, we managed to start enough of a small rockslide sufficient to deter the villains from trying to climb up to us. It bought us enough time to run. We got back to the horses and rode for town as though Satan himself was nipping at our heels.'

He gave an odd, regretful smile. 'I expected to be punished when we returned to town. I was just a mercenary, not some lord, and we had failed. Perhaps our emir was a truly insightful man. I like to think so. He thanked us for our efforts, despite our failure. More than that, he paid us half our due fee, which was beyond generous. I went and drank myself stupid on the back-garden liquor the Christians made in contravention of our masters' laws – *horribly* drunk, the way only young men do. I was still inebriated and maudlin when the guards found me and I was hauled before the emir once more. I truly thought I was doomed then, a failed drunken mercenary under arrest. I suspect the emir did not know I was drunk because he had never seen it on a man, and I suspect I hid it well. Or perhaps he understood why I had resorted to the bottle. Whatever the case, it turned out that my companions had informed our lord that I was the only reason they had survived.'

Despite it being one of the seven sins men must avoid, Arnau could see a touch of pride puffing out Balthesar's chest as he took up his tale once more. 'That was how I left the city the next day as a freshly equipped mercenary captain at the head of a new group of fifty men, with a remit to complete our unfinished job.'

His shoulders sagged. 'And finish it we did. I was implacable, barbaric, even insane in my vengeance. We took their heads as proof, with their turbans nailed in place, and we delivered them to the emir. I will not say that he was overjoyed with my new demeanour, but he paid us well and we soon had another commission.'

He sighed. 'Perhaps we could have done very well serving under him, but the next year the Almohads came, and with little difficulty managed to persuade the emir to submit to their growing caliphate. I tried to serve under the new Almohad regime, but they had no interest in a Christian working for them, and I found myself instead poor and begging, too proud to go back to life as a common craftsman.'

He gave a wry smile. 'Isn't it odd how sometimes it is the most ridiculous chance, which beggars belief, that changes everything? I fled north. I found myself back outside Almohad lands once more. I made it to Balansiyyah, one of the greatest of all the *taifa*, which we know as Valencia, the land of El Cid himself. There I sought an audience with the local emir, Abu Muhammad of the Jyaddid. Of course, I was a nobody there. I stood no chance, and that meant seeking out a small group of swordsmen and signing on once more at the very bottom. Chance, though, played its part. As I stood in the ornate palace of Valencia, who should walk in but the emir I had previously served in the south. It seemed that Almohad domination suited him even less than it did me. We reaffirmed a friendship, and he secured me my audience with the Emir of Valencia.'

Arnau looked at the man beside him with a whole new level of respect. He had suspected the man's origins were within Moorish lands, which, of course, suggested he had no noble background, but his tale was more astonishing than the young sergeant had ever suspected. No wonder Balthesar knew the Moorish lands and language, and their people and history too. He had fought under them, and lived under them.

'I spent good years in Valencia,' the old knight continued. 'For some reason, though he had long since died, the spirit of El Cid lived on in that place, and in those days Christian, Jew and Moor lived in relative peace there. We worked together and learned together. And for my part we fought together, too. Once more I was a mercenary, killing the enemies of the Valencian emir for pay. *Good* pay, too. And life in Valencia was different. The difference there between my kind and the Moor was so much less pronounced. I found myself bellowing *Allāhu akbar* as I rode into battle, and it seemed only right. I may pray to the Trinity, and not speak of God by the name of Allah, but it is just a different language, in truth. *God is the greatest* is a good thing to shout in any tongue.'

It struck Arnau as odd that he had never considered this point in such an oddly prosaic manner. Why would it be any different praising God in Arabic than in Spanish, or German, or Italian?

'I fought for years,' Balthesar went on, dragging the young sergeant back into the tale. 'Well over a decade. I served the Emir of Valencia and built up something of a reputation. I think perhaps my faith had become oddly enmeshed with those men I fought for and with. I had begun to see little difference between us. By the time things began to change there, as they had in the south, I was not only a mercenary captain, but I was called *sidi*: a minor lord in my own right. I had hundreds of men at my command, and I fought with a fervour that only grew with each passing year.'

He gave Arnau a strange look. 'I think I had reached my apex. Or possibly, looking back, my nadir. I was as rabid a believer as I could ever be, though I was no longer certain where my spiritual allegiances lay. I fought with the cross on one shoulder and the crescent on the other. I fought Christians for Moors and Moors for Christians. I fought Christians for Christians and Moors for Moors. But be assured that I always fought bad men for good, no matter how they prayed. And my dreadful reputation from the days we brought back dozens of African heads to my lord in the south only grew. I was a butcher of renown. I was a killer of men supreme. I was… well, can you guess it, young Vallbona?'

Arnau frowned in confusion for a moment. Then suddenly things fell into place.

'You were the Pious Killer. The—'

'The *Qātil wari'a*. Quite. So now you know what it is. The *Qātil wari'a* is me. A name earned in three decades of mayhem, bloodshed and bellowing the love of God in whatever tongue I was using at the time.'

'Heavens above and saints bless us,' breathed Arnau. Somehow old Brother Balthesar looked different to him now. Just how many men had the old man killed in his long life? He felt cold at the mere thought.

'Perhaps now you understand why I am reticent over my past. Why I said that some things – some *names* – should stay buried.'

'But what of the Lion of Alarcos?' Arnau said suddenly. 'I assumed he was part of your tale.'

'My story is far from done,' Balthesar sighed. 'But the last part should be saved for the campfire.'

They rode on for the rest of the day, high into the mountains now. The mountains around them were beautiful, not dissimilar to the lower southern slopes of the Pyrenees near Arnau's home, but the trail was hard, and he could not imagine what they would do if they met a local with his cart coming the other way. The sun began to sink as they entered a new type of terrain, where oddly shaped rocks jutted from the earth all around, as though the world's skin had shrunk and the bones protruded. They stopped at a small dell formed by a natural circle of the rocks and made camp. While Arnau set up their blankets and gathered wood for a small cooking fire, Balthesar disappeared and came back with a rabbit, thank the Lord, which he then skinned and began to prepare. He smiled at Arnau, knowing how grateful the young man would be not to face that old fish yet again.

Once they were settled in their small camp and eating delicious roasted rabbit with bread and fruit, Balthesar smiled. 'This is most pleasant, but I will warn you that these mountains are barren and home to much animal life. There are wild cats up here that are of a size not to normally pose a threat, but if they are starving and we are unwary, we could very well fall foul of them, so listen and relax, but always keep your eyes open.'

Arnau did so, nerves pinging at the thought of meeting a savage, starving wild cat who was so desperate that he might bite a man.

'It changed again, as it always must,' Balthesar sighed. 'Valencia had been strong and glorious, and a bastion for tolerance and reason, as Mayūrqa is now – the very last, in fact. But all of Al-Andalus had fallen beneath the zealous heel of the Almohad caliph, and Valencia was a prize of some importance. The emir knew he was being targeted. He reached out to the Christian lands, but who among the godly kings was going to aid a Moor against his enemies in those days? Short-sighted and foolish. When the Almohad forces came to Valencia, we had only our own men, including all those mercenaries like myself who had fought for the emir for years.'

'The Almohads. They are a plague,' Arnau grunted.

Balthesar snorted. 'All invaders are a plague, Vallbona. Iberia softens invaders, though. The Carthaginians came here as overlords, but became part of the land. The Romans came in conquest, but soon Iberia became a second home to them after Italia. The Vandals came with destruction, but stayed as Iberians. The first waves of Moors were no different from the Almohads we see now, rolling their new religion across a conquered land, but they soon came to be relatively tolerant and calm. They became children of the peninsula. Successive waves of invaders now have come from Africa, for there are *many* kinds of Moor, and yet they have all, in the end, become the same. So will the Almohads one day, I suspect, but their belligerence is likely to force Armageddon before then. They will push for the battle for dominance in the peninsula and begin the war that will engulf us all. But I digress. Yes, it was the Almohad plague that came to Valencia.'

He leaned back in his blankets in the warm summer night, the canopy of stars opening up above them. 'We could not win. I doubt anyone who fought for the emir believed there was a hope of holding the caliphate back from Valencia, but such was the need that we tried anyway. Once more I took up the sword and fought for the cross and the crescent. Once more I was *Qātil wariʿa*. For the *last* time, in fact. In those days I became *Malak Al-Mawt* – Azrael, the angel of death – which is another name I wore, and which I pray never resurfaces. I made the Almohads pay for every foot of land they took as they closed in on the city of Valencia. Finally, when we were beneath its walls, fighting out last great fight to keep the *taifa* independent, I made a mistake.'

He rolled onto his back. 'We fought like lions. Oh, and in those days the Lion of Alarcos did not exist, for the disaster at Alarcos had not yet happened. Abu Rāshid Abd al-Azīz ibn al-Ḥasan was just an Almohad lord then, albeit a dangerous one. He was one of the lesser commanders in that army that came to force Valencia to submit. One afternoon, we sortied from the city gates in the latest of many awful fights, thousands of us under arms, refusing to submit to their domination. I was a lord myself then, a vicious killer with a name that was used to frighten children.'

'God forgives such things.' Arnau said, impulsively.

'I pray daily that he does. Time will tell.' The old man scratched his beard and yawned. 'I saw one of their leaders through the press. My sword bit into steel and leather and flesh, and sometimes horses, as I carved a path. I wanted him. My vanity as a warrior was truly ascendant. I wanted that leader. I would see if I could buy another day for Valencia with his death. You know who he was, of course?'

'Abu al-thingy. The Lion.'

Balthesar nodded. 'Abd al-Azīz: a lord of the Almohad. I almost had him, too. I went for him, and I almost had him. At the last moment, one of his more impressively garbed men got in the way, screaming curses to my God, and spitting bile. He was a good warrior but only a young one. I, on the other hand, was *Qātil wari'a*, and I had killed more men than leprosy, or so it was said. I feinted once or twice before I gutted him and pushed the gurgling, dying warrior from his horse.'

He sighed. 'That warrior was little more than a boy, really. He should not have been on a battlefield. I have regretted sending him to his paradise every single day since then. He was just a boy, Arnau, years younger than yourself. But he was in the way of that which I sought, and I killed him without a thought. Sadly, I was swept away then. You have been in battle, I believe? Not a simple fight or a duel, but true battle? Battles are tidal; they have ebbs and flows, and a single man cannot fight the current. I was pulled away after I finished the boy, long before I could kill Abd al-Azīz.'

He sighed. 'Valencia capitulated the following day, and with it the last *taifa* of the mainland fell to the ever-expanding caliphate. Reason had died in Al-Andalus and my world was gone. That was more than twenty years ago now, young Vallbona. And it was only on the next morning as I fled north among the survivors, hearing fragmented tales of the aftermath, that I discovered that the boy I had killed protecting his lord was Rāshid.'

He paused, clearly expecting Arnau to understand. When the young sergeant simply lay silent and blank-faced, the old man frowned. 'The Lion of Alarcos is Abu Rāshid Abd al-Azīz ibn al-Ḥasan: Father of Rāshid, Servant of God, Son of Hasan.'

'You killed his son?'

'Quite. He harbours more than a little hatred for me. I was the enemy, and a Christian defying his caliphate, and that was all before I killed his boy.'

'Jesu, he will never stop hunting you.'

'Actually, he did not pursue me then. I heard nothing of him for a long time. You see, since the day I abandoned the lathe I had always been a man of the sword, living by the purse, but I had never really seen the Moor as evil. Even the Almohad. They were people as were we. Growing up among them perhaps changes a man's perspective. When I fled from Valencia, I was seeking a new chance to fight. A new war and a new border. Perhaps stupidly, I came to these islands, for they are close by ship. Here I found the last *taifa*, the last emir, and I thought to fight for the remains of my dying world. But the emir – a proud man called Ishāq, of the Ghaniyid – did not want warriors. The sea was his rampart, and he felt sure he did not need to defend himself from Almohad advances. I tarried a while on this island, unable to earn a crust as a warrior, but the strangest thing happened. My pride began to wither, and while I was here and becoming poor and hungry, I fell back upon carpentry as the only skill I had. I lived well for a while, and with every chair I made my need to fight and to kill drained from me. I began to become something new. I was a man who created instead of destroying.'

A look of odd contentment struck him. 'I was happy. But the legend of *Qātil wari'a* followed me like a bad smell. Abd al-Azīz finally sent men. He had, I am sure, sent men to every quarter of the world to find me once Valencia was settled, and find me they did, on Mayūrqa. I fled back to the mainland, unwilling to confront the truth. I was not that man any more. In fact, I would say I had become a lost soul. Carpentry was seeing me through and had been something of a catharsis for me, but I had no real purpose and no goal. I was a killer no more, but the world seemed unwilling to let me disappear.'

He propped himself up on an elbow. 'I met a priest, who changed it all: a man called Diego.'

Arnau blinked. 'Father Diego from Rourell?'

Balthesar nodded. 'At the time he was a local priest and teacher in a village near Tortosa. He took me under his wing. I found true peace for the first time under his care. I renounced the sword, spoke my vows, and took up the poor habit of a mendicant priest, living by the charity of good folk and preaching peace and understanding. After two years with Diego, I began to move through Iberia as a wandering holy man in the border lands, where our two peoples clashed. I sought, perhaps in a blind way, to heal the division between the Moor and the Christian, for I could see like no other the bonds between us. I did good work. I began to put my life right, healing wounds I had helped to create with my sword.'

He took a bite of cold rabbit. 'Sadly, while I had changed, Abd al-Azīz had not. He devoted every moment of his free time now to hunting me. I evaded killers and assassins every month for years, despite my obscurity and anonymity. I had stopped being the Pious Killer, but my past was still with me. Eventually all Moorish lands, being Almohad-controlled and far too close to Abd al-Azīz for comfort, became too troublesome for me. I ended up fleeing north permanently to Christian lands. It was exceedingly odd for me. I was born and bred a Christian, and had been reborn under Diego, but the simple fact was that I had spent most of my life in Moorish lands. Moving into the Christian kingdoms of the north was utterly alien and bewildering for me. I spoke Arabic far better than Aragonese. I still have an Almerian accent in both languages.'

He lay back again. 'I looked for Diego. He had left his church near Tortosa, but he had left a trail that a clever man like me could follow. I found him within the year. He too had gone north. Something had happened at his church. He would not say what, and has held his tongue on the subject as long as I have known him, but it had pushed the very model of a man of peace to take up the sword. I found Diego at Rourell. He had signed on as a sergeant, albeit a rather old one.'

Arnau tried to imagine the old, mad-haired priest in the black of a Templar sergeant. The image did not sit well.

'I almost left him to it,' Balthesar said quietly, 'but because it was late at night I was given accommodation in the guest quarters – the very room I think you yourself first slept in – and I spent that evening in the company of two men.'

'Who?'

'Ramon de Juelle and Lütolf of Ehingen. One night with my brothers, and I never left. I signed on the next morning, and affirmed my vows within the month. I was grateful to have found the Temple, and I think the preceptor at the time was pleased to have me, for manpower was scarce and I was a warrior, tried and tested. The rest is history. I am still there.'

'And Father Diego? How did he come to discard the sergeant's robes?'

Balthesar nodded. 'We were at Alarcos together a few years ago. Many Templars were. It was perhaps the most appalling battle of all time, and certainly the worst in my memory, even considering what I lived through in Valencia. Whatever had driven Diego to seek the sword, he laid it to rest on the field of Alarcos. When he returned to Rourell with our despondent, beaten column, he became a simple priest once more, attending to our spiritual needs.'

'And the Lion?'

Balthesar smiled. 'It would be nice to say that I fought him on that field and that I achieved some sort of vindication. But the simple truth is that I never even laid eyes upon Abd al-Azīz at Alarcos. It is the battle where he made his name, though. At Alarcos he became the Lion, as I had become the Pious Killer at Valencia. We never met on that field and he returned to Almohad lands in triumph while I limped north in defeat. In truth it has been three or four years since I gave any thought to the man. I assumed him to be busy plotting his part in the next great expansion of his caliphate. But then, that was perhaps not so wide of the mark. Perhaps he was, for here we are in the last *taifa* – the lands of the last independent emir – and so is he. Where else would the Lion of Alarcos be than the one land that holds out against the caliphate? Mayūrqa is his new Valencia. So is it bad luck that he and I are here, Arnau, or is it fate?'

CHAPTER SIX

SUNDAY, 6 JUNE 1199

S omehow the revelations of the previous day had not brought the clarity and focus that Arnau had expected. There had been such mystery surrounding the history of Brother Balthesar and the man known as the Lion of Alarcos that Arnau had expected, when he knew the answers, that all things would fall into place. In fact, little had changed, though now perhaps he understood more of why they had not.

They were still hunting the relic of a saint which had been lost to human knowledge for seven centuries, and it still seemed like a pointless and doomed exercise to the young sergeant. And though he now knew the history of the Almohad lord and his connection to Balthesar, it did not alter the fact that they were still on the island together and that the Lion posed the most appalling, constant threat to them. Furthermore, it would appear that if Abd al-Azīz was here on the island, then Mayūrqa was plunging into the same disastrous struggle as Balthesar had lived through in Valencia: the unforgiving, conquering might of the caliphate and the struggle of the beleaguered *taifa* to remain independent. That thought alone was far from encouraging.

But the most important concern right now was that they were poorly provisioned, crossing a difficult mountainous wilderness on beasts that had very definitely seen better days, following Balthesar's approximation of a route that *might* once have been taken centuries ago by a priest they only knew by name, and who had disappeared without trace. It was not a reassuring thing upon which to ponder, and the uncertainty was at the heart of Arnau's growing disaffection with their quest.

They rose the next morning in that rocky dell with the charred remnants of the rabbit's carcass over a pit of ash, ate the few parts of the previous day's bread that were not so stale that they resembled the surrounding rocks, drank sparingly from water flasks the old man had bought in Al-Bulānsa, and set off once more into the wild, hungry and thirsty.

The terrain did not change. The path meandered along the edge of frightening drops and occasionally crossed ridges with the most astounding view where tantalising glimpses of the sea could be seen to the north between high, grey, severe-looking peaks and crags. Those same weird rocks jutting from the ground became ever-present, and the road occasionally wound between them.

The morning passed in relative silence, with only occasional exchanged pleasantries against a background of humming bees, chittering birds and rasping cicadas. Balthesar had seemingly used up all his words in the telling of his tale the previous day and, now rather taciturn, seemed unlikely to launch into further dialogue. Even if he did, Arnau did not feel up to it anyway. His own morale was suffering too much for light conversation.

Why had the preceptrix agreed to send them on this fool's quest? Why did Balthesar not see the lunacy of it? The uncomfortable thought struck him that perhaps Balthesar simply needed time away to finish healing and this was his excuse, and that perhaps after all the trouble he had brought to Rourell, the preceptrix was trying to get rid of Arnau for a while. While he continually brushed that idea aside as unworthy and unlikely, it kept creeping back in like a thief in the night.

They plodded on in silence, and as the sun began to climb high, filling these valleys with sizzling warmth, the next major worry began to gnaw at Arnau. Whatever the older knight had said about the thriving wildlife of this region, Arnau had seen virtually nothing other than large birds circling above that looked alarmingly like vultures. Their bread was gone and there seemed little chance of catching another rabbit. If only a man could eat bees and insects they would feed well, but real meat seemed unlikely. They would therefore be extremely hungry by the time darkness fell. At least the horses were eating well, thanks to the many small dells of greenery between the rocks, and they had found small streams here and there in which to refill the water flasks. But the gurgling in Arnau's belly indicated just how hungry they would yet become.

Still they moved through the landscape slowly and silently, Balthesar perhaps in mournful reverie, and Arnau in a worried huff. It was as they crested another slope and were treated to a distant view of yet more green and grey mountains with the road winding off into the distance that he finally snapped and spoke.

'This is *ridiculous*.'

'Oh?' Balthesar turned, his expression unreadable. 'How so?'

'We have no idea whether we are in remotely the right place. We could be on entirely the wrong side of the island. You've never travelled this road before, and we can't be certain the ancient priest did. We're hungry and we're out of supplies, there is nothing around to hunt, and this entire quest is beginning to look utterly doomed. And even if we get to the end of this stupid, difficult road, I would not be surprised to find your old friend from Valencia waiting for us with his men.'

'You paint a bleak picture, young Vallbona.'

'I prefer to think of it as realistic.'

'But once again, you seem to be distinctly lacking in faith. The Lord will provide.'

'Then he'd better send a roast chicken and a signpost our way soon,' Arnau grumbled bitterly.

'How about a village?' the old knight asked.

'Even better,' snapped Arnau. 'Or perhaps a thriving town with a full market and a cheerful innkeeper with a mug of beer?'

'No. Just a village. Like that one.'

Arnau's brow furrowed as his gaze followed the old knight's pointing finger. The young sergeant had been so focused on the peaks ahead in the distance and the high road crossing them that he'd not looked closely. The path from here descended into a deep valley, and at the bottom was a small area of cultivated greenery with orchards and groves, and a small collection of grey stone huts clustered around a central square. A village.

'You knew it was there,' accused Arnau as he turned and saw the wide smile on Balthesar's face.

'No, young man, but I had faith in the Lord and he provided. Come. Let us replenish our supplies and seek information. And remember to be quiet, respectful and circumspect. You are still a poor mute. We know nothing of this place or its inhabitants, after all.'

Despite the apparent change in their fortunes and the possibility that starvation had been staved off, Arnau remained tense as the two men descended into the lush hidden valley. This was still an unknown world for him and he could not anticipate its potential dangers, other than starvation and the unlikely, but always possible, sudden appearance of the Lion of Alarcos. Balthesar led the way and soon they were in the flat farmland, riding along between a well-irrigated field of already golden wheat and a small orchard of apricot and citrus trees.

'Well, well,' said the older knight in a surprised voice, and Arnau leaned out to look past him, blinking in astonishment. They were now approaching the square, which was surrounded by squat stone houses, and the focus of the village, at the very centre of that open space, seemed to be a small stone cross.

'Is that what I think it is?'

Balthesar chuckled. 'The Lord will *always* provide, young Vallbona. I tell you repeatedly: have faith.'

Wide eyed, Arnau followed the older knight into the small village, which in reality was little more than nine or ten houses surrounded by worked farmland, yet felt like a metropolis after a full day of trekking through mountainous terrain with no sign of human life. As they walked their steeds into the dusty square faces appeared at windows, and two of the doors opened to reveal stocky farmers wearing expressions comprising equal parts surprise and suspicion.

Brother Balthesar reined in and sat straight in the saddle, seemingly weighing it all up. Finally, he spoke in Arabic, to Arnau's surprise, given the cross in the square. It was a greeting, but not the usual Moorish one he recognised. There was a long pause and finally a man stepped out from his house, a stout wooden stick in his hand, his eyes narrowed. He replied in Arabic, with that same regional inflection that Arnau had begun to recognise as native to the island. This initiated a brief exchange, and finally the man's suspicion seemed to fade and he reached up and took Balthesar's hand.

The knight slid from his saddle, landing with a grunt, and spoke with the man some more before turning to Arnau. 'We are in luck. It seems that someone in this village has a passing command of Spanish. Come on.'

The local led them to another house, and they walked their horses in his wake, a small crowd of locals following them in an interested cluster, murmuring breathlessly.

'I suspect they don't get many visitors at all, let alone foreigners,' Arnau said.

'Quite,' Balthesar agreed. 'In fact, I suspect the only visitors they see at all are the Moorish tax collectors.'

They left their horses outside with one of the villagers, who nodded and smiled, and entered a small house that looked identical to all the others in the village. A small family sat awaiting them, the man a stocky fellow with a leathery complexion and an interested expression. His wife and two children looked nervous, sitting close together in a corner, watching with beady eyes.

'Good day,' Balthesar said slowly, in Aragonese Spanish.

'Hello,' the man replied. 'My Spainish not so good, no? I not use it often.'

The knight laughed. 'Your Spanish is considerably better than the Arabic of my friend here. Allow me to introduce myself. I am Balthesar d'Aixere, a scholar of the Church from the Crown of Aragon, and this is my companion Arnau de Vallbona, formerly of Barcelona. I must say I was surprised to find a cross on my journey. Surprised and delighted, in fact. Might I ask your name?'

'My name Yaqoub. Or Jacob, as you say.'

'Well met, Yaqoub. This entire village is a Christian community, I presume?'

'Yes. Since forever. Always Christian.'

'How fascinating. I had no idea you were here. I met a small community in Mahón across the water, and in earlier years I have known other Christian communities on the island, but always as a minority within a Moorish town, never as a sole isolated village. Are you left alone in peace here?'

The man nodded. 'Pay taxes. Leave in peace.'

'Excellent.' He turned to Arnau. 'Faith, my young friend.'

Arnau waited until he turned away and then rolled his eyes.

'I would be most grateful,' Balthesar said in a friendly tone, 'if we could purchase from you and your fellow villagers supplies for our journey – some food and perhaps an extra blanket or two?'

The man nodded. 'Yes. *Give* you supplies. Where to you go?'

The old knight smiled. 'Currently to the fortress of Alaró to the west of here, and from there I am unsure. We follow a rather obscure and uncertain path.'

Yaqoub shook his head. 'Alaró run by hard man. Not go there. Not friendly.'

Balthesar shrugged. 'I am afraid we must. We are seeking something, you see, and that place is the next known landmark on our trail. I always thought this island was still very tolerant. Is the Lord of Alaró not so, then?'

'Years ago,' the man said, '*all* good. Now days, not all so good. Moors becoming hard. Not trust us like before. Some do,' he added with a shrug, 'some not.'

'That is a shame for a place I remember as a home, once,' the knight replied. 'We have encountered Almohad soldiers on the island, and they are most certainly *not* peace-loving men like the locals I remember. Might I ask, is the cross in the square your gathering place for worship, or do you have a chapel too?'

The man shook his head. 'No chapel. Not any more.'

'Not any more? There was one, then? I am a monastic scholar, you see, travelling with my novice here. We are seeking evidence of the early Church on the island, but there are so few reminders left to be found. I know of a ruined basilica many centuries old in the south of the island that is little more than low foundations now, and I have found a few sanctuaries, unused but remaining untouched and whole.'

'Sanctuaries?' the man asked, trying his mouth around an apparently unfamiliar word.

'Hermitages?' Still a blank look, and Balthesar pursed his lips. 'Like a small chapel that is lived in by one religious man as his home too.'

'Ah,' the man nodded with a smile. 'Once was santry here.'

Balthesar turned a raised eyebrow to Arnau, and then swung back to Yaqoub. 'Was there, indeed? A long time ago?'

The man, clearly eager and excited now, nodded. 'Come, come. Show.'

Arnau, baffled by this entire exchange, hurried out in the wake of the local and the old brother. They strode across the square, the gathered crowd still there and watching them with interest, and stopped in front of another house. Arnau failed to see what was interesting about it, and the door opened a moment later to reveal a small, wizened old man.

Yaqoub lifted a hand and pointed. Arnau studied the indicated place above the crude hut's door. It took him a long moment to spot the cross carved in the stone, for it was so aged and weathered that it had almost disappeared. It had been carved roughly, clearly by the hand of an ordinary man, and not a master stonemason.

'Fascinating,' Balthesar smiled. 'So we have a small Christian community grown on the site of an ancient sanctuary. God is pointing the way, young Vallbona.'

'It could still be nothing,' Arnau replied, though there was little conviction in his voice. The small, tantalising signs were enough to rekindle that spark he had felt back across the water. He could feel his scepticism ebbing once more, and his excitement growing. Had Balthesar actually been right about Father Lucas's route after all? Had the priest been here with the relic?

'Look, look,' urged the man, gesturing to the old resident, who shrugged and stepped out of the way. Yaqoub led them inside and turned. Balthesar and Arnau followed suit and looked up as indicated to the same stone. This other side had badly weathered carving on it too, but much more of it.

'Lord of Grace and Mercy,' Balthesar said in a breathless whisper.

'What?' asked Arnau.

'Look,' Balthesar said, running his fingers over the marks in the stone. 'SANC... TVS... STE... PHA... NVS. Sanctus Stephanus,' he repeated in a reverent whisper. 'The remains of the blessed first martyr were here, Vallbona.'

As he removed his finger, Arnau squinted. The light was not good in here, but still he was less than convinced. The carving was ancient and worn and, while it could quite conceivably have said Sanctus Stephanus, it could as easily have been a recipe for soup, as far as Arnau could see.

'I think that could be wishful thinking,' he said quietly.

'You may think what you like, Vallbona. I believe that somewhere here was a sanctuary, centuries ago, to Saint Stephen, which has to be more than mere coincidence if Father Lucas passed through here with the arm of that very same saint. Sadly, I would be most surprised if anyone here had any knowledge of those days. These are not descendants of the community that was here, as were those we spoke to in Mahón. This is a fledgling community that has grown up around a once sacred site. Consequently there will almost certainly be no ancient tales passed down to point the way from here.'

He fell silent and, despite his misgivings, Arnau could feel that excitement building once more. It was such an attractive idea, and the simple fact was that if a sanctuary *was* built here and dedicated to Saint Stephen, then not only was it likely that the relic had passed through here, but either something of import happened here, or even perhaps this was where the bones came to rest. Why else build a sanctuary and go to all the effort of carving these stones?

'But where is the sanctuary now?' he asked.

'A very good question.' The older knight turned to Yaqoub. 'Where did this stone come from, do you know?'

Yaqoub turned to the wizened old owner of the house and there was a brief exchange. Balthesar clearly understood what they were saying, but he waited politely for the man to nod and explain to them in his stilted Spanish for Arnau's benefit.

'Great-great-grandfather build house. Take stone from field near. Show you.'

Again, Balthesar flashed that smile at Arnau, and the young sergeant couldn't help but reciprocate. Leaving their horses with the lad in the square, they hurried after Yaqoub and the old local, who led them past the houses, between two fields that had been cleared of rocks and stones, and over a small wooden plank bridge into an area of relative wilderness. They had to stamp down the summer growth of weeds and forge a path into an overgrown area dotted with occasional trees and prickly bushes, and after perhaps five minutes the two locals stopped. A brief discussion in Arabic ensued, and finally Yaqoub nodded to the two adventurers.

'Here. This where stone from.'

The two locals gestured around them, and then threaded their way back past Arnau and Balthesar until they reached the edge of their compressed undergrowth, where they stopped, turned, and began to watch the two travelling monks with interest. Arnau felt rather odd under their scrutinising gaze, but Balthesar was ignoring them and had already begun to search, using hands and feet to comb the greenery, bending almost double.

Arnau, not entirely sure what he was looking for, joined in. He kept finding lumps of stone, though whether or not they were parts of an ancient sanctuary or just some random lump like all the others in these mountains, he simply could not tell. He could hear excitable noises from Balthesar as he searched, but no distinct indication of discovery.

He was about to give up entirely when his foot tripped over a stone and, as he glanced down in irritation, he noticed something odd jutting from the ground, jammed between half-submerged rocks. Crouching down with a creased brow, he peered closer at it. Misshapen and covered in muck, it was hard to tell what it was, but there was a hint of the human form about it. His frown deepened and he felt the hair rise on the nape of his neck. He couldn't see what it was made of or make out its true shape. It would be very hard to tell unless it was removed from where it was half buried between rocks and then cleaned, but for a heart-stopping moment, Arnau thought it might just be a statue of the Virgin herself. It definitely wasn't remains, or a casket containing them, but it could be something important. Something connected.

He rose to his feet, ready to call to Balthesar and point it out, but as he did the old knight leaped up excitedly and called him over. With a last, fascinated look at the buried object, Arnau hurried over to Balthesar.

The older knight had cleared a small area of long grass and weeds. What he had uncovered was a corner of a wall, or at least the lowest courses of it. It was, at best, unimpressive, but Balthesar seemed to be treating it as though he'd had a visitation from the saint himself.

'A wall,' Arnau commented.

'Two walls, complete with a corner.'

The young sergeant frowned. 'It could be anything. Could be something only fifty years old. Could be an old animal shed or something.'

'Use your eyes, Vallbona. This is the sanctuary, for sure. Father Lucas was here, I know it.'

Arnau chewed his lip sceptically. 'It's just a corner of stones. How can you be so sure?'

'Evidence. Not faith this time, Vallbona, but logic once again. See the stones? These are shaped and worked in a very old manner. You can see each and every chisel mark, just like that lintel in the old man's house. That stone came from here. It is the same work. This was the sanctuary of Saint Stephen. And looking at the rough workmanship, I believe the occupant, which can only have been Father Lucas, built it with his own hands over some time, or at least began to build it.'

Arnau tried not to get too excited. It all still seemed just a little far-fetched, but he remembered that buried lump that might just have been a statue of the Virgin, although more likely a piece of old refuse. He felt his pulse quicken. If was a lot to assume, but even though it seemed fanciful, it was still most definitely *possible*. This *could* have been a hermitage built by the fleeing priest with his precious cargo. But if so, why did he stop here instead of going on to the fortress of Alaró, and what happened after he stopped?

He voiced those two very questions as he crouched and peered at the shaped stones.

Balthesar tapped the side of his nose. 'I think I know. See here?' He showed him where one stretch of wall ended in a distinct squared-off shape. 'This was for a door. There is no stone beneath it, but this can only be the opening for the door. And yet the doorway has only one side. Where is the other?'

'Probably in the old man's fireplace,' Arnau suggested.

Balthesar nodded and crouched. 'There is that possibility, I admit, but I do not think so. If you look at this other wall, you can see where our friend over there's ancestor, and the other villagers, took apart the stones to add to their own houses. They took very basic ones to use, and yet left the shaped door frame. If they left this side, why would they take the other?'

'Because they only needed one?'

Balthesar cast an exasperated look at him. 'Prosaic and possible, but your explanation gives us nothing to go on. If this is simply a ruin plundered for local houses and I am wrong, then our trail of breadcrumbs ends here. If so, Father Lucas probably grew old and died in this place, and the fate of the arm of Saint Stephen will forever remain a mystery.'

Arnau's eyes narrowed. 'So what is *your* theory then, Brother?'

'I think that side of the door is not there because it was never built. I think the hermitage is incomplete. I think our friend Father Lucas created an altar for the relic, the focus of which is now that lintel back in the village, and I think he was interrupted before the hermitage could be finished.'

'Interrupted?' frowned Arnau. 'By who?'

Balthesar shrugged. 'The most likely explanation is that he stopped here, and soon afterwards the invaders found him. You see,' he said, straightening, 'following their initial conquest of the islands, the Moors will have taken some time to fully subjugate the place. I know of old tales that fortresses like Alaró, and a similar place once called the sanctuary, held out against the invaders for months. Years, even. But as the Moors subjugated the Christian populace, they likely dismantled churches and sanctuaries, or converted the better ones to mosques as they did elsewhere. I have seen the results of their handiwork in the ruins of ancient basilicas elsewhere on the island.'

He pointed down at the stones below him. 'This is an unfinished hermitage because while Father Lucas was building it – perhaps thinking that this remote location was the safest place, or perhaps upon hearing something of the fate of Alaró – the Moors came for him. Whether they were actively hunting the man who had fled Mahón with a relic, or whether perhaps they were simple marauding invaders who stumbled across him, the result I think would be the same.'

'And that would be?'

'He was likely killed out of hand, his unfinished hermitage abandoned, and anything of value taken away. We heard back in Mahón that the relic was kept in a silver case. Likely, being a reliquary, it would be an ornate one. And Father Lucas having built an altar for it, it would be easy enough for the invaders to find. I am in no doubt that the Moors came here, dealt with the priest and took away the arm of Saint Stephen.'

Arnau stepped back and folded his arms. 'If I accept your idea – and I have to admit, though it sounds a little implausible to me, there is no reason to deny that it *could* have happened – then where did the Moors take the relic afterwards? Soldiers like precious metals, Balthesar. They're often base creatures. They could have taken it themselves, tipped the bone out onto the ground and melted down the box to pay for their next whore.'

Balthesar snorted. 'While that *is* possible, I do not believe it to be so. Remember that the invaders were new to these lands and full of the faith that drove them to conquer. They were pious zealots, even the general soldiery, and this was a Christian reliquary. I think it would have been too important for them to see it as mere silver. Whether it was something to be respected or something to be reviled, I do not think it would be simply destroyed or cast aside. No, it will have been taken from here and probably to a superior, who would have passed it on to his own master, and so forth until it eventually reached the hands of the ruler, who by that time would have made his court in Madina Mayūrqa. Whether immediately or by a circuitous route, I now believe the relic will have gone to Madina.'

Arnau tried to remember the map he'd studied. 'Madina is at the other end of the island, yes? On the south-west coast?'

'It is.'

'And it's the capital of the island?'

'Quite so.'

'So you're saying that our next crumb on this increasingly vague trail is in the island's capital city.'

Balthesar smiled, took two steps forward and gave Arnau a slap on the back. 'Quite right. Madina Mayūrqa is where the relic will have gone, and therefore it is where we shall follow. We are going into the viper's nest, Vallbona. Into the emir's city.'

Arnau closed his eyes and breathed deeply, keeping his calm. The very idea seemed insane, and yet Balthesar's logic, while the evidence was interpretable in more than one way, lacked holes. It was a leap of faith, and a leap potentially into the fire, but the old knight had been vindicated time and again. If a leap of faith was required then perhaps it was time Arnau exhibited that very faith Balthesar kept urging him to have. He sighed and straightened.

'All right, how far is Madina?'

'Via these roads?' Balthesar replied. 'Four or five days.'

'Very well,' Arnau said, 'but I cannot go on as I am without even a smattering of Arabic, and I'm sick of playing the mute. I've learned a few small things from listening to you, but I need to know more. I need to know the basics before we go into Madina, because that cannot be a place to wander blindly.'

Balthesar nodded. 'Agreed. I shall teach you all I can in the time we have. It will make the miles pass easier.'

As the old man smiled and turned away, heading over to the two locals to tell them what he had found, Arnau stood and stretched. Into the very home of the emir, the heart of Moorish power on the island. A dangerous proposition, he was sure, made more so by the locals' assertion that attitudes seemed to be changing.

Ah well. Madina Mayūrqa awaited.

CHAPTER SEVEN

TUESDAY, 8 JUNE 1199

7.30 A.M.

Madina Mayūrqa was impressive. The road that had led the two travellers down from the mountains, then through lower hills, and finally into flat, cultivated lands full of villages reached the capital city at a powerful gate in the high walls. The ramparts stretched from here both to the east and the south, tall, pointed battlements atop them, while the gate itself consisted of a high pointed arch within another even higher one, the stonework decorative and picked out in designs in two colours, all flanked by massive, heavy towers. Artistic in design, but also very, very strong.

Arnau's first thought was that the Almohad caliphate would be utterly insane to even attempt to take Madina Mayūrqa from its emir. Beside the gate, the river flowed into the city, thundering through low arches too small and close to the water's surface to allow access for a boat. There were two men on guard at the gate in elaborate uniforms with very fine mail and decorative helmets, their pikes tall and gleaming.

The two travellers had been on the road for two hours since they had broken camp on a small hill overlooking the plain and the distant city, and now the heat of the day was beginning to assert itself. They had dismounted as they closed on the walls and walked the horses. The road was not theirs alone, and Arnau had settled sensibly, if unhappily, into the role of mute once more. Balthesar had assured him there would be Christians in Madina, and they were permitted to live and worship there, but the visitors could still draw interest and probably suspicion, so they would be best served, in the old knight's opinion, by continuing to masquerade as poor Moorish nobodies until they were surer of the situation. Thus with all the other people and traffic on the road heading in and out of the city, silence would be the order of the day.

For the last few hundred yards to the gate, with the river rushing alongside them, they moved at snail's pace as the guards funnelled the mass of people in through the archway, occasionally pulling someone aside and checking them over or asking questions. The majority, though, were just herded through as speedily as possible.

Arnau ran mentally through the various phrases he had learned from the old knight in the past few days. He had practised them over and over again until they sank in, or at least until he hoped they had. Arabic was, he realised, a very difficult language to study, for it shared almost nothing in common with his own, and was utterly alien even in its sounds, while the writing would clearly forever remain a mystery. Still he had picked up some basics, and Balthesar was shrewd in selecting what he believed would be the most important phrases for Arnau to know.

Finally, in the wake of a merchant who smelled of spices and sweat and some farm animal's manure, they reached the gate. Balthesar touched his forehead and greeted the guards with the traditional phrase, which Arnau now knew to mean 'Peace be with you,' and the guards replied in kind, giving the old man and the shabby youth with him only the briefest of glances before waving them through. As they passed beneath that high dark arch, Arnau breathed out slowly. He'd not realised he'd been holding his breath until he felt the freedom to exhale.

Inside, Madina Mayūrqa was not what he'd expected at all. He'd anticipated passing through the gates into winding narrow streets and a packed urban mass. What actually greeted his eyes was something wholly different. The river continued on within the city walls, carving its path into the centre, but to either side of it lay open cultivated fields and orchards, all well irrigated with channels that led off from the main river. It was something of a gardener's paradise. He could see small areas of housing and structures in places here and there among the gardens and fields, like independent villages within the massive loop of the city walls.

The road they took forked inside the gate, one path crossing the river on a wide bridge, the other marching off to the left, where he could see that it entered a more built-up region and turned, making for the south where the main heart of the city lay on the hill at the very centre of the fortifications. He was twitching to ask Balthesar about the place, but remained safely silent instead, watching everything, taking everything in. It was a fabulous bit of civic planning in military terms. If Madina was besieged, it could hold out more or less forever. The river supplied ample water, and there was clearly farmed land inside the walls to feed a multitude.

After a short distance, they reached a crossroads where the urban area truly began, a small outlying bathhouse sitting directly opposite a mosque, both flanked by crowded housing. To the left a lesser gate in the walls lurked some distance away, a cemetery beside it, but Balthesar took them right, away from the walls. Close to the corner the older knight motioned for Arnau to pass over the reins of his horse, and when the young sergeant did so the old man delivered the mounts into a place that had both the smell and sounds of a stable, and returned without them, shouldering his pack and passing the other to Arnau. Now without their horses in tow, they walked on.

Though the two men were now taking the direct route into the city's centre, the bulk of the inbound traffic had instead gone straight ahead at the crossroads, to where a large market was in full swing. Leaving the majority of the visiting traffic, Arnau and Balthesar continued along the street, which climbed a gradual incline, the river occasionally visible through side roads off to the right. They passed another mosque, this one larger and more impressive, and continued to climb. Finally, they seemed to reach the densely populated built-up centre of the city, the streets becoming something of a tangle, and then, to Arnau's surprise, they emerged into another area of open gardens hundreds of yards across, with another mosque slap-bang in the centre. On the far side was a huge market square that was currently unoccupied by stalls and yet still seemed to swarm with people. Arnau peered about, fascinated. Far away to the left, along a long, wide street, he could see a huge, powerful gatehouse, marking the entrance to some separate fortress or compound. Ahead the urban mass closed in once more, the slope rising to the cliff above the sea.

Balthesar led them to the right and Arnau followed dutifully, still silent. He was busy paying attention to the side streets when voices suddenly attracted his attention. His head snapped round in surprise to see an important-looking man in rich red and white clothes, accompanied by a small group of the emir's soldiers and a number of clerks and servants, apparently giving an audience to several Jews. As he listened and observed, he definitely heard Hebrew, and now noticed the traditional beards and pointed hats among the plaintiffs. Another group who looked like ordinary non-Jewish citizens were also arguing with the official in Arabic. One of the lackeys was continually translating the words of the Jews to his master and sporadically the well-dressed man would give an answer, or a judgement, or whatever it was.

Arnau tore his eyes from the scene as they rounded another corner and instead settled them on the sight at the end of the next road. He could see another battlemented wall, though this one was considerably more decorative and elegant than the city walls or those of the other fortress he had seen earlier. As they closed on this place, Arnau's gaze eating it all up, they emerged into another wide space of well-tended gardens that pleased the eye. Off to the right he noted that the street descended the hill rather steeply and he could see the glittering water of the river over there, the city extending beyond it on the other bank.

But it was the place in front of them that really drew the eye. The fortified walls were high but spoke of beauty and style as much as defence. He could see the roofs of buildings behind them, and they too were clearly of a far superior quality to the bulk of the city on this side of the wall. A small, almost unobtrusive gate pierced that wall on the left-hand side, and beside the great complex there stood a mosque of a style and size that surpassed any such building Arnau had ever seen.

Balthesar was gesturing now, pointing to someplace in a line of shops facing the great walled compound on the far side of the gardens. Arnau followed him stoically, and was relieved and pleased as they crossed to the buildings that the indicated place appeared to be some kind of inn, with tables both inside in the shade and outside in the sun. As they neared the place, Balthesar selected one of the tables in the searing hot sun, and dropped his pack next to the table. He pointed at the seat and then walked off inside.

Arnau dutifully sank to the seat, grateful to rest his legs for a while, and sighed with relief, though he was instantly jealous of those men inside in the shade. The place was packed within, but there were still seats available. Out here in the searing sun, the tables were empty. It came to Arnau in that moment *why* they were outside: comparative privacy.

After a long pause, the old knight reappeared carrying two cups which he placed on the table, sliding one across to Arnau.

'It would appear,' Balthesar said suddenly in Spanish, 'that we might be best advised to use our native tongue right now.'

Arnau's eyes widened. This was unexpected. 'Why?'

'Because while we might draw attention in doing so, it will mostly be idle curiosity, and the simple fact is that hardly anyone in the city will speak this tongue. It is entirely possible, in fact, that the majority will not even recognise what it is. The Jews here speak Hebrew, but the Christians all speak Arabic. And outside, in this heat, we will not meet too many prying folk. Additionally, several things I noticed upon our walk through the city allayed the worst of my fears and convinced me that tolerance and ease still prevail in Madina. I do not fear as much for our safety.'

Arnau sighed. He couldn't imagine what the old man had spotted that Arnau had not, but he was grateful nonetheless. 'Thank the Lord,' he said, 'I was becoming tired of the silence again.'

'I can imagine. Get as many of your inanities as you must out of the way now, since this may just be temporary. There are things

I want to discuss that I would rather passers-by could not understand.'

'First, though,' Arnau replied, 'what is this?' He indicated the cup.

'Tea. It is the main drink here.'

'It smells like sweetened feet.'

'Tastes a little like them too, but you'll not get beer or wine here. Well, *probably* not. Some places will serve a very thick, sweet wine made from dates, but to be honest if you think the tea tastes like sweet feet, you had probably best avoid the wine altogether.'

'They make wine? I thought it was illegal?'

Balthesar shrugged. 'This is not the Almohad caliphate, but an old-fashioned *taifa*. Here, even the Moors follow differing versions of their beliefs. Some hold that all alcohol is forbidden by their holy book. Some tolerate certain concoctions, citing the ingredients of the drink as to whether it is forbidden or not. Some recognise alcohol as sinful, but just choose to ignore that and drink anyway.' He chuckled. 'Back in Valencia in the old days, you'd be surprised just how many very pious and faithful Moorish soldiers could be found in certain dens throwing back thick date wine until they wouldn't know their mother from a camel. That is the beauty of tolerance, Arnau. That is why the *taifas* were and are important, and that is why the Almohads are wicked. They remove all choice from their own people.'

'I saw Jews back there arguing with an official,' Arnau said, taking a sip of the tea and wincing before privately admitting to himself that it wasn't at all bad, really.

'Jews *and* Christians,' Balthesar replied, 'though you'd not have realised they were Christians, for they were speaking Arabic. I saw the same scene and it was one of those that reassured me we were still on relatively safe ground. The man was a tax official, a *wazir*. The authorities don't hold court like that, so I suspect he was on his way somewhere when he was spotted by unhappy taxpayers. It is a sign, as far as I am concerned, that the lands of Mayūrqa are still tolerant and just, that this is allowed to happen. If the Christians in Qurṭuba in the south of Iberia accosted an official in that manner, they would likely be peeled and left out for the scavengers.'

Arnau shivered, glad suddenly that Balthesar had chosen these islands and not some other place for his quest.

'On the whole, Christians have always been tolerated and even respected here. I am not sure how well those who speak the tongue of the mainland will be received, though, and I doubt it will garner a neutral response. We will be welcomed or shunned, and it is a gamble right now as to which. If those Almohad warriors are here by popular choice, then we will be very unpopular ourselves. If they are here uninvited, it is possible that we will actually be *more* welcome. It's a simple matter of who is less reviled, us or them.'

'So this is something of a brutal test of opinion? Speaking Aragonese openly?'

Balthesar smiled. 'If people start to glare at us, we might have to reconsider our position.'

'I'm just grateful to be able to talk again.'

They paused at the sound of footsteps and a man in a turban appeared from inside, bearing a tray. He placed his burden down and removed from it a plate for each of the visitors, placing it before them along with a spoon.

'*Šukran,*' Arnau said with a slight bow of the head, earning a delighted smile from Balthesar, who followed suit, similarly thanking the man. When he had disappeared back inside with his tray, the old knight nodded. 'Well said. Your accent needs work, for you sound like a Syrian. But it was good.'

Arnau looked into the plate. Brown lumps sat next to a pile of rice and mixed vegetables. 'What is this?'

'Lemon mutton. Try it. You'll enjoy it.'

Arnau did. And he did. He took another sip of the cooling tea and smiled. This all felt rather civilised after days on that mountain path.

'So,' he said, 'now that we are here, how do we follow up on your somewhat ethereal breadcrumb?'

Balthesar smiled. 'What we do is a matter of the utmost simplicity. It is how we do it that will be the complicated part. We need to look for records of what happened to the relic.'

'Records?'

'Yes. The Moors are more of a slave to record keeping even than the Church. There will be little that has happened since the conquest of the island that has not been kept documented in their records office. The office – the *diwān* – will have everything we need. And if we cannot find it, then the *kātibūn* – the secretaries who work there – will.'

Arnau's eyes narrowed. 'How we do it is the problem, you say?'

Balthesar nodded. 'I did not select this tavern at random. Those fortifications before us are the walls of the Al-Mudaina. Somewhere inside there will be a small collection of *diwāns*, one of which will be the one that contains the records we seek.'

Arnau's eyes widened. He thrust out his hand, rice falling from his spoon onto the table, pointing the implement at the walls across the gardens. 'There? The office is in there?'

'Yes.'

'But that's a fortress.'

'No,' Balthesar smiled. 'That is a palace.'

'A *what*?'

'Al-Mudaina is the palace of the Emir of Mayūrqa. Naturally, his government and bureaucracy share the same complex.'

Arnau stared. 'You want to walk into the emir's palace and ask to look at some old records?'

'Something like that. Are you sure you won't try some date wine now?'

Arnau stared at the walls. What lunacy would the old knight suggest next?

They passed another half-hour at the tavern eating the rest of their meal and drinking another cup of the tea, though all calm had gone from Arnau now as he sat and pondered the fortified palace before them. Breaking in was clearly out of the question. Sneaking in might be possible, but would be extremely difficult, and the price of failure would likely be very high. That left only trickery and bluff or open invitation. The latter seemed somewhat unlikely.

He watched intently. There were four guards on the wall top facing them, and they had a regular pattern of patrol, but not one in which Arnau could identify any weak spot. Whenever the small door opened or closed to admit or release a servant or official or soldier, Arnau could see at least two guards within, manning the door, though at this distance he could make out little more than their outlines. If only the tavern were closer to that gate.

'It's well protected.'

'That it is,' Balthesar agreed. 'Fortunately we do not seek to use force in any way, so that need not concern us. What we need is to be asked inside, or at least to have someone there who is amenable to our presence. We could, conceivably, simply request admittance, although whether we would be welcome in the current climate I cannot say. We must gain access to that records office.'

'How would you suggest we do it, then?' Arnau asked bitterly, sipping the last of his tea.

'Very simply,' the old knight smiled. 'I intend to use the truth.'

'What?'

'I may have spent my youth in Moorish lands, Arnau, but I have been a boy, then a carpenter and then a mercenary. I was never a scribe and I have never set foot inside a records office. I would not know where to start looking, and I cannot imagine that you have any more of a clue. So even if there were a way to sneak inside we would likely come up against immediate problems. We would have to find the office itself before we could find records within it. We would be as likely to bump into one of the emir's wives as one of the records offices. No, the only truly feasible solution is to speak the truth and seek the help of one who works there.'

'So we're going to go up and knock on the door and ask to see records?'

'Basically, yes.'

'We've spent days sneaking around the island, pretending to be Moors and with my lips glued shut, and now that we're in the heart of the place, we're going to drop all pretence?'

Balthesar shook his head. 'Not quite. Our true identity I think should remain a secret. We cannot be certain about attitudes to the order. But we can be relatively open, yes. I would not have suggested as much before, until I was comfortable that we would not be instantly seen as enemies.'

'I've been mute round half of Mayūrqa,' Arnau reminded him with more than a little frustration in his tone.

'I know. But we did not know we would be coming here, and I could not have anticipated these circumstances. Be grateful that Madina is still a place where we *can* do this. Now come on.'

Arnau, still irritated that he had held his tongue for so long in case of discovery only to now walk up and announce himself to the local soldiers, rose from his seat and grasped his bag, following Balthesar across the gardens towards the gate.

The old knight's gaze kept slipping this way and that, attracted by a variety of scenes and folk, but Arnau, trying to fight back his irritation and see this new approach as a boon, kept his own eyes on their goal. From that small door, which had opened several times while they sat at their table, had issued forth occasional servants, a noble and a guard or two, but they had always seen them from a distance. Now, as the two knights moved through the garden and closed on it, the door to the Al-Mudaina opened once more and Arnau was treated to a much clearer view. What he saw stopped him dead in his tracks.

Another servant had left the complex through the door, but as this one emerged from the darkness within he was angry, his face a storm of ire, and he wagged a finger at someone as he left, stomping off down the street with a document of some sort under his arm. But it was neither the man nor his anger that had struck Arnau. It was what he caught sight of in the shadowy interior, in the blink of an eye before the door closed, that shocked him.

A figure in black and white.

It happened so quickly that he almost believed he'd imagined it, but a glance at the angry clerk storming off down the street reassured him. He *had* seen the man.

'This way,' he said suddenly, tapping Balthesar on the shoulder and veering off their course, angling away from that door and more in the direction of the angry servant. The older knight looked around in surprise, but without argument turned and hurried after him.

'What is it?' he breathed quietly.

'That man ahead in the green and white with the red hat left the palace all but spitting feathers in anger a moment ago, and I swear that as that door closed behind him, the man he had been arguing with was wearing black and white.'

Balthesar gave him a blank look.

'The Almohad soldiers,' Arnau reasoned. 'The Lion's guardsmen. They wore black and white. It was one of them, I would stake my life on it, and he's riled one of the emir's clerks. Suddenly I didn't know what to do, but I felt certain that knocking on the door and coming face to face with one of the Lion of Alarcos's soldiers would not be a good idea'

The old brother frowned deeply. 'That's fairly vague,' he said. 'Not much to go on. You saw a brief flash of black and white and leaped to the assumption it was an Almohad soldier. We don't even know there are Almohads *in* Madina Mayūrqa.'

Arnau shook his head. 'I beg to differ. Most people favour colours, and I think I've only seen the Almohads in black and white. Think back to that fight in Al-Bulānsa. There were enough Almohads at the top of that street to ride us down and kill us three times over, and yet they didn't. It wasn't fear. It was the presence of the emir's guards at the bridge. The emir's men shouted something angrily at the Almohads and they didn't chase us. I reckon the Lion was there to meet someone, and that someone was part of the emir's guards or his retinue. The Lion came from Mahón and crossed to the larger island, and they were heading this way. While we were moving slowly through the mountains and hunting signs of Father Lucas's passage, they could just ride along the main road. To my mind they seem to have been destined for this place, and they may have been here for three days already. Plenty of time to start getting in the way and annoying the palace functionaries.'

Balthesar stared at his young companion for a while, then broke out into a smile. 'And just like that, after weeks of complaints and doubt, suddenly you entirely justify my having brought you along. Very astute, young sergeant. Good. Let us assume, then, that these Almohads and their master Abd al-Azīz are in the Al-Mudaina and that they are interfering and irritating the emir's staff. We still need to secure access to the records office. How do you recommend we approach this?'

Arnau blinked. 'Me? What do I recommend?'

'You have proved that you have a thinking head on today. I need that mind working for us. How do we approach the palace now?'

'We…' Arnau took a deep breath. 'We lie in wait, we use the angry clerk, and we still tell the truth.'

'We do?'

The young sergeant wavered, doubting himself now, without the immediate confirmation of the old man. 'Well, yes. I can see three reasons. Firstly, we will need his help to find the office and possibly the records in the office even once we're inside, and the truth will make it far easier to do so.'

'True. A very plausible point,' Balthesar replied.

'Secondly, the enemy of my enemy is my friend. You have spent all our journey teaching me the distinction between this *taifa* and the Almohads. I cannot imagine the emir is in any way enamoured with these men who want to dominate his island, and therefore the same should hold true of his court. If they dislike and distrust the Almohads, then we, as representatives of the only other great power that opposes the Almohads, might just have an advantage.'

'You stretch reason there, Arnau,' the old man warned. 'Because the emir will have no love for them does not mean his court do not. It is a staple of all ancient court stories that the man who serves closest often wields the assassin's knife. It could be that there are men in that palace who would see the Almohads as a path to personal power and riches at the expense of their lord.'

Arnau nodded. 'Agreed, and I take the point. But a mere clerk is probably too lowly to hope for such a thing. And the anger of the man at his departure suggests that he hates them. Perhaps he hates them enough to support us? To help us?'

Balthesar grinned. 'I like this new Vallbona. He is a machine of reason. Quite right. You have sold me on your thoughts.'

'And there's the third thing.'

'Which is?'

'That at least I don't have to play the stupid mute and I can be a useful part of it all.'

That brought a laugh from the grey-bearded knight. 'Most true of all, and if I have learned one thing in the past five minutes it is that you are more valuable with your tongue wagging than silent.'

They had reached the edge of those well-tended gardens now, and there they paused, Arnau watching 'Red-hat' disappearing off into the city with a hint of regret. 'If we follow him now to secure his aid,' Balthesar pointed out, 'then it will look very odd and suspicious, as though we targeted him. It needs to seem like a chance meeting.'

'As he returns from whatever trip he's on now,' Arnau added.

'Perhaps a touch more tea and a pastry or two is in order?' The old knight smiled, and Arnau, flooding with relief for several reasons, joined him. The two men returned to the tavern and Balthesar, as promised, secured more tea and several sweet, pleasant pastries. They sat for some time, keeping themselves busy, all the time watching both the door of the palace for any sign of a black-and-white-clad zealot, and that road down which the clerk had gone for a red-capped, angry servant.

As they waited, and in order to give them something to do that did not require their eyes and distract them from their observation, Balthesar continued his linguistic training. Arnau struggled with two of the three new phrases, but the old knight's contentment over the level of tolerance in Madina seemed well founded when the innkeeper came out to see if they wanted anything else and went away with not just an order for more drinks, but having corrected Arnau's pronunciation with a friendly smile.

It was long after noon when it happened, and both men had become so used to sitting at the table discussing the Arabic tongue that they almost missed the arrival of the very man for whom they were watching.

Red-hat appeared from that same street, making for the palace doorway. The only thing that bought them adequate time was that the man moved slowly, dawdling often, seemingly reluctant to return to the palace, probably still angry. Arnau and Balthesar, having paid for their fare, simply abandoned what was left and grabbed their packs, running across the street and through the gardens, attracting only that level of interest that men running in a city generally do: a brief glance, quickly forgotten.

'Follow my lead now,' the old knight said as they hurried into place. 'We are thwarted and innocent. We seek only help and we are somewhat irked, yes?'

Arnau grunted his agreement. 'He's definitely the man? Definitely from these offices?'

'Yes.'

'Then let's make a new friend.'

They hurried into place just before the clerk arrived. As Red-hat emerged from the crowd, making for the door of Al-Mudaina, he found two foreign visitors in conversation at the palace's corner. Paying little attention to them, still angry, he stalked on past, but then the old grey-bearded traveller beckoned to him. The clerk slowed, intrigued despite his irritation, and the old man called out. 'You are a *kuttab* of the *diwān*, yes?' At least, that was how Arnau translated with his meagre grasp of Arabic.

The man nodded.

'I do not suppose you speak the language of the mainland kingdoms, do you?' he tried earnestly in Spanish.

The clerk frowned, but answered after a moment in a neutral, if suspicious, tone, 'I do.'

'Splendid,' Balthesar grinned. 'My friend and I here are travellers from the mainland researching the history of the islands. We are particularly focusing on the early days of the Umayyad caliph, and even the later days of the Romans before him, and I suspect there are records in the palace that would be of immense interest to us.'

The man shrugged as he replied. 'The archives are not sealed. Any document that is private is kept locked away and the bulk of public records can be accessed with the permission of the appropriate *kuttab*.' He pointed to that door. 'You may approach the palace quite openly.'

Balthesar nodded. 'I understood as much. There are problems, however. I hear rumours that the palace currently plays host to the Almohads, and as I am sure you will understand, the men of the caliphate are not lovers of my kind.'

The clerk nodded his understanding. 'Yes, the caliph's dogs prowl Al-Mudaina as though they own the city and the emir is nothing. I can imagine your reluctance to meet them.'

'I wondered whether I could enlist your aid, for any appropriate fee you name, in accessing the *diwān* and searching for the records we seek, preferably without coming into contact with your visitors. I am fluent in Arabic, so it would simply be a matter of directing me to the appropriate place and leaving me to it. Would that be possible, do you think?'

The clerk frowned for a moment, flicked a gaze at the doorway, and finally nodded. 'This gate is watched by a dog with the taste of the caliph's balls still in his mouth. Come. I will take you through the servants' access and show you to the *diwān*.'

As the man turned and marched off down the shady side of the palace wall, seeking a second access, Balthesar grinned at Arnau. 'The Lord will always provide, Arnau. It just has to be remembered that the Lord is sometimes Allah.'

CHAPTER EIGHT

TUESDAY, 8 JUNE 1199

12.45 P.M.

The Al-Mudaina was breathtaking. The outer walls had hinted at decoration and style despite their military function, but the interior was truly something to behold. The side gate through which the clerk led them, without more than a passing question from the guards, opened into a courtyard decorated with beautifully carved stone lions and delicately sculpted trees and shrubs, pots of brightly coloured flowers arranged at precisely the right position to please the eye. At the centre of the courtyard a fountain with more carved lions threw sparkling diamonds of water high into the air to be collected by a wide marble bowl below from which it ran along narrow channels to irrigate more flowers and fill small troughs.

One channel ran through another doorway in the courtyard, and through it Arnau caught a glimpse of the most magnificent gardens, with pergolas and lawns, pools and fountains. He also caught a glimpse of the inside of the gatehouse they had been watching from the tavern. Sure enough, three figures in black and white with gleaming steel armour stood close by, the only thing to darken Arnau's mood in that moment.

But then they were moving again. Passing servants, nobles and soldiers all in bright colours and rich apparel, they crossed the courtyard and entered the palace itself, a perfectly proportioned and well-appointed complex of golden, honey-coloured stone, punctuated with windows topped by horseshoe arches and decorative panels emblazoned with the indecipherable, yet beautiful Arabic script. The door they passed through was small and with a delicate pointed arch, positioned in a shady spot beside a staircase, and it took a few moments for Arnau's eyes to adjust to the darker interior after the brilliant sunlight outside.

He had been in a palace only once in his life – the palace in Barcelona that had belonged to the counts of the region before the union with Aragon. It had been the most magnificent residence Arnau had ever seen, filled with rich tapestries and ornate fireplaces, thick pelt rugs and ancient dark wooden chairs. He had wondered what it was like to live with such opulence.

The palace of the Counts of Barcelona looked like a hovel next to the Al-Mudaina. The walls were only visible where there was architectural beauty to be revealed. Where they were plain and functional, they were hidden behind rich, colourful hangings and painted or ceramic panels of Arabic script. The floors were of marble, the ceilings delicately vaulted with the ever-present Moorish arches. Furniture was all uniformly dazzling, every seat and table, chest and cupboard formed of delicate fretwork and inlaid semi-precious stones.

As they passed through corridors that seemed to have been created for the glory of their architecture rather than simple functionality, and rooms devoted to servants and menial tasks that would make an Aragonese don jealous, Arnau's gaze nipped here and there, taking in every delicious sight, unable to settle on any one thing for too long. It was as he was marvelling at the most elaborate ceiling he could ever have imagined and dropping his gaze to a chair that was more deserving of the term 'throne' that he saw the visitors.

He experienced a moment of confusion, looked away and back as if his eyes had deceived him the first time and a second look might prove him wrong. But no, they were definitely there. Balthesar's gaze was on them, too: half a dozen very well-dressed Christians from the mainland, garbed in the latest expensive Aragonese manner. They all wore swords, though three were clearly more court swords for show than for actual use. The others, carried by younger, more ferocious-looking men, were swords designed to maim and kill. Three noblemen and three warriors, then, all horribly out of place here.

Yet it was not so much their presence that made Arnau boggle, but rather the fact that he recognised two of them. Baron Alberto de Castellvell, still impossibly gaunt and cadaverous, seemed to be leading the party, and the very sight of him made Arnau shiver. A man who had been della Cadeneta's sponsor in many ways, who hated Rourell and its preceptrix, and had all but set himself against the Templars there. Castellvell had threatened the preceptrix in those tense days before the siege, had had the temerity and certainty of his power to actually threaten the Order of the Temple. Few had the will to do such a thing, and the man remained a dangerous thorn in their side, yet he was also a powerful nobleman and close to the king, which perhaps explained his presence here.

The other figure he recognised was considerably more welcome. Among the three knights accompanying the high nobles was a young man with neat black hair, clean-shaven and energetic. He hadn't seen the young man for several years, when the knight had accompanied his father to Barcelona and to Santa Coloma, and the intervening time had clearly been kind to him, for he seemed to be wealthier and more powerful than ever, given his dress and the company he was keeping.

The six Christians did not spare a glance for the two shabby men across the room, and they were gone, out of sight, when the Templars turned a corner and moved into the area of the palace that was clearly reserved for the offices.

'Did you see them?' Arnau said quietly, dropping back so that the clerk leading the way would not hear.

'Castellvell, Gaston de Béarn and Pelegrino de Castellarzuelo. Leading figures in the Crown of Aragon. They can only be here on official business for the king. Would that we could speak with them, but I fear the presence of Castellvell negates that possibility. He would have me strung up if the chance arose. Perhaps it is better that he remains ignorant of our presence lest he stir up the emir's court against us.'

Arnau nodded. 'I know one of the knights with them, too. Guillem Picornell. He's the son of a Pyrenean nobleman. Actually, looking at him, I suspect he's inherited his father's domain now. Spent time at court in Barcelona and Santa Coloma. Good man. I always got on with him.'

'Still, it might be better if you did not reacquaint yourself. Drawing attention to us will simply alert Castellvell. Come. We are not here for political chicanery. The order has to remain above the dealings of kings and noblemen as far as possible. We serve the Lord and our task is to locate the arm of Saint Stephen.'

The young sergeant nodded again, though he could feel something building in Madina Mayūrqa. A beleaguered independent emir playing host to a deputation from the most powerful Christian king on the peninsula at the same time as a lord of the Almohad presaged great and terrible things.

'They and the Almohads…' he said under his breath.

Balthesar crossed himself. 'May the Lord bestow peace on this place, for I fear no *man* will in the coming days.'

Ahead, the clerk had paused at a doorway. A small office stood beside it with several more clerks and two soldiers in the emir's colours.

'You must leave your swords and bags here,' the clerk said, 'and your admittance will be recorded. When you leave, you will be checked for documents, I'm afraid, but will then be signed back out and your weapons returned.'

Balthesar bowed his assent and unfastened his sword, handing it to one of the guards. Arnau did the same, feeling a tinge of worry and regret as he relinquished something he thought he might need in this place. Balthesar gave their names to the appropriate clerk, though without their titles or ranks, and they were admitted to the records department.

Arnau was impressed at the organisation of the place, which had numerous rooms, though he couldn't tell what they were for since the written language was to him utterly baffling. After a few moments their guide came to a halt beside a door that looked identical to all the others, and tapped his finger on the sign in Arabic beside it.

'Here are the earliest archives. Documentation from the year two hundred and eighty for approximately two centuries. Anything newer than that will be in the appropriate divisional *diwān*, and we do not have records from before the arrival of the Umayyads, I am afraid. Is this the room you require?'

Balthesar smiled calmly. 'That is perfect, my friend. *Šukran gazīlan.*'

'Will you require aid in your search?'

The old knight shook his head. 'I believe we will be fine. Thank you.'

'When you are done, return to the place you left your swords and bags, and you will be escorted from the palace. Good luck with your research.'

The man hurried off to his own work and Balthesar turned to Arnau. 'Here we go. Our next clue awaits.'

He pushed open the door and stepped into the room, Arnau following and closing the portal behind him. The room was arranged in a square, all outer walls filled with delicate racks of carved wood, inlaid with what appeared to be marble, except for a small and intricately glazed window. Each compartment in the racks contained several scrolls, and each had a small label in Arabic below it. The centre of the room was occupied by a large table which contained an open book.

'Date,' Balthesar mused, tapping his chin. 'What date to begin with? It was the year of our Lord nine hundred and two when the Umayyad invaders arrived in Mayūrqa. I think we must assume that it was that same year that Father Lucas fled his church in Mahón with the relic, and likely the same year he stopped in that place along the mountain road and began to build his hermitage. On the assumption that it would take him many months to get even as far as he did with the construction, then we are probably looking for records starting in nine hundred and three, but I think we will begin at the beginning for the sake of certainty, yes?'

Arnau shook his head in confusion. 'The clerk said this room started in two hundred and eighty, and covered two centuries. We're in the wrong room.'

'The Moors do not measure time from the birth of the Saviour, Vallbona. Use your head. They date their calendar from the time Muhammad left Mecca. So by Moorish time, the year we need is two hundred and eighty. This is our room, but where do we begin?' he muttered, peering at the book.

Arnau leaned back against the table. The language was meaningless to him, the dating peculiar, the scrolls unreadable. He could be of little help here. Instead, he strode over to a window and looked out as the old knight pored over the book, murmuring as he went.

The window looked down upon the city's port, and there was much to observe. Arnau's gaze stretched from the city walls to the docks below at the mouth to the river. They were bustling, and he could see many ships there. Most bore the white lateen sails of Moorish vessels, but there were a couple of traders there clearly of Christian design and ownership. Trade tended to ignore politics at all times except the height of war.

His gaze strayed down, coming back towards his own location. He found another ornamental garden just inside the walls above the riverside port, and then the seaward edge of the Al-Mudaina complex. A high, ornate brick arch formed part of the palace's walls there, and the sea flowed in beneath it to create a small, square, sheltered harbour directly beneath this window. A private dock for the palace, and at it sat the ship in which the Christian visitors had clearly come. The pennants of Aragon – stripes of red and gold – snapped and fluttered in the breeze.

'Castellvell's ship is in the palace harbour,' he noted.

'Perhaps that explains why the Almohads landed at Al-Bulānsa and crossed the island by road,' Balthesar replied, still bent over his book. 'Perhaps the emir is doing his best to keep the two groups apart. A sound decision, I might add.'

Arnau nodded. Would the two forces actually openly oppose one another, even in the court of an independent lord of whom they were guests?

'I can find no record of the bone coming here,' the old knight announced, which did not surprise Arnau in the slightest. 'But there is another reference I can find that might be pertinent. Dated to what would in our calendar be perhaps one thousand and twenty. Less than a century after the conquest. Let me see what I can find.'

Arnau continued to peer out of the window, taking in the strangeness of it all as his companion scoured the shelves looking for the section indicated in the book. Finally locating it, the old knight began to sift through the scrolls in the wooden compartment.

'Marvellous,' he said quietly. 'They may be heretics, but they could teach the Church a thing or two about archiving documents. There is one scroll here that I can only assume is original, from more than two hundred years ago. It's a little delicate and faded, and some clerk has attached a note, marking it for replacement. The others all appear to be faithful copies of ones that have fallen apart or become faded. They even have an iterative copy number on them. The clerks continually renew all records so that nothing is lost. Imagine the mind behind all of this.'

Arnau grunted his passing interest, though he was more fascinated by the city outside

'This must be the scroll,' the old knight said suddenly. 'Come and look.'

Arnau reluctantly tore himself away from the window and crossed to the table, where Balthesar had placed a scroll tied with a silk ribbon. Almost lovingly, the man untied the ribbon and unfurled the scroll.

'Hold the top for me.'

Arnau did as he was asked, pinning the upper edge of the scroll to the table with his thumb, while the grey-bearded brother pulled it flat and anchored the bottom with his own finger. He then proceeded to run another digit along the strange, beautiful text from right to left in the Arabic way. Arnau had no idea what it said, and the older brother simply muttered so quietly under his breath as he read that it came out as little more than a hum.

'What is it?' Arnau said, more to relieve the boredom of complete bafflement than to prompt an answer.

'Shh,' hissed Balthesar, and Arnau waited as patiently as he could while the knight ran his finger back and forth until he was somewhere in the middle of the page, when he uttered a bark of triumph.

'Aha. Here we are. Faith – remember, young Vallbona. We have another breadcrumb.'

'Tell me.' That familiar surge of excitement in the blood suddenly returned. He'd been swept up in the exhilaration of finding the stones back at the mountain village and had doggedly continued to follow and assist Balthesar, without voicing any further negative view on the quest until now. But privately, deep down, with every mile they travelled from that hermitage the young sergeant had become less and less convinced that they would find anything here. Balthesar's whole theory as to what had happened to the relic seemed to rely so heavily on guesswork that the chances of picking up any further trail had seemed minute. More than that, on the discovery that the Almohads were in Madina, and now Castellvell too, it would almost be better not to find anything, as they would then have ample excuse to disappear and leave this increasingly dangerous city. But no. It would appear that despite Arnau's private scepticism, the old knight had been correct yet again.

'This is a record on the construction of a mosque within the city – the Al-balad mosque. Helpfully it records almost everything about it, from the architects and the masons to the quarries that were the source, the *imam* appointed to it upon its opening, and so much detail that it is, in fact, quite staggering. But here is the interesting part.'

His finger tapped somewhere in the middle, and he moistened his lips. 'There seems to have been some local debate over Saint Stephen. Remember that he was connected to Manûrqa, since that was where his miracles manifested. As such, he came to the attention of the Moorish conquerors. Saint Stephen has never been a popular figure with the Jews – remember that they stoned him for berating them – and their actions towards his worship in Mahón were harsh. It seems at least that one *imam*, the one assigned to this new mosque, lobbied for Stephen to be considered a *nabī* – a minor prophet in their religion. After all, though we Christians only regularly hear of Muhammad, there are many thousands of prophets respected in their faith, and few know them all. The thing is, miracles are one of the things that mark out a Moorish prophet, and so there was actually a surprisingly strong case for it.'

'Fascinating,' Arnau said, and meant it. 'But what of the bone?'

'I was coming to that,' the old knight replied. 'I can see no record of the relic being found or brought to Madina, but this very document records its placing in the new mosque at the bidding of the *imam* there, with the consent of the emir. It would appear that with the death of Father Lucas and the destruction of his hermitage, the bone of the blessed Saint Stephen disappeared from records for a century only to reappear in a mosque in Madina Mayūrqa.'

'Can we find the mosque? Is it still here?'

'Patience, young Vallbona. That question is very easily answered. Come.'

With care and reverence, Balthesar rolled up the scroll once more and slipped the ribbon around it, tying it neatly before replacing it in the compartment in the rack. Satisfied that they had got what they sought, the pair left the office and strolled back to the main door. There they were given a brief search, cursory enough to remain polite, but thorough enough to determine that no scroll had been stolen from the archive. As soon as the guards were happy that all rules had been obeyed, the two names were marked in the ledger and their swords and bags returned.

As Arnau fastened his sword belt around his middle, the grey-bearded brother gestured to one of the nearby clerks. What he asked, Arnau couldn't translate, but it clearly included the name '*masjid Al-balad*' and so the young sergeant presumed it to be an enquiry about the mosque.

As they finished with their swords and shouldered their kit, one of the clerks sidling past them to escort them from Al-Mudaina, Balthesar smiled. 'The road to the town of Manaqûr leads out of the city via a gate to the north-east. It is called the Al-balad gate. The mosque is nearby in an area of fields and orchards.'

Arnau grinned. 'Sounds idyllic. And a long way from here.'

The two men followed their clerk guide through the warren of the palace and finally out into the courtyard. He was about to lead them out into the gardens when Balthesar engaged him in further conversation, steering him away, and instead they crossed towards that lesser servants' entrance.

As they turned, heavy footsteps suddenly drew Arnau's attention. He turned along with the old knight and his heart thumped, his blood turning cold at the sight of the Lion of Alarcos at the top of the stairs beside which their own door had opened. The Almohad lord was accompanied by several of his veiled, monochrome henchmen, and a man in very expensive clothes beside him had two of the emir's men at his shoulders. Arnau's immediate thought that this must be the emir himself was quickly dashed as he realised that life was still going on around them, and not even the servants had stopped to bow. Still, he was plainly a figure of importance in the court to be attended by guards and escorting the Almohad nobleman.

Balthesar cleared his throat meaningfully and turned his face away, subtly suggesting that Arnau do the same, but it was too late. The man at the top of the stairs had clearly seen them. Arnau registered surprise for a moment that the Lion of Alarcos did not simply bellow out orders for their death, and then realised that the Almohad could hardly initiate such a fight in his host's own courtyard, especially with so many of the emir's guards present.

The struggle in the man's face was fascinating. Despite clearly being prevented from having his men rush to detain the two scruffy figures below, his lips were moving, trying to force out the words regardless. He was patently almost willing to start a war with the emir just to get to Balthesar.

'Come on,' hissed the older knight, grasping Arnau by the shoulder and pulling him along. They followed the clerk across to the small postern door, where it was opened for them with a smile. As Balthesar thanked the man profusely and stepped out into the street, Arnau turned and looked back. The Lion of Alarcos was on the move. He had clearly made his excuses to the emir's man and he and his soldiers were now trotting down the staircase in almost casual-seeming pursuit, trying to move fast yet without drawing too much suspicion from their hosts.

'They're following us,' Arnau breathed as he himself stepped from the door.

Behind them the door shut with a clonk; they heard two bolts sliding home and then, with barely a pause, a muffled shout and the sound of the bolts sliding open once more.

'Run,' Balthesar said, and Arnau did not need to be told twice. They disappeared around the edge of the mosque that stood beside the palace just as they heard the door slam open. Shouting echoed from the palace gate, but Arnau was too busy running to pay it a great deal of attention. He wondered for a moment if they could have simply hidden in the mosque and let the Almohads run past, but logic intervened. There were plenty of witnesses around watching them run. It would not be hard for the Lion and his men to follow the trail. Their only hope was speed and subtle evasion. Lose them, and lose them fast.

Balthesar ran between the trees in a small square dotted with palms and at the far side jogged left into a street between shops selling all manner of wares. Arnau hurtled after him, leaping any goods that had been placed too far out into the street and running like a madman. At the bottom of the street the old knight turned left again, and Arnau followed once more. He could hear urgent shouting behind him, back up that last cluttered little commercial street, which proved how close the Almohads were on their trail.

As they ran up this new street, Arnau suddenly realised they had come out of the palace in such a way that a left and a second left had sent them back towards the front wall of the Al-Mudaina once more. Had Balthesar planned on that, or was it the unhappy accident of running blind?

'Quick,' shouted the old knight, short of breath, and ducked in among those perfect gardens where many others were now strolling. As Arnau darted in behind him, Balthesar threw down his bag and ran on, yelling, 'Drop your kit.'

Arnau did so, though with no small regret, and the two men hurried past the next set of manicured hedges where the old man suddenly slowed to a sedate walk. As he did so, he brought up his hand with his *ghifara* hat that had been stuffed into his belt while they were inside the palace, and jammed it on his head. The transformation was simple but extraordinarily effective. In but a moment Balthesar went from a running, bare-headed man with a pack on his back to a strolling local in a traditional cap. Arnau noticed also that somehow during the run, the old man had managed to slip the sword beneath the folds of his off-white burnous. The sword was quite obvious if you were looking for it, but at first glance a passer-by would probably miss it.

Balthesar had gone, to be replaced by an average local. Arnau immediately tried to hide his own sword but failed dismally, tangling it and getting his own burnous caught in the belt. Moreover, he had not thought to put his hat in his belt like the old man, but had stuffed it into his bag, which now lay on the ground back across the gardens.

'Stop fidgeting,' hissed Balthesar, and Arnau reluctantly left his sword hanging only half covered. The two men strolled through the gardens, and suddenly they heard a commotion behind them. The young sergeant almost turned to see what was going on, but stopped himself just in time. He could hear voices raised angrily in Arabic. Questions being bellowed. No answers forthcoming.

Keeping his gaze locked on Balthesar in front and trying to move as casually as possible – and only now did he realise how difficult it was to walk casually on purpose – they moved out of the gardens and across the street. Arnau had wondered where they were going, but now he realised. Ahead sat the tavern where they had first rested, eating lemon mutton and watching the palace. The outer benches were still shunned by guests due to the blazing sun of midday.

As they approached, the noisy commotion still going on behind them, seemingly heightened somewhat by the discovery of their kit bags, the innkeeper emerged from the door and greeted them cheerily. Arnau marvelled at his companion's relaxed manner as Balthesar responded in kind and politely ordered tea and two more pastries before sliding back into his former seat. Arnau was about to sit next to him, but the older knight lifted his foot and pushed out the chair opposite. 'Sit with your back to the square.'

Arnau did so, obediently. They could hear the noise coming closer.

'Do you remember the Arabic you learned these past few days?'

'I think so.'

'Then whenever I tap your left leg with my foot say something negative and banal, and when I tap your right, agree with me.'

Arnau nodded.

Balthesar began to expound on some unknown subject in Arabic, rattling it out fast, yet no signals came. Moments later the innkeeper returned with food and drink. Arnau took a bite of the pastry, which now tasted like ashes in his mouth, and Balthesar lifted his cup and cradled it in his hand, turning it this way and that and looking into it as though it might answer a question. He paused in his monologue and then suddenly picked it up again.

When was he going to demand an answer in his speech? Worry hit Arnau. Had the old man already nudged his leg and he'd somehow missed it? Was that what the cup swirling was about? And if so had he drawn suspicion upon them by blithely not answering? His tense gaze lifted under heavy brows, glancing this way and that at the people nearby. Two were looking at him. Had he messed it all up by missing a cue? He looked at Balthesar and almost jumped to see the old knight glaring at him meaningfully. He almost blurted something out before the old man resumed, and the sergeant realised that Balthesar was silently reproving him for looking about so suspiciously.

He was lowering his gaze once more as he caught a glimpse of black-and-white figures among the crowd. He looked down at his food, bending with infinite slowness, certain that by trying so hard not to be conspicuous he was inadvertently becoming more so with every second.

Balthesar continued in mild tones. How could the man be so *calm*?

More tea. More pastry. Arnau's leg began to tremble with the sheer tension of it all. Balthesar paused once more, drawing breath, and in the momentary lull, Arnau heard a brief angry exchange not twenty paces from where they were sitting, and the shush of chain mail as two men came closer and closer.

Arnau's head remained dutifully lowered, but his gaze flitted hither and thither like a panicked butterfly, taking in anything he could make out in his peripheral vision, working out how he would react when the men reached him and something went wrong.

He could see the mailed calves of the Almohad soldiers now, tucked into hard-wearing leather boots. They were so close. There would be room to leap up and draw his sword if he was fast, but he would have his back to them and he would be between them and Balthesar, which was inconvenient. The door. He could probably get across the table and in through the door, though that would again leave Balthesar in the lurch. Perhaps as one of the soldiers reached for him he could draw his blade and stab backwards?

The tension was becoming unbearable. His whole world now seemed to consist of a melody of three strains: Balthesar's lilting conversation, the low shush of Almohad chain mail, and Arnau's pulse, which beat out a tattoo loud enough to drown out almost everything else.

The two warriors had to have been right behind Arnau when Balthesar stopped again, his speech ending in a questioning tone. Arnau felt the tap on his left leg.

Sweat poured from his brow. He couldn't remember a *damn thing*. The Almohad soldiers were maybe two or three feet away, and he couldn't remember a single word. He felt panic course through him.

Balthesar frowned and repeated that same last refrain.

'*La 'aetaqid dhlk*,' Arnau said suddenly, surprising himself

Balthesar threw him a worried frown and said something else, kicking his left leg again.

'*La*,' said Arnau firmly, hoping he was going down the right path with this. '*La, la, la.*'

Was this too much? The sweating was becoming unbearable. With a metallic shushing noise, he heard the soldiers moving on. They peered briefly inside the tavern, checking its patrons as Balthesar went on doggedly in his Arabic diatribe. Arnau felt his right knee being kicked.

'*Ah*,' he replied, as if to close a conversation, hoping to God he was right.

Balthesar seemed happy, and the two soldiers walked on, checking out the next few shops. Once they were some way down the street, Balthesar sighed. 'That was rather close, was it not? Congratulations on your first convincing Arabic conversation. I can see Abd al-Azīz still, standing close to the Al-Mudaina door again. He does not look pleased.'

'What were we talking about?'

'Whether your wife was ugly,' grinned Balthesar.

They stayed at the table for another ten minutes as the search concluded fruitlessly, and then remained for another half-hour just to be sure, and then Balthesar paid for their food and drink, and they left the tavern.

'I hope this is the last breadcrumb,' Arnau said as they headed towards the Manaqûr road. 'I don't think we're going to remain in this city for much longer before the killing starts.'

CHAPTER NINE

TUESDAY, 8 JUNE 1199

2 P.M.

The journey across town was tense. They had clearly given the Almohads the slip by the Al-Mudaina, but the very fact that the Lion and his men were in Madina Mayūrqa, and knew that so too was Balthesar d'Aixere, the *Qātil wari'a*, meant that now no alleyway or door could be considered safe. It was astounding, having now seen the Lion of Alarcos's face in more than one encounter, just how much the man wanted Balthesar dead. Arnau was privately of the opinion that despite his piety and the zealotry of his people, Abd al-Azīz would renounce Allah and break every rule in their holy book to skin the old Templar.

The Baron de Castellvell would react little better. An enemy of the Christian, and a Christian himself, both set stolidly against the Templar house of Rourell and its knights. The longer they stayed in Madina, the more dangerous it would become. And so, as they crossed the city, Arnau's eyes slipped this way and that, paying attention to every possible shadow.

Still, soon they found themselves on the Manaqûr road. As they descended through a street that seemed to be mostly home to haberdashers, silk merchants, clothiers and hatters, Arnau could see the gate ahead that bore the same name as the mosque they sought. It resembled strongly the gate through which they had first entered the city, at one and the same time beautifully decorative and militarily impressive. Once again, a small cemetery sat beside it, but they turned off before then into the fields.

The mosque was a squat, heavy building with a large welcoming arch, an odd apsidal end, and a small tower that looked more fortified than sacred. It definitely resembled some sort of castle more than it did a place of worship, and Arnau already had misgivings as they approached. The door stood open, and Arnau followed Brother Balthesar towards it with a certain trepidation.

As they reached the door, and Arnau peered inside, he was surprised to see the floor covered in expensive carpeting, deep and rich and of a duck-egg blue colour, rather than the bare, unforgiving stone flags of a Christian church. It occurred to him as the older knight stepped inside that he, Arnau de Vallbona, had never been inside a mosque. But then, why would he? Had a single mosque remained standing in Iberia when the Christians had taken the land back? His perceptions were certainly being tested on this journey.

The first thing that struck him as he stepped into some sort of porch area was not the wealth of differences between this and a Christian church, beyond simple carpeting. It was, instead, the unsettling similarity behind it all. On the surface this was a heretical, dreadful parody of the Church, loaded with anti-Christian symbolism and celebrating a version of God that denied the Bible.

And yet, as he relaxed and felt the atmosphere flood into him, he realised to his surprise that he got the very same feeling here as he did in a Christian church. Perhaps it was simply a matter of faith? Balthesar kept telling him to have faith, after all. But what was faith? The priest in the village when Arnau was growing up had believed that faith was the force in all men that drove them to believe in the Lord. Yet faith was clearly also what drove the Moor to bring his beliefs to the world. Was it perhaps more important to *have* faith than to worry what that faith was in?

His religious musings were pushed aside as Balthesar nudged him and indicated that he should remove his boots and his sword. Frowning, he did so. That would make any quick getaway all the more difficult, for sure. Balthesar then made his way inside, barefoot and unarmed. Arnau followed suit and was surprised as they rounded a corner at the strange homeliness of the Moors' temple. The churches of northern Iberia were at once both severe and austere, yet golden and opulent. It had always seemed to

Arnau odd that his local priest had harangued the nobles over the fact that a rich man had far less chance of entering heaven than a poor man, and yet the Church had contained more gold and silver than the castle of any noble knight Arnau had seen.

The mosque was different. It seemed built for comfort and community more than self-aggrandisement. The decor was light, airy and comforting, despite the strong presence of the Arabic script that Arnau could not translate and which had for decades signified his enemy.

The *imam*, a reedy figure in a black robe with a simple hat, was polishing the rail of his pulpit. Another thing Arnau noted there – he couldn't imagine most Christian priests lowering themselves to cleaning their own church. As they approached, the man in black bowed. He had a strange smile that looked a little to Arnau like a man trying to eject a particularly difficult turd, but he seemed friendly. He approached with the traditional greeting.

'*As-salāmu 'alaykum.*'

Balthesar replied in kind and Arnau, aware that he was unlikely to understand a single thing said here, played the mute once more, standing back well out of the way. He paid attention to the decor and the architecture as the other two men chattered away in Arabic, wondering why the place felt so spacious and airy until he realised that there were no seats. Of course, the Moors knelt for their services, and faced east, he seemed to remember. Recalling the route they had taken to get to this place from the centre of the city, he turned slowly until he thought he might be facing east and was interested to note that he was now looking directly into a strange, arched and very decorative alcove in the mosque wall. Though he couldn't imagine precisely what its significance was, it clearly had a purpose.

'*Kam,*' Balthesar said suddenly, and from the tone, Arnau realised the command was meant for him, one of the words he knew: 'come'. He did as requested, turning and following the old man, who was already on his way out of the mosque's main room. They gathered up their boots and swords in the porch and re-equipped swiftly before leaving under the benevolent if constipated smile of the *imam*.

As they emerged into the street once more, the bulk of the population had retreated from the streets for the *qaylulah* – the afternoon rest – and they were more or less alone, barring a beggar sitting nearby at the roadside, his legs ending in stumps at the ankle. Balthesar automatically crossed the road and fished his purse from his belt, removing one of the precious few remaining coins and dropping it into the grateful beggar's hand.

'It did not go well, then?' Arnau said quietly.

'Not entirely satisfactorily, no,' Balthesar sighed. 'We have not secured the bone of the blessed Saint Stephen, but equally we have not reached a definite failed end to our quest. The *imam* has the history of his mosque committed to memory in great detail, almost as thorough as the records office in Al-Mudaina. He confirmed that the relic was brought here by the first *imam*, who considered Stephen a possible prophet and was therefore unwilling to simply dispose of the bone. He kept it secured here in a new container, for the original had been melted down and recast by the emir's administration.'

'So they were here, but now they are not?'

'Precisely. It seems that at the height of Almoravid control of the island...' He noted a glazed look fall across Arnau's face, and pursed his lips. 'Mayūrqa has been a *taifa* twice. When the Almoravids first built their caliphate some eighty years past, they seized control of the islands in the same way as the Almohads threaten to now. It then became an independent *taifa* once more, which it remains to this day. But when the Almoravids first came, they brought a new wave of Islamic zealotry and there was a great deal of unrest on the island.'

Arnau nodded. He'd always seen the Moors as just Moors, some good and some bad, until coming face to face with the Almohad raiders that day by the Ebro. Now, he was beginning to understand that there had been as many divisions, dynasties and empires among the Moors as there had been among the Christians.

'The first Almoravid ruler of Mayūrqa,' Balthesar continued, 'was a hard and unforgiving man – Muhàmmad the First. The *imam* tells me that under his rather oppressive reign, the Christians and Jews on the island revolted more than once and there was serious bloodshed. Muhàmmad put down the revolts and initiated a sweep of the entire island, increasing his military presence, building a series of fortresses and removing all traces of Christian worship. By his orders the bone of Saint Stephen was removed from the mosque. This happened sometime around the year eleven hundred and thirty something – the *imam* is a little vague on the precise date. He is also unaware of the fate of the bone once it was removed.'

'I would assume it was simply disposed of,' Arnau said, feeling a little deflated. 'Assuming it was caught up in anti-Christian fervour.'

Balthesar nodded. 'That is a very distinct and disappointing possibility. For the sake of our mission, though, we must cling to the hope that it remained cared for somehow.'

They began to walk back up the street, still talking. 'But who would care for it?'

'That is what we must seek to discover,' the old knight replied. 'We must find out what happened when it was removed. We have leaped forward another century in our story. We know the bone was in that building less than seventy years ago.'

'But how will we learn anything further?'

Balthesar turned a pained expression on his young companion, and Arnau shook his head. 'No.'

'Yes. The only place where there might be any further record is back in the *diwān* of the emir's Al-Mudaina.'

'We cannot go back there, Balthesar. You *know* how dangerous that place is now.'

'We have little choice other than to abandon our mission entirely and return to Rourell as failures. While there is still a chance to recover the relic, it is our God-given duty to attempt to do so. This is my own fault to an extent. I should have thought of this while we were last in the office. The fact that I was reading from right to left – back to front – should have made me think of it. For some blind, idiotic reason I began my search with the earliest reference in order to find out what happened when the bone was brought to Madina. What I *should* have done was to begin with the latest records and work backwards. What use was it finding out how the bone arrived in Madina? What I needed to know was what had happened to it most recently.'

Arnau nodded again at the sense of that, but the very notion of returning to that place seemed insane. 'Then we were in the wrong office to begin with?'

'Quite. Though since the more recent documents are not gathered into one place but divided by category, it will be difficult even to know where to start. I suspect that this time we will need to enlist the aid of a friendly clerk after all.'

'Going back into the Al-Mudaina is still lunacy,' Arnau reminded him.

'Yet it is necessary. As God's chosen we have a duty.'

Arnau fell into a gloomy silence. The very last thing he wanted to do right now was step back into that nest of vipers, but the grey-bearded brother was quite right that the only alternative would be to leave the island and return home empty handed, knowing that they had not done all they could.

The first he knew of trouble was when a short, chisel-bladed knife thrummed through the air and missed his face by less than an inch. The weapon had been thrown with enough force that it thudded into one of the poor quality wooden houses in the long street and jammed there, vibrating slightly.

The young sergeant's eyes swept left in the direction from which the knife had come, his hand already going to his sword hilt. They were passing a narrow alley, which Arnau automatically assumed to be the source of the attack. Sure enough, as he took a few steps forward, drawing his sword, and managed a direct view into the alley, he could see two figures. One was already hefting a second knife, and Arnau ducked back as it hurtled from the darkness and hissed past him again.

'Watch your back,' Balthesar called, and Arnau spun. Two more figures were stalking up the street behind them, the direction from which they had come. With a sinking feeling, the young sergeant turned and looked up the street. Sure enough, two more figures emerged from a side street and began to edge down towards them.

They were trapped. Six against two. Fortunately the others all carried swords, and it appeared that the man in the alley was out of knives, for he too was now drawing the blade at his side. Still, the odds were not good.

What to do? If they stayed here they would inevitably end up surrounded and fighting back to back. Their chances if that happened would be poor. Rush the ones up or downhill? Likely they would not be fast enough to break through, and they would end up once more surrounded. The alley, then.

Arnau peered into the narrow lane at the two men stepping cautiously towards them. The place looked a little tight for the swinging of swords, but the two villains both brandished theirs, so it was just about possible.

'The alley,' he shouted, and began to run. Balthesar said nothing, but Arnau could hear the older knight running behind him, so the knight had both heard and understood.

The two men in the alley were almost out into the street now, and Arnau picked up the pace. They had to get into that alley if they were to stand a chance. He wondered for a moment what kind of men these were. They were dressed in ordinary clothes and without armour. They seemed to be common criminals or thugs, which was a relief. That meant they were not trained fighters, and might get a nasty surprise when they realised they were attacking experienced swordsmen.

The lead figure in the alley, the one who had thrown the knives, reached the street just as Arnau ran at him full pelt. He tried to bring his sword up, but by the time he had, the sergeant, moving at an impressive pace, was inside his reach. Arnau cannoned into the man and both the figures in the alley were thrown back. The rear one fell, and the nearer one stumbled backwards over his friend, only just managing to remain upright, shocked at the impact of Arnau's collision.

Recovering his balance, the man warily stepped back a few more paces and Arnau, his momentum stalled, stepped forward menacingly, making sure to stand on the head of the man who had fallen and who now yelped in pain. As the young sergeant continued to advance on the former knifeman, he heard behind him the sound of a blade slamming through flesh and a cry of agony, and prayed that it was Balthesar despatching the man on the floor and not a sword slicing into the older Templar.

The ruffian ahead gripped his sword with both hands and waved it this way and that threateningly. Arnau was relieved to note that there seemed to be more enthusiasm than skill on display. He feinted to the right with his sword and sure enough the man inexpertly thrust his sword that way to parry.

'This is not your day,' Arnau smiled.

The thug glanced nervously over his shoulder for a second, perhaps pondering his chances of flight. He appeared to come swiftly to the correct conclusion that if he even attempted to run he would die with a sword in his back in moments.

The ruffian licked his lips and took another step back, then suddenly lunged with his sword, aiming for the sergeant's belly, an easy target and a central strike that made the most of the minimal space in the alley. Arnau, though, had watched the man's feet. Days of practice last year against the implacable German knight had taught him well to anticipate an opponent's moves, to look for his 'tell'. The moment the man stepped back but braced his left foot, the sergeant knew the lunge was coming and, with the distinct lack of room here, it would almost certainly be a central strike. Consequently, it was a simple thing to sidestep the blow. The sword whispered through the air where his belly had been moments earlier and its wielder, taken by surprise, staggered forward. Arnau lifted his own sword as the man lurched past, and brought the pommel down on the back of his neck, the best blow he could achieve in the tight space. He was rewarded with a cracking noise and a scream from the villain who tumbled forward, sword dropping from his fingers.

Arnau's satisfaction was short-lived. He'd thought only of his own predicament but the falling man, suffering agonising and paralysing neck pain, fell into Balthesar's back, sending the older knight staggering into his own opponent.

Somehow the old man managed to keep his footing, but the mistake cost him dearly. A lucky strike from the lout in front of him tore through Balthesar's side. The knight yelped, his free hand going to his middle. Blood blossomed on his torn *gandura* and *burnous*. Guilt washed through Arnau at the knowledge that the wound was entirely his fault.

Hurriedly, he bent and swept up Broken-neck's fallen sword, pausing only long enough to ram his own blade into the man's back to put him out of his misery and stop him shaking. A shaking body underfoot could cause havoc in a fight.

Despite the wound to his side, Balthesar was still engaging with the man before him, swords clashing, teeth bared. The old man let go of his side to better deal with his opponent, and the blood flow into this clothing increased worryingly. The grey-bearded knight stooped with a grunt of pain as his opponent lunged, and Arnau realised the manoeuvre had gone wrong in an instant. Balthesar had intended to duck under the attack and drive his own sword upwards in a killing blow, but it was not to be, for as he ducked the pain lanced through his side and he gasped and failed to lift his sword.

Arnau was there in a heartbeat. Before the ruffian could recover and strike at the hunched knight, the young sergeant swung both swords down in a chop. It was not an elegant move and would never appear in a manual on swordsmanship, but with such limited space with which to work and no time to plan, his reaction bore fruit. Both swords slammed down into the man. The right, Arnau's common sword arm, smashed into the man's left shoulder so hard it almost separated the limb, crushing the joint that held it on. The left sword also smashed into his right shoulder, though with less force, being his off-hand.

The man screamed and fell, knocking Balthesar to the side.

Arnau was now facing another Moorish thug with a sword, though he realised with a great deal of respect for his comrade that this was the last man facing them. While Arnau had managed to deal with the two in the alley, Balthesar had already despatched the front two of the men who'd followed them in.

The last criminal looked extremely nervous, and well he might. He was alone and a poor match for a knight. He began to step back, slowly, carefully and gingerly, across the bodies of his fallen comrades and out towards the street. Arnau advanced on him implacably. The man reached the end of the alley and, seizing the only chance he was likely to get, turned and ran.

Arnau couldn't quite get to him to stop him and so, trusting to the Lord and praying for accuracy, he threw his sword.

It was not a good throw. Swords were not meant to be thrown weapons, of course, and he'd never expected a serious hit, but he achieved what he'd intended. The sword slammed into the man's back, side-on, the crosspiece hitting first. The man stumbled in surprise and fell to the road. Arnau was on him before he could rise.

'May the Lord Jesus protect you and lead you to eternal life,' Arnau said quietly, and thrust his blade down into the man's back.

The ruffian squawked, then gurgled and slowly passed from the world of men. Arnau collected his own sword, noting with irritation a nick it had picked up when it fell on the road. He briefly considered keeping the other blade, but decided that it was a poor quality weapon and not worthwhile.

On the way back to the alley, he checked for movement among the fallen, but they were all lifeless. Balthesar was on his feet now, wiping his sword on a piece of material torn from one of their assailants.

'A struggle full of accidents, both happy and *un*happy,' the old knight declared.

'I am so sorry I caused that,' Arnau said, contrition filling him.

'It is of no consequence. Such things happen in battle. I have survived, and I consider that a boon, given the odds. Your choice of the alley for our battleground was inspired. I suspect it saved our lives.'

The old knight sheathed his sword and staggered out of the alley, wincing as he touched his side.

'We need to find a doctor,' Arnau said.

'No. We need to get out of here before we become the centre of attention, and we need to lie low for a while.'

Arnau frowned. 'You don't think this was a random attack?'

Balthesar shrugged, wincing again. 'It may very well be, but we cannot discount the possibility that these men were somehow retained by Abd al-Azīz. We may have escaped him earlier, but even with you muted we are not too hard to find, for we tend to stand out, especially when we speak Aragonese as we are now. And whether they were or were not sent by the Lion, we still need to be away from them. Once the authorities learn of this, questions will be asked, and I think we would be far better served not being the subject of those questions, don't you?'

Arnau nodded. 'Do we have time to search them?'

The grey knight shook his head, nodding towards the windows of the street where nervous faces were appearing, perusing the carnage in their neighbourhood. 'They will have nothing incriminating and likely no valuables, so a search would be fruitless. Let us move.'

The two men hurried off up the street at the fastest pace the old warrior could manage, turning several corners until they were far away from the site of the attack. At last, after a quarter of an hour of climbing the steeper streets, they rounded a corner and Arnau realised they were facing that second great fortification he had seen when they first arrived.

'The Gumāra fortress,' Balthesar breathed, nodding towards it. 'A recent addition to the city's defences. They were building it when I was last here. Now help me.'

The old man staggered over to the edge of the street and sank onto the side of a water trough. Carefully, he undid his sword belt and propped the weapon by the stone tank. Then he grasped his clothing and pulled it up at the side, hissing with pain, to reveal the wound.

Arnau was relieved. Though there had been a lot of blood, the blow had been a poor one, causing a flesh wound – just a small slice in the side that did not look as though it had gone deep enough to do any real damage.

'Doesn't look too bad,' Arnau said, peering at it.

'I do not think it has injured me permanently. It is painful, but the blood is a normal colour and I am not experiencing discomfort or difficulty inside. If I eat and it fails to come out of the other end, we will know that my gut has been cut, though other than that I suspect it will heal in no time. But I need you to stitch it.'

Arnau stared. 'What?'

'I will see a doctor in due course, but for now I am bleeding badly. It needs stitching so that I will last long enough to seek proper attention. Quick now, or I will lose too much blood and become faint.'

Arnau shook his head. 'I've never stitched a wound. In fact the only time I've ever stitched anything was the tunics and robes of the order after the siege last year. And I did such a bad job I was told to find something else to do.'

'I cannot stitch it myself, because I cannot reach there. And I do not wish to faint. If you have no thread, you will find that I carry needle and thread in my pouch.'

Arnau, feeling faintly nauseous already at the prospect of what he must do, found the old knight's pouch and fished around until he rather painfully located the needle and thread. His tongue protruding from the side of his mouth, he inexpertly threaded the needle and then looked back down at the wound, feeling a little sicker with each moment.

'I can't see it properly. It's so messy. So much blood.'

Balthesar cast a scathing look at him. 'Have you not noticed what I am sat upon? Use your head, Vallbona.'

Arnau nodded unhappily and tucked the needle carefully into his sleeve as he scooped up water from the trough and splashed it over the wound. Four times he repeated the process before he could clearly see the rent in the old knight's flesh.

'All right. Here I go.'

He leaned close and, wincing, pushed the needle into the skin. He almost lurched back at the yelp of pain from his companion, and fresh blood welled up from the wound.

'Damnation, but I cannot see it again. More blood.'

'Then use more *water*,' Balthesar hissed. Arnau did so, washing the wound clean again, and then braced himself and pushed the needle through and up, back, out of the skin on the far side of the wound. The old man breathed heavily and grunted, but sat still. Arnau made the second stitch and was then forced to pause and use more water. Having done so, he pulled the stitches tight, making Balthesar hiss in pain. With a deep breath he went in for the next stitch.

It took him a quarter of an hour in total to put in ten stitches and seal the wound. When he had finished, he leaned back to appraise his handiwork.

'How does it look?' the old man asked.

'Like you were attacked by a blind seamstress. Not good.'

'Is it leaking?'

Arnau splashed another handful of water over it. The last of the red washed away and only a few droplets remained on the wound. 'I don't think so.'

'Then it will do. One last piece of work and we can move. See that shop over there?'

Arnau looked where Balthesar's pointing finger indicated. A small shop sat between heavy-walled houses, selling all sorts of culinary delights. 'Yes?'

'Take money from my pouch and buy honey.'

Baffled, the young sergeant did as he was commanded, crossing the street. The shopkeeper was sitting far to the back in the shade, filling jars with olives from a large bowl. Arnau ignored him and looked around for only a moment before he spotted what appeared to be honey. He took it to the man and greeted him politely in stilted Arabic.

'Honey?' he asked. The man looked at him blankly. Arnau pointed at the bottle and placed it on the table before attempting a childish impression of a bee, buzzing as he walked in circles, flapping his hands up and down.

'*Assel*,' grinned the shopkeeper and nodded, chuckling to himself.

Arnau handed over his coin, took the change and the bottle and thanked the shopkeeper before leaving. Once more across the street, he held it up.

'Smear it on the wound and then use it to stick a strip of torn material on it. It will act as a dressing until a doctor can work his miracles.'

Arnau, frowning, did so, washing the sticky substance from his hands afterwards in the slightly pink water trough.

'It is an old method. Older than Christ, in fact.'

'What now?' Arnau said as he let the clothes drop back into place and the old Templar rose to his feet stiffly with a grunt.

'Now we find a place to stay. The day is moving on. I think we need to ponder on our next move with the Al-Mudaina, and we would be better doing that somewhere safe.'

'You have somewhere in mind?'

The knight nodded. 'I do.'

CHAPTER TEN

TUESDAY, 8 JUNE 1199

3.20 P.M.

'This place will be safe?' Arnau asked. 'You realise that the Lion and his men will be investigating? Looking into our presence.'

'It is, I promise you, the last place Abd al-Azīz will ever look.'

Something about the way he said that worried Arnau even more. 'Do you really think those thugs were in his pay?' he said by way of a change in subject.

Balthesar made a 'so-so' motion with his hand. 'Let's just say that I am not ruling out the possibility.'

'But why would he send criminals after us when he has perfectly good soldiers?'

'Do not forget, Vallbona, that he is not free to do as he pleases in this place. Mayūrqa is still the emir's domain. Setting his soldiers on someone without permission from the emir could just be the sort of provocation that triggers something he cannot afford to start with so few men on the island. No, I think his chasing after us was impulsive and he quickly reined his men in. I suspect he made a few swift enquiries of local eyes and ears and sent out men to pick up our trail. We spent long enough nursing our tea that it is possible we picked up a tail even then and they followed us, simply waiting for us to be out of the public's eye somewhere. No, it is too coincidental, I think, to be anything other than Almohad work.'

Arnau sank into gloomy silence once more. 'That suggests that nowhere we go will be truly safe.'

'No,' Balthesar agreed. 'Nowhere is truly safe. But we must do what we can with what the Lord gifts us. This would be an excellent time for you to practise a taciturn nature. Where we are going we will once more be Moors.'

'Where *are* we going?'

'Do you know of *waqf*?'

'Of course I don't know of *waqf*,' Arnau said, faintly annoyed at the way Balthesar seemed to have sunk naturally into the culture while expecting Arnau to keep up.

'*Waqf* is the practice of donating property to religious groups for charity. They are a little like Christian almshouses. Often, *waqf* results in hostels that are maintained under the administration of the local *imam* and are used to house the poor, the sick and the wretched. We are both poor, and I am sick,' he added, gesturing to his side.

'Are you perchance intimating that I am wretched?' Arnau sighed.

Balthesar just smiled. 'There is a *waqf* institution not far from here. I stayed with them when I first came to the island. I am not sure what their regulations would be about charity to Christians – I suspect the subject has never arisen – but whether they would be agreeable or not, we need to disappear from the public eye right now, and being poor Moors in a hostel seems a good choice. Certainly a *waqf* house would not appear on any list of places Abd al-Azīz will think to look.'

Arnau acknowledged the point unhappily. The prospect of evenings spent in silence listening only to constant chatter in an unintelligible tongue was not a pleasant one. A thought occurred to him.

'If we're Moors, we will have to pray.'

'We will,' the old knight agreed. 'Fortunately even the most rabid zealot would not expect a mute to speak the words, so you will simply have to go through the motions. So long as you can kneel, bow, raise your hands and suchlike you need not worry too much.'

Arnau glanced ahead. The ritual early-afternoon nap had begun to end, and people were emerging from their houses and shops. The streets were starting to fill once more and Arnau fell silent as they moved unnoticed through the crowd. His eyes continually flitted this way and that furtively, attempting to identify anyone who might be watching or shadowing them with malicious intent. Logic said no one was currently following them. Even if those attackers back near the mosque had been in the Lion's pay, none had escaped with their life, so the trail must now be truly lost. Yet it did not do to be complacent.

The *waqf* house lay not far from the Gumāra fortress at the edge of town, nestled close to the powerful walls. Arnau was somewhat surprised by its appearance. As a charitable property to house the poor and the hungry, he had pictured somewhere run-down and similarly impoverished, perhaps an old house that had seen better days.

The Moor who had donated this place to the mosque had clearly been a very wealthy man, if he could afford to part with such a place. Its façade was of decorated stone, three storeys high and with delicate arches and many glazed windows. As they approached from the south, he caught a view of the side of the building, which was of timber construction but similarly decorative and rich regardless. It appeared to be square-shaped, constructed around a courtyard, and the only word Arnau could easily find to describe it was palatial. This place must have been a noble's home before he generously donated it.

The young sergeant tried not to goggle, wide eyed, as they moved towards the entrance, a doorway with a red and white stone horseshoe arch and a sign above it in elegant Arabic script. He wanted to speak to Balthesar, to question him, but he needed to remain silent.

Inside, a Moor in a simple white robe emerged from some gloomy side door and greeted the older man who stood to the fore, nodding respectfully at Arnau also. The young sergeant returned the gesture. Had it not been for the danger inherent in their situation, he would have found the place fascinating, but he was dreading the call to prayer, certain he would get something wrong. While he fretted, the two older men had a brief exchange in friendly-sounding, high-speed Arabic.

At one point during the exchange, Balthesar showed his bound wound to the man, and elicited sympathy, suggesting that it was the old man's injury that had bought them admittance, or at least that and the poor stupid mute he relied upon. When the conversation apparently reached some sort of satisfactory conclusion, the man in white beckoned and led them in through another archway. This one opened into a wide hall, set up with long tables and benches. The administrator explained something to them which, of course, flew entirely over Arnau's head, though he was willing to wager it was something along the lines of this being the refectory. Another arch from here admitted bright sunshine, and it was through this they next moved out into the courtyard. Arnau's awe reached new heights at the delights of the courtyard. A wide, paved space, it was surrounded on three sides by wooden balconies with delicate arcades and many doors, and on the other by that high stone frontage. Colourful plants grew in shapely terracotta pots around the edge, but the bulk of the courtyard was occupied by a large pool. Some fifty feet across by perhaps forty long, it also looked surprisingly deep, a more than adequate home to the myriad fish swimming around in it. A fountain at one end fed into the pool, its drain presumably hidden beneath the paving, for of it the young sergeant could see no sign.

This was a home for the poor? Arnau had stayed in well-appointed mansions that looked impoverished by comparison. His fears about staying here were gradually abating. He'd have to be silent and careful, yes, and he would have to wear the mask of a Moor, but at least it would be comfortable.

Through another arch at the far end they reached another large hall, this one well carpeted and elegant. Realising what it was in time, Arnau stopped before walking into it, as did the other two for, if not an actual mosque, this was clearly a place to pray and therefore no place for his boots.

They went back out into the courtyard, following an explanation by the administrator, and then moved through a side arch and found a staircase that climbed both wooden storeys of the building. On the upper floor they were led to a room overlooking the street outside, with a view that took in a small bathhouse and part of the city walls. Another brief chat between the other two men and they were finally left alone.

Balthesar waited a score of heartbeats after the door closed, and then also closed the shutters on the outer window before sinking onto one of the two beds.

'This will be more than adequate,' he smiled. 'And with so many rooms, it appears that occupancy is not high. We have no neighbours – I told the man that you snored terribly and it bought us extra privacy. So, as long as we check the balcony outside beforehand and keep door and shutters closed, we can talk quietly.'

Arnau breathed a sigh of relief. 'I am worried about the prayers.'

'Do not be. I know the form, you do not need to. Just follow the actions of those around you and remain silent. We shall stay at the rear so we are not observed, while you can see all those in front. Very simple. And we have missed the *dhuhr* prayer. The next call will be *asr*, and we shall be absent for that, and possibly also for the *maghrib* call at sunset. The only one you need concern yourself with is the final prayer of the day, when it is dark.'

'Why will we miss the next two prayers?' Arnau frowned.

'Because, my young friend, I need now to see a doctor, and then we shall return to the lair of the Lion. It is time to search the records once more.'

With a sigh of regret at having secured such comfortable lodgings and then leaving them immediately without a chance to rest, Arnau rose to his feet once more. Following Balthesar from the room, they descended the stairs and crossed the courtyard once more, through the refectory and out into the sunshine. Balthesar clearly knew where he was going, perhaps directed by an earlier comment of the administrator, and they found the house of a doctor three streets away.

The man, whose house backed on to some sort of communal hospital, accepted a nominal payment from Balthesar and examined the wound briefly. Though Arnau clearly could not understand his words, his manner and actions suggested that Arnau's stitching left a great deal to be desired, and would leave an impressive scar. There was some probing, and many questions, but the doctor seemed on the whole satisfied that his patient would heal in due course. He spent some time cleaning up the wound and then re-dressing it in a more professional manner. In the end, after half an hour, the two men left the small hospital satisfied.

They then, at Balthesar's instigation, took a somewhat circuitous walk, close to the walls and past the Gumāra fortress, to the southern ramparts that overlooked the sea, though from their perspective all they could observe was the inside of the high, powerful walls. Here was yet another area of agricultural land, crops growing in abundance, confirming how easily and for how long Madina could withstand a siege. They passed into a built-up area once more, and then, ahead, Arnau spotted the high, square brick tower of the great mosque in the centre.

Biting down on his rising nerves, he followed Balthesar past the street of shops down which they had run for their lives mere hours ago. As they neared the mosque, a voice began to ring out from its minaret. The lilting chant that rose in the call to prayer was instantly joined by other voices across the city and rose like an aural tide. In every street, the city's population finished off what they were doing, locked doors and began to move towards their local mosques. Not all went, Arnau noticed. Clearly the emir's guards he could see on the walls would not abandon their duty to attend, and there would clearly be many others who could not spare their time.

Such was clearly the case at the Al-Mudaina. They approached the palace from the south-east, making for that second door through which they had entered with the disgruntled clerk.

'What do we do?' Arnau whispered as they passed the mosque, his low tones muffled beneath the surge of people heading to their prayer and the warbling call of the *imam* above.

'I don't think we have much choice this time,' Balthesar sighed. 'Danger or no danger, we are in no position to wait. The chances of seeing our friendly clerk once more are impressively small, and there is no real chance to sneak in. I fear our best option is to brazenly approach and beg permission to search the archives.'

'Drawing attention to ourselves might be a terrible idea, especially here.'

'Agreed, but we are forced to play off peril against speed. To make ourselves known is certainly more dangerous than to be subtle and circumspect, but means we can be in and out faster. Waiting around for a better option as we did last time is less perilous, but every passing hour carries the risk of discovery, and with Abd al-Azīz now aware that we are in the city and have been in the palace, he will be watchful. Come, and button those lips once more.'

Arnau unhappily followed the older brother over to the gate, where Balthesar lifted the heavy iron knocker and rapped it twice on the door. There was a pause, and a hatch in the door protected by a solid iron grille clicked open. The face of a swarthy, clearly ill-humoured guard appeared and barked a question at them.

Balthesar greeted the man and spoke at length in Arabic. The guard grunted and the hatch clonked shut. There was a long pause, during which Balthesar seemed disinclined to move and Arnau could not enquire what was happening, and then finally the hatch opened once more. Whatever the guard said sounded positive, and bolts were thrown back and the gate opened.

The grey knight stepped inside, bowed and thanked the man, and Arnau followed him in with a polite nod of the head. His eyes immediately raked the courtyard, searching for the Lion of Alarcos and his men. The Lion himself might not be watching for them, but a black-and-white figure stood not far from the gate. By the merest chance, he had been engaged in an argument with one of the emir's soldiers and had his back to them, oblivious to their passing. Nevertheless, Arnau attracted Balthesar's attention with a tug of the sleeve, and they hurried through the courtyard before the man turned and saw them. As they moved onwards with a guard for escort, the only other sign he could see of the vile black-and-white-clad Almohads was through that second arch, out by the main gate once more. There were men on both gates now, watching who was coming and going. The Lion of Alarcos was not going to be taken by surprise again.

The guard led the way, though Arnau was sure he and Balthesar could probably find their own path, this being their second visit in a day. Still, they were in a royal palace, and it was probably not permitted to let wandering vagrants poke around. At least they were inside now, and not under the potential scrutiny of those men by the gates. That alone was a comfort.

Arnau heaved a sigh of relief as they passed from the busiest areas of the palace and into the part where the records offices were to be found. They approached that first doorway and their escort gestured for them to continue on, then spun and returned to his place outside. The two men stepped through the arch into the area where the clerks and soldiers dealt with visitors, and Balthesar spoke briefly.

Arnau and his companion both saw the man at the same time: a soldier with a chain veil, garbed in black and white, stood silent and menacing at the rear of the room. Arnau immediately lowered his gaze, though it would clearly be too late now. The soldier had seen them enter and there could be no other reason for him to be in the records offices than to specifically watch for the pair of them. So the Lion was being thorough enough to post eyes wherever he suspected they might appear. Likely there would be men in that tavern and down by the Al-balad mosque too, then. Arnau felt his nerves flutter. A more dangerous situation he could not imagine.

He was surprised when Balthesar blithely gave their names to the clerk and removed his sword, they no longer having bags to hand over. Arnau did the same, pulse thumping loud in his ears as he did so. To his growing astonishment, Balthesar gave the Almohad warrior a respectful bow before turning and speaking to another clerk. In this, Arnau did not follow suit.

Handing over his sword with the deepest misgivings, he followed the old knight along the corridor, seeking a room that would undoubtedly look like all the other offices. Arnau watched over his shoulder as they went and was totally unsurprised to see the black-and-white warrior leave the records offices swiftly and with purpose, no doubt to report to his master.

'We're in trouble,' Arnau said.

'Not yet. Later, perhaps.'

'Why?'

'Remember, we are still in the emir's palace. Abd al-Azīz cannot simply attack us. He is bound by etiquette and simple common sense while we are all here. It is when we leave Al-Mudaina and move into the poorer streets of the city that we will be in extreme danger, for he will not let us slip his leash twice.'

'So we stay in the palace until we go home, then? *Real* home, I mean. Rourell.'

Balthesar gave him an encouraging smile. 'Come on. I have located the archives of the emirate's more recent staff. My first thought is to find the senior clerks who served under Muhàmmad the First. If they were as thorough as I suspect, then someone would have been charged with recording all the property impounded or destroyed during the reprisals for the Christian uprisings. Somewhere, someone will have mentioned what was taken from the Al-balad mosque and what was done with it. I am positive the records will contain at least a clue.'

It sounded like a long and involved task to Arnau, though admittedly he was in no hurry to leave the palace now, knowing what probably awaited them when they did. So he followed the older knight along the corridor to one of the many almost identical record rooms. They entered and Arnau was relieved to discover that they were alone. Perhaps it was because of the afternoon prayer that there were so few clerks in evidence. Whatever the case, Balthesar busied himself with the large book on the table once more, while Arnau, starved of anything useful to do, moved over to the window and peered out.

This room must be on the same wall of the palace as the one they had been in during their morning visit, for it also afforded him a good view of the port and the seaward walls. He could not quite see the palace dock that played host to the Aragonese ship, but his view of the rest of the port and the city was unimpeded. There was a noticeable lack of folk in the streets, since many would now be in the mosques praying, and he could see in places, especially in the garden nearby, people who simply did not have the time to visit their mosques, who had unrolled a small mat and were kneeling upon it, facing east and praying. They were obviously as regimented in their prayer as the brothers were bound by the liturgical canon in the monastery.

Behind him, he could hear Balthesar muttering as he turned page after page.

His own gaze roved the landscape, taking in everything, in particular any place that might conceivably serve to conceal two running fugitives. There were many places in the city that might suffice, and he tried to commit the best of them to memory, but his gaze was inevitably drawn back to the one place he would prefer to go above all others: the port.

Ships from all over were docked there, including Aragonese merchantmen, French ones, Genoese and even Byzantine. From here, passage could probably be bought back to somewhere safe. His laughed bitterly at the notion that just because Aragon was a Christian land it was safe. The Baron de Castellvell still hated them and held sway there. And the house of Rourell would never be the most popular establishment. Still, he would give all he had – which admittedly was not much right now – to be back across that sea and in Rourell. Somewhere where vengeful Almohads were not watching them like hawks, waiting for the opportunity to swoop.

He sighed wistfully as he took in the variety of colourful sails, each of which held the promise of somewhere safer than here. Three new ships were even now coming into port, heading for a cluster of empty jetties. These, though, were Moorish vessels, from the setup of their sails and their general shape. They turned as one, in formation, making in a line for the three jetties, and that was when he saw the design on their sails.

'Saints preserve us,' he breathed, and turned a worried face on his fellow Templar.

'What is it?' asked Balthesar, lifting his gaze from the book for a moment and leaving his index finger marking his place.

'Three Almohad ships. Just coming in to dock.'

The old knight pursed his lips, his eyes taking on a worried cast. 'That cannot be good. Three ships is far too many to be mere merchants or another deputation. On the other hand, it is too few to signify an invasion, so at least we are not about to find ourselves in the midst of a war.'

Arnau nodded, though he wasn't sure that even Balthesar believed that from the tone of his voice.

'Have you found anything?'

'Not yet. This is troublesome. It seems that there was simply too much disturbance and not enough order during those risings and their aftermath for record keeping to be up to its usual impressive standard. I may have to try another tack. Let me think.'

'Think all you like, Balthesar. I'm in no hurry to leave.'

His gaze went back to the port, where he could now see yet more of those gleaming soldiers in black and white gathering on the dock. This did not bode well. Not at all.

'Have you—?'

He was interrupted by a click as the *diwān* door opened, and both occupants turned as one.

Two green-garbed soldiers stood in the doorway. One gestured at Balthesar and bowed his head before he spoke. When he did, it was in Arabic, of course, and Arnau had no idea what he said, other than that his tone carried a certain level of respect but also an element of compulsion. Balthesar answered in their tongue and also bowed his head before turning to Arnau.

'It would appear that the presence of the *Qātil wari'a* has come to the attention of the emir. We are summoned to an audience.'

Arnau's heart lurched. The emir?

His eyes slid back towards those ships in the port. It would very much appear that they had chosen the most troubled time imaginable to visit Mayūrqa.

CHAPTER ELEVEN

TUESDAY, 8 JUNE 1199

4.30 P.M.

Brother Balthesar seemed remarkably calm and collected on the walk through the palace, which felt to Arnau more like a trudge to the gallows. They had not had the opportunity to exchange more than a few bland words since the emir's soldiers had appeared, or at least not useful, private ones. Arnau's mind had raced, though, with each new room or corridor through which they passed.

The summons had not been an immediate response, that was clear. The emir knew that they were in the palace, and he knew who Balthesar was – or at least who he had been years ago, while he was still fighting for the Moors and before he took his vows. And if the emir knew all that, then he can only have learned it from Abd al-Azīz, the Lion of Alarcos. And why would the Almohad reveal this information to the emir? There were several possibilities that arose in the young sergeant's mind, and none of them boded well.

Perhaps the Lion had managed to put pressure on the island's ruler and had more influence and freedom than Balthesar suggested. If that was the case, then perhaps the Almohad was simply using the emir and his administration and guards to arrest and detain the two travellers. Result: they were in the Lion's grasp.

Or the Lion had discovered what it was they were seeking, had denounced them to the emir as undercover Christian treasure hunters sneaking around the islands. Arnau didn't know the emir, obviously, and Balthesar seemed to consider him a solidly independent ruler, but would any Moorish ruler find such a thing acceptable? It seemed unlikely to Arnau. Result: they were arrested by the emir.

Perhaps the Lion had somehow become aware that they served the order. If that was the case then they would undoubtedly be doubly unpopular. Result: the emir and the Lion *both* got their hands on them.

It was even possible, if far-fetched, that during that fleeting moment they had passed in the Al-Mudaina that morning, Baron de Castellvell had spotted and recognised them. After all, it had been less than a year since he had been at Rourell issuing barely veiled threats. If he was working to some political end with the emir, might he sell them out? Result: unthinkable.

Nothing seemed to produce a happy conclusion for them in Arnau's mind, and so he continued to picture a noose at the end of their journey, probably being strung by the Lion. Or Castellvell. Or the emir.

The opulence of the place did not insist itself upon the young man this time as he passed through it. They climbed a staircase that was grand and magnificent with Arnau tramping along like the condemned man, and emerged before a door that contained so much intricately carved woodwork it was more art than function. The guards knocked once and then stepped to the side as though planning to prevent any attempt at escape.

The doors were opened from within by more of the emir's green-clad guards. The room inside was not as magnificent as Arnau had imagined, given the other rooms in the palace. An open space with wall hangings of flags in many different designs – all Moorish, though – surrounded a marble-floored room with a single focus. The dais upon which the emir's seat rested was ornate and well appointed, and carved beasts reared at the corners. It was reached by three steps, and more of the emir's guards bristled close by.

The Lion of Alarcos stood to one side with two of his black-and-white-clad men, though his presence came as absolutely no surprise to Arnau. The emir sat upon his throne, eyes locked on the new arrivals, and Arnau found himself studying and judging the man instantly, though with a great deal of difficulty. The ruler of Mayūrqa, Abd-Allāh ibn Ishāq ibn Ghāniya, was darker-skinned than many of the islanders Arnau had seen, closer in complexion to the Lion and his men, which struck Arnau as odd. He was dressed soberly, without affectation, and his personal jewellery was minimal. He wore a turban and his beard was neat. His eyes were absolutely unknowable. Arnau had seen men who looked shifty and men who looked true, he had seen angry and jolly and proud. What he had never seen was a man who looked *nothing*. There was nothing about his expression and eyes that gave Arnau anything to work with. That alone moved this powerful man into the 'worrying' bracket for the young Templar.

They came to a halt equidistant from the emir and the Almohad deputation, and Balthesar nodded briefly at the Lion before bowing his head respectfully to the island's ruler. The emir looked the old man up and down and said something in Arabic, and then suddenly followed it up with: 'Or would you prefer the tongue of Aragon?'

Balthesar bowed his head again. 'I am proficient in both languages, though my companion has only a few words of your tongue. If it would be acceptable, Spanish would be of great help for him.'

The emir nodded and flashed a momentary look at the Lion of Alarcos, who barked out a harsh-sounding reply. The emir gave a weird smile. 'The *Qa'id* here refuses to, as he says, sully his tongue with your infidel language, though be assured he can understand it.'

Again, the emir's manner failed to clarify whether he was joking at the Lion's expense or having a joke *with* him at theirs. Unreadable. Ineffable. Arnau realised now just how clever, and probably dangerous, the emir was.

'So you are the infamous "pious murderer", then. When I was but a young man, parents frightened their children with your name. You are not the horned demon of those tales after all.' He smiled that odd smile again, which seemed to teeter somewhere between a savage snarl and a warm grin.

Balthesar nodded, but replied calmly. 'I was a terror of the Almohads and of bandits and criminals. Never of the men of the emirs. A man can change, *Sidi*. After all, I was born a poor Christian peasant in a Moorish land.'

'Which is what you now appear to be.'

Another laugh. 'Granted. But I am far more than a simple peasant, as you know. And you are far more than a *wāli*. You rule as an emir of old. The only one, in fact. The *last* emir. You control the only *taifa* in the world now. No, I think you are far greater than an Almohad.'

Arnau's eyes flicked to the Lion of Alarcos, whose face reflected the subtle digs at his status Balthesar was making. Still he remained silent.

'Tell me,' the emir continued, 'what the most distinguished Monster of Valencia, the soul-child of El Cid, has been doing for near three decades? It is a magnificent tale to begin with: the rise of a nobody from a downtrodden faith to become the champion of a powerful emir and a lord of men, a demon on the field of battle. And then, when Valencia falls, you disappear. I heard tales once that you had come to Mayūrqa to die.'

Balthesar chuckled again. 'I am old, yes, but as you can see I am far from expired. In fact, despite the years that hang heavy upon me, I would say that I am in a position to best many a good man. I have not spent my time in dotage, *Sidi*. Far from it. However, given the somewhat strained history between myself and Abd al-Azīz here, I would prefer not to delve into my personal life in front of him.'

The emir nodded. 'Quite. Then if you will not reveal your past, perhaps your present? I do feel that an explanation of your presence on my islands might be in order.'

'I am travelling as a mendicant with my novice here, Arnau de Vallbona. We are on personal business, though it is a matter that has no bearing on your rule, the politics of the islands and the caliphate, or even the good *Qa'id* here,' he said, indicating the Lion.

'Personal business that involves sneaking around in my palace?' urged the emir.

Balthesar took a breath and straightened slightly. '*Sidi*, there are ears here that are more than merely unfriendly. I cannot, and shall not, say more in front of them, even if pushed to it.'

The emir sat back and rubbed his beard thoughtfully. A moment passed and then he turned to the Almohads and issued what sounded like a very peremptory command, somewhat at odds with his earlier familiarity with them. Again, Arnau was struck by how difficult to read and to predict this man was.

With a blank expression, though clearly smouldering with hatred, the Lion of Alarcos gestured to his men and they strode from the room, the guards opening the doors to allow them egress and then firmly closing them afterwards.

'So, terror of Valencia and slayer of Almohads,' said the emir with that smile that wasn't a smile, 'we are alone. You are out of earshot of your unfriendly ears. Tell me why you are here.'

The older knight nodded and straightened slightly again. Somehow he looked more virile and slightly less old now, through a simple exercise of standing straight and proud with chin lifted. Arnau tried to emulate it as the older man addressed the emir once more.

'Despite the Almohad blood that runs in your veins, *Sidi*, it is known far and wide that you rule the *taifa* of Mayūrqa as an emir of old, and it is said that you are a fair and wise ruler.' Arnau noticed an amused twinkle in the emir's eyes. 'This is not sycophancy,' Balthesar said, 'and not flattery. It is simple fact. I do not seek to inveigle my way into your court, for I am a temporary visitor to these islands on an entirely disconnected matter, and had Abd al-Azīz not been at the court now, you would have been entirely unaware of our existence, even after we left and returned to the mainland.'

'Agreed,' the ruler replied with a bow of the head. 'Now tell me.'

Balthesar sucked his teeth for but a moment. 'My name – my true name and not some title heaped on me by my peers or enemies

– is Balthesar d'Aixere, and has been since the day I let that vicious name that clung to me fade and die. My companion here is Arnau de Vallbona. We are, as you are aware, Christians from the mainland. I am searching for a sacred relic that we know was on Mayūrqa in the early days of the Umayyad conquest. That is the entire and sole purpose of our visit.'

'You are looking for a Christian relic centuries old in my lands? That is all?'

Balthesar nodded. 'That is all.'

'The Lion of Alarcos seems convinced that there is more to your presence than that, given your shared history, the impact your name still carries in our courts, the presence of the Almohad deputation and – as you may not be aware – an ambassadorial party from the court of the Crown of Aragon. Your timing does seem strangely coincidental, yes?'

'And yet, *Sidi*, coincidental it is. We seek only the bones of a man a thousand years dead, and to take them back to the mainland. I cannot conceive of any reason your eminence or any *imam* or scholar on the island would not wish us to do so.'

'Why, then, come in the guise of a poor Mayūrqan and not as the men you are?'

Balthesar chuckled. 'I have not been on the island since the days of your predecessor. Though your reputation is good and you rule in the Ghaniyid name, your Almohad connections, combined with my history, made it prudent to be careful. I had the misfortune to pass through a market at the same time as Abd al-Azīz when an old veteran, presumably from Valencia, recognised me and drew attention to me. Without that, I would have continued on unnoticed.'

'Tell me of your relic.'

'It is the arm of Saint Stephen, brought here from Hippo Regius in the days before Muhammad. When the caliphate came to Mayūrqa, it was carried from its church in Mahón and hidden in a shrine in the mountains. It would appear that the shrine was destroyed before it was completed and the relic brought to Madina. It rested in the *masjid* Al-balad for some time, as the relic of a potential *nabī*, but after the Christian risings in the reign of Muhàmmad the First, it was removed again. After that we do not know its movements, which I was busy tracing in the records here when you sent for us.'

'This relic is clearly of great value to you to risk all you have risked.'

Balthesar nodded. 'It is beyond price, *Sidi*. Though to Allah's faithful it has no value.'

'Except clearly as a bargaining tool,' smiled the emir. 'And that brings me to my current purpose.'

He gestured to the pair of them. 'You are mendicants, you say?'

The two men nodded and the emir gave a throaty laugh. 'Mendicants of the sword, then. You were reported to be bearing blades on arrival.'

'These are dangerous times, *Sidi*.'

'Quite. But the *Qātil wari'a*, here, bearing a sword and claiming to be a mendicant? I am no naive child, d'Aixere. You may fool many of the folk in my court, but I know a crusader when I see one. That is the term, is it not, that your holy men use for their own sacred warriors? Are you now the "pious killer" for the Christians? You have the bearing of a knight, not a beggar, and your man here. He is your squire, no?'

Arnau felt his blood chill. Heavens, but this man was sharp. The important question, then, was how he felt about all this.

Balthesar sighed. 'There is no fooling the emir, clearly. Though I am both less and more than you believe. I am no crusader, determined to wipe the Moor from the peninsula. I remember halcyon days of coexistence, after all. But nor am I a beggar-priest. I am a brother of the Order of the Temple, and my companion here is a sergeant. I presume you are aware of our order?'

'I am quite certain that all the world knows of your order,' the emir replied, his face still unreadable but a certain tension creeping into his general appearance now.

'The hunger for glorious battle is far behind me now,' Balthesar said quietly. 'Unlike Abd al-Azīz, I do not cling to the past, and I have sought in my later days the peace of the cloister and the clarity one can only achieve through dedication to good works.'

The emir's smile reappeared. 'And you maintain that your presence here is simply in search of the mouldering bone of an ancient heretic?'

The old knight nodded. 'My identity is revealed; my path remains the same. I seek the bone. If the emir would graciously allow me to continue my research in the record offices, I am certain that within a day, perhaps two, I will find anything there is to find there and we shall either know the history and current location of the relic, or we will confirm that it is no longer here to be found.'

The emir frowned for a moment, then drummed his fingers on the chair arm. Finally, he leaned forward again. 'Not all records are in open rooms, Templar. Many of the records, especially ones that have a bearing on the actions of the emirs themselves, are kept locked away. It is highly likely that the details you seek will be unavailable.'

'Unless we had the emir's express permission,' Balthesar replied.

That smile again. 'Permissions can be bought or bargained for, as well as simply given. Indeed, rather than simply giving you access to records, my people might be directed to aid you in any possible way. I may even be inclined to bend all our efforts to locating your bone for you.'

Arnau's eyes narrowed, as Balthesar spoke the same words as were on his lips.

'In return for what, *Sidi*?'

'An exchange of favours is all I ask. A promise from you. I will find you your saint's arm, in return for a service from you. I mentioned just now that we are host to a deputation from the Crown of Aragon, yes?'

Balthesar replied. 'We have observed them. The Baron de Castellvell among others. A powerful man, well connected at court but not, I would say, an easy or understanding man. He is not the noble I would have chosen to send as an ambassador to a foreign nation.'

The emir nodded. 'I have noted much the same in his manner. His companions are more amenable. The baron seems determined to treat me as an enemy, despite the fact it was I who sought the visit from Aragon, rather than King Pedro sending it. They are here at my invitation. Come.'

He suddenly rose from his seat and strode across the room towards a large, decorative window, where he came to a halt and gestured for them to join him. They did so, and Arnau was interested to see that this was much the same view as from the offices, though from a loftier position and slightly further east, giving him an excellent view of the Al-Mudaina's private dock, and then a distant vista of the port and the lower city.

'Tell me what you see,' the emir said. Arnau noted that the guards had flocked with their master like ducklings after their mother, clustering close enough to protect the emir should the two Templars try anything.

'The port,' Balthesar said. 'The sergeant here has already noted the ships.'

Arnau nodded. 'Three Almohad ships in port, newly arrived. And the Aragonese vessel in the private dock.'

'That last made the Lion of Alarcos fume,' smiled the emir. 'That I gave precedence to a Christian deputation and made them land at the far end of the island and travel by land. It was my hope that the Aragonese would have left Mayūrqa before Abd al-Azīz arrived, but the timing was unfortunate. Castellvell was delayed in his arrival and the Lion of Alarcos came earlier than expected. I was forced to shuffle matters to keep them apart. And despite my best efforts, they are both in my court, circling one another like hungry wolves over a fat carcass. Needless to say I find myself in the position of *fat carcass*.'

Balthesar gave the emir a sympathetic look. 'It is never easy to be the sole voice of reason in a world of zealots, nor to remain independent between two great empires. You are to be commended for having lasted this long without either Almohad or Aragonese artillery battering your walls.'

The emir sighed. 'Once, to rule this island was a joy. Now I spend every hour of my life playing the game of politics and oratory, pitting one wolf against the other so that I can lie and moulder a little longer before I am eaten. It is a sad state of affairs.'

'But,' he said with sudden fresh energy, 'the balance has begun to change. Since your disaster at Alarcos, the caliphate in Al-Andalus is ascendant on the peninsula. They are becoming too powerful to resist.'

'Abd al-Azīz is here on behalf of the caliph?' Balthesar prompted. 'To urge you into his domain?'

The emir issued a short bark of a laugh. 'Friend Templar, I am all but in his domain already. For years now I have been made to pay homage to Qurṭuba. It seems a trivial thing, I know, to acknowledge a superior without any other ill effect, but it damages my authority, and we all know that it is but the first rung on a dreadful ladder.'

'The second being tribute?' Balthesar noted.

'Yes. In monetary and military form. And then interference in governance and law. Soon I will find my court full of men from the caliph who claim more right to pass laws and judgement than I. I will become nothing but a figurehead. And then, finally, when I have too little power to resist, I will be moved aside and the islands will be annexed by the caliphate officially.'

'It is a sad thought.'

'It is,' the emir agreed. 'And the only viable alternative is to refuse their overlordship and resist. That, of course, would put me directly at war with the Almohad caliphate, and I think you know how that would end.'

Both Templars nodded. It would be brutal and bloody, and likely with the same end result as capitulation.

'You see, then, my dilemma.'

'We do.'

'And now,' Arnau put in, 'the Lion and his caliph are twisting your arm? Sending more men to strengthen their presence here?'

'Quite,' the emir agreed. 'And worst of all, the ordinary folk of my island are wavering. Particularly the nobles and the senior officers in my military. The Christian defeat at Alarcos and the clear rise in power of the caliph has convinced many that Allah's will is the domination of Al-Andalus. I know of men who already murmur in support of Almohad control. And if there are men of whom I know, then how many are there of whom I do not?'

'You fear an uprising? A coup?' Balthesar asked.

'It is not impossible. My control of Mayūrqa comes largely from my unassailable position as emir. Should I fall to an assassin's blade, then few in these islands would resist the Lion stepping into my place as a *wāli* of the caliph.'

'And so you sought an alliance with Aragon? That is why they are here, is it not?'

'Quite so. My one remaining hope for the survival of the *taifa* is that King Pedro will see the clear importance of these islands not falling to the Almohad. With Aragon's support, we can resist the caliph's advances and remain independent. I am willing to give money, trade preferences, even bend my knee – almost anything Aragon can ask barring outright control – in order to maintain our independence.'

'And I cannot imagine it is going well.'

'No,' the emir sighed. 'Above and beyond Castellvell's open dislike of my kind, which I fear unduly influences the position of the embassy, I am told that the King of Aragon will not lend me his support. It is, in the words of the diplomats, "simply impossible at this time". I am informed that the losses at Alarcos were severe enough that the Christian monarchs are forced to look to the security of their own borders and have precious few military resources to deal with that, leaving them devoid of strength and resources to offer a potential ally.'

Balthesar chewed his lip for a moment. 'This comes as no surprise, sadly. It is true, to an extent. The north is still in disarray, and Pedro is a new king, making sure his hold on his lands is secure. With increasing belligerence from Al-Andalus, should he weaken the borders to any extent to send you support, his own nobles would make him regret it. I do not agree with the decision, for we both know the critical value of these islands, but I also understand why the decision was made. Castellvell might revel in delivering the decision, but I believe that decision will have come directly from the king.'

'The Order of the Temple were not at Alarcos, no?'

Balthesar snorted. 'Not as a serious force. A few of us were there, committed in return for deals with the king. But no, no great Templar force such as was seen at Hattin or Acre in the Holy Land. I doubt, in truth, that they would have made a difference at Alarcos, though Pedro already seeks our support against the possibility of a future similar conflict.'

'Of course he does,' the emir said, and stepped away from the window now, walking back towards his seat. 'But there are possibilities here. The King of Aragon needs the Order of the Temple and all the strength her can gather in case the caliph attempts to push for a repeat of Alarcos. If that happens, the north will crumble and nothing will stop the expansion of the caliphate. So the king is receptive. And you, the hero of Valencia and the terror of the Almohad, must have influence within both your own order and the court.'

'I think you overestimate that.'

'Nonsense. I believe that you could persuade your order's masters to intervene with the Crown of Aragon and persuade the king to accept an alliance with Mayūrqa. It may not even need a great deal of military support. The simple flying of a few flags, a few ships, a detachment of men lent to my garrison could be enough to state that Aragon will protect Mayūrqa. That might just be enough to keep the caliph at bay. It is certainly worth King Pedro's consideration, because the alternative is to risk Al-Andalus enveloping these islands, which lie in a strategic position, either a boon or a nightmare to trade, depending upon who controls them.'

Balthesar came to a halt in front of the throne as the emir sat once more. 'You wish me to attempt to persuade the order and the Crown of Aragon to seek alliance with the *taifa* of Mayūrqa. And,

I presume, in return you will find the bones of Saint Stephen and grant them to us?'

'That is my proposal, yes.'

Arnau felt an odd sense of pride and pleasure that one of the most powerful men he had ever met had enough respect for the order that he believed them capable of changing the mind of a king. And that it might bring them what they sought into the bargain, too. But most of all, what Arnau felt was a flood of relief that the emir had not sought their arrest and demise, but rather friendship and alliance.

'I could not promise that my efforts would be successful,' Balthesar warned the ruler of the islands.

'And I cannot guarantee that the bones are here. But we are men of honour and men of faith, and all I seek is an oath to try.'

Balthesar nodded again, thoughtfully.

'Go for now,' the emir said, waving a hand at the door. 'Go and consider my proposal. Shortly, I must make one last attempt to persuade the Aragonese diplomats to my cause, and if they remain steadfast, then I must send them away. Their very presence here alongside the caliph's men is courting disaster. Go and think, and when you have made a decision, return to me. And when you do I will tell you what my *wazir* can find of your old bone.'

And with that dismissal, the doors to the room were opened behind them.

Balthesar bowed low. 'It has been an honour and a pleasure to make your acquaintance, *Sidi*. I am enriched by your friendship.'

The emir smiled that weird smile again. 'Likewise.'

Arnau bowed his head in respect and turned, following the older knight as he strode back across the room and out of the door into the chamber beyond. Behind them the emir's door was closed with a click by his guards. Arnau's near elation at having survived the encounter, and even having been left in a strangely positive position, was shattered a moment later at the sight of the black-and-white soldiers standing menacingly off to one side, white eyes shining out above the chain veils they wore. The Lion of Alarcos himself seemed to be simmering with vile rage. As they emerged, the Almohad rattled off something in Arabic at them in acidic tones.

Balthesar gave the man a cold smile. 'I know that you understand me, Abd al-Azīz, so heed my words: no good will come of the vengeance you seek. I am not the man who stole your son from you. I am not the man who fought for Valencia in a sea of blood. I am a man of God now. A man of peace. I have no desire to plant a blade in your heart as I once did. But pursue your current path and you and I *will* end up facing one another over a sword. And if that happens, Allah had better shield you, for no other power will save you. Go back to your caliph and stay there. Grow old and fat in peace.'

The Lion's lip twitched repeatedly and his nose wrinkled slightly; Balthesar simply bowed his head at the man and strode out. A green-clad guard was suddenly with them, escorting them through the palace and returning their swords to them. They crossed the courtyard and passed that other Almohad soldier, through the gate and emerging back into the city once more, close to the mosque. The prayers were done with and the streets were once more flooded with people.

'What now?' Arnau said.

'Now we go and think it over,' Balthesar replied, 'just as the emir suggested. Perhaps back at that same tavern. I favoured their lemon mutton and would be interested to see what they might have for an evening meal.'

'You said the Lion might have men there watching for us.'

'He likely does,' the older man replied. 'But now we are no longer kept to the shadows. The emir is aware of us and we have his approval. That more or less places us under his protection. Abd al-Azīz will not make an open move against us now, even out here, because to do so would bring down the wrath of the island's ruler, and even with three ships full of men at his command, the Lion of Alarcos is not yet strong enough to challenge the emir.'

'No *open* moves?' Arnau prompted.

'Quite. We should continue to keep a wary eye on doorways and alleys. More criminals and hired thugs who cannot be traced back to their master very likely wait in our future.'

Arnau sighed. Every time things got a little bit better, they promised to become a little bit worse too. He stumped unhappily away from the palace.

'Vallbona?'

Arnau and Balthesar turned as one at the call, uttered in a very distinctive voice, thick with a jagged Pyrenean accent in a land of drawled Arabic. Arnau felt his heart jump at the sound and then chided himself for being needlessly panicky. Mere hours ago, someone drawing attention to them could have triggered the worst, but now, since their presence and almost everything about them was known to both the visiting Almohads and the emir of the island, what need had they to worry about such things?

They had not yet passed the mosque on their way out of the Al-Mudaina, and a figure had emerged from the gate behind them, waving to catch their attention. Arnau was surprised to see Guillem Picornell calling to them.

'I thought it was you,' the young knight called in French-inflected Aragonese.

'Guillem?'

Balthesar cast a surprised look at the knight behind them, and Arnau felt his emotions whipping around like a whirlwind. On one level it was excellent to see a friendly face in this dangerous world, and yet adding recognition by the Aragonese embassy into the mix could bring with it even more dangers and complexity. Certainly the frown of the older knight suggested that this was how *he* saw it.

Unable to make this encounter conveniently unhappen, the two Templars came to a halt and waited as the young knight hurried over towards them. They were raising a small buzz of interest among the townsfolk nearby. Nothing untoward or important, but *any* interest would become common knowledge in time, and Arnau doubted that news of conversations between them and the Aragonese diplomats would be a good thing when it reached the ears of the Lion of Alarcos. Picornell stopped next to them, a smile on his face as he heaved in breaths from a swift run. Despite the heat he wore a mail shirt and his surcoat, featuring two black crows facing a tree on a field of gold.

'I happened to be passing with a colleague,' he said by way of explanation, 'when I caught sight of that most loathsome Almohad fellow and his dour companions. I turn my gaze away from them for fear of attracting their attentions, and what do I see but a man that resembles an old friend hurrying past as though the Almohad might try and eat him as he passes.'

Arnau nodded. 'The Almohad are certainly no friends of ours. But I am surprised you recognise me, Picornell.'

The young knight laughed. 'It takes more than a beard and a beggar's apparel to hide the Vallbona looks. But tell me, what are you doing here of all places?'

'Not a discussion for open streets, I fear,' Balthesar put in.

Picornell nodded, his brow creasing. 'I imagine not. This place is a nest of vipers, I believe. May I join you?'

Arnau glanced at his older companion for an answer, to which Balthesar simply shrugged. 'You would be most welcome,' the young sergeant replied, ignoring the brief look on the older knight's face that suggested this might not be so. 'Have you eaten?'

'Only a brief repast of what passes for food in this place.'

'Come, then.'

They crossed the ornamental gardens and closed on the tavern in which they had spent their time earlier. Slipping into the seating of the table out front, Arnau worriedly noted two locals sitting at another outside table, though Balthesar seemed to be paying them no heed.

'So, tell me,' Arnau said, determined to take control of the exchange before any difficult questions might be asked, 'what brings you here?' In truth, he knew the answer, had done so since he first spotted the Spanish visitors, and the emir's explanations had clarified it further, but Picornell could hardly know that.

The young knight shrugged. 'The Emir of Mayūrqa sent to the Crown of Aragon, requesting a dialogue with his representatives.

The king has gathered four of his more influential nobles for the task. His Majesty is concerned with more pressing matters that prevented a personal meeting, but he felt that the situation required a showing of some of his most powerful officers. And needless to say, with the Catalan nobles still a little touchy at Aragonese hegemony, the inclusion of representatives of Barcelona and the County of Roussillon seemed prudent.'

'So you are here negotiating between rulers? How far have we come, Picornell, since days sitting wishing for tourneys and watching our fathers at the table arguing over lands.'

The knight laughed again; he seemed to do so easily and often. 'How far indeed? I to escorting barons and counts into the courts of kings, and you, apparently into the gutter? Now come, tell me how you ended up here? I know that Vallbona is not the richest of lands, but to descend to such poverty?'

Arnau snorted. 'I am not brought quite that low, Picornell. In fact, I am here with my companion on a quest of the most pious kind.'

The light that rose then in the young knight's eyes spoke of both fervour and unadulterated excitement, and it suddenly occurred to Arnau just how tedious it might be being an armed escort for a diplomat. Suddenly the constant danger in which he found himself took on a strange allure he'd not realised was there before.

'A pious quest? How bold and fascinating. Are you venturing into the desert to be tempted by Old Nick, or something similar?'

'Hardly,' Arnau said and, catching Balthesar's eye, realised that the safest way to play this was to play down the interest of their mission so that Picornell swiftly forgot it, and hopefully the pair of them into the bargain.

'We simply seek a relic that has resided under Moorish domination this past millennium. A lot of dusty research and some negotiation. Nothing like your story, clearly.'

Balthesar nodded and took the reins now.

'Tell me, young sir knight, of your mission. Wherefore did the emir seek your visitation?'

Picornell, clearly a man given to openness and not to dissembling, shrugged. 'The emir seeks an alliance with the king. It is a hopeless cause and a fool's notion, though I find myself wishing the king would concede. It seems to me that this ruler is strikingly good for a Moor.'

True words, if roughly spoken, and Arnau nodded his approval. Picornell had always struck him as a sensible young man, if prone to fits of exuberance as were all the Pyrenean breed.

'And you think the king will refuse, then?' Balthesar was pushing, Arnau realised. Shortly he would have to give an answer to the emir, and their own quest rode upon the answer he gave.

'How can he not?' Picornell replied, sadly. 'In truth I very much doubt the king ever had any intention of even considering the matter. I fear he sent his most powerful men in order to take the edge off the disappointment of his refusal. The king can no more afford to send men and supplies to Mayūrqa than he can send men to the Holy Land to capture the heart of the world, Jerusalem, as the Pope keeps hoping. There are not enough mailed fists with a red cross on the heart to save Aragon from its enemies, let alone lend support to others, especially Moors.'

'Aragon is that pressed?'

Picornell gave a strangely embarrassed look. 'I cannot say from my own experience, but those with whom I travel suggest strongly that if the caliph manages to send an army north within the year, Aragon will not have the power to resist him. The king gathers every man he can to keep the border secure and attempts to grow alliances with his fellow kings to east and west. He appeals to Rome, and it is said that his crown will be blessed by the Pope himself. King Pedro must look to Aragon, and simply cannot afford to pledge support to a Mussulman, no matter how important.'

Balthesar shook his head. 'It is short-sighted. If he agreed, the king would have haven here and trade, and an ally. If he refuses and the Almohads gain Mayūrqa, the king will be forced to invade, and it will be far costlier than a few men to support a garrison.'

Picornell's eyes narrowed.

'What kind of travelling mendicants are you? You press for information on the king's plans, and you yourselves are at court? There is more to this than meets the eye, I fear.'

Arnau shrugged. 'We are here, in this Moorish world, yet we are from Aragon. It is worth keeping abreast of developments.'

Picornell's gaze turned upon him, and betrayed complete disbelief. 'Whatever you say, I fear it would be best if I stayed out of your way for the moment. I somehow cannot imagine my socialising with you going down well with my superiors.'

Arnau glanced at Balthesar and realised the older man was expecting him to resolve this. He swallowed and tried not to look nervous. 'On that score, might I ask that you keep knowledge of our presence from the noblemen of your embassy?'

'What have you done, Vallbona?'

'Nothing,' reassured Arnau, 'and we are in absolute truth and honesty here to seek a holy relic and nothing more. There are just... there are complications, and the Baron de Castellvell is one of them.'

A cloud passed across Picornell's eyes. 'Castellvell is nothing *but* complications. Do not repeat this, I beg of you, but I fear half our deputation's job since arriving has been pouring water on the fire of Castellvell's anti-Moorish convictions. Even men who fought and fled from Alarcos are more respectful of the emir than he.'

'Castellvell is also our enemy for a number of reasons,' Arnau breathed. 'I would regard it as a personal favour if he were not to hear of my presence.'

'Yes, well...' Despite having eaten nothing and the owner not having yet arrived to offer food and drink, Picornell rose. 'I'm afraid my appetite is not what it was a few minutes ago. I think perhaps it is better that our paths cross as little as possible right now. I do appreciate your friendship as always, but our mission is tense and balanced on a knife blade as it is, without this to add to the weights. I shall take my leave and return to the noblemen. We have a little more dilly-dallying to do before we can leave. But when I return to the mainland, and you do too, please do look me up, Vallbona. It would be good to catch up, and I miss the days of faux jousts in the orchards of Santa Coloma.'

Arnau rose and clasped hands with him. Balthesar simply watched him with one raised brow.

The young sergeant sighed as his old friend left. Things were becoming more complicated by the day here.

CHAPTER TWELVE

TUESDAY, 8 JUNE 1199

6 P.M.

The two knights spent some time in silence, mulling things over until the tavern's owner appeared suddenly, asking what they wanted. Deferring to the older knight's judgement, Arnau waved the questions aside and left it to him. Twenty minutes later they were served something that was once more brown and unidentifiable, yet tasted tangy, spicy and very flavoursome. Two drinks were brought, one of which was the pleasant, light tea, the other something pungent and dark with the consistency of fresh cow manure. This, Arnau suspected, was the date wine of which the older knight had spoken.

They ate, still in silence, and finally, unable to bear the tension any more, Arnau cracked.

'What will you tell the emir?'

Balthesar pursed his lips and paused for a while, a forkful of something brown hovering close to his chin. 'I am not entirely sure.'

'We are at an impasse.'

'We are.'

Arnau breathed deeply. 'Yet you deliberate?'

'The emir sought only my oath that I would *attempt* to persuade the king to his cause.'

Arnau frowned. 'But you said yourself you could not succeed. And what Picornell revealed confirms it. You will never change the king's mind. Even the grand master of the order could not change the king's mind.'

'This is true, but the emir did not ask for a promise to change the king's mind, just a promise that I would *try* to do so. It is a promise I could live up to.'

Arnau shook his head. 'That is a world of half-truths and wickedness. I cannot believe you would consider such a thing. This is surely not what being a brother of the Temple is about? Lütolf would not dissemble so, I am sure.'

Balthesar levelled him with a look that the Israelites could have used to crumble Jericho's walls. 'Our poor, fallen brother was exemplary in almost every aspect of life, but even in the short time during which you knew him, you must have discovered that there are lances that are more pliable and flexible than he was. Lütolf was the best of us, but he did not live in the real world as we surely must.'

'But—'

'Listen, young Vallbona: if we seek to rebuild Rourell, we must draw support in terms of both finance and manpower. We are unpopular enough that we currently cannot rely on either, but the presence of relics will draw both. Think how such a place as the great sanctuary of Santiago became more than just a village. The landscape? The priest? No, it is what is to be found and revered there, and we shall emulate that. Rourell will become the home to the arm of Saint Stephen, the first martyr. Knights from as far afield as Scotland and the Bulgar mountains will flock to Rourell, taking their vows and donating their lands. Soon we could eclipse even our mother house. And with a possible crusade against the Almohad looming as King Pedro perhaps plots, strength at Rourell could be a serious advantage.' He leaned back in his seat and took a sip of the probably-wine. 'So am I willing to give an unsupported and possibly false promise to the emir? I would rather not, for I truly feel for the man, but I must put our needs above his, and the man is sadly doomed, I fear. So, yes.'

'And will the emir simply help us in return for the mere offer of your aid?'

'That was his request.'

'And you can live with that?'

'You would be surprised what the *Qātil wari'a* can live with.'

'So your answer to the emir will be yes? You will pretend you can try and change the king's mind in return for any lead on the bone of Saint Stephen?' Arnau was not at all happy with this idea. In fact, he was a little disgusted at the base falsehoods to which his fellow brother would apparently stoop.

'Yes. Yes, I will. Though to allay your fears for my eternal soul a little, bear in mind that I *will* bend every effort to the king's persuasion. On that I do not lie. I simply do not expect success in my endeavour.'

Arnau fell silent and ate the rest of his brown stuff – with lighter brown stuff and green stuff – in silence, unwilling to breach the uncomfortable silence in order to ask what it was he was consuming, which was perhaps for the best. He followed it by downing his tea and then drinking the bittersweet, sticky date wine, and wishing he'd done so the other way around.

The silence continued to reign, becoming ever more meaningful and heavy as Balthesar similarly finished his food and drink, visited the innkeeper and dealt with payment, then led the way away from the tavern.

Evening was beginning to approach now. They had missed a call to prayer while out on their task, and the next one began as they made their way back through the city. Immediately, Arnau became utterly confused about their route through the streets.

'Where are we?' he asked as the distinctive warble of the sundown prayer call echoed across the skyline. 'I thought we'd reach that fortress again quickly.' As far as he could tell, they had left the tavern in a southerly direction, which took them far from the route that had first brought them there. His suspicions were confirmed when, before the older knight could answer, they turned a corner and found a bridge across the river awaiting them.

'Laying as complex a trail as we can,' Balthesar replied. 'Beyond the bridge take the third exit to the right and then the first left. If things are as they were last time I was here, it will bring you to a fruit market. Pass through it along the side of a mosque, look for a second bridge and cross it, then make for the bathhouse by the river. I will meet you there.'

'Are they following us?' Arnau breathed, turning and looking back. He'd been casting his eyes over his shoulders all the way and had seen nothing untoward as yet.

'Without a doubt. I have not seen anyone, but be sure they are there. When you cross the river, they will probably follow me. They might split up. Move fast and you can lose anyone tailing you. I know somewhere to discourage pursuit. See you at the bathhouse.'

And with that he was gone, dipping into a side alley. Arnau's gaze raked the streets behind them, and he could still see no one, but he picked up speed anyway, crossing the bridge. The old man's memory was good, and the market was still there as he'd recalled, and soon the young Templar found himself crossing the river once more and spying the bathhouse beyond. He hurried over with still no sign of pursuit and ducked into the entrance.

He almost made to kill Balthesar as the grey-bearded brother slapped a hand across his mouth from the shadows, wrapped the other arm round his middle, and bundled him inside.

'Did you see them?'

Arnau, still shocked, shook his head. 'No.'

'Then perhaps they all followed me. I *saw* no one, but I could feel their presence. They're still on the trail like hounds on a hare. Fortunately, this place has a rear entrance which only regular patrons know.'

And with that Arnau was dragged into the mysterious world of the bathhouse. A few had survived here and there in the north, of course, in cities conquered and cleared largely of Arab influence. Those that had not been destroyed in the fervour of reconquest weren't used. The places were weird, heretical complexes. A good Christian bathed in a simple tub in plain water and that was that. The common view in the north was that the fripperies of Moorish baths were made for men who were more feminine than women – that last brought a touch of unexpected guilt given the impact two strong women had had on his life.

They moved through rooms where normally there would be attendants and bathers. Fortunate were they that the call to the *maghrib* prayer had emptied the baths of both workers and patrons, with only the one guard left at the entrance, who had clearly accepted sufficient coin from Balthesar to let them in unrecorded. They finally emerged through a shapely door into a lush garden, and the older knight led them through it like an expert, suggesting that he had been here more than once.

They passed through two more doors, connected by a small passage, and back into the late afternoon's light by a small plank bridge over one of the small side irrigation streams. Without a word, Balthesar led them up the road and through several narrow alleys, jinking this way and that. Finally, they stopped in a small square with a trough of water.

'What can you see? Smell, hear, feel?' the old man asked.

'Nothing,' breathed Arnau looking around and drinking in everything he could.

'Same here. We've lost them. Let's move on before they catch up with us.'

Ten minutes later, by some circuitous route that Arnau could never hope to replicate, they reached the *waqf* house. Somehow, bless him, Balthesar had managed to time it so that the sun had sunk into darkness and the sundown prayer was over when they arrived. The poor and unloved shuffled through the building back to their rooms, and the two knights fell in among them as driftwood in the pious tide. Before long they were back in their room.

Arnau was contemplating the strangely haunting idea that the Moors returning from their prayer with the air of a good deed done and an opportunity to move on and deal with the day-to-day tasks of life was so like the routine of most Christians that it made something of a mockery of the supposedly huge gulf between them.

He collapsed on his bed and lay there for a moment, still fully clothed. After a moment more of contemplation he removed his sword belt and boots, letting them drop to the floor, then did the same for all his gear except his undertunic. Suitably attired for sleep, he lay back with his hands interlaced behind his head and failed to get to sleep, his thoughts awhirl.

He and Balthesar sought the relic. They had no power or influence, and a ready supply of enemies. The emir might be a friend, but only on a temporary political level, and even then only in a conditional manner. Picornell was a friend, but with insufficient influence or power to make a difference. The emir sought an alliance with Aragon that the king would not grant and Balthesar could not secure, but if they promised to attempt to secure it, he would give them what he could on the relic. The Lion of Alarcos could not overtly move against them without earning the ire of his host. So he hired thugs instead. And Balthesar was confident that the Almohads had as yet insufficient power to pressure the emir. That brought images of the ships landing, mind, and Arnau wondered just how many men it would take to secure the Al-Mudaina, and with it the island. And finally there were the Aragonese diplomats. They were here for little more than consolation, to mop the emir's brow and tell him how sorry they were the king could not help. One of them might be Arnau's friend, but a more important one was his enemy.

Lord, what a mess. They had come here as two simple travellers seeking a relic, and it had led them into a world of political turmoil. And though Arnau was about ready to admit defeat and return home empty handed, clearly Balthesar was not.

'Forgive us our trespasses
as we forgive those who trespass against us.
And lead us not into temptation,
but deliver us from evil.'

'What are you muttering about?' mumbled Balthesar.

'Just praying. I seem to have missed the chance rather often of late. Prayer seems more important than ever right now.'

'Lucky you, then, for the evening prayer is little more than an hour away.'

'Can we not skip it?' Arnau sighed. 'I've noticed that not all Moors go anyway.'

'Not all go, but it is considered correct form to pray together with others when possible, and alone only when necessary. Given our precarious position here, let's not aggravate our hosts. The whole process of the *salat* takes less than ten or fifteen minutes, including the ritual washing and all preparations. You can spare that long.'

Arnau grunted. 'I might sleep through it yet. I'm exhausted.'

Balthesar nodded as he too lay on his back with a sigh. 'It has been a busy day. Hard to believe that this morning we were still in the hills and blessedly ignorant of so much. But fear not, sleep if you will, the call to prayer will awaken us, for certain.'

'Oh good.'

The two men lapsed into silence, and Arnau rolled onto his side, wishing that sleep might enshroud them both so solidly that they missed the coming call. Sadly, though his body felt drained and his eyes heavy, his mind continued to churn with all they had learned and seen that day. No matter how many times he contemplated the many aspects of this entire mess, nothing changed, and he was graced with no clearer solution to any of it. Still, he lay in silence, in the darkness, turning and sighing. His irritation with the absence of sleep only grew when Balthesar began to snore gently in the next bed. The old knight had removed his boots and sword belt but otherwise remained fully attired.

Another sigh.

Another turn.

Sleep was fighting back.

It didn't help that this place smelled lightly of spice and sweat, which seemed to be the overpowering odour of the town as a whole. Spice and sweat and—

His eyes sprang open and he sat bolt upright, shivering. Perhaps he had imagined it. Perhaps he had fallen asleep after all, and his dream state had created the scent.

No, there it was again. For a fleeting moment he wondered whether it was part of some Moorish ceremony of which he was not aware, in a similar manner to the thurible of the Christian Church, but again, no. This was not incense.

Slipping sideways from the cot, wincing as his aching muscles held him up once more, he hurried across to the other bed and shook Balthesar. The old knight started awake with the suddenness and ease of a warrior used to sleeping light and being ever ready.

'What is it?'

'Smoke,' Arnau replied.

'Are you sure?'

'Believe me,' the young sergeant said firmly, 'I know the smell.'

Trapped inside a burning mill, sacks shoved up against the crack at the bottom of the door, rafters ablaze, enemies outside and no escape.

Yes, he knew the smell right enough.

'Could it be a cooking fire or something?' Balthesar asked, though he was already sitting on the edge of his bed and reaching for his boots. Suddenly aware of how lightly dressed he was, Arnau hurried over to his own pile of clothes and began to dress swiftly.

'If that's a cooking fire, then it's a big one.'

As the older man strapped on his sword belt, Arnau slipped into his burnous and hurried across to the window. He threw back the shutters and became aware now of shouts of alarm. They were muffled, not coming from the street, but from the other direction, beyond the door, in the building itself. He wasted not a moment at the window but slipped into his boots and ran to the door as the older man now rose, fully dressed.

The sergeant noted with sinking spirits the wisps of smoke now curling under the door. Not again…

He braced himself and undid the catch, swinging open the door. The din of urgent, panicked shouts suddenly became clear, along with the roar of flames and the crack and spit of burning timber. The *waqf* hostel was ablaze in a dreadful conflagration. His gaze took it in immediately. Only this wing of the structure was alight, though the blaze was already spreading into the rear of the building and also threatening the ornate stone frontage. The balconies were on fire, and the stairwell was wreathed in burning golden flames.

'Mother of God, we're trapped.'

Balthesar appeared at his shoulder. 'Abd al-Azīz's hand grows stronger.'

'You think this is the Lion's work?'

'A blaze begins in a place that belongs to the mosque, and happens to start below our very room, engulfing the stairs we need to escape? If this fire is an accident, then it is a most specific and unlikely one. No, agents of the Almohads are behind this, mark my words.'

'But to burn down a building just to get to us?'

'An unhappy incident that rids him of me and cannot easily be traced back to him? Think, Vallbona. This is most assuredly his work. Now use that mind of yours. You are inventive, young man. You escaped an impossible fire at the mill last year. Get us out of this.'

Arnau felt the claws of panic tearing at him. He had so often followed the old man's lead on these islands, for Balthesar was the fount of knowledge and the senior man. Now, when their lives hung in the balance, suddenly it became Arnau's task to save them. His mind raced. To go up was impossible. Most of the balcony was aflame now, and he could see ripples of flame above. Whoever had set the fire had been thorough. Outside the door, only the few paces around this room remained untouched. Above, below, and to both stairwells the fire roared. Perhaps…?

He hurried over to the window once more and leaned out. The drop was considerable and onto cobbles. While it was possible to jump, it carried a high risk of broken legs. He turned and looked up. This side of the roof was still dark, though he could see the orange glow cast by the flames on the other side. There was an overhang, but if he could just manage to get his elbow over the edge, he could pull himself up and onto the roof. Perhaps then he could also pull Balthesar up. The knight might be remarkably fit and strong for his age, but Arnau couldn't see him achieving such a troublesome climb. And if…

The arrow came so close to ending his life that it tore a tiny piece from his ear in its passing before it thudded into the wall, close to the ceiling. Arnau blinked. The second arrow would have killed him had Balthesar not grabbed him by the burnous and hauled him back from the window. This second shot thrummed through the air, whispering above his head as he fell, and thudded into the ceiling. Arnau lay on the floor in shock as the older knight slammed the shutters to swiftly and dropped the catch. Two more thuds shook the shutters as the unseen archers targeted them once more.

'I think that confirms that this is no accident,' Balthesar said grimly. 'And perhaps your timely prayer tipped the Lord towards your salvation. Pray on, young man, pray on.'

The notion of taking time now to pray as the inferno closed in around them was ridiculous. Instead, Arnau found himself rushing around like a chicken without a head, dashing back and forth between the door that offered only a blazing balcony and a shuttered window that threatened barbed death, pausing in between each time to gather up another piece of his kit.

Yet as he ran and worried, his mind churning, the old knight watching him patiently as though fully believing that Arnau was planning and not panicking, still the young Templar found his mind drifting into his mother's favourite Psalm, the one that had risen unbidden to his lips more than once during the horror of last year.

The Lord governeth me and nothing shall fail me. In the place of pasture there he hath set me. He nourished me on the water of refreshing and he converted my soul. He led me forth on the paths of rightfulness, for his name...

His mind whirred as something clicked into place. What was it? Something he'd just thought of. Something in the song of David. Something on the tip of his tongue.

A moment later he was at the door once more, but this time full of purpose. The fire was almost at the threshold now, and the timbers of the balcony were too hot to touch, even through boots. Still, he stepped out onto the precarious walkway, feeling the ends of his hair singe in the heat. He reached the balcony edge, eyes streaming, skin parching and sizzling, and without thinking grasped the rail. Yelping, he let go, his hands pink with pain. But it was *over* the balcony he was looking.

Then he was back inside, heaving in smoky breaths.

'How far can you jump?'

Balthesar frowned, looking over the courtyard with the central pool at the balconies beyond. 'Not far enough to get to the other side.'

'But far enough to reach the water?'

The old knight's eyes sparkled as his gaze dropped to the pool. 'Let's find out.'

Arnau nodded. They were out of time. Even now tongues of flame licked at the door frame. Any longer and they would be trapped in this bonfire. With a deep breath, he turned in the middle of the room and ran. Years of activity and martial training as a knight and then a sergeant in the order had left him as fit as any young man of his age could possibly hope to be, and yet he still only just cleared the steaming timber of the balcony.

The world roared past him as he plummeted. Half the building was now wreathed in fire, the other playing host to those few residents who had not already fled the premises but instead remained to gawp at the disaster.

He hit the water hard, not in an easy dive, for his run had been instinctive and designed primarily to clear the rail and carry him as far beyond it as possible, rather than brace him for landing. He felt the impact in every joint and every bone, and his sword came round uncomfortably and slammed into him during the fall, bringing more heavy bruising. Yet the water, despite the pain, was a balm, soothing the burning in his lungs and the sizzling pink of his skin.

He was alive.

He broke the surface of the pool, coughing violently, not from the water, but from the smoke that still sat heavy in his pipes. With desperate, thrashing movements and grateful above all that he was not wearing chain mail, he powered to the side of the pool and threw his elbows over it. He was leaning over the edge and heaving in breaths when Balthesar hit the water behind him. The impact sent a wave over Arnau and set him off coughing again, but the young sergeant was faintly peeved that the older man had landed with far more poise and grace than he himself had.

Moments later, Balthesar was leaning over the side of the pool with him, elbows up, breathing in deep, calm breaths. 'The good Lord provides, but when he is busy elsewhere, the good Vallbona sits in for him.'

Arnau laughed and then exploded in another coughing fit.

'What now?' he asked when it finally subsided.

'It is too much to hope that they believe us expired, but we have to at least try and maintain that fiction. At the worst it might buy us some time. The locals will extinguish the blaze before it consumes the whole building, for they cannot afford it to spread to other blocks. The exits will be watched by men with bows. We are confined, but if we find a small, dark room in the stone-built front wing of the place, we can shelter there tonight, away from the fire and out of harm's way. Then, when dawn comes, we can leave, for surely the Lion's archers will presume us dead by then.'

'And then what?' Arnau felt he knew the answer to that, though he would much prefer to head to the port he'd seen so often from the palace windows and secure a voyage back to the mainland.

'And then we go back to Al-Mudaina and deliver my reply to the emir. A promise for a relic.'

Arnau sighed and nodded.

CHAPTER THIRTEEN

WEDNESDAY, 9 JUNE 1199

11.30 A.M.

It was startlingly late when Arnau awoke in their dark, smoke-scented corner of the *waqf* house. Though there were no windows here, he could tell from the lengthy golden beam of light in the next room that the sun had been up for some time – long enough to have climbed high and peek over the roofs of other buildings.

'What time is it?' he said in muffled tones, making out the shape of Balthesar next to the doorway.

'Late. Approaching noon, in fact.'

'You let me sleep this long?'

Balthesar nodded. 'I felt that after the exertions of yesterday you likely needed the rest. Worry yourself not. I have made full use of the morning thus far.'

Arnau blinked, his eyesight slowly focusing in the gloom. He could see the old knight sitting in the dim light of the doorway. His heart lurched as he noticed the huge dark stain at the man's side.

'Your wound!'

'Quite,' Balthesar replied. 'The leap into the pool. I ruined most of the stitching, and when I woke it was in a pool of blood. I have forayed out into the town and visited our friendly doctor close by. He was less than impressed, but has done an exemplary job of repairing the wound once more.'

'You went out?'

'I did, and was not attacked. I suspect that the thugs responsible believe we died in the blaze, for that entire wing of the building is little more than charred timbers and ashes. Abd al-Azīz will not believe as much without visible proof, but it has bought us precious moments to act with impunity. And I intend to do so. Now you are up and I am repaired, we shall make for the Al-Mudaina.'

Arnau stretched and paced, urging life back into tired and stiff limbs, and soon thereafter the two men emerged once more into the city of Madina Mayūrqa. The sun was indeed approaching its zenith as they moved away from the part-ruined *waqf* house. Balthesar chose their route even more carefully than usual, and they moved from the building through three backstreets until they came upon the Gumāra fortress.

As they approached, Arnau frowning, he realised that the great heavy gatehouse and the tall walls stretching to either side of it were more than just a fortress. They were a massively defended entrance in the main walls. One of the old city gates had been given an inner barbican and formed a small enclosure. This being in theory a time of peace, those gates were currently both open, and people were being allowed in and out of the city through the Gumāra.

Following the older knight and lowering his face to prevent easy identification, Arnau passed beneath the first gate, through the heart of the small fortress, and then through the second gate and out into the extramural area of the city. Here, Balthesar swung sharp left and began to make his way somewhat laboriously around the city's northern edge. It was a slow and tiresome journey, but eventually they passed inside once more through the same gate at which they had first arrived, crossed the river on the bridge just inside, and then passed around the edge of the city inside the walls until they were almost at the port. Finally, having taken the most indirect route possible, they headed towards the river once more, crossed the lowest bridge and headed for the high walls of the Al-Mudaina on the hillside above, confident that skirting almost every neighbourhood in the city would have discouraged any potential pursuit. Still, with every step closer to the emir's palatial fortress, Arnau's nerves increased, his disquiet more than mere worry.

'This feels wrong,' he said finally as they climbed the slope towards the Al-Mudaina. 'Dangerous in the extreme.'

'Without sufficient cause,' reassured the older knight. 'Abd al-Azīz will surely not act within the palace of the emir. We are more at risk from him in the city outside, as the residents of the *waqf* house discovered.'

Arnau nodded his understanding of the reasoning, though the nerves remained and his uneasiness continued to increase as they approached the walls. His gaze strayed upwards and alarms sounded in his mind. He reached out and grabbed Balthesar by the sleeve.

'What?' the old man said.

'Look up. That's not good.'

And it wasn't. The emir's men in green and shining steel were in evidence patrolling the wall top as usual, but here and there, interspersed among them, were figures in black and white. Balthesar made a low rumbling noise in his throat, and Arnau recognised it as a rare indication of worry from the old man.

'A troubling sign.'

'Yes, first a worry to find them on the island at all, then many times worse to find them unopposed in the emir's presence, but to see them in positions of strength and authority in the palace...?' Balthesar nodded, yet he began to walk once more towards the gate. Arnau, eyes flickering nervously about, followed. He was immensely relieved when Balthesar rang the bell and rapped on the small door in the gate and the portal was opened by one of the emir's own men and not an Almohad soldier.

Balthesar exchanged swift and polite words with the man, and Arnau could tell by the way his expression changed that he was not receiving the answers he expected and that something was amiss. After a few moments the old knight bowed his head and thanked the man, and they turned and left, the door closing behind them.

'Don't tell me the emir has changed his mind?' the young sergeant said.

'The emir is not there'

'What?'

'It appears that he departed both the Al-Mudaina and Madina Mayūrqa with his entire retinue earlier this morning. The guard refused to elucidate, but his manner suggested that it was an unplanned and desperate flight. I fear the balance of power in Madina has just shifted, and not for the better. Vallbona, I fear the *taifa* of Mayūrqa teeters on a knife edge. The reason for the Almohad presence on the island is becoming clear.'

'Did he say where the emir went?'

Balthesar shook his head. 'Not as such, but there are two or three estates on the island that are reserved solely for the emir, and some of them are fairly remote and defensible. Perhaps he has retreated to one such. A worrying thing is that the guard intimated that the city is currently under the control of a *wāli*, a governor of some kind. If reason prevails, then this governor is the emir's second in command, the *wazir*. If not...'

'You don't think the Lion could have seized control?'

Arnau felt his blood chill at the very idea.

'It is not outside the bounds of possibility if the emir is losing the support of his people and Abd al-Azīz is strengthening his own position. We are two knights on a giant chess board, Vallbona, and the game is a fraught one.'

'What do we do?'

'I need to think,' the old man said, which further worried Arnau. One thing that had been constant throughout their time here was that Balthesar had never faltered in his certainty of their path. To see the old man nonplussed was a new and troubling development.

'The tavern.'

Balthesar nodded and the two of them crossed the open space and passed once more through the ornate gardens, making for that tavern in which they seemed to have spent half their time in the city. Still, Arnau's gaze followed every movement around them, tense and expecting disaster at every turn, and it was with both surprise and relief that it fell finally upon the figure of Guillem de Picornell seated at their usual table at the tavern, his surcoat announcing his lineage to all around. As they neared the table, however, the young sergeant's breath caught in his throat at the sight of his old friend.

Picornell had been beaten savagely. His lip was split and swollen, his right eye welded shut with gore and bruising, his cheek covered in welts and his hair matted with drying crimson. Whoever had attacked him had been unrelenting.

They made for the table and slipped into seats opposite, and the young knight's eyes danced across them, just as tense and nervous as Arnau's own.

'Thank all the saints,' he said through thick, painful lips, his battered face twisting with the pain of speaking. 'I was concerned for you, despite everything.'

Arnau shook his head in wonder, eyes drinking in the damage to that once handsome face. 'What happened to you?'

'Thugs set upon us as we left the palace this morning. There were too many to put down, though we made good show. We fought them off, and somehow managed to prevent the barons suffering, but we paid for our valour.'

'Thugs attacked you? Attacked six armoured men from a foreign country?'

'Quite,' Picornell agreed. 'It seems outside the bounds of probability to me too. Fortunately for you, the Baron de Castellvell remains unaware of your presence. He puts this morning's attack down to failings in the emir's rule and the increasing instability of the island. Me? I think it was not the barons they were after. I think that was why the barons escaped without injury. They were after me in particular, and I think it was because I was seen talking to you yesterday.'

Arnau felt another chill. Surely not? But it made sense. Unidentifiable ruffians were attacking them, so why not their friends? 'We have enemies,' he said. 'Powerful ones, but I had not anticipated them spreading their net so wide.'

'Whatever you're up to,' Picornell said flatly, 'seems to be causing trouble. The emir is losing control and your interference may well be tied into that.'

Balthesar leaned forward. 'You were concerned for us why?'

'Have you not heard?' Picornell gave a humourless laugh. 'The emir has left the city. He took his entourage and many of his soldiers and retreated to one of his villas. Castellvell is of the opinion that he only just slipped out of the Al-Mudaina in time.'

'Why?' Arnau put in. 'What happened?'

'Have you been hiding under a rock, Arnau? The Almohads.'

'Three ships arrived yesterday,' the young sergeant nodded.

'And four more this morning – not long after dawn, just as we were limping back to the palace covered in blood. The city is flooding with Almohad soldiers. The emir's vizier is nominally in command now, and there has been no confirmation of a change in government. Mayūrqa is still an independent *taifa* in name, but I doubt anyone is under any great illusion as to what is happening. Whatever name is applied, the vizier rules Mayūrqa only by Almohad consent, and it is Abd al-Azīz whose law now applies in these islands.'

Arnau felt his stomach churn. An Almohad coup! No siege or invasion needed, if the enemy were already in the heart of the emir's palace. The Almohads had snaked their way into Madina and to the Al-Mudaina, and once there, had wrapped their coils around the *taifa*'s heart and begun to squeeze. God, but they had been swift. The idea that the Lion of Alarcos could rise so easily to control this land was alarming enough. The fact that Arnau and Balthesar might now be trapped on an island controlled by a man who harboured burning hatred for them made it many shades worse.

'We are leaving,' Picornell said, breaking his uneasy train of thought.

'Leaving?'

'There was nothing more to be said here, diplomatically anyway. The king will not support the emir, and we remained in the court merely as a minor mollification for that refusal. With the emir now fled and a raging anti-Christian in power, dallying seems foolish. As soon as the ship is loaded and the conditions are favourable we are bound for Aragon once more. It is my heartiest recommendation that you do the same. This place will be far too dangerous for any of us very soon. Castellvell believes that the emir has lost control of his land irretrievably.'

Balthesar nodded unhappily. 'It is looking increasingly true. I fear the Almohads are insinuating themselves into control here, and the emir is beating a retreat into private life. It is a sad day for Mayūrqa and heralds potential disaster for the West. Without the support of Aragon, which is not forthcoming, the emir would seem doomed. It is only a matter of time before these islands become little more than a province of the Almohad caliphate from which their ships can strike at our merchants bound for Italy and the Orient.'

'We will be gone with the tide,' Picornell said, 'and the next time a lord of Aragon sets foot upon these islands, I suspect it will be at the head of an army of conquest. You are not safe here. Despite your personal rift with the baron, he would not dare deny succour to men of the Temple in front of his peers. If you come to our ship before we sail, I will see you safely on board.'

With that, Picornell rose, hissing at various unseen pains.

'God be with you, Vallbona, and you too, Brother knight.'

Arnau nodded. 'Travel safely. May the blessed Saint Christopher shelter you until you touch a friendly shore.'

Balthesar gave his own valediction and the young knight stepped away from the table, exhibiting a strong limp, and left the tavern, making for the Al-Mudaina where the private dock still held the Aragonese ship. Once he had departed, Arnau and Balthesar sat in silence for some time. Finally, unable to stand the mounting tension, Arnau spoke.

'Is the emir finished?'

Balthesar shrugged. 'No man is finished until he has passed Peter's gates and is at the Lord's side. The emir is shrewd and still has supporters, including his own private army, but he is also sensible and realistic. He can see how precarious his position is. I fear he recognised threats rising in his own court and removed himself from them. On his private estate he will be surrounded only by those he can trust, and that is the only position from which he can possibly attempt to regain full control. Things may have gone too far now, of course. He may be in a position from which he cannot return, but there was little he could do to prevent this happening. He could have denied the Almohad ships the right to land, but that would have exacerbated the situation and likely would have urged the Almohads into outright war, which the emir could not hope to wage without Aragon's support. This is a true miasma of military politics, Vallbona, and we are in the very murk of it.'

'But you think that perhaps the emir still stands a chance?'

'It is largely a matter of support. Abd al-Azīz is currently ascendant because he is visibly strong and becoming ever more so. Strength begets strength. His power attracts others to his cause. Conversely, every day the emir seems weaker and so his supporters leech away and add their voices to the Almohad chorus. I fear the only solution for the emir now would be the fall of the Lion of Alarcos. Without him, there would be no powerful Almohad head for the island to support and the emir would become the strong one once more. Of course that would only buy him a little time. He might regain control in Mayūrqa, but the Almohads now have these islands in their sights, and the death of one of their own more prominent nobles would only goad them into further action. He might fight off Abd al-Azīz, but it will not be long before they come back, and in greater strength. Without the support of someone like Pedro of Aragon, the end is inevitable.'

Arnau nodded sadly. That support would not come, of course. Mayūrqa had become too dangerous for the two knights to continue, and there was little chance of matters improving in the foreseeable future.

'So what do we do? Can we realistically get to the Aragonese ship? It's all well and good Guillem offering us a place on it, but that vessel is in the Al-Mudaina's private dock, and if the Lion is in control of the palace, I fear we would not reach the gangplank alive.'

Balthesar raised an eyebrow. 'So ready are you to give up on our quest?'

Arnau stared at the older knight. 'You are surely jesting? You intend to continue on this fool's errand?'

'Where would our Church be if the men of faith who created it had simply conceded the game because the situation became tough? Those apostles who spread the word of the Lord following his ascent to heaven – who took the word into the heathen world that hated them, despite the dangers? Paul and James who were beheaded, and Peter, Philip and Andrew crucified. James stoned and Matthew and Thomas butchered. Matthias burned, Bartholomew skinned, and Simon sawn in two. Only John of the sacred twelve escaped with his life. What if those brave followers of Jesus had been cowed by fear?'

Arnau nodded unhappily in the face of the old knight's fervour. Personally, he felt that their own quest and contribution could hardly be compared with the Fathers of the Church, but it seemed a poor show to point that out.

'Every hour longer we spend here will become more dangerous,' Arnau reminded his older companion.

'Which means that when we prevail and succeed we may be rightly proud of our achievement.'

Wasn't pride a sin?

'So what do we do now?'

'We resume our search, of course.'

'What?'

'We were interrupted at the records offices of the Al-Mudaina. I still need to find the last reference to the relic. And if the emir was true to his word and set his people to examining those records before his sudden departure, then perhaps the information has already been uncovered and our work half done. Have faith, Vallbona.'

Faith, again.

'Have you any idea how dangerous it could be going back into the palace now?' Arnau pressed. 'No matter that the *wazir* is officially in control, you know it is the Lion of Alarcos who commands here. Walking into the Al-Mudaina is tantamount to walking into the Lion's maw.'

'Do you think us any safer here, Vallbona? Quite ignoring the fact that we have been set upon by unidentified swordsmen and had our lodgings burned down around us, look at the faces of those around you.'

Arnau did so, curious and still struggling against the impulse to flee this place. It was only now, at Balthesar's urging, that he noticed it. While they had been on the island these past few days, and in Madina for two of them, he had felt constantly the sizzle of hatred from the Almohads, and had remained nervous of the emir and his men, for they held the power of life and death in Mayūrqa, but he had felt nothing but peace, acceptance and even a little curiosity from the ordinary Moors in the street. Something had changed, though, now. Something indefinable and strange had changed. It was hardly noticeable unless you were looking for it, but there was a slight narrowing of the eyes among anyone who regarded these two men speaking in foreign Christian tongues in their midst. There was a slight increase in tension in the way they held themselves. It was barely visible, but now that Arnau had realised it was there, it became clear to him that the people of Madina had become tense and suspicious.

'It feels dangerous.'

'Yes, doesn't it? Yesterday these fine people welcomed us. Today things have changed.'

'But that is so swift. Surely the Almohads cannot have spread their poison so fast?'

Balthesar snorted. 'Opinion and rumour spread faster than a forest fire. This is the work of Abd al-Azīz. Since his arrival in Madina, I would wager that he has pursued in every waking moment a path of winning over those men of power and import in the emir's court. That is how he has so swiftly suborned the man. And you know how it works. The nobles and the priests: they are the men who tell the common folk what to think. The good people of Madina are being turned against not only us, but *all* outsiders – your friend's bruises speak clearly of that. And I fear soon that those same suspicious glares will be cast even at supporters of the rightful emir, neighbour against neighbour. Politics can be a poisonous thing. Power is slipping into Abd al-Azīz's hands and without a fight.'

'And nothing can be done to arrest that slide?'

Balthesar shook his head. 'Probably not. This is how persecution and oppression begins: one clever and charismatic man with a single purpose. Remember how easily Rourell's farmers were turned against us despite years of being well looked after?'

Arnau cast his mind back to those dreadful days last year. Farms lying empty. A body revolving slowly in his own home, dangling from a beam with glazed eyes and a swollen tongue...

He took a deep breath. One last try.

'Brother, let us away on a ship. Forget the arm of Saint Stephen. There will be other relics. When the armies of Aragon roll over the caliphate's lands in retribution for Alarcos, other lost relics will come to light and perhaps we can secure one of those.'

'Vallbona—'

'No, it needs to be said. This entire journey was founded on the belief that the relic would be invaluable in bringing gold and manpower to Rourell. But if we sacrifice ourselves needlessly then all we are doing is wasting the money with which we were sent and diminishing the house's manpower by two. I do not believe the preceptrix would approve.'

Balthesar frowned, clearly caught by those last words. It was an argument that seemed to have hit him hard. Finally, he nodded.

'I will strike a deal with you, Vallbona, since your words are honest and valid, for all I disagree with them. Boarding the ship of Castellvell *would* be troublesome. Abd al-Azīz will not willingly let us join the deputation, as you pointed out, and even if he did I have no great desire to share a ship with the good baron for a voyage. But there are other Christian ships in the port. Traders come here from all lands, and with what is happening in Madina the next few days will see them all evacuate back to their own nations. It is with them that we shall secure passage home. One more day is all I ask. One more trip to the Al-Mudaina and one more search of the records to determine what can be learned of Saint Stephen's bone. A matter of hours and I will know what happened to it, or at least I will know if it is lost. One last attempt to retrieve that for which we came, and then I will relent and we shall take ship from this place with those merchants fleeing a change in the regime.'

It was not a perfect solution, certainly, but Arnau knew the old knight now, and he knew that this was the best he was going to get: an acknowledgement that his opinion was valid and a promise to leave after one last attempt to find the relic. Of course, that meant stepping into the lair of the Lion of Alarcos once more.

He sighed and nodded. 'All right. One more time.'

As they passed through the gardens again and made for the palace, Arnau found himself wondering how Balthesar planned to get them into the Al-Mudaina. It seemed unlikely they were simply going to walk inside, especially now, with the Lion's men in control. It surprised him greatly, therefore, when the older knight simply walked up to the door through which they had entered and left several times and knocked and rang.

They waited for a few long, nervous moments and then the hatch in the door clacked open and wary, narrowed eyes looked out at them, a comment barked in Arabic. Balthesar replied politely and there was a tense pause. The guard snapped something else out, Balthesar responding once more, and though Arnau couldn't understand the words he most certainly comprehended their import. The older knight had remained polite, but there was an edge of command and determination to the tone. It was now, as the nerves began to shudder through the young sergeant, that he realised he had not relieved himself since rising that morning, and as his bladder contracted with the mounting tension the need to do so was becoming paramount. He shifted his weight from foot to foot uncomfortably as the guard and the old knight argued, the emir's man seeming ever more insistent, but Balthesar sounding increasingly convincing.

Whatever the old man finally said in tones of velvet-coated steel clearly worked, for the door opened with a click, and the green-clad guard bowed his head as he motioned for them to enter. Arnau followed the older brother into the courtyard within and his gaze swooped cautiously around the square. His breath caught in his throat. In addition to the emir's men and several palace functionaries and nobles in a variety of colours, there were three men in monochrome colours and armed with lethal spears, watching the two newcomers with barely contained aggression.

'What did you tell them?' Arnau asked, only then realising that perhaps this was one of those times he should have been playing the mute. Too late now, anyway.

'That we were invited companions of the Aragonese delegation. It is the truth, after a fashion, since your young noble friend did indeed invite us aboard his ship. It took a little persuasion to make the man see sense, but even in the emir's absence none of his people are going to risk angering the representatives of one of the strongest Christian kings. We should be safe under their nominal protection. Even the Almohad soldiers seem to be constrained. Likely Abd al-Azīz has enough on his platter undermining the island's emir without risking war with Aragon. We walk a knife edge here, Vallbona.'

And it felt like it too. Passing beneath that vicious scrutiny, they made their way into the doorway beside the stairs and through the now familiar rooms and corridors to the various *diwāns* that made up the palace records offices. As always they paused at the entrance and handed over their weapons, and then Balthesar asked directions of some clerk and they moved off along the corridor and into the rooms.

Balthesar seemed immensely satisfied with the office to which they had been directed, though to Arnau it was indistinguishable from any of the others, except that the window from this room did not offer a view of the palace dock and the city ports, but rather of the main gardens of the Al-Mudaina, where nobles and servants moved about in colourful garb, all under the stoic watchfulness of the Almohad soldiers. Shuddering, he turned away from the window and instead stood bored, contemplating the room itself.

After some time, the older knight retrieved a set of records from one alcove and began to pore through them, his manner becoming more irritable as he read. Finally, he straightened and stabbed a finger at the document.

'This is the only reference I can find so far. It is recorded that Muhàmmad the First, following the Christian uprisings, had any remaining churches and places of worship pulled down and the materials reused in his own projects. But sadly it intimates that all Christian, or as they term it, *heretical*, materials were made illegal and destroyed. There is no direct reference to the saint's arm as far as I can see, but a blanket statement. It is not a hopeful sign, I'm afraid, but I cling to the hope that, because of the status of the bone as potentially a Mussulman relic, it might have been saved. I shall not give up on it yet. We are here among the records and while that is the case I shall make sure I have scoured them thoroughly.'

Arnau nodded. There was so little he could do to help, even if he had a clue what to look for, which he didn't. The discomfort pressed upon him once more, and he had to change the way he stood, clenching himself.

'My bladder is straining,' he admitted finally.

'Have a word with the clerks. They'll direct you. I'll be at least another hour.'

With a sigh, Arnau slipped from the room and returned to the front desk. Only as he arrived did he realise he had no idea how to ask about latrines. He motioned to his groin, raising some amusement from the gathered clerks, and then, flushing a little, asked the way in Spanish. One of the men clearly had sufficient command of the tongue to understand his query and gestured a sequence of directions. Arnau was trying desperately to remember the sequence when he caught the word *ḥammām* and recognised it as the Arabic term for a bathhouse. He remembered seeing what appeared to be the door and changing room of a small bathhouse on their various visits to the offices, part way along the route. Clearly the baths would be a sensible place to look for a toilet, and so with a nod of thanks Arnau turned and set off towards that place. He rounded the first two corners as directed by the clerk, and was standing, tapping his lip in contemplation of where to turn for the third, when the pommel of a sword came down on the back of his head and sent him spinning into sickening blackness.

CHAPTER FOURTEEN

WEDNESDAY, 9 JUNE 1199

The blackness failed to recede. Arnau awoke with a start, eyes jerking open, heart lurching and panic coming in a flood at the apparent blindness that had been inflicted upon him. Not blindness though, but soul-shrouding darkness all around, he realised as the very faint edges of things appeared. Not enough to identify anything, but enough to show that something was there in the darkness. As that panic receded, new realisations came.

First was the excruciating pain in his head. The rear of his skull felt as though someone had driven an iron piton through it, and his brain felt woolly and strange. Memories came. The bathhouse. Desperation for the latrine and a hurried walk through corridors to… a thump on the head. Yes, he remembered now being hit from behind, unaware of the assailant until it was too late. Damn his idiocy, but he should have clenched harder and stayed in the office with Balthesar.

He made to reach up and test the back of his head, and was suddenly acutely aware that his hands wouldn't move. Fresh panic now. He was bound somehow. His wrists were pressed together and strapped tight behind his back. There was no pressure, though – he was just bound. What about his legs? A little exploration confirmed that his legs were still there and that he was in a heap on the floor. They did not seem to be bound like his arms, which came as something of a relief.

He stood. Or at least he tried to stand and failed. His legs held no strength whatsoever, probably from hours of being folded uncomfortably beneath him. Rubbing his legs together he could feel the sensation and nothing appeared to be broken, or cut, which was yet more of a relief. In fact, he seemed to be unharmed apart from the pain in the back of his head where he had been struck.

That was not enough of a relief to make him relax, though. Unharmed as he was, he was still bound and clearly held captive in some dark place, and that never boded well. So where was he, and by whom had he been captured? The answers were fairly obvious. Only two men on the island had reason to imprison him: Castellvell and the Lion of Alarcos. And Castellvell would be constrained by the presence of the other lords of Aragon and by Guillem Picornell; plus the only place he could realistically hold someone would be aboard their ship, while this place was silent as the grave and lacked all the creaks and groans of a floating vessel. So he was clearly in Almohad hands, which he would have assumed anyway. And that being the case, he was almost certainly still in the Al-Mudaina where the Lion now prowled.

He opened his mouth, wondering suddenly if he could speak or whether he'd been gagged. No, his mouth opened wide. His tongue felt a little swollen and his mouth arid and rough, and when he tried to speak it came out as a rasping cough. After a few attempts, he found a dry, uncomfortable voice deep inside that intoned the Psalm of David.

'God, hear thou my prayer, when I beseech; deliver thou my soul from dread of the enemy.'

He fell silent, dreading the enemy still, and a moment later became aware of a muffled noise: a repetitive tapping which he soon realised was footsteps that were becoming louder as they approached. Two voices in Arabic – low, hushed tones. An exchange. The rattle of keys. The door.

Arnau snapped his eyes shut at the sudden intrusive light. It might only be lamplight from some dingy corridor, but after the oppressive darkness of the prison room, it felt like the brightest of noon suns. Slowly he became accustomed to the faint glow through his slitted eyelids, gradually opening them as new sources of illumination sprang into life in the chamber. Someone was lighting oil lamps.

'I would tear out your tongue to still it shaping your heathen invocations,' said a familiar and sour voice, 'but I have need of that tongue yet.'

His vision focused a little more in the dull golden light and Abu Rāshid Abd al-Azīz ibn al-Ḥasan, the Lion of Alarcos, stepped into view from the right, his face a mask of hate, his clothing rich and fine, his aura murderous.

'I do not fear you,' Arnau spat.

'Yes you do,' replied the Lion, in a truly matter-of-fact tone. 'And you are right to do so. I am a fearsome creature, a blade of God's will, a son of the Prophet and an instrument of righteous vengeance.'

'You are a zealot and a would-be despot. Little else.'

Was that a smile that passed across the Almohad lord's face? If so it was considerably less pleasant than even his frown of hate.

'This land is mine now, Christian. What little influence Abd-Allāh ibn Ishāq ibn Ghāniya retains will soon melt away in the face of the true caliph's power. And you can call me despot if you wish, but I am just a governor for the caliph, and it is he who *truly* rules. So forget any hope of rescue or survival you cling to. There is no succour or safety on Mayūrqa for you or your kind now.'

A black-and-white-uniformed soldier brought forth a chair and placed it before Arnau, and the lord sat in it and steepled his fingers. 'I am not here to gloat, and I am not a man to unduly waste time and effort, so let me come to the point. Your life is forfeit, heathen, as it was the very moment you set foot on the soil of the Faithful. What remains to be decided is the manner in which you pass from this life.'

Arnau felt himself shiver. The man was so straightforward and direct in his evil.

'I will do nothing to help you.'

'Oh you will,' the Almohad lord replied flatly. 'You will spin me every yarn for which I ask, but you must decide how precious is your faith and how dearly you value your companions, for preserving them will come at a high price. You may refuse my requests, but to do so will bring agony. Comply readily and you will be fed and watered until this is over, whereupon you will be granted a swift and clean death. If you are particularly helpful, I might even consider sending your body back to your people for them to perform their heathen rites upon, rather than tossing you out upon the rocks for the scavengers and the gulls. You must decide how readily you can weather the pain through which you will be put. I urge you to acquiesce immediately and save yourself the agony and us the trouble.'

Arnau felt the dread rise in his stomach. Torture. He had faced death plenty of times, in battle and even face to face with della Cadeneta, but torture was entirely different. Not to face wounds that were intended to kill, but injuries meant simply to cause the maximum pain with the minimum of actual damage. He pushed down the fear. Pain was just a reaction, not injury in itself, and therefore it could be overcome. Like those apostles of whom Balthesar had spoken, he would be tough and weather all storms in the knowledge that the Lord would protect him, and should he suffer agonies at the hands of the wicked, his soul would dwell with the Lord in glory.

'What is your answer?'

Arnau cleared his dry, scratchy throat.

'The Lord governeth me and nothing shall fail to me.'

The Lion's lip twitched upwards as Arnau squared his shoulders defiantly.

'In the place of pasture there he hath set me. He nourished me on the water of refreshing.'

'Your faith will be rewarded only with pain,' the Almohad snarled.

'He converted my soul. He led me forth on the paths of rightfulness, for his name.'

'I shall give you no other chance to co-operate. From this time there will be only pain and interrogation.'

'For why though I shall go in the midst of shadow of death, I shall not dread evils, for thou art with me. Thy rod and thy staff; those have comforted me.'

The Lion's sneer returned and he made a flicking gesture with two fingers.

'Thou hast made ready a board in my sight against them that trouble me. Thou hast made fat mine head with oil, and my cup that filleth greatly is full clear.'

Suddenly the reason for the bound wrists became clear as they were jerked up sharply behind him, putting immense pressure on his shoulders. He winced and gave a yelp before biting down on it, refusing to give the man the pleasure of his audible pain.

'And thy mercy shall follow me…' he gasped, 'in all the days of my life. And that I dwell in the house of the Lord… into the length of days.'

And then speech was no longer possible, for to open his mouth would be to scream as some unseen hand hauled on the rope that ran through a large iron ring in the ceiling and Arnau was jerked from the floor to hang by the wrists, his shoulders groaning and shrieking with pain as muscles stretched and threatened to tear, the joints aching as they were brought close to separation. He remembered hearing once about ancient peoples tearing their victims apart with wild horses, and he wondered if that was to be his fate. His shoulders were afire, every muscle tearing with infinitesimal slowness so that each heartbeat brought a continual stream of pain, pulsing through him, making him grit his teeth and huff through them.

Just as the agony was becoming truly unbearable and the possibility that his arms would dislocate and tear away became startlingly real, the rope was let go and he plunged to the ground once more, his legs folding painfully under him. Clearly the Lion and his men were experts at this. They had waited as long as they could before inflicting permanent damage, and had released him in time for his shoulders to heal in a matter of hours. Arnau knew that a skilled torturer could do this sort of thing indefinitely without killing their subject, and that knowledge brought him absolutely no comfort.

'That was by way of a demonstration,' the Lion said as Arnau breathed heavily in a heap on the floor. 'I have time to devote attention to you. I will not push hard and break you, for that would not be productive. We shall work slowly so that you survive intact through everything we do, with time to recuperate before the next agonies are visited upon you. You will not be damaged, just put through much pain. You understand now?'

Arnau nodded and silence reigned for a moment. He realised that the man was waiting for him to beg, or perhaps to capitulate. In truth, the possibility had at the very least passed through his mind. The pain of being hauled up by the wrists had been so intense he was not sure he could cope with it again, let alone any other horror the Lion dreamed up. Still, he was not going to bow to this man, at least as long as he was in control of his mind and his tongue. As long as he could hold out, he would do so.

'The Lord hear thee in the day of tribulation; the name of God of Jacob defend thee. Send he help to thee from the holy place, and from Zion defend he thee.'

Arnau cried out then in fresh pain as the rope was hauled on sharply once more and he rose from the ground, shoulder muscles tearing, feet kicking wildly. This time he was only there mere moments before he fell once more with a thud. The pain of landing roughly on the stone floor felt like luxury compared with the pain of dangling.

'See how readily you suffer. And this is but the beginning. Now let me explain my purpose, for I am not a cruel man and I do not make men suffer for the simple love of it. I have reason for my actions. You are aware of my history with the *Qātil wari'a*?'

'He killed your son in battle,' Arnau managed before gasping and clenching his teeth once more.

'Yes, I felt certain he would have boasted of his prowess in killing young men. He was ever a killer in the saddle, long before my son met his end. But yes, though the caliph maintains a fatwa demanding the head of the Monster of Valencia, it is not this that drives me. I owe him for taking my son from me, and I have lived with that debt owed for much of my life while the *Qātil wari'a* hid in obscurity. Now he is here, and I have wrestled for days with how I should proceed. For years I thought to take his head in revenge for my son and to hand it to the caliph as is my duty. But now, despite that duty, I find simply killing the Monster of

Valencia to be inadequate punishment for the crime. He should suffer for the rest of his years as I have, and die a lonely and broken man. That is my purpose now. That is my goal.'

'Your goal is to let him live?' Arnau laughed. 'How easily achieved.'

'Mock me as you wish,' the Lion responded, 'but I will visit upon my enemy the worst of all pains: loss, regret and guilt. For he will lose everything he loves, and will live the rest of his miserable days knowing that this is the case and that all his suffering is solely due to his own deeds.'

Arnau felt that shiver again now. What wickedness was this? How cruel to ruin a man for one act committed in the heat of battle.

The Lion of Alarcos steepled his fingers once more. 'Now, I will find out everything you know about the *Qātil wari'a*, and I will use what I discover to strip him of everything for which he cares. We shall start by learning what you know of him since he disappeared at Valencia, who you are and your connection to him, and what you are doing in Mayūrqa. I think to begin with, tell me who you are.'

'Piss on you,' Arnau spat.

The Lion of Alarcos sighed. 'This is the simplest and most innocuous of questions, I'm sure. If you baulk at this one, I cannot imagine how you will feel about the rest. But let me demonstrate once more how I shall respond to such defiance.'

Arnau braced himself for the agonising lift once more, and was more surprised than shocked when some unseen figure behind him instead lifted his *gandura* and *burnous* and wrenched down his braies, exposing his bare buttocks to the cold damp cellar air.

The first thwack from the switch was like having liquid fire poured in a line across his posterior. What the weapon was made from he could not tell, but the pain was extreme and he immediately felt a tiny trickle down his buttock, confirming that the blow had drawn blood. His eyes watered, and he had to bite down on his lip to stifle the rising whimper.

The Lion frowned and barked something in Arabic. Arnau could quite imagine what he was saying: upbraiding his man for doing too much damage. As Arnau began to recover, his breathing returning to normal, the second blow landed. Once more the pain was excruciating, but he suspected it had been delivered to leave a red stripe rather than tear into skin.

'We have such an array of torments,' the Lion said now. 'In the catalogue of man's history, he has devised ever more means of causing pain, and now we have them all upon which to draw. Rest assured that we have only just begun to explore the many methods of loosening your tongue.'

Arnau was breathing sharply again now, still biting his lip. The second blow might not have drawn blood, but his teeth certainly had. He was now horribly aware of how easily he was going to break. That last blow had almost been enough to make him talk, and he had no doubt that the Lion had much worse yet in store.

'Your name.'

'Lord, reprove thou not me in thy strong vengeance; neither chastise thou me in thine ire.'

In a flurry of the worst pain Arnau had ever experienced, he was suddenly jerked from the floor once more, his arms screaming in agony, and he was just clenching his jaw to prevent himself crying out anything that might stop this when the next stripe was torn across his posterior with the switch, making him spin sickeningly, drawing ever more pain from both shoulders and wrists.

'Vallbona,' he cried out suddenly. 'Arnau de Vallbona!'

As he landed in a heap, sobbing, he felt utterly wretched. He'd not meant to say it. It had somehow slipped out against his will. He had been broken. It had been less than ten minutes since he'd been unconscious, and already he had talked. And the Lion had only just begun.

He sat on the floor, whimpering, as the Almohad lord sat back once more, arms folded. 'That is much better. And I'm sure we can do even better than that. Your name is interesting, Vallbona, but of little use to me in the long run without more detail. Are you now willing to see reason and simply answer my questions without the need to resort to such inhuman measures?'

It took a good minute for Arnau to recover enough to speak, and when he did he could feel the blood from his bitten lip dribbling down his chin.

'Go… fuck yourself.'

The Lion of Alarcos simply sighed. 'Very well, Arnau de Vallbona. We shall work to draw more from you. Now that I have your name, I would know *who* you are. You claim, I believe, to be some sort of itinerant preacher, though even the most gullible fool would not credit such a fiction. I wish to know *what* you are. A knight perhaps, but in whose service? If you are the king's man, then why are you not with the embassy, but rather exploring the island as a pair? And if you are *not* the king's man, then how come you to know the young knight in the embassy so well? So tell me, as succinctly as you can, who you truly *are*, Arnau de Vallbona.'

Something was suddenly looped around Arnau's throat and he felt it snap tight against the skin and begin to pull ever more taut. Panic gripped him, making his body shake, his eyes bulge, his mouth dry out. He gasped and realised that he couldn't draw in air. His windpipe was closed.

Insanity! How was he expected to talk if he could not breathe?

As if reading his thoughts, the Lion of Alarcos leaned forward, his face expressionless.

'A strong and composed man can hold his breath for a minute or so,' he said knowledgably. 'A weak man, or a panicked man such as yourself, is likely to fail at perhaps half a minute. But rest assured that you can survive at least a minute longer than you would manage voluntarily before you suffer any ill effects. This is how my method will work: we will loosen the cord after one minute. You will then have only the blink of an eye to decide upon your next course of action. If you immediately answer my question, you will be allowed respite. If you do *not* immediately do so, you will be allowed three breaths and then we shall repeat the procedure for a further minute. In my experience a man will usually speak immediately whether they intend to or not, for the body sometimes overrides the mind at such times. If you are exceptionally strong you might manage another minute, but I guarantee you that you will then talk. So spare yourself that discomfort and capitulate now.'

Arnau realised that the Lion was now counting down on his fingers.

Three...

Two...

One...

The cord loosened and Arnau choked in a breath, coughed one out, choked another back in, gagged a little, and then threw a defiant look at the man before him.

'A Templar?' snarled the Almohad, and Arnau blinked. He'd not said anything! He'd done nothing but draw breath. But as he stared in shock, he suddenly felt certain that he'd choked that very word out even with his first exhalation. How weak was he proving?

'A knight of the Temple,' the Lion said again. 'How it must gall you to know that your Temple church in Jerusalem is now once more a house of the Faithful, its crosses torn down and the *miḥrāb* returned, showing the way to Mecca. So you are one of their knights. And if you are, and you travel with the *Qātil wari'a*, then clearly he is also one of your order now. Fascinating how the butcher no longer delivers halal, but wields the same cleaver regardless, eh? He has spent his time hiding in your mysterious monasteries, and now he travels with you. You Christian knights, you have servants... *squires*, I seem to remember. So you are surely his squire. Fascinating. Already I have so much upon which to build.'

Arnau sagged, breathing heavily, tears streaming down his face. He had been tested, and had been found wanting at the earliest of stages. He had never felt so wretched. The cord was no longer around his neck and he felt no pressure on the rope. He was in a heap on the floor, his nethers exposed, stinging pain still across his backside, thumping aches in his arms and shoulders, throat sore as though he had swallowed a misericorde dagger.

'You also have much to think upon, Arnau de Vallbona, knight of the Temple. I shall leave you for the time being, and will return when you have recovered sufficiently to begin afresh with my next set of questions. I trust that when I return you will have reflected upon what has happened thus far and will simply co-operate without the need for such unpleasantness.'

As the Lion rose, Arnau's eyes upon him, the unseen figure moved around from behind him, clothed in black and white, and began to snuff out the lamps. When only one was left, the Almohad lord stepped towards it and indicated what could be seen by its glow. Arnau felt his stomach churn at the sight of a brazier filled with dark coal and a table full of things that gleamed gold in the lamplight.

'We are only at the beginning. Pain can always get worse. Think on your future and how much you value your pride,' the Lion said, then turned and left the room. After him, the guard snuffed out the last lamp and then exited, closing the door and shutting out the last of the light, plunging him once more into darkness.

The room – a cellar or something like – was cold and dark and damp, but none of that got through to Arnau, who burned with fury and shame. He lay for some time in the damp, the discomfort of the hard floor nothing after the agony of the Almohad's torture.

What could he do? He had to somehow fight back. Balthesar would not come for him; he couldn't. The old knight would now have finished in the records office, and he would know that something was wrong. He would know that Arnau was no longer with him and would surmise that he had been captured, but with the emir absent and the Lion of Alarcos in control of Madina, the old knight could hardly search the palace for him. In fact, Balthesar would be best served getting away from the Al-Mudaina as fast as he could and going into hiding. He hated the thought, even as he acknowledged that it was the best option and that Balthesar would be mad to try anything else.

He was on his own, and that was that. His chances of escape were miniscule. He was locked in a cellar, with only one barred door and no window. There was probably a guard outside the door, too. And even if he could somehow get out, he was in an unfamiliar palace full of enemies. He would never escape it. All that remained, then, was to fight back. He spent some time struggling to free his hands, but whoever had tied the bonds had been thorough. His hands were too tightly secured and in such a position as to make struggle painful and futile.

His legs were free.

With pain and difficulty he rose to his feet. His movement was hampered by the braies around his knees, but he could walk with difficulty. He began to move carefully in the darkness but was soon jerked to a halt. The rope was tied somewhere, restricting his movement. Over half an hour's trial and painful error, he discovered that his captors had been equally thorough there. Despite being free to stand and walk he could not reach the brazier, the desk with the metal implements, the door, or wherever the rope was fastened. In fact all he could do was walk within a small, empty circle.

Hopefully, when they began the torture again they would do so with the lifting from the floor. He resolved that when they next did that, he would bite down on the pain and use the swing of his legs to kick either the lord or his man who held the rope. One way or another he would fight them however he could. And when he ran out of strength to fight or ways to do so, he would do the only thing left: he would dash out his own brains on the stone-flagged floor.

He had no idea how long he lay on the ground before blackness claimed him once more, and no idea how long he then slept despite the discomfort. All he knew was the cold dread that filled him from nave to chaps when he was roused from slumber by the sound of approaching footsteps out in the corridor. He was on his knees by the time the keys jingled and the door groaned open. A single figure stood outlined against the glow, and this time there were no guards with him. Arnau wondered for dreadful moments what the Lion now had planned, before the figure moved into the room and lit one lamp only, close to the door, carrying it with him.

It was with some surprise that Arnau realised it was not the Almohad lord. In fact, the man was naggingly familiar, though it took some time for him to place the features. Finally he remembered seeing this wise-looking old Moor standing close to the emir on several occasions. The *wazir*: the man who served the emir and who now nominally ruled in Mayūrqa, held in check by his new Almohad master.

Hope flooded into Arnau, and his fresh optimism seemed borne out as the old man swept up a blade with a serrated edge from the table and said 'Hold up your hands,' in good Spanish. When Arnau did so, the man gave several expert cuts, then stood back.

'This has to appear to be your own work. I will not suffer at the hands of Abd al-Azīz for you. I have weakened the bonds, but you must use your strength to break them, so that it is not clearly the work of a second man. Do so now.'

Arnau strained for some time, and was beginning to think it impossible when suddenly they gave with a tearing noise and his arms came free.

'Why?' was all he could find to say.

'Abd al-Azīz already considers himself the *wāli* of an Almohad Mayūrqa. Not all of our people are so blinkered as to want to fall in line with a callous and dangerous master such as they. The emir must return and retake his land before it is too late. Somehow he trusts you and your companion. He believes you are men of power and influence. You may be able to help. I will get you out of the Al-Mudaina, and then you will find the emir and bring him back with his army to oust the Almohads. You will do this because I have saved you, and you will do it because you know it to be the right thing to do.'

Arnau nodded as he pulled up and tied his braies, wincing and hissing at the pain in his arms and shoulders and the fiery stripes across his buttocks.

'The emir is a good man,' he said through a sore and scratchy throat. 'If I could bring all the might of Aragon to bear for him, I would, but I will certainly do what I can.'

The old Moor nodded his understanding. 'When you emerge from the Al-Mudaina, you must move swiftly away from the city centre. Go past the port and find the westernmost gate from there. Beside the gate is a stable where you will find a horse waiting for you, held under the name Abu Mansur. Leave the city and ride for the emir's estate in the hills at Al-Fabia. All my hopes for the future of the *taifa* will go with you. I will leave first, and I will loosen the lock on the door. Wait five minutes and then hit the door with all your strength and the lock should give. But before I go, listen carefully, for this is how you will find your way out of the palace...'

CHAPTER FIFTEEN

WEDNESDAY, 9 JUNE 1199

6 P.M.

After the requisite five minutes Arnau braced himself, took a deep breath and ran at the cellar door, left shoulder to the fore. He hit it hard and bounced off, cursing sullenly. The pain in his shoulders from being dangled on the rope was still raw and unpleasant, despite the sleep he'd managed since, and the jarring thud of hitting the heavy and immobile door brought it all back and then some. Pausing and breathing, recovering slightly from the blow, Arnau braced himself, gritting his teeth. The cellar door was strong and still fastened, and even if the *wazir* had sabotaged the lock to give him a chance, it was still heavy and his shoulders still weak and damaged.

He hit the timber at a run again, and this time there was a sharp cracking noise. Pain rolled through his shoulder once more, and tears streamed down his face, but the knowledge that something at least had given brought fresh hope and determination, and he retreated across the room, panting, and prepared once more. The third time he barrelled into the door it flew open with a crack and banged against the corridor wall outside.

Despite having been partially rescued, he still half expected to see a troop of Almohad soldiers awaiting him in the corridor. If they had been there he'd not have seen them anyway, for the corridor was as dark as the room had been.

Shoulders throbbing, he began to set off, but then stopped and turned, identifying the faint change in the gloom that showed where the doorway was. He made his way back through it and felt his way along the wall. As he'd anticipated he quickly came across the table that sat below the lamp shelf. Briefly, he contemplated taking the lamp, but there did not seem to be any method of lighting it on the shelf, so he passed on that idea and instead returned to his original plan. His fingers danced lightly and carefully across the table, feeling the shapes. He shunned the hooks and the heavy, serrated saw blades, and settled on a narrow-bladed knife that had a long, tapering blade, sharp as anything he'd ever come across, which made him grateful that his questing fingers had been so careful.

Further across the table, he found three hammers of different sizes and selected the middle one, a hefty wooden affair with a solid grip. Armed with blade and mallet, he turned and left the cellar.

He moved carefully along the corridor, pacing steadily on the balls of his feet, aware of every shuffle and creak. The silence was oppressive and he wondered how half the world had not been attracted by the sound of the breaking door. It was only when he came to the first junction that he realised he had been concentrating so much on getting through the door and collecting weapons that he'd stopped repeating the mantra of the old man's directions and had consequently forgotten more than half of them. He cursed silently. Left. He was sure it was left. Though the more he thought about it and attempted to recall the directions the more he began to worry that he'd got it wrong.

No second guessing. He would have to rely on instinct. He turned left. He made it perhaps twelve paces along the passage before he changed his mind, returned to the junction and turned right instead. This corridor quickly jogged left and he followed it a short distance, anxiously, when suddenly he turned another corner and the air in the darkness changed. There was the distinctive feel of clammy warmth ahead and a faint smell of wood smoke.

Good. He had clearly chosen correctly in the end. That smell and sensation grew as he moved down the passage, and he was surprised how quickly the smoke thickened and the heat rose. He was close. Another corner, and he could now see a faint golden glow. He approached the turn carefully, and became aware of a growing rumble, too. Peeking around the corner he found the next stretch of passage to be empty, but the light was much brighter, forcing him to narrow his eyes to slits. Equally the smoke was now more visible, and the heat was becoming more and more intense.

He moved at a measured pace now, worrying over the time he was taking even as he slowed. Sooner or later the Lion of Alarcos would visit his prisoner once more and would discover he had gone. Arnau was under no illusion what would follow. The palace would be turned upside down and inside out looking for him, and he needed to be outside and running through the city by then, but equally he could hardly rush now, for he could so easily stumble blindly into disaster.

It seemed to take an age to reach the next corner and as he did so he prepared himself, for as well as an increase in all sensations, another thread had joined the subterranean tapestry: a voice. It was low and seemed to be singing a repetitive refrain in Arabic. Perhaps it was a prayer, or possibly simply a song. Whatever it was, it betrayed the presence of another human being, and Arnau would have to deal with him.

His fingers tightened on the mallet and the knife. The *wazir*, in giving his directions, had extracted from Arnau the promise that he would spare whatever lives he could in his flight. The vast majority of folk in the Al-Mudaina, he was reminded, were ordinary, innocent people who had no more love for the Almohad visitors than he. That was both true and fair. The words of Balthesar in Arnau's earliest days with the order came flooding back:

We protect the innocent and the God-fearing from the wicked, Brother Arnau. We live in turbulent times, but the order is not about the Christian and the Moor. Or the Jew. It is simply about the good and the wicked. It does not do to see the world in such a basic manner as good Christians and bad everyone else. Sometimes, Vallbona, the wicked wear a cross. Sometimes the innocent do not.

Quite. And nothing had brought that to the fore as much as witnessing the difference between the tolerant world of the Mayūrqan emir and the violent zealotry of the Almohad lord.

He approached the next turn and lifted the hammer, ready.

No wonder the cellar door crashing open had gone unheard in the populated areas of the palace, for as he turned the corner, the roar of the furnace thundered along the corridor. A man in ragged clothes, stained with sweat and soot, was digging around in an alcove stacked with logs, filling a basket, his back to the young Templar, blissfully unaware. A bath slave, tending to the furnace. He could be Christian, Jew or Moor, since their colouring was almost identical in these lands, and they all by necessity spoke Arabic.

With a profound sense of regret that he needed to do this, Arnau paced quietly along the stone floor, approaching the slave. The ragged man collected two more logs, turned to put them in his basket and looked up, wide eyed. Before he could utter a word, the young sergeant smacked him on the forehead with the wooden mallet, pulling the blow considerably, hoping simply to knock the man out rather than crack his skull like an egg. Clearly he had pulled the blow too much, for the slave staggered, a shocked expression crossing his face, and fell back against the filthy wall, struggling to stand. Before he could recover, Arnau hit him again, and could not tell whether it was the mallet blow that knocked the sense from the man, or the fact that his head then ricocheted off the wall. Whatever the case, the man fell in a heap. Nervously, Arnau checked the slave and his chest continued to rise and fall, so he lived.

He contemplated for a moment taking the basket and masquerading as the slave, but to do it properly he would have to change clothes, and if he carried the logs, he could not wield the weapons. Moreover to do so would waste precious moments. Instead, he gripped his blade and hammer and moved on.

He remembered the directions from this part of the palace, and quickly slipped through the bathhouse's support system, briefly noting a side passage that led to a door which would emerge into the main bath area, hoping that with this being only a small complex there would be only one slave down here. A beam of white light, dazzling in the gloom, pierced the darkness mid-corridor, and Arnau paused, blinking, and looked up. Ladder rungs were pinned into the side wall, rising up into the light, and the temptation to climb them was strong. Up there was the roof of the baths, the access here for the slave to reach the top where he could open all the small, star-shaped windows above the rooms to vent steam and cool the chambers below. To emerge on the roof would see him out of these tunnels, but he would then be trapped in the heart of the Al-Mudaina, visible to all.

Reluctantly, he passed the beam of light and moved on. He slipped past a side junction, which glowed gold, blasted him with heat and carried the roar of the furnace, and wondered briefly if he would fit through the narrow hole that was used to empty the place of spent ashes. Possibly, but like the ladder going upwards, he had been warned that escape that way would simply lead to another trap.

He pressed on, the heat and noise diminishing now as he moved away from the baths. Three more corners, which he hoped he remembered correctly from his instructions, and there it was.

A door.

Not just any door, though, since this one was etched all around with a narrow line of silvery light. A door to the outside. Of course, if he had gone wrong in his directions since the baths, and this was not the door he had been sent to, then he could easily emerge into the waiting arms of Almohad soldiers, and he knew exactly how much chance he would have to escape a second time. He dithered for some moments, nervous about even trying it. If it was the wrong door…

Lord, bow down thine ear and hear me, for I am needy and poor.

Keep thou my life for I am holy, my Lord, and make thou safe thy servant hoping in thee.

In the day of my tribulation I cry to thee, for thou heardest me.

Lord, lead thou me forth in thy way, and I shall enter in thy truth; mine heart be glad, that it dread thy name.

Not the full Psalm, of course. Surely the Lord would forgive him brevity and omission in the circumstances, but while he felt the need to beseech God for aid in this moment, he was equally aware of how little time he now had before his absence was noted, and his trail would not take too long to discover, given the unconscious bath slave he'd left in the tunnel.

Knife or hammer? He'd been warned what would await him, and he needed a hand for the door, so the choice had to be made now. Could he – *should* he – kill? But then, would the mallet be enough?

The thirty-fourth Psalm crept into his mind.

Turn thou away from evil, and do good; seek thou peace, and perfectly follow thou it.

The eyes of the Lord be on just men.

Carefully, he tucked the knife away in his belt and hefted the mallet. His free hand went to the door. He probed it in the gloom, searching for locks and latches. There was indeed a lock, but his keen gaze noted no bar interrupting the narrow vein of light surrounding the heavy wooden door. Unlocked. Perfect. His hand found the handle and he turned it, pulling the door towards him.

At first he tried to just inch it open gently, but the door was old and warped for all its strength, and it gave a long groan like an ancient giant rising from his chair. Realising that his cover was already blown with that noise, he yanked it wide and leaped out.

He was momentarily blinded by the brightness as he emerged into the open air. The light was so intense and all-consuming that the soldier was almost on him by the time the shape had resolved in the dazzling blur.

He was not an Almohad warrior, but one of the common palace guard, a green garment covering his mail shirt. He wore a sword, sheathed, at his side and his head was protected by a pointed helm surrounded with a white, turban-like covering. He had levelled his spear as the door croaked open, and even as Arnau's sight cleared, he realised that the man was deliberating whether to strike. While the guard had not been expecting anyone to emerge from the substructures through that door, clearly slaves sometimes did, else why have a door at all, and why leave it unlocked?

Had the man been certain Arnau was an enemy the blow would have come fast, and the Templar would likely have died, skewered here in the doorway. Instead, by the time the guard had made the split-second decision that Arnau was not supposed to be here and lunged with the weapon, the young Templar had reacted, ducking to the side. The spear shaft whispered past his ribs, and he swung the hammer high and hard, not pulling his blow at all this time. The wooden weight smacked into the man's head with a ding, denting the helmet within the turban. No matter how much his fellow brothers had tried to persuade Arnau that the sword was the weapon of a knight, he still favoured his mace above all; this mallet might be crude and rough, but its usefulness in combat was much the same. The guard staggered and spun, one hand falling free of the spear which swung wildly in an arc, scraping along the wall of the Al-Mudaina.

The man was a professional. He was dazed, but otherwise unharmed. Aware that he was now in danger from this unexpected visitor, the guard stepped back once, twice, thrice, letting go of the spear entirely as he drew his sword, shaking his head to clear it of the ringing. Arnau pressed forward, unwilling to let his momentum slow and the guard find sense.

The sword came free of the sheath and Arnau leaped, his hammer swinging once more. The guard had backed away too far now and hit the wall, his elbow striking stone and the sword flailing uselessly out to the side, but even as Arnau's hand came round wielding the hammer, the man ducked and the wooden head of the mallet missed him, thudding hard into the stone of the wall and sending shockwaves up the Templar's arm and into his shoulder, bringing back waves of the pain that had begun to dull until now. All right, perhaps that would not have happened with a sword…

The two men both staggered now, one still fighting the ringing in his ears and the difficult position of being backed against a wall, the other shaken and suffering from intense pain in the shoulders. It took precious moments for them to strike once more, and when they did so, they parried one another, the weapons bouncing away harmlessly. Another strike and this time Arnau had his hammer in place, descending, the guard's sword blocking it, and the two became locked in that position, Arnau forcing his weapon down towards the man's face as his arm slowly buckled under the pressure. The hammer would do little damage at such speed, but the man's head was against the wall, so the Templar stood a chance at least of causing sufficient damage. The guard's other hand came up now and gripped his sword blade, pushing back, and suddenly Arnau's mallet was moving up and away again, the balance of strength shifted. Arnau threw his own left hand into the struggle, trying to force the mallet down, but that shoulder was the one he'd thrown three times against the cellar door and it had become far too weak, strained and achy even beyond the damage done by torture. It made no difference. The guard was pushing him back, and Arnau, tired and injured, was almost out of strength. Damn it, but what would Lütolf think? He was fighting like a street urchin now, like a wrestler or pugilist in the back alleys, and not the sergeant he was. He was going to lose this struggle, and when he did, there was little chance of recovering enough to win the fight.

With a sigh of regret, he dropped his left hand once more from the hammer. The guard redoubled his effort and forced Arnau back, grinning a savage rictus of victory which suddenly fell away into shock. The Moor's eyes widened in horror and all the pressure against the sword disappeared as his gaze slid downwards to where Arnau's left hand had slipped his narrow blade from his belt, turned it in a single, smooth move, and thrust it between the man's ribs. The chain mail shirt the man wore would have turned most blades, and even arrow points, but the knife Arnau had taken from the cellar table was so slender and sharp as to resemble the point of a bodkin arrow, and had slid with surprising ease into the mail, snapping links as it sank into shirt, then garments, then flesh, like a misericorde, designed to deliver the *coup de grâce*.

Arnau stepped back, his hand falling away from the knife handle. It had taken every ounce of strength he commanded to punch the knife in through the armour, and now he was spent, so weak that he no longer had even the power to pull the blade back out.

Blood ran from the man's wound down the knife and dripped from the hilt. Arnau staggered, weak and feeble, away. He'd truly not wanted to kill the man, but in the end it had come down to that simple equation: him or me. He had to fight not to collapse to his knees, and watched with distaste as the guard did just that before toppling face first to the stone with a final sigh.

For the first time, Arnau looked around and took in his surroundings. He was indeed outside the Al-Mudaina, and exactly where the *wazir* had said he would be. Before him stretched the private dock of the palace. To his right he could see an ornate gateway leading into the public areas of the palace. Directly in front, the Aragonese ship wallowed at its jetty, rising and falling gently with the low waves. To the left, through that great brick arch, lay open sea.

He realised with a shock that figures were standing on the foreign ship, halted in their work by the sight of the brutal fight across the dock, and panic flittered through him. He'd been seen. Not by the Almohads or even the palace guard, mind, but even the common sailors of the Aragonese vessel would carry dangerous news. Word of this fight would undoubtedly reach Moorish ears swiftly, and from there the news would spread through the Al-Mudaina until someone important heard.

He had to go, and he had to go now.

Swallowing his fears and summoning up reserves of strength he didn't believe he possessed, he staggered across the dock and toppled gracelessly into the water. The cold, salty sea closed over him, and far from bringing fear it felt more like a soothing balm as it washed his dirty and bruised skin, though the salt as it seeped through his braies brought a stinging sensation to the stripes of pain on his rear. It was long moments before he began to kick and rise through the dark currents towards the air once more.

When he finally broke the surface and heaved in a breath, he was surprisingly close to the prow of the ship. Realising that the closer he was to the vessel the harder he would be to see from it, he closed on the hull and then swam slowly around the prow to the far side. Every pull of the arms through the water was almost cripplingly painful and he knew even as he rounded the ship that he would not be able to do this for long before his strength failed and he began to sink unstoppably to a watery end.

Heaving in breaths and forcing every last ounce of strength from his ravaged shoulders, he pushed on through the water. At the far side of the dock lay another pier with two small warehouses, presumably where supplies could be unloaded for the Al-Mudaina's ancillary structures, but to the left of them, where the dock opened out to sea beyond the arch, it was protected from the worst waves by a breakwater, which, as the *wazir* had suggested, was connected to the harbour walls of the main city port.

He reached the stone jetty even as the last of his strength ebbed away, and it took him four painful attempts to haul himself up onto it. Even then, he could not stop, though his body shook with effort and pain. He was not being watched from the ship now. They had not seen him slip around the prow and to the far side of the dock, but sooner or later someone from either the ship or the palace itself would spot him lying on the stone and all would be swiftly undone.

Exhausted and fragile he forced himself up, first to his knees and then to his feet, and staggered and limped away. At the end of the private dock, he took a small jump out onto the breakwater, almost failing to make it and plummeting back into the water. Wobbling a little, he regained his balance and staggered a few more paces. Then succumbing finally, his energy sapped, he sank to the ground and lay there, shaking, chest rising and falling in ragged breaths.

He was free.

He had no idea how long he lay there. Sleep was not possible, even had he wanted it, but his body needed to stop moving and rest, and would not even allow him to rise to his knees for some time. He simply lay there, shivering, staring upwards like a washed-up corpse, watching the sun move across the sky with infinitesimal slowness. He tried to estimate the time. Late afternoon, he figured. Perhaps an hour and a half from sundown.

It took him some time to realise what it was he was hearing. There was a muffled cacophony around him, of sailors and port activity, the creaking of ships and the lapping of waves, the shrieking of gulls and the general hum and drone of life. But over it all there was a more urgent melody now, and hearing it brought back his sense of urgency. The body of the guard had been brought to the attention of someone who mattered, and the palace had burst into frantic life as investigations ensued. Perhaps they had already found the unconscious body of the bath slave? It would not take long before the furnace heat dropped without being fed, and the baths cooled. And the dead guard, the open door and the battered slave would inevitably lead to the cellar and the knowledge that the Templar had escaped.

He had to go. He was outside the palace and free, but they would soon know exactly who had left and where he had exited and it would not take long for a search of the dock area to reveal the prone form of Arnau de Vallbona lying on the breakwater. Gulping in air and praying that he had strength to go on, Arnau half crawled, half rolled across the breakwater and down to the far slope, on the city port side, where he lay half submerged in the water for precious seconds.

The shouting at the Al-Mudaina had increased in volume and urgency. No time to stop, though he felt almost willing to fail now rather than push any more.

I slept and rested and I rose up, for the Lord received me.
I shall not dread thousands of people encompassing me.
Lord, arise thou; my God, make me safe.

Arnau pulled himself wearily to his feet and staggered towards the port. He counted every step as he went, all the time alert to the rising tension and troubles in the palace off to his right, and at the thirty-third step, he passed a wall and the Al-Mudaina disappeared from view. Still, he would not be safe for long. He had to keep moving. Had to run.

But at least he was free. He had escaped the Lion of Alarcos's grip. He had escaped the dungeon of the Al-Mudaina. He would never again have to visit that fortress and place his head in the Lion's mouth. He continued to stagger and reel as he moved up onto the dock, passing a fisherman who seemed only half surprised to see an exhausted, bewildered and bedraggled man emerge from the breakwater. Arnau ignored him and moved across the port, passing along the dock, threading between seamen and merchants heading this way and that, unburdened or carrying documents, or weighed down with ropes or sacks. He ducked between stacks of cargo and gradually passed across the huge port to the far side, where he clenched his teeth against possible danger and made to pass inside the city walls. He could so easily have just disappeared into the wilds without entering the city again, but the *wazir* had been shrewd enough to prepare a horse for him, and Arnau was under no illusion as to how far he would get on foot today.

Braced against potential danger, Arnau limped and staggered towards the gate. There were no black-and-white Almohad figures there, at least, but even the emir's men could be dangerous now that in the city they answered to the Lion. Had word of an escaped prisoner already spread from the palace to the city walls? If so, this would be a very short walk.

He approached the gate into the city chewing on his lip nervously, but as he neared the portal his fears abated somewhat. The two guards looked thoroughly bored, and were making no attempt to stop or interrupt the flow of humanity passing back and forth between port and city streets. In a trice he was through, past the walls and into the heart of Madina once more. His pulse slowed again, and his shivering subsided to just that caused by standing in cold, wet, clinging apparel.

It did not take long to move through the streets and locate the next gate. He raised barely a look from the busy populace, and as he neared that exit the buildings thinned out to farmland and orchards once more. Only half a dozen structures huddled close to the gate, and the stable was easy to identify.

Trying to straighten and look less like a bedraggled vagrant, Arnau strode across the open space and into the stable. A short, wizened man with a pointy grey beard and a pale yellow cap hurried over to him, hands clasped together and head bobbing like a water lift. He rattled out an enquiry in Arabic and though Arnau was sure that he knew two or three of the words the man used, he was far too tired to consider any attempt at translation or reply. Instead, he placed all his trust in the old *wazir* who had proved to be correct at every turn thus far.

'Abu Mansur?'

The grey-bearded man looked as though he might argue for a moment, frowning as he looked Arnau up and down. Then he gave a strangely enigmatic smile and nodded. 'Abu Mansur. See. Knight from *wazir*, yes?'

The young Templar nodded, relief flooding through him. Despite everything, he had harboured a faint worry that the horse would not be here and he would fail at the very end, but the emir's man had proved true and good once more. The man with the pointy beard led Arnau through the stables into an enclosed stall, where the young sergeant was overwhelmed to see that his benefactor had thought of everything.

His horse was already saddled and she was a magnificent grey, some fourteen hands tall, with a darker mane and tail. She had already been saddled and tacked up, Arab style. But more than this, a pack pony stood ready in the same stall, tethered and with saddlebags already in place and filled with provisions. On the bench to one side lay a chain shirt, pointed gleaming helm, green *burnous* and a sword with a soldier's belt, even a pair of good heavy boots. The *wazir* had given him not only a steed, but a disguise and gear for his journey.

Arnau found himself thanking not only God, but also the old *wazir* at the palace, the older man in this stable, and even Allah, in his outpouring of gratitude. He was hardly surprised to realise that he was actually crying with both relief and thanks.

He began to strip from his damp clothes and the little man made no attempt to leave and grant him privacy. Arnau didn't care. He was alive and safe, and now about to climb into dry clothes and tuck into whatever food the *wazir* had had packed for him. His promise to deliver the message to the island's self-exiled leader now seemed a small price to pay for such generosity. As he dressed once more, he gestured to the stable owner.

'The emir. His villa. Al-Fabulous?'

The grey beard's eyebrow rose and he gave a smile. 'Al-*Fabia.*'

'Yes. Where is it?'

'Al-Fabia. Musuh Bunyula.' He pointed, and Arnau estimated it to be north-east, back towards those mountains he had crossed when he arrived with Balthesar. Nodding his thanks as he dressed, Arnau continued to repeat to himself his new mantra.

Al-Fabia. Musuh Bunyula.

Al-Fabia. Musuh Bunyula.

Al-Fabia. Musuh Bunyula.

There he would find the emir, and for the sake of all right-thinking folk of any faith on these islands, he would persuade that clever, strong man to return and fight for his throne. And maybe, just maybe, the emir would be able to find Balthesar, too.

To the emir's estate, then…

CHAPTER SIXTEEN

THURSDAY, 10 JUNE 1199

1 P.M.

The journey took far longer than it really should have done. By the time Arnau climbed the last slope towards his destination, he surmised that he had only actually travelled some ten miles or so from Madina Mayūrqa, yet he had probably ridden more than twice that, maybe even three times as far, though by a very winding and curious route. Moreover, he had stopped regularly and once, cautiously, for the night.

Taking his cue from Balthesar even in the old man's absence, he had left the city by the coast, laying a false trail, should anyone manage to identify him leaving Madina, however unlikely that might be. Then, to be absolutely sure, he'd ducked off the road, spent two hours as night set in waiting until anyone who might be following him passed, then doubled back and skirted Madina's walls once more at half a mile's distance before passing into the hills in the island's heart. There he had camped beneath a tree for the night in a nicely hidden dell. He had explored the packs on the pony and discovered everything he could want for a journey. He had set up his tent and cooked a hearty meal and then lay there on his side and let his aches and injuries heal a little more in a warm, comfortable bedroll.

Though his shoulders were sore and would be for a long time now after being suspended in the cellar, and his throat still felt scratchy, it was the stripe of raw scabbing on his buttocks that caused the most discomfort, for every bounce in the saddle had brought fresh pain. He had forgone ease of riding in favour of dulling the pain, and wadded up two blankets between saddle leather and braies to dull the shock. Still his backside felt as though it had been minced when he rested for the night.

After so long as his companion, the hole left by Balthesar's disappearance was tangible and left Arnau with far too much opportunity to think. Throughout the ride over late afternoon and evening, he had worked through things with a depth and concentration that had been impossible during his imprisonment and tense flight. They had come to Mayūrqa seeking an old bone, and it had been only Balthesar's will that kept them to their quest as danger closed in around them over the days.

But things had changed now. Arnau's repeated fears that they had been chasing ghosts when they should have been running for home seemed to have been borne out, for though the emir had promised them information on the relic, he had now been forced from his palace into exile and the island was under the de facto rule of a monster. There would be no chance to pursue their quest further.

And all that had taken a secondary place now in Arnau's mind, for his primary concern had become the Lion of Alarcos. The man was clearly intending to pursue his vengeance against Balthesar to the ends of the earth, and Arnau and everyone close to him would forfeit their life in that mission. The Lion had to be stopped.

He tried to reason that it was not personal. The Lion needed to be removed for so many reasons. The *wazir* had been quite correct and quite clear that the emir needed to return and the Lion removed for the future peace and security of these once calm and tolerant islands. He needed to be stopped before Mayūrqa became a bastion of Almohad power in the middle of the sea and a haven for seaborne raiders that would plague the Christian coastline. He had to be removed before he purged every soul that meant something to Balthesar, including all those wondrous souls at Rourell. It was clear that he had to be stopped. But deep down, a small, cankered part of Arnau's soul knew that the Lion had to die because of what he had done, and what he had planned to do, to Arnau.

That, now, was his mission. He would, as the *wazir* asked, persuade the emir with all his will to return and face down the

Lion. It was the dying agonised face of the Lion of Alarcos that Arnau pictured as he slipped into slumber that night.

The next morning he had felt a little easier, physically at least. Stiff from his exertions in the escape and the ensuing ride, of course, but his shoulders were on the mend and his backside healing, with the best part of a day having passed. He had packed his camp up into the saddlebags and set off once more, determined now to find the emir and begin the task of bringing down the Lion somehow. Knowing that he had to find the rural estate somewhere north-east of Madina, he then made his way back down out of the hills, cutting back across the plain, zagging where he had zigged the previous day.

There had been a moment of panic that morning when he realised that he could not remember the names the *wazir* and the stable master had given him, and it was only after an hour's riding that it came back to him. He had grumbled and snarled at his own stupidity and finished by announcing, 'Fabulous. Now I don't know where I'm going.' But that brought back *Al-Fabulous*. Another half-hour's cycling through every permutation of sounds he could think of brought him *Al-Fabia*, and he was content that this was the place. *Moos Banal* was the best he could manage for the area in which it was to be found, and he knew it was not correct, but he simply couldn't get any closer.

He had passed across what appeared to be the main road through the island between Madina and Al-Bulānsa, and stopped in a small village half a mile to the far side whose name he could neither read nor pronounce. The locals there seemed fascinated by a man dressed in the emir's colours but with a mainland accent and no command of Arabic, though they seemed eager to help nonetheless. Here he tried Al-Fabia a few times with the local peasants, and then moved on to Moos Banal, which raised some mirth before the clarification that he referred to Musuh Bunyula. This, a farmer explained in incomprehensible Arabic with plenty of gestures and a pointed finger, lay in a valley to the north of the village, perhaps five miles distant. Thanking the man, Arnau moved on.

The route indicated was clear enough. While there were plenty of other valleys to be found in this area on the edge of the mountains, this particular one was wide and deep, and though it naturally narrowed as it marched north, it also became impressively deeper with towering peaks to each side, the slopes terraced expertly to grow fruit, olives and grain. Small farms were dotted around, and he passed into another village perhaps two miles into the valley, and asked for directions once more. He learned that the village was *in* Musuh Bunyula, while the town of Bunyula itself lay a mile up a side valley to the east from the village.

Al-Fabia, though, lay ahead. Through much gesturing, Arnau surmised that the emir's estate lay at the head of this valley on a hill a further two miles away, where the road curved to the left, heading for a place named Sûlyâr. One of the villagers offered to guide him, and though he declined gratefully, he distributed a few of the coins that had been thoughtfully provided by the *wazir* among these folk who had been so much help. He was all but forced to stay for a pre-noon meal, and then thanked them all and left as the local *imam* began to call to the *dhuhr* prayer. Grateful as he was for their hospitable nature, Arnau remained aware that his passage would be remembered and the trail would remain for anyone who happened out this way seeking the escaped Templar, even if he was dressed as one of the emir's men.

Consequently, rather than heading the way they had indicated, he explained that he had something to do at Sûlyâr first, and, leaving the locals thus confused, headed out of the village across the valley. At the far side, where he found another farmstead, he asked for directions to Sûlyâr, laying as much of a false trail as he could manage. A mile up the valley, he crossed back, rejoined the road, and started up the hill to what could only be Al-Fabia.

It was mid-afternoon, a day after he had languished in the dark, licking his wounds, when he climbed the final slope to the emir's rural retreat.

Al-Fabia was impressive. A complex of golden walls with delicate arched windows and balconies topped by red-tiled roofs, it was easily the size of a substantial country house, and the estate itself was surrounded by a high barrier, though it appeared to be a simple wall rather than a fortified one with a rampart walk atop, and the only guard visible was a man in a single slender tower at one corner, surveying the surroundings. As Arnau turned off the main road and climbed the long white drive lined with slender pines in ordered rows, the man atop the tower clanged a bell, and by the time the young Templar slowed his horse and pony some twenty yards from the ornate door, it had swung open and two green-clad men stood before it.

Arnau reined in and dismounted with a hiss of pain at his various aches and injuries, stamping life back into his feet and wondering if his posterior would ever be a friend to the saddle again. Clinging on to the reins, he used his other hand to sweep the helmet from his head and announced in Aragonese Spanish that he had come from Madina and required an audience with the emir on behalf of his *wazir*.

The two guards exchanged interested looks and one retreated inside. Arnau stood there for some time under the scrutiny of the other guard, wondering whether he was likely to be admitted, wondering whether the emir would want to see him, wondering even whether the guard had understood him or had simply gone to find someone who spoke his language.

Finally, the guard reappeared and fell into position by the door. Heavy, booted footsteps clumped inside the building, increasing in volume as they neared the door. Arnau's mind cast back and he recalled the emir from their one encounter in the palace throne room. His memory of the man included soft calfskin shoes and a light tread. This, he was sure, was not the emir, and he braced himself to argue his case and demand an audience with the emir from whatever soldier was coming to deny him.

He opened his mouth to forestall any barrage of Arabic denial from the green-clad, mail-shirted officer who emerged from the doorway and, given the apparel, it took him precious moments to recognise the features of Balthesar beneath the turban, his grey beard neatly trimmed to a short, more Arabian style and his hair hidden beneath the folds of yellow cloth.

Arnau floundered, his voice failing him.

'It would appear that the Lord and Allah both watch over you, Vallbona.'

Arnau stared, and Balthesar's face cracked into a grin. 'I worried for quite some time,' the old man added, 'but I was impotent at Madina, and so I placed my faith in the Lord and he has seen me right once more. Come.'

He rattled something in Arabic to one of the two guards, who nodded and reached for Arnau's reins. The astonished sergeant handed them over and followed the older Templar as he turned and passed back through the arch of the door.

'You came here?' he managed, as they moved into a wide, high vestibule, an open courtyard bathed in the early afternoon sunlight visible ahead.

'I found nothing in the office,' Balthesar said, coming to a halt inside. 'No records specifically relating to the relic, and those to Muhàmmad the First's purge were vague and, I suspect, incomplete for some reason. When you did not swiftly return, I gave up my search and asked a *kuttab* from the desk to find you. He was gone for some time, and I began to worry then. When he returned he confirmed that he could find no trace of you. The bath attendant had not seen you, which was where you had been bound, and there was a rumour flittering around the Al-Mudaina that the Almohad guards had arrested a trespasser. I knew then that Abd al-Azīz had seized you.'

The old man scratched his chin. 'The realisation struck me that if you had been taken, then I would almost certainly follow shortly. They knew where I was, after all. While I deliberated over what could be done for you, I decided that I had to absent myself swiftly from the place they would immediately search. I thanked the men at the desk and left, though I went only a short distance and stepped into a dark corner, where I waited. Sure enough a few minutes later four of the Almohad guards came looking for me. When they were told I had left, they raced away to seal the gates and put out an alarm. I worked through every scenario I could come up with and could simply see no way to find and rescue you, and with you caught, I realised that my time was also up. I had to leave, else we were both caught.'

'As it happens,' Arnau said darkly, 'the Lion was not seeking to capture you any more. He wanted me, for his plans for you have changed and become ever more brutal and dark. I will explain shortly, but how *did* you get out?'

'In the end it was simple and elegant, if I say so myself. I took off my cap, turned my *burnous* inside out so it showed a different colour, wrapped a cloth around my head turban-style and then when the next call to prayer went up a little while later I watched the bulk of the palace staff flood past in a huge group, heading to the grand mosque. They swept past my dark corner, and I slipped in among them and accompanied them out into the city amid the flow, unnoticed by anyone.'

'Clever.'

'I thought so. I changed my clothes for any I could find in the backstreets nearby, may God forgive me for petty thefts, and then spent a couple of hours keeping an eye on the palace to see if you somehow emerged. Finally, when I was left with no conclusion other than you were captive and there was no way to reach you, I did the only thing I could: I sought the emir. I have been here since yesterday evening and the *Sidi* generously allowed me a change of clothes from the vagrant's rags I wore upon my arrival.'

'The emir *is* here, then?'

'He is. We have exchanged pleasantries but he has yet to discuss the relic or Abd al-Azīz with me. I fear he skirts the subject. I shall take you to him and perhaps together we can draw information from him. And then you can explain what you mean about the Lion no longer seeking my head.'

Arnau looked around himself, relieved that he had made it to his destination, had been admitted and, best of all, had been reunited with the old knight. The vestibule was airy and elegant, even in the shadows, with a beautiful coffered wooden ceiling and decorative panels on the walls displaying Arabic script.

'Allah is great. Allah's is the power. There is no other God but Allah,' said Balthesar, noting his gaze.

'I find that faintly offensive.'

Balthesar chuckled. 'Of course you do. And I'm sure the emir is *overjoyed* at the Holy Bible's similar claim. Exodus, chapter twenty, verse three: "Thou shalt not have alien gods before me." Or verse five: "Thou shalt not bow down to them, neither worship them, for I am thy Lord God, a strongly jealous father." Come on, Vallbona. Enough theology. We have much to discuss.'

They walked through the charming courtyard, through another vestibule and then out into the gardens, which Arnau had to admit were certainly the most magnificent gardens in which he had ever found himself. Walkways and long pools, high jets of water and fountains, ornate stepped cascades, neat hedges and lines of exotic-looking trees, with small pavilions here and there set up for seating. The whole place seemed to be built on a number of levels and every time they turned a corner in the gardens, they were treated to a new and unexpected vista.

Several times as they descended the levels, he caught sight of the watchtower with its solitary guard, and he half expected at any moment to hear the bell clang, announcing the approach of the Lion of Alarcos and his men, hunting their escaped prisoner. Yet no bell rang out and no army arrived.

They paused at the bottom of a flight of stairs where a green-clad soldier impeded them until Balthesar spoke to him and gained them access to the estate's master.

The emir sat on an octagonal patio at one end of a long esplanade, his seat offering an excellent view down the valley back towards the coast. A dozen guards stood close by, near enough to react to danger but not close enough to be intrusive. A small table held a bowl of fruit and a jug of water with ice floating in it. Arnau tried not to puzzle over how they had managed to find ice in this balmy climate and instead turned as they approached and peered down the valley. He half expected to see Madina from here. Still half expected to see a small column of Almohad soldiers, too, though in fact he could see neither, just the beauty of this splendid location.

Balthesar greeted the emir and the two exchanged words briefly in Arabic before the island's ruler rose and bowed his head to Arnau, who bent at the waist in respectful response. Then, the old brother pressed for something in rattled Arabic, which seemed to irritate the emir, who waved him aside. Still, Balthesar insisted and finally, with a resigned slump, the emir turned to Arnau. His face changed suddenly to an expression of companionable interest.

'You escaped the clutches of the Almohad intruders, then, young Templar? I am suitably impressed. I myself slipped away, narrowly avoiding a similar fate.'

Arnau sighed. 'I did not escape without aid, Majesty. It was your *wazir* who found me bound in a cellar, tortured for information. He freed me and explained how I could exit the palace through the slave tunnels and out into the private dock. He also supplied me with horse and uniform and I travelled here by a roundabout route to discourage pursuit, carrying a message for you from him.'

'And what does my faithful *wazir* say?'

'He begs you to return to Madina Mayūrqa, Majesty, and retake your throne from the Lion of Alarcos.'

The emir nodded slowly. 'Of course, the Lion does not actually sit upon my throne, young man, for all the power he currently exerts. He threatens to rule, but he does not yet do so. Not while I live as emir, which is precisely why I took myself out from under his grasp.'

Arnau shrugged. 'An absent ruler is powerless, while a present usurper controls all. Look at what happened in England just a few short years ago: their king held captive by Duke Leopold and his despicable brother ruining the country in his absence. You cannot allow a similar situation to develop here.'

The emir looked at Balthesar. 'The young man is almost as persuasive as you, *Qātil wari'a*. You teach him well.'

The old knight laughed. 'He was taught by a better man than I. But he is correct, *Sidi*. Blunt, but correct. The longer you leave

Abd al-Azīz in command in Madina, the more power will drain from you until you are little more than an empty title and the Almohads rule these islands.'

'What you ask is neither practical, nor even possible, for all its truth,' the emir replied sadly. 'Do you believe that if I could have retained a hold on my throne, I would have left the city and exiled myself here?'

'Why, though?' demanded Arnau. 'If your *wazir* thinks you can fight back, why not?'

'Because he is an able administrator, but not a politician or a warrior, and the practicalities of what such an action would entail escape him. While I am here there is still a chance, young Templar. If I return to Madina, though, I will die, and then there will be no impediment to Abd al-Azīz's rise. He ships in men daily now, bolstering his force while my own army diminishes as men defect to him. And I had precious few to rely upon even before they began to seek his approval. Earlier in the year, I launched a campaign. Did you know of this?'

Arnau and Balthesar both shook their heads.

'It was my presumption that brought about Almohad interest in the first place. They controlled the island of Yabisah sixty miles south-west, which had historically been ruled from Mayūrqa, and so I launched a campaign to seize it. I mistakenly believed that it was of such little value to the caliphate that they would surrender it rather than devote strength to its defence, since they were still consolidating against the north. I was wrong. They fought like lions and threw together an armada from the mainland with which they massacred my invading force. I failed to take the island and in doing so lost the bulk of my veteran fighting men, while drawing the ireful attention of the caliph.'

Arnau shivered at the thought of such a disaster.

'So you see, I have only a diminished guard now. I do not have the strength to fight off the Almohads if they decide to come to Mayūrqa in force, while they have a sizeable garrison on Yabisah. Military action is simply not possible without the support of another leader, which is why I sought Aragon's aid – in vain, sadly. I have treaties with Pisa and Genoa, but only commercial ones. They will not supply men or ships for my cause. No, we cannot fight the caliph. But as long as I stay in Madina I risk a knife in the night, and my death will leave Abd al-Azīz unopposed. I stayed as long as I could, but with the failure of the Aragonese embassy and the rise in strength of Abd al-Azīz, things were becoming untenable. Two nights ago, I narrowly avoided meeting my maker when one of my own guard, his loyalty swayed by Almohad coin, tried to slip a knife in my ribs. I left that morning, taking only those men of whom I could be certain.'

Balthesar nodded. 'It is a thorny problem. Madina is not safe for you. And perhaps Aragon could be persuaded to aid you, especially with the aid of the order, but such help would not come swiftly, for the Christian kings will not risk weakening their southern borders for your sake. No aid will come in time to help you against the Lion.'

'Murder,' Arnau said suddenly.

'What?' Balthesar turned a frown upon him, and the emir too furrowed his brow.

The young sergeant shrugged. 'If you were murdered in your sleep, you say the island would fall unopposed to the Lion of Alarcos.'

'Yes. Mayūrqa would become a vassal of the caliph.'

'But the same is as true of him as of you. He is the one with the authority in Madina, who draws troops over from this other island and seeks to supplant you. Without him, there will be no more ships brought and his men will still not significantly outnumber you. If the Lion were to die, you would regain your throne without a great deal of effort, I believe.'

Balthesar and the emir shared a look, then the older knight turned to Arnau once more. 'What you suggest is not only against the rules of our order, but it is forbidden by all ethical powers, both Christian and Moorish. War can be justified, but murder is still murder. You could be expelled from the order for even suggesting it.'

'No, Balthesar. Perhaps according by law and custom it is forbidden, but by ethical codes it is not. You once told me that the Order of the Temple was not about Christian and heathen – it was about protecting the good from the wicked. And if the death of a wicked man protects the good on a grand scale, then that is the very duty of the order. That is why the order exists, is it not?'

Balthesar chuckled. 'I fear you missed your vocation, young Vallbona. You should have studied law.'

'Is it not?' pressed Arnau.

'I suppose it is,' the older knight agreed. 'Though it still sits badly with me, for regardless of the reason, murder is still murder and I will not be a party to knives in the dark. That is not the Christian way.'

'Nor will I,' Arnau said. 'And in fact, the shadowy death of the man would not be enough, I think. He has to be *seen* to die, and to die hard and for the right reasons. I used the wrong term. It is not a murder, but an *execution*, of which I speak.'

'What are you suggesting?' the emir probed.

'We need to kill the Lion of Alarcos, man to man, in the open and both armed.'

'A duel?' Balthesar frowned. 'You cannot believe he would accept such a proposition?'

'No, probably not. Se we must corner him and force him into it.'

The old knight chewed on his lip. 'You seem curiously keen on this, Vallbona. Little more than a day ago, you wanted nothing more than to flee Mayūrqa altogether and abandon our quest.'

Arnau's face hardened. 'It's astounding what a few hours of torture will do. It rather focuses one's mind. I would love to be back in Rourell, and I still believe our quest to be a failure, but mark my words: if it is remotely possible to leave this island having sent the Lion of Alarcos to his grave, then I will not board a ship until it is done.' The determination that had been growing on his journey from Madina was now burning like a brand.

The emir smiled. 'You are a rare jewel, young Templar. Such valour. Beware the lure of vengeance, though. It is a heady drug, but like all drugs, it leaves you hollow and poor in the end.'

Arnau shook his head. 'Revenge is a drive, certainly, but this is more than that. This is duty. It is right. It is necessary.' *And after all, revenge was what had turned the Lion of Alarcos into the hollow monster he was.*

Balthesar folded his arms. 'You are correct, I think. But it needs careful planning, and it needs to be a proper response to a usurping noble. He needs to be dealt with formally, and the emir here should be present in the city, ready to step in and take control, suppressing any dissent when it happens. We need to be seen to be doing the emir's work, not our own.'

'We?' Arnau said archly.

'Of course.'

'And what of your own quest – *our* quest,' Arnau reminded him. 'What of the relic?' he turned to the emir. 'Will you still give us the arm of Saint Stephen if we do this?'

A look crossed the emir's face now, and it took Arnau a moment to realise what it was: guilt. His brow furrowed, and he bit his sore, tender lip. 'There *isn't* one, is there? The relic. It doesn't exist.'

The emir nodded slowly. 'It did not take long to find the record. The clerks located it swiftly. The bone was taken away in the purge of Muhàmmad and added to the rest of the confiscated Christian artefacts, which were classed as refuse and dumped somewhere. Their location will forever be a mystery, for the location of their disposal is not recorded. They could be anywhere on Mayūrqa, or even out to sea.'

Arnau huffed. 'You found this out straight away. Were you planning on telling us this, or continuing to hold the information against us aiding you?'

Balthesar leaned in. 'I believe the emir intended to show us the record. It was removed from the office and taken to him. That was why I could not locate it in my search. But it matters not, right now. The relic is gone and that quest is over. And whether we could ever find it or not, we would still lend our aid to the emir, because it is the right thing to do. Do you disagree?'

There was a difficult silence as the three men looked at one another, the emir oddly chastened, Arnau simmering, Balthesar determined. Finally, Arnau nodded. 'You are right. We should help the emir. And I never believed we would find the arm anyway. What we are doing now is far more important than the reason we came here in the first place. You kept telling me to have faith, and I do. I think your whole quest was always a fool's errand, but I see now how God set us upon the path so that we could be here to do his true work and battle the evil to be found on Mayūrqa.'

Balthesar straightened, his face working through a number of expressions before settling on a smile. 'Faith. 'Tis an odd thing, eh, Vallbona? We must plan our course of action, then, and afterwards you can tell me why the Lion no longer hunts me.'

CHAPTER SEVENTEEN

FRIDAY, 11 JUNE 1199

10.30 A.M.

It felt like war – like a campaign of invasion, if only on a minimal scale. The emir's guard numbered less than fifty on the rural estate, those men upon whom he claimed he could faithfully rely, and they had set out as a small military column, armed and armoured for trouble, at dawn. The dust from the road rose like a grey curtain behind their horses as the party closed on the walls of Madina once more, the emir and his close advisers to the fore, his guard behind, including Balthesar and Arnau, both still clad in mail and green *burnous.*

This was not what Arnau had ever envisaged upon taking his vows. Far from defending Christian pilgrims from the machinations of wicked men, he was now dressed in the colours of a prince of the Moors, denying his own cross as he prepared to fight both against the crescent and *for* the crescent. Would Lütolf have agreed to do such a thing? He doubted it, though somehow in Balthesar's company such things seemed so reasonable, so acceptable. He shuddered to think what the preceptrix would think. And yet, as he had reasoned a hundred times since he had dressed that morning, no matter that he now wore green instead of black, he was still fighting for the good against the evil. And that was what counted. Still, a small part of him yearned to strip this *burnous* from his torso and return to the red cross of the order.

So much could go wrong. The success of the day relied upon the persuasiveness of the emir himself, the loyalty of his people, the strength and stealth of the two Templars, and even, when it came down to it, basic luck.

The first obstacle would be the city walls. Nominally, the emir still had authority in Madina, and certainly his *wazir* held official control in the city in his absence. But the fact remained that the real power in Madina was the Almohad lord Abd al-Azīz, and if his influence and power had grown sufficiently, it was at least possible that he could seal the city against its own ruler.

Thus it was that Arnau felt the tension rise as they approached the gate. It was late morning now and plenty of people filled the road, surging in through the gate on foot or on horseback, unburdened or bearing baskets or hauling carts of goods, the two green-clad men at the gates only occasionally taking an interest in someone who drew their attention.

As the emir's party approached the gate, two riders moved out in front of their lord to make sure the populace moved respectfully out of their ruler's path, and as the crowd parted the gate guards peered at the approaching group. Arnau tensed yet further, his teeth indenting his lower lip behind the chain mail veil attached to the pointed steel helm. Not all the soldiers were so veiled, but some were, and Arnau felt considerably more comfortable behind the mask than in open view.

The last of the public shifted aside and waited on the verge, close to the riverbank, leaving the party of guardsmen with their master closing on the soldiers at the gate. Arnau watched between the heads of the men in front, half expecting a shout to go up from those above the parapet and the gate itself to swing shut. It came as a great relief when the two soldiers at the side of the huge doorway instead bowed deeply. The emir nodded his acknowledgement to them and the party rode through the gatehouse and into the city without incident.

Inside, they passed first between the stable where Arnau had first collected his horse the previous day and a small knot of houses, then into open arable land, spotted with fruit orchards. Gradually they moved on into the urban centre, approaching the bridge across the river, the heart of Madina rising on the slope beyond. The people in the city streets swept out of the way of the mounted party, waiting with respect, surprise and thankfully joy in many cases, as their ruler passed by. The city's residents came to their doorsteps and windows to see their emir as he returned to his palace.

Up the slope they rode, approaching the Al-Mudaina. Arnau shifted uncomfortably in the saddle. Since he was ostensibly a soldier of the emir, hidden among others, he had foregone the two folded blankets between his rump and the leather, but had managed one smaller garment folded beneath him which did not look as out of place yet relieved the worst of his posterior pain. Fortunately those wounds had healed further overnight and he was no longer in quite the same pain or discomfort. Even his shoulders had recovered a little, though they'd stiffened up again with clutching his reins during the ride.

The young sergeant's eyes now swivelled up to the walls of the palace. Men in green stood there along with men in black and white. Unlike the city gate, which stood open during the day in times of peace, the palace gates naturally remained shut until they were opened for someone, then closed again. The question was whether they would open for their master today. The green figures atop the walls did outnumber the others, but that was no guarantee that their loyalties continued to lie with the emir. The sheer power of the Lion of Alarcos would have swayed more of the island's people than mere gold.

It was a bad sign, if not an entirely unexpected one, when the gate failed to swing open at the approach of the emir's party. The wide street outside and the gardens that lay beyond, between the palace and that pleasant little tavern, had been thronged with people as the riders first crested the slope but now, as they bore down on the closed gate, the entire area had miraculously emptied as though the populace expected some kind of fight. They might get one, too, pondered Arnau as the lead riders came to a halt before the gate, the rest of the party slowing behind them.

The number of figures atop the wall had gradually increased over the past minute, and there were clearly officers and higher palace functionaries among them.

One of the leading riders untied his chain veil, allowing it to drop to the side, cleared his throat and barked out a long order, which included among its commands the name 'Abd-Allāh ibn Ishāq ibn Ghāniya', and the words 'emir' and 'Mayūrqa'. A command to open the gate, as Arnau knew full well. Though he still could translate only a few basic words of the language, he was comfortable with whatever was said here, since it had all been planned in his own tongue back at the Al-Fabia estate, with Arnau present and participating.

Silence greeted the order and Arnau could feel the tension rising in the air, prickling his skin, as men atop the gate huddled and argued. The gate remained resolutely shut. The rider who had spoken was counting under his breath. His lips moved with each iteration, and finally he took another deep breath and then barked out a second order, this time adding a little force and sounding more than a touch angry.

The arguing atop the wall became more frantic, and many of the figures disappeared from view. Arnau felt sure he heard a muffled scream, gagged as it emerged. He noticed the parapet had emptied of black-and-white figures, though whether that was a good sign or bad, Arnau couldn't tell. Almost certainly things would follow the course predicted by the emir and Balthesar. It was just a matter of whether they were admitted to the palace first or not.

The time was almost upon him. Arnau glanced across at Balthesar, who gave an almost imperceptible nod. The young sergeant slipped his left foot from the stirrup and made sure he was loose in the saddle and his sword was swinging free in its sheath. Lastly, he checked the hang of the weapon they had each been gifted at the estate.

Whatever had been discussed atop the wall, the result clearly came down in favour of the emir, for moments later the gate to the Al-Mudaina groaned open. The column of riders began to move once more, guards to the fore as well as behind, four in particular staying very close to the emir with their heart-shaped shields up, ready to protect him from any would-be assassin with a bow.

Arnau and Balthesar, close to the rear of the column, readied themselves. As they neared the gate in line with everyone else, Arnau passed over his reins to the man beside him and, with only moderate pain in the rump, slipped from the saddle and down to the ground with a gentle thud and shush of mail that was lost in the din of the walking horses. Balthesar did the same a moment later, and then they were both off and moving.

Walking swiftly along beneath the palace walls, the two men were virtually invisible from the parapet unless the guards leaned over to look straight down. That, added to the fact that the bulk of attention would now be on the head of the column and the emir himself who had emerged through the gate into the gardens within, meant that the two Templars were as hidden from the palace soldiers as they could hope to be. Still, they hurried. Time was almost as important as stealth. The road and gardens had cleared of the bulk of pedestrians and those who would be watching the palace and the activity with interest would likely make nothing of two of the emir's guard separating from the column and moving off down the slope.

The last of the riders disappeared inside the palace behind them, and the gate clonked shut with ligneous finality. This was it. They had gambled on several things being the case, else what they were attempting would fail. There was nothing they could do now but carry out the plan and pray that all fell into place. As they headed west, down the slope towards the river and the corner of the Al-Mudaina, Arnau could hear the emir's raised voice in the gardens of the palace. He couldn't understand the words, of course, but it mattered not, for he knew what the man was saying. That had all been part of the plan.

All ambassadors, nobles, servants and soldiers of the Almohad caliph were being ordered to leave Mayūrqa on those ships of theirs docked in the port. They were being given just one hour to do so. The emir was reminding them, and his own people besides, that Mayūrqa was an independent *taifa*, with no fealty and no obligation to the caliphate, and was declaring that any attempt at resistance and any refusal to depart would be considered a criminal act and a provocation to war. That, of course, would not worry the Lion of Alarcos or his men too much, and Arnau couldn't imagine any of them complying readily, but it would certainly make any of the emir's former supporters who had thrown in their lot with the Almohads think again. Loyalties would waver once more with control of Madina and the island itself in the balance. To strengthen his case, the emir claimed publicly that the Crown of Aragon had taken a personal interest in the island's future and that with Aragon, Genoa and Pisa in support, Mayūrqa would become a bastion of independence. A complete untruth, of course. Genoa and Pisa had no intention of supplying men or ships in the defence of the island, their interest being purely commercial, and Aragon would sympathise and perhaps even speak in favour of the emir, but they would simply not commit militarily. Still, the crown had sent ambassadors, and most of the palace's population would know only that, and not what had been concluded with them. Moreover, the Aragonese ship would now be long gone from the dock, and so no Christian mainlander would be there to deny it.

The emir finished his announcement and silence fell in its wake. Arnau and Balthesar, though, would hear nothing further, for they had rounded the corner of the Al-Mudaina's walls and were now hurrying down, no longer worrying about stealth or noise, towards the small postern gate that abutted the walls and gave out into the port. As they neared, they slowed. A single guard stood beside this gate, which was a military one and not open for the public. They could have made for the main port gate, of course, but that would add precious minutes. Instead, as they approached the small postern, Balthesar rattled off something authoritative in Arabic, and once more Arnau heard the emir's name invoked. The guard, clearly still a man loyal to his true master, nodded and swung open the gate, and the two Templars, disguised as the emir's men, emerged into the corner of the city port beneath the walls of the Al-Mudaina.

It had been a gamble moving this far through the city with the emir and then trying to disappear right outside the palace walls on their clandestine mission, but with every discarded plan it had become clearer that it would be the only feasible way. They could not have been certain whether they would make it through the city walls or safely through the streets on their own, whatever they wore. Two of the emir's men on their own might be suspected by the current power in Madina, but in any other guise they would be in even greater danger, their descriptions undoubtedly having been circulated by the Almohad lord to every pair of watchful eyes in the city. The only way they could realistically guarantee their safe arrival at this place was among the emir's men.

And so now the emir was in the Al-Mudaina itself, awaiting compliance with his demand, or more likely lack thereof. There was no din of violence arising from within the walls, although all sound would be muffled and distant from here. But still, no signal blast had rung out, and so the Lion of Alarcos remained in control of the palace proper. Both the emir and Balthesar had been convinced that even if they were admitted through the outer gate of the palace, the building itself, shaped around its small courtyard, would be sealed against them on Almohad orders. If the soldiers loyal to the emir that remained there wished to throw open the doors to their master, they would have to overcome the might of the Lion's men to do so.

There was, therefore, an impasse. The Lion would not depart and abandon his plan, and the emir did not have enough might to storm his own palace, and so the Almohads remained besieged inside the building, the emir locked outside, facing one another as the hour the emir had given his enemy continued to count down.

An hour should be long enough, though, unless something went horribly wrong.

Balthesar now stepped aside and allowed Arnau to take the lead, as he was the man who knew this area. Feeling cold nerves tingling at the memory of the last time he had been here, the young Templar pushed on, walking fast around the edge of the port, past a couple of old men mending a net and out onto the breakwater. Here, they clambered across the large, heavy stones that comprised the sea defence until they were close to the palace's perimeter wall and the waterside of the private docking facility.

Arnau slowly turned the corner first, pausing at the wall to look ahead at their destination. He gave a strangled groan.

'What is it?' Balthesar hissed from behind.

'I thought the dock would be empty now the Aragonese ship has gone, but there's an Almohad ship in there instead.'

'People?'

Arnau peered around again. There seemed to be precious little activity. Likely the ship had been in dock since the Christian vessel left the previous day, and all loading or unloading would already have occurred. All there would be on the ship was whatever skeleton crew or watchmen had been set there by its captain. A few figures moved around aboard. He could also see a couple of palace functionaries at the far end of the port messing with a pile of baskets. What was happening on the far dock, he did not know, for it lay behind the ship from here.

'Not many.' He paused, listening carefully. Whatever the men on the ship and those around the other end of the dock were doing, he could not hear it over the lap of waves, groans and clonks of the ship timbers and the cacophony of screeching from the ever-present gulls. He thanked the Lord for that small mercy. If he could not hear anything of them, then they in turn would not hear him.

'We shall just have to chance it until we get to your warehouses,' Balthesar whispered.

Arnau nodded, largely to himself. Dressed as they were, they had legitimate reasons to be within the palace, yet there were certain places and certain activities that would draw unwanted attention. Leaping from the port breakwater to the private dock was one of them.

Moab is the cauldron of mine hope. Into Idumea I shall stretch forth my shoe, aliens being made friends to me.

Who shall lead me forth into a strong city? Who shall lead me forth into Idumea?

Whether not thou, God, that hast put us away; and, God, shalt thou not go out in our virtues?

Fortified with prayer, Arnau took a deep breath. He rounded the corner of the wall and without pause ran three steps and jumped to the private dock. He landed with a thud and a jingle of mail and harness and was off and running. The morning sun was high enough that its glow filled the dock uninterrupted and there was no real shadow to keep to. This was about speed now, anyway. Arnau hurried off to the large doorway of the nearest of the two huge warehouses on the western dock. Once inside, he quickly scanned the place and heaved a sigh of relief to find it empty. As Balthesar hurried in behind him, he then peered out towards the Almohad ship in harbour. There was no more activity aboard than there had been while he prayed on the dock. It appeared they had not been seen, and the alarm had not been given.

'We cannot hope to maintain this sort of luck,' Balthesar hissed. 'Something will go sour shortly. Be prepared.'

Arnau nodded. He was already sure of that and prepared for it. For now, the next step was to move to the far dock beyond the ship, and that would be a simple bare-faced stroll. The two Templars nodded to one another and, adjusting their equipment, they emerged from the warehouse at a casual pace, striding out onto the dock and making for the end, where the workers unloaded the baskets.

The Lord God remained watchful over them, for the bored and tired-looking slaves at work gave them not even a glance, continuing on with their mind-numbing work as they strolled past them. The two interlopers moved past the stern of the Almohad vessel and rounded it, heading for the far dock.

'One guard,' hissed Arnau, spotting a black-and-white figure not far from the door whence he had emerged yesterday, battered and bruised, and for which they now made.

'He cannot be allowed to raise the alarm,' Balthesar reminded him, somewhat unnecessarily. Arnau nodded. There was, of course, a good chance that the small door that led into the slave tunnels was locked anyway. A *lot* of today's activity depended upon luck. But the emir had reasoned that with the disappearance of Balthesar and Arnau, there was little need for that door to be so secured, and furthermore the slaves used it several times a day. To keep it locked would be inconvenient, and posting a guard before it would probably be deemed enough. Arnau prayed he had been right. But even if the door *was* unlocked, one call from the guard and someone could rush to lock it, even if he didn't slip inside and do so himself.

'One guard,' Arnau said again, 'but I can see three men on the ship. Can they raise the alarm?'

'Possibly,' Balthesar replied. 'They don't have the same authority, but enough clamour and they'll get the attention of someone who does. I fear we must deal with them.'

'Then the time is now, but the guard has to come first.'

They continued to stride forward, and the Almohad soldier over near the door turned his mailed face to them, expression hidden by the chain veil. Arnau could not see the eyes within that shadowy gap between helm and veil, but he could picture them widening in surprise and perhaps horror as the two soldiers of the emir striding towards him suddenly slipped the light, powerful composite bows from the bow-quiver at their belt and drew a narrow-pointed arrow of Damascene style from the far side.

The guard's hand went to his sword hilt, his protective, heart-shaped shield coming up in defence as his head tipped briefly towards the wall top. Somewhat inexpertly, the two Templars pulled back the strings with the unfamiliar thumb hooks. Arnau raised the weapon, closing his eye in the manner he'd done the few times he'd used a bow, hunting in the Catalan woodlands, arrow nocked on the right of the shaft over the thumb, as Balthesar had told him to. Sighting briefly, he released.

The young Templar was unfamiliar with bows in general, for the skill was not one usually taught in the cloisters of the order, and certainly not these strange Arab designs. His arrow, released poorly, struck the stone flags of the dock some two feet in front of the guard, skittering off between his legs in a bounce. Balthesar's, on the other hand, flew true, and as the old man gathered and nocked a second arrow, Arnau noted that the older man was not sighting along the arrow, but raising the bow to chin level, both eyes open, and releasing with an almost instinctive aim. The old knight had fought for decades as a bandit hunter and mercenary among the Moorish armies and likely this was far from the first time he had handled such a weapon.

Balthesar's first arrow would have been a good shot but for the fact that the guard managed to put his shield in the way and the missile tore through fabric and leather and lodged there, the point inside but with insufficient momentum to carry on and pin the shield to its wielder. The guard bellowed something as he brandished the transfixed shield, and Arnau felt cold fear that the warning had now gone up. Even as the older man's second arrow flew free, Arnau nocked and raised his own, feeling oddly uncomfortable with simply visualising his target as he prepared to release.

Balthesar's second shot had been higher this time, while Arnau's had been once more accidentally low, though considerably better this time. The guard reacted urgently and sensibly, his shield rising to ward off the greater threat of the old man's projectile, which would have taken him in the throat had the shield not moved into place and caught the arrow, robbing it of sufficient power to punch through to the inside.

Despite his improved aim, Arnau had been aiming for the man's chest, but the arrow instead thudded into his thigh below his mail shirt's hem. The guard howled in pain, though the cry was somewhat stifled by his veil. Shouts were now also going up from the ship.

'Finish him,' Balthesar snapped as he turned and began loosing expert arrows at the figures visible aboard the docked vessel.

Arnau nodded and simply dropped the bow, drawing his sword. The guard had staggered back but miraculously had not fallen despite the shaft protruding from his thigh, though he was clearly in pain and struggling, his sword dipping and waving as he tried not to collapse.

Arnau was on him in seconds, attacking with uncharacteristic silence, determined to keep the alarm from going up any more than he had to. His sword came down and the guard managed to throw his shield in the way, blocking the blow. The sword thudded into the heart-shaped, decorative shield and left a huge long dent in it.

The guard yelped again as the shield splintered into his arm, possibly breaking it and certainly causing fresh agony.

The blow was enough to fell the man. Driven back and without the strength in his wounded leg to hold him up, the guard fell back with a metallic crash, grunting. Arnau was on him once more like a savage, sword hammering down again and again as the desperate, wounded guard tried to defend himself. The third blow finished it, skimming off the rim of the battered shield and smashing into the man's chest. The blade's edge would never penetrate the chain shirt, of course, but Arnau heard the ribs crack and the man gasped, his arm spasming and the sword falling from his grasp.

Arnau rose. For a moment he contemplated mercy, as a good Christian, but these were not men who deserved mercy. These were invaders and murderers, torturers and usurpers. Arnau snarled and delivered the killing blow not with his blade but with his boot, slamming it down onto the man's chest, where the ribs were already broken. He felt the man's weakened chest collapse under the weight of the sudden blow, organs crushed within.

The guard died in three gasps as Arnau stepped back, half relieved that it was over, half reviling himself for his own brutality. Breathing heavily, he lifted his head. They had made far more noise than he'd intended, but there remained no figures atop the wall above them. Likely what was happening on the other side of the Al-Mudaina was occupying everyone's attention.

He turned, suddenly recalling the men with the baskets who must have seen all this, and noticed that they had disappeared. Perhaps they had rushed inside to give the warning, or perhaps they were cowering out of sight. Likely they would stay as far out of all this as possible. As slaves they probably held no allegiance as such, and if they did it would likely be to the emir in whose uniform Arnau was dressed rather than to the Almohad invader he had killed.

He turned again, to see that only one of the men on the ship remained standing, hands cupped around his mouth, bellowing up to the walls, seeking to warn his countrymen of this new danger. He managed just a few words before Balthesar's arrow struck him in the chest and threw him back to the deck, dying even as he fell. The old knight's arrows were unnervingly accurate, and the sailors were entirely unarmoured.

In moments the two men were alone on the dockside with just corpses for company. Arnau shivered as the old man dropped his bow too, since the weapon would be of little use inside the palace itself. Both men also unfastened their quivers as they hurried over to the small door, letting those too fall away.

The young Templar, once more taking the lead as the man familiar with their route, closed on the door, again intoning that line from Psalm 108.

'Who shall lead me forth into a strong city? Who shall lead me forth into Idumea?'

His fingers fell to the door's handle and he grasped and tried it.

His relief when the door groaned open was expressed in a sigh.

'You can remember the way?'

Arnau nodded. That journey in the choking dark tunnels was ingrained in his memory forever. He could remember every corner and every brick between this door and the cellar in which he'd been incarcerated. 'I can get us past the baths. From there, there was a side passage that led to the public area. If I'm right, that door will emerge somewhere in the long corridor with the wall hangings we've passed through several times outside the baths. From there it should be easy enough to locate the stairs up to the throne room. You think that's where he'll be?'

'It is as good a guess as any,' Balthesar murmured. 'The Lord will see us right. Have faith, Vallbona.'

Arnau threw the old man a sour look, then pulled the door wide and stepped inside.

CHAPTER EIGHTEEN

FRIDAY, 11 JUNE 1199

11.35 A.M.

It took time for the two men's eyes to adjust to the gloom of the passageway, and despite the urgency and importance of their quest, Arnau slowed to a halt just half a dozen paces in.

'What is it?' hissed Balthesar at his shoulder.

Arnau shivered. 'Nothing,' he replied, though it took a supreme effort of will to force his foot another step in. Every pace he traversed of that dark corridor brought him one pace closer to the cellar where the Lion of Alarcos had tortured him, and where he had realised how swiftly he would break. Where he *did* break, in fact, on their very first session of interrogation. Shame, anger, fear and hunger for revenge all flooded through him at the memory of what had happened in these tunnels, and that heady combination made it ever more difficult to push on.

He forced resolve upon himself.

Revenge. Exodus over Matthew. Old Testament over New.

Soothly if the death of her followeth he shall yield life for life, eye for eye, tooth for tooth, hand for hand, foot for foot, burning for burning, wound for wound, sore for sore.

Of the swirling and powerful emotions coursing through him, he grasped hold of the mane of revenge and rode it to the exclusion of the other beasts. Fear, anger and shame swiftly fell behind, and once more he was pacing down the corridor, for of all those feelings that had hit him as he entered this place, revenge was the only one that might drive him forward rather than hold him back.

Picturing the Lion of Alarcos, wide eyed as he clutched a spear that transfixed him through the middle, Arnau felt a silent feral snarl fall across his face and pressed on. He passed several turns or side passages, certain of his course, and quickly felt the rise in temperature and the smoke begin to build as he closed on the baths.

Despite his new-found resolve, he began to wish that he had agreed with the notion that the entire emir's guard could have entered the palace this way and simply taken the complex from below by stealth. Just the two of them entering the place now felt very foolish. The fact remained, though, that they had rejected such a plan for twin reasons: that the emir needed to be seen by his people to do things nobly and honourably, and also that a force of fifty men in these tunnels would be about as stealthy as a drunken ape in a nunnery. It would not have taken much for the Almohad defenders to trap them down here and neutralise any threat they posed.

No, they'd had to go in alone, while the emir was seen to make reasonable and honourable demands at the gate.

Damn it.

Favouring alertness and stealth over protection now they were inside, Arnau unfastened the chain veil with his free hand as he walked, pulling the helmet from his head and dropping it to one side. The roar of the furnaces came thundering in with his hearing freed, and the choking smoke made him momentarily wish he had kept the covering on. His heightened alertness made itself manifest, though, as Arnau noticed the slave before the man even heard him.

The young slave, dressed in poor and basic, hard-wearing clothes to serve in the tunnels, turned in shock as an armoured man in the emir's colours suddenly emerged like some demon from the black cloud of smoke. He cowered back as Arnau bore down on him, face locked in a grimace, soot-stained and furious with a naked blade in his hand.

But Arnau was set upon his course and would be no demon to this man. The two men were not here to kill indiscriminately. Not even to kill Moors, for after all, was he not now working for a Moorish emir as a mercenary sword, much as Balthesar had done in his youth? Today, Arnau was a Templar and a servant of God *second*, and the emir's man first.

Only Almohads would die by his hand today.

The shaking, quivering slave stared as Arnau leaned very close and placed a finger to his lips in the age-old gesture for silence. The slave, baffled but grateful at this seeming reprieve from an agonising death, simply nodded over and over as Arnau slipped past him and a second figure followed, an older man in the process of removing and discarding his helmet.

Ahead, as the smoke began to clear somewhat, Arnau could see the log store and the corner that would carry the passageway back towards the cellars where he had been kept. Despite his sense of purpose, he still faltered for a moment then, shivering at the memories, feeling that pain in his shoulders, his throat, his buttocks, as he peered ahead into the gloom. With great effort, he turned away from that dark place and its darker memories and took the side passage that led to the door he'd spotted during his escape.

He took a deep breath, coughed at the smoke still swirling in the air, and approached the door. The last time he had been here he'd been focused solely on escape and on the directions he had been given by the *wazir*, and so had paid only passing attention to this door, assuming – *determined*, even – that upon escape he would never again set foot in the Al-Mudaina. He had presumed that the door would lead out either into the front of the bath complex where the small store and the changing room stood, or otherwise into the corridor close by, which they had traversed several times over the past few days. He could not, of course, say for sure whether that was truly the case. Moreover, he could not be certain that the door would not be securely locked. Just another aspect of this task that relied upon luck.

He could make out the door in the gloom, largely thanks to the faint light around the edges, but it took some feeling around to locate the lock and handle. There was an empty keyhole, and above it a handle shaped into a slender grip and decorated with geometric patterns. Arnau marvelled once more at the Moorish devotion to art. Even here, in the dark, where only slaves would grip such a handle, still it was delicately and beautifully designed.

His heart in his mouth, aware that here, once more, he was at one of those junctures where simple chance could ruin everything, he reached and gripped the handle, pushing it down. It moved easily without a sound, and as he pulled hard, the door swung open with the gentlest of creaks.

Breath held, teeth clenched, and ready for anything, Arnau stepped through. The corridor into which he emerged was a wide, decorative one, with hangings on the walls displaying the arms of the emir, his dynasty, and every region, town and noble line of Mayūrqa. It was indeed that one that they had used time and again. For a moment as he peered left, past the entrance to the baths and towards the complex of offices where they had spent so much of their time, he thought that by God's grace they had emerged into an empty corridor.

But as he stepped further out and Balthesar appeared from the dark and the smoke behind him, Arnau turned to see a servant in the centre of the passageway, a bundle of folded linens in her arms, her face pale and eyes wide in fright, her mouth opening into a wide O, ready to scream.

Even as the young sergeant felt a momentary panic of indecision, the older knight leaped past him and grabbed the woman, one strong arm pinning her to him, the other slapping across her mouth to stifle the howl of terror that tried to escape. The linen fell to the floor, forgotten, and landed in a heap as Balthesar leaned close to the woman's ear and murmured something to her. Still he held her tight, stifling a scream, until she nodded. When he finally released her, she stepped back and, though clearly still frightened, bowed her head and scurried off.

'We are the emir's,' the old knight explained. 'She is also the emir's. We are not enemies.' Balthesar smiled, and they turned to head into the heart of the palace.

Pausing at each door as they went, and carefully peering ahead, they moved through eerily empty halls and corridors. Arnau felt the tension building as he recognised that they were close to emerging into the courtyard. Clearly all the tension of the emir's arrival and ultimatum had drawn the bulk of the palace's population towards the outer gardens. At the penultimate door Arnau paused, and they could now hear voices in the distance, outside.

At a signal from Balthesar he stopped for a moment, the old man listening intently.

'It is the emir,' the older knight confirmed. 'His deadline draws close. Half an hour has passed and he is reminding them of his demand.' Other voices were raised also. 'There seems to be much heated discussion within the palace buildings. I cannot imagine the Almohads intend to relinquish their position. There is—'

The whispered conversation went unfinished as a figure suddenly rounded the corner of the doorway beside which Arnau lurked as he paid attention to Balthesar. The young sergeant caught the warning in the old man's eye and turned in a flash to see an Almohad warrior in his black-and-white *burnous*, white eyes burning in the darkness of his mailed face. There was no cry of alarm or anger from the man, and even as Arnau prepared to defend himself he surmised that this warrior probably had no idea that these two were anything but ordinary guards from the palace. They wore the emir's colours just like everyone else, after all. He remembered then, though, that they were no longer wearing helmets and their features would most certainly be known by the Lion's men. Moreover, even if he could not be recognised, the fact that these two men of the emir's guard were filthy, faces streaked with soot and sweat, would raise an alarm of some sort in the man.

They were too close for Arnau to immediately bring his sword to bear, which, of course, meant the same applied to the Almohad, and they each reacted on instinct. The enemy warrior reached down and wrenched a small knife with a gentle curve from his belt, preparing to stab the Templar.

Arnau was not armed with any such weapon. His sword hung useless in his hand, too long to swing here. His instinctive act was as effective as it was unwise.

He slammed his head forward, butting the enemy warrior hard in the face.

He regretted the move immediately. The Almohad wore both helmet and chain mail veil, while Arnau's head was bare. His forehead smashed into the mail, and he felt the edges of the man's helmet scrape the skin at his temple even as the links of chain bit into the skin of his face. The pain was shocking, and the only relief from the blow was the fact that the damage must have been equally bad for the man he had butted, as there was a distinct crack, muffled by the veil, and the warrior gasped in shock and pain.

Arnau staggered aside, stunned by the pain in his face, unable to recover fast enough to do anything more, but his unorthodox attack had been enough and he watched the fight end even as he reeled and blinked away the pain. The Almohad similarly staggered, blood soaking the mail of his veil from the ruined face beneath, and he had little chance to do more than sigh with regret as Balthesar, further back and with more room to manoeuvre, simply swung his sword with all his might into the man's torso. The Almohad warrior folded over the blow, which failed to penetrate the mail shirt but pulverised the chest beneath.

The man fell, unable to shout, gasping for breath from his ruined lungs, and the older knight reached out with his free hand to steady Arnau. 'Are you all right?'

'Urgh,' was all the young sergeant could say immediately, reaching up and probing his forehead. His hand came away covered with blood where the chain links had scored bloody lines in his face, but he appeared to have escaped real wounding, and nothing was broken. His mind began to recover from the daze, and he nodded. 'Nothing serious, I think. Am I still pretty?'

Balthesar snorted. 'Prettier, in fact,' he laughed. 'Not that that would be hard. Come on,'

The older man was now in the lead, since they were once more in the open areas of the palace and not the tunnels that only Arnau knew to navigate. They peered around the corner, and the room appeared empty. They could both see the next doorway that led to the small inner courtyard with the lion fountain and the staircase leading up to the higher level. Possibly there was some other way up, but they could not be sure and could hardly afford the time and leisure to thoroughly search the place. Thus they concluded that they must brave whatever dangers lay in the way and take the route to the throne room along which they had been escorted for their interview with the emir.

They passed into that empty room and approached the door. Arnau felt his spirits plummet at the sight of a small knot of nobles standing out in the courtyard, accompanied by soldiers in green and also in black and white.

There was no chance of them reaching and ascending the stairs unnoticed and, with the best will in the world, in the state they were in they were not going to pass as ordinary palace guards without being questioned over the soot and blood. It appeared that the time for stealth had now passed, and the time for bare-faced bravery and confrontation had arrived. Arnau looked at Balthesar, an unspoken question in his eyes, and the older knight nodded. They stepped out into the sunlight, walking with speed and purpose through the doorway, across to the foot of the stairs and then turning to climb them. They did not run, in order to draw as little attention as possible and yet get them as far as possible before the inevitable alarm was raised.

They were on the third step when an angry, alarmed shout went up from the men in the centre of the courtyard. There had been more than a dozen of them and both knights knew that, strong and skilled as they were, two men against twelve or more was a death sentence.

'Run,' barked Balthesar, and they did, pounding up the steps towards the upper floor. Behind them, the Almohad warriors in the courtyard bellowed their war cries and charged after the intruders, two of the green emir's guard joining them. The other green-clad soldiers remained with the nobles in the courtyard, driven to stay either by loyalty to the emir or perhaps by duty to protect the courtiers with them.

At the top of the stairs, the two Templars burst into a wide corridor and Arnau pulled himself up short as Balthesar stopped at the threshold.

'Help me,' the old man said as he swung shut the doors at the head of the stairs. Arnau turned and grasped the other side, heaving the door closed. The doors were more ornate and artistic than robust, designed here in the middle of a palace to be decorative rather than defensive, but there was still a latch and Balthesar dropped it into place just as the soldiers reached the other side.

There was a series of thuds and shouts in Arabic, and the doors shook, bending inwards until only the iron latch prevented them bursting open.

'That won't last long,' Arnau said.

'Not against such force,' agreed Balthesar, 'so let's move.'

They turned and ran along the corridor, but before they could reach the far end, where another flight of stairs led to the antechamber and the throne room, another party of soldiers suddenly emerged from the bottom of the steps and, catching sight of Arnau and Balthesar, shouted and drew their blades.

'Shit,' said Arnau, with deep feeling.

'In here,' the older knight said suddenly, grabbing Arnau's arm and directing him to a side door. For a moment the young sergeant wondered why they were running, but common sense quickly told him. Half a dozen men now lay between them and the stairs, and any time now the far doors' latch would give and the men chasing them would also flood into the corridor. There was simply no hope of fighting their way through that lot.

Balthesar pulled him forward, pushing open the door and slipping through. They were in a vestibule with doors in all the walls, those ahead seeming to be the main ones, larger and more ornate than the others. Balthesar moved quickly, ducking to the right and trying that door. It opened instantly and they found themselves in a small chamber with a narrow stairway leading down. Balthesar closed the door behind them and they ran on, clattering down the steps to the lower level once more, taking the pair ever further from their goal, which worried Arnau.

They emerged at the bottom of the stairs into a gloomy room and Balthesar stopped, finger to his lips. They listened. The door of the vestibule upstairs must have opened, and the soldiers were arguing as they thudded around upstairs, making for the various doors. As quietly as he could manage, the old man paced across the small room and pulled at the door. This one again opened without trouble and with little sound and Balthesar slipped through it, beckoning to Arnau, who followed in a similar manner.

As the young sergeant entered, he was surprised to see three servants or slaves huddled to one side, shying nervously away from the two intruders. Balthesar gestured for Arnau to deal with the door, while the old man held up his hand in a gesture of calm and peace and stepped over to the three figures, speaking calmly and quietly in Arabic.

Arnau closed the door and was immensely relieved to see that it was lockable and that the key sat in the hole. He closed it, turning the key and sealing the pursuers out for now. By the time he had done so, the three servants seemed to have calmed down and were in quiet conversation with Balthesar, nodding here and there as they spoke. Arnau looked about. The room was not large, and was clearly some sort of servants' access. From here a second door led out and, if Arnau's sense of direction and memory were to be trusted, headed off into the areas of the Al-Mudaina where the slaves and servants would be concentrated: store rooms, kitchens and the like. With the stairs leading up to the more noble areas of the palace complex and a trapdoor that should lead down into the cellars, the servants would have easy access to most of the palace from here, enabling them to move without offending their masters with their presence.

Balthesar seemed to come to some agreement with the three and rose, turning to Arnau.

'We must move fast, but we are in luck. God is with us – or perhaps Allah. These three are most loyal to their emir and loathe the Almohad invader. The young man with the beard will lead you by a subtle route to the throne room. The older one will stay here and protest to any who follow that he has not seen us pass this way, buying us precious time.'

Arnau nodded, then his brow folded in concern.

'And what about the third? What about you?'

'We are running out of time, and if we cannot find Abd al-Azīz and put him to the sword, then the emir will be forced into an impossible position, having to besiege his own palace against difficult odds. The girl here will direct me to the gate, where I will find a way to open it for the emir.'

Arnau stared. There would be a score of hardened Almohad soldiers at the gate. How the old Templar could hope to get the gate open, Arnau could not conceive, but there was no time to argue as in that moment of silence there was the muffled and distant, but distinctive, sound of the door at the top of the stairs opening.

'Don't argue, Vallbona. Have faith and go. Find Abd al-Azīz and kill him honourably and openly.'

The bearded young servant crossed to Arnau and gestured to the other door, while the girl led Balthesar over to the trapdoor. The old servant paused but a moment and then unlocked the door to the stairs through which they had entered.

Arnau felt his stomach twist at the fact that they were separating, leaving him alone to face such a dangerous opponent, and also a flicker of irritation at yet another of the older knight's exhortations that Arnau trust to his faith, but there was no time to waste lest the Almohads be on them. He followed the bearded servant as the man crossed to the door and opened it, slipping through. He had to hope and pray that the old man they had left behind managed to convince their pursuers that they had not come this way.

The young sergeant swallowed his nerves as he passed through another room in the servant's wake. He was committed now. Balthesar had gone on his own mission and Arnau was left alone to deal with the Lion of Alarcos, the only hope of reaching him being the servant that led him along. He only hoped that the bearded man could be trusted.

With ever-growing anxiety he followed the slave through corridors and rooms, occasionally passing another slave or servant, none of whom paid the pair any attention beyond mild interest, and was surprised when they emerged into an even smaller courtyard – little more than a light well in the heart of the complex. Here, they passed another pair of slaves who merely nodded acknowledgement of their existence, before reaching a small and functional staircase, which they climbed, emerging once more back inside the palace itself. A long corridor led to another door, and then a second staircase.

They climbed this latest set of steps and at the top the slave turned a handle, opening the door wide and gesturing for Arnau to go through. Gripping his sword tight and holding his breath to steady his nerves, the young Templar stepped through the door.

He was now in the chamber where the Lion of Alarcos had stood glowering at them as they'd left the emir's presence. To his left the staircase descended to the corridor where he and Balthesar had almost been trapped, while to his right lay the double doors of the throne room. The bearded servant had been true to his word. Leading Arnau via the hidden ways of slaves and servants, he had brought the young Templar to his destination without encountering the enemy, and without even raising more than passing surprise from anyone. Arnau turned and thanked the man in his limited Arabic, hoping he had remembered the correct word.

'*Šukran*.' He bowed his head respectfully, and the servant beamed happily, confirming that Arnau had got it right.

Nodding repeatedly as he retreated, the servant passed back through the door, leaving Arnau alone in the antechamber. The young sergeant swallowed noisily and felt his breathing become shallower, his pulse faster. Nerves. Beyond that door lay the throne room and, with luck, the Lion of Alarcos. He would likely be well defended, but Arnau had a feeling that if confronted the man's odd mix of perceived honour and pride would demand that he face Arnau alone. What the young man really wanted was to do so in public. Perhaps he could challenge the Almohad lord and back away, leading him somewhere more open and visible, though at the very least it seemed likely that some of the emir's people would be witness wherever it occurred.

He had not planned that far ahead, of course. None of them had. In truth, though they had agreed to the plan, none of them, he suspected, had ever truly believed that the plan would work this far, so reliant was it upon chance. And once at the throne room they could hardly plan further anyway. The variables were just too myriad at this point.

Faith. Damn Balthesar, but he would just have to trust in the Lord.

Lo! I made a smith blowing coals in the fire and bringing forth a vessel into his work, and I have made a slayer.

Each vessel which is made against thee shall not be directed, and in the doom thou shalt deem each tongue against withstanding thee. This is the heritage of the servants of the Lord, and the rightfulness of them at me, saith the Lord.

Isaiah be praised. Arnau was the Lord's slayer of the wicked this day. He reached up and grasped the handle of the throne room door, pushing. The door swung inwards, into that wide, spacious room where they had initially met the emir. The first thing he registered was that the room was not empty. The second, with some deflation and anger, was that the Lion of Alarcos was not one of those inside.

The *wazir* kneeled on the floor close to the dais upon which the throne sat, his hands behind his back, presumably bound. A Moorish nobleman in a rich blue *burnous* stood close by, a green-clad soldier beside him, and a black-and-white-garbed Almohad warrior loomed at the room's centre, sword in hand as he wagged an angry finger at the *wazir*, snarling something in Arabic.

Something snapped inside Arnau at the sight of the arrogant Almohad, and instead of contemplating his best options, or simply backing out of the door and hoping to remain unseen, he began to run, raising his sword as he did so.

The Almohad warrior turned in surprise at the thundering feet behind him, and Arnau snarled as he pulled back his blade. The soldier, shocked, threw his own sword up to block the swing, but it was a last-moment attempt and Arnau's blow had been powerfully delivered, infused with the force of anger, hate, frustration and thirst for revenge. The young Templar's sword hit the parrying blade of the Almohad with such power that it smashed the other sword aside and slashed at the man's face.

The Almohad realised what would happen even as he blocked, and was leaning back as far as he could to be out of the way of the sword as, even robbed of strength, it continued on its deadly course. Only that instinct saved the warrior's life, and even then it cost him dearly.

Arnau's blade tip smashed into the Almohad's mailed face, ripping the veil free from its fastenings so that it flopped loose, revealing the horrified face of a dark-skinned man only for a fraction of a second before the blade ruined that too, carving a line through his nose and taking an eye before smashing against the orbital socket, then the helmet, then flying free.

Howling, the disfigured Almohad fell back, sword out to the side, staggering backwards from the savagery of Arnau's assault. The young Templar, still enraged and gripped by the fury of righteous battle, pulled back his sword and advanced on the man. The Almohad turned his blood-soaked, ruined face to Arnau, and the young man was impressed to see the defiance that still gleamed in the remaining eye. The wound must have been agonising, and yet the warrior was pulling himself up into a combat stance, ready to face Arnau once more.

'And lo! I have given to you power to tread on serpents, and scorpions, and on all the virtue of the enemy, and nothing shall harm you,' Arnau growled, crossing himself with his free hand.

The Almohad, unlikely to understand anything but Arabic, frowned at Arnau in utter incomprehension, though he clearly recognised the intent behind the words, for his sword came up ready.

'The book of Lucas,' Arnau snapped, and swung his sword down in a powerful chop. The Almohad pulled his blade into the way, but once more it only robbed the Templar's strike of a little strength, and the sword came down hard, biting into the man's shoulder. He bellowed in pain.

'Chapter ten,' Arnau growled once more, pulling his sword back to the side. He swung with all his might and the Almohad failed to react in time, reeling as he was in agony and partial blindness.

'Verse nineteen,' added the young sergeant as his sword point dropped, the Almohad falling back, blood gushing from a face now ruined a second time, this time fatally.

Still emitting a low rumble of rage, Arnau turned to the other occupants of the room. He gestured to the *wazir*.

'Your master has returned and stands outside the gate, which will be opened to him and his men shortly. The lifespan of the Lion of Alarcos is now measured in hours at most.' He turned to the nobleman with the emir's guard. 'That you stand here with the emir's trusted adviser bound and even one of the Almohad dogs in attendance suggests that you chose to favour the hated invader over the island's rightful ruler to whom you took an oath.'

The guard in green clearly had no idea what Arnau was saying, but the facial expression of the nobleman suggested that even if he did not have a strong grasp of Spanish, he grasped enough of what Arnau had said, or at least the emotion behind it, that he had the grace to look utterly foolish and chastened.

'Release him.' He pointed at the *wazir* with his sword, and the nobleman barked an order to the soldier, who hurried over to the emir's second in command and untied the man's hands.

'May Allah and his prophets send you favour and strength, young man,' breathed the *wazir*, standing and rubbing his hands. 'Thank you.'

Arnau simply nodded his head, then pointed at the other two. 'Good men, who owe allegiance to the rightful emir, are busy working to open the gate and deliver this palace to him. I know your faces. When this is over, if I learn that you were not part of that effort, I will make your failings known to your emir. Do you understand?'

The nobleman nodded, but there was no need for him to pass on the ultimatum to his guard, for the *wazir* was already effortlessly translating Arnau's words like an echo. Seemingly hungry to absolve themselves, the nobleman and the green-clad soldier hurried off, heading for the stairs. Whether they would help Balthesar, or even try to do so, Arnau did not know, and in truth he would never recall their faces, but he would not kill a man who could be saved. Besides, he had his gaze set upon greater prey.

'Where is the Lion of Alarcos?' he demanded of the *wazir*, once they were alone in the throne room.

'You will find him at the highest level,' the *wazir* replied quietly. 'Atop the battlements of the tower, whence he commands his temporary kingdom, and from where he can see everything.'

'Not *everything*,' Arnau said, in tones of serrated steel. 'He cannot see me.'

CHAPTER NINETEEN

FRIDAY, 11 JUNE 1199

11.50 A.M.

Arnau climbed the stairs slowly but purposefully, the *wazir* four steps below him and following on close. The Templar had almost argued when the old man had left the room in his wake and followed him, worrying that he had no time to look to the safety of civilians right now, but had said nothing in the end. Not only did he have at least as much vested interest in what happened here as Arnau, if not more, but on a purely practical level, the *wazir* would know the palace well and could direct Arnau to his destination, diverting him around any trouble spots. The upper levels of this place were a mystery to the young sergeant after all.

Strangely, as they passed through half a dozen rooms and corridors and climbed towards the roof, he picked up an entourage. No one of practical use, admittedly – no green-clad emir's guards loyal to the end and able to put down an enemy with a blade – but palace slaves who, in the chaos and panic of the confrontation between emir and Almohad interloper, had spotted the *wazir* and flocked to him as a symbol of stability and authority, regardless of the crazed-looking warrior with him.

By the time Arnau approached the door that would lead out onto the battlemented roof, there were five people with him, all nervous and weak and clinging on to his tail. It felt oddly thrilling to gather an entourage, even if they were really here for the old man and would be of little aid. At least it gave him a little extra spirit to know he was not alone.

Psalms and prayers flitted through his mind as he climbed, none of them willing to settle long enough to be of comfort as his tension grew. He was about to face the most dangerous man on the island, and it had been gratifying to do so when he had expected it to be both he and Balthesar. Now, it felt somewhat different. Arnau could handle a sword – or a mace for preference, though his skills with the blade were improving all the time – but he was under no illusions that there were not much better swordsmen in the world, and instinct told him that the Lion of Alarcos was almost certainly one of them.

Fragments of prayers and Psalms, just odd lines, flickered into his thoughts.

Blessed be my Lord God, that teacheth mine hands to war; and my fingers to battle.

Thou hurtlest down to me the instruments of battle.

For the armours of our knighthood be not fleshly, but mighty by God to the destruction of strengths.

And suddenly, as the door that would lead to confrontation loomed close, Blessed Paul's Epistle to the Ephesians came to him, a passage the army's priest had intoned before the kneeling ranks of knights and men-at-arms before that fated clash at the Ebro where the Lord of Santa Coloma had died.

Clothe yourself with the armour of God, that ye may stand against the assailing of the devil. For why battle is not to us against flesh and blood, but against the princes and potentates, against governors of the world of these darknesses, against spiritual things of wickedness, in heavenly things. Therefore take ye the armour of God, that ye may stand in the evil day, and in all things stand perfect. Therefore stand ye, and be girded about your loins in soothfastness, and clothed with the habergeon of rightwiseness, and your feet shod in the making ready of the gospel of peace. In all things take ye the shield of faith, in which ye may quench all the fiery darts of him that is the most wicked, and take ye the helmet of health, and the sword of the Ghost, that is, the word of God.

The words flowed from his mind into his veins and thundered around his body, filling every part of him, bolstering his courage. He was clothed in the armour of God, even though he wore the mail shirt of a Moor, and he was here to do the Lord's work as well as the emir's. Wickedness had to end, whether a man marched for God or for Allah.

Arnau's fingers tightened on the hilts of his weapons, his sword and a short stabbing knife he had purloined from the belt of the dead guard in the throne room before he left. Now, as he closed on the door, he reached up and slipped the knife temporarily between his teeth, freeing up a hand.

His left hand reached the door handle. He had no idea what awaited him outside and would have to trust in the Lord to see him through. If the Lion was confident – something on which Arnau was relying – then the bulk of his military strength would be down below facing the emir, where Balthesar would have to deal with them. If he was nervous or being cautious, on the other hand, then there could be a number of black-and-white-clad soldiers on this roof, and Arnau might find himself having to fight through a small army just to get to the man he had to kill.

Lord, watch over me.

Speed. Right now, he had only one true advantage, and that was the element of surprise. The Almohads could not yet know that he was in the palace, and would not be expecting danger to strike from so close a position. If he hurried, he could take advantage of that, but once he lost that surprise, he lost all advantage. As soon as the door opened, he had to take in everything in the blink of an eye and be on his enemy in a trice.

Steeling himself, he turned the handle and pushed.

I shall stand in the evil day, and in all things stand perfect.

The door flew open, and Arnau took in everything in an instant. They were on a tower top, one of several at the summit of the Al-Mudaina, and there was a lot less room than he had anticipated. In fact, from the door he was only twenty paces from the battlements at the far side, which looked down upon the troubles below. There were but four figures on the rooftop, which came as something of a relief.

Abu Rāshid Abd al-Azīz ibn al-Ḥasan, the Lion of Alarcos, stood at that far parapet, facing away from him, observing what was happening down by the gate. Off to one corner, also looking away and down, was a courtier of some kind in bright red and green, oddly the colours that seemed to be favoured by the emir and the Lion. The remaining two figures were in the ubiquitous monochrome of the Almohad guards, one standing to the right of the door by a different parapet, and the other at the tower's centre, inconveniently between Arnau and the Lion, and facing the door, to boot.

Speed. Surprise. Instinct.

The man to his right would have to wait. The first target had to be that guard who stood between Arnau and his prey, who was prepared and alert, whose eyes had already widened in shock and perhaps even recognition of the man who had emerged from the door.

The guard managed to get out a strangled squawk and half draw his sword before Arnau was on him. As the young Templar ran, he whipped the knife from his teeth, delivering a tiny cut to the corner of his mouth in the process. He concentrated on his left hand now, aware that his sword was of limited use against such an armoured man, especially when speed was of the essence.

A panicked and fading scream suddenly arose behind him and to his right, and he realised with grim satisfaction that the small group of civilians following him had tipped the other surprised guard over the parapet. The doomed Almohad soldier landed with a crunch some distance below, raising a cry of alarm from the other enemies down near the gate, but Arnau had his own issues to deal with.

He hit the guard at the tower's centre hard with a shoulder, knocking him back. His left hand came up as the two men fell back, seeking his difficult target. The tip of the sharp knife found the opening he sought fast, though, and he stabbed. The standard form of the chain veils worn by such guards was a flap that was an integral part of the chain hood, and could fold across the lower face and tie to one side. It was as protective as any other area of chain against a standard attack, but a strike launched carefully from so close was a different matter. The tip of the blade slipped easily between the veil and the hood, into that narrow opening, and sank into the throat beneath. The guard choked mid-cry, white eyes almost glowing in the dark space between veil and helmet.

Arnau let go, momentum still with him. The mortally wounded Almohad solider fell away, knife still lodged in his neck, blood spraying out around the weapon and between the folds of mail. But Arnau had not stopped moving. He had hit the guard hard, knifed him, and kept going.

The odds had changed in an instant, thanks to a combination of surprise and the civilians in his wake. There had been two guards here protecting the Lion of Alarcos. Arnau had swiftly despatched one, and the slaves had dealt with the other. Now only the Almohad lord himself, and the nobleman in the corner, remained.

Arnau pointed at the unarmoured courtier, and heard the footsteps of the others behind him veer off as they went to deal with the man, leaving just Arnau and the Lion.

He slowed.

This was not about a swift kill, utilising surprise, like the attack on the guards. As they had planned at Al-Fabia, the Lion had to die cleanly, honourably, and preferably in a public place in full view of anyone whose opinion made a difference. For just a moment, though, Arnau contemplated keeping going, picking up the pace once more. He knew what had to be done, and *how* it had to be done, but the sight of that man as he turned, his baleful face so emotionless, inflamed Arnau. This man who would see Balthesar suffer an agony of anguish and loss through his dotage, and in doing so would kill Arnau, and Ramon, and Ermengarda and Titborga, and anyone about whom the old knight cared. This man who had taken Arnau and restrained him in a cellar, torturing him and inflicting pain and humiliation. This man who sought to ruin what had proved to be the last bastion of the tolerant Moor in Iberia and usurp it on behalf of the hated Almohads. This man deserved to die badly, but also quickly, to be despatched from the world as swiftly as possible to halt the sickness he and his kind spread.

It would be so easy to kill him, too. All the young Templar had to do was run and hit him hard. The two men would tip over the parapet in the blink of an eye and fall to the courtyard below, where their skulls would crack like eggs. He would die horribly. Arnau would die too, but it would be worth it to save everyone. To save even Mayūrqa. And he was fairly sure that in the eyes of Saint Peter, in whose hands lay the keys to heaven, such a thing would not be considered taking one's own life. In fact it would surely be more along the lines of blessed martyrdom. Lord, he might even be able to stop himself following the bastard over the top.

No.

They had discussed everything for hours at Al-Fabia, and that was not how it had to happen. The Lion of Alarcos had to die not unseen and for revenge, but openly and for defying and usurping the Emir of Mayūrqa. Arnau wore the emir's colours. He represented the rightful ruler of the island, and he had to put that ahead of himself.

Resisting the urge to speed up and thunder into the hated man, he instead stopped, facing the Lion as the man unfolded his arms, his fingers dropping to rest on his sword hilt. Out of the corner of his eye he saw the courtier waving his arms madly in panicked defiance as four slaves closed on him.

'You have more lives than a cat, Templar,' the Almohad lord said quietly.

'And you are at the end of your only one,' Arnau replied in flat tones of finality.

'I do not fear you, Templar, for Allah guides my hand.'

'Odd, for the emir down there seems to think the same of himself, and I cannot picture God favouring two enemies. I fear you live under the same delusion as all Almohad fanatics: that God loves a monster.'

'Are you done with your prattling?' the Lion said, sliding his blade from its sheath with a metallic sigh. Arnau wondered for a moment whether this place could be considered public enough to finish it. There were a few witnesses, though they were the *wazir*, who needed no persuasion, and slaves, whose opinion would count for nothing anyway.

As silence fell in the wake of the various scuffles and the verbal sparring of the two men, Arnau became aware of a commotion below. Keeping a wary eye on the Lion, who was shifting and testing his grip on his sword, Arnau edged around towards where the nobleman was busy being mercilessly beaten by four slaves, his cries little more than muffled gasps in the press. Ignoring him, Arnau reached the parapet and glanced sharply down, just long enough to see what was happening there but not long enough to put him in danger from the Lion.

He felt his spirits buoyed by what he saw. Green-clad figures fought and struggled with black-and-white ones in the courtyard. Against all odds, the gate had fallen and the emir's men were in the palace now. Even as he tore his eyes away, he saw the emir himself ride into the courtyard through the archway, returning to his place of rule. All was falling into place, and at least a dozen pairs of eyes were locked on the tower top, now aware that something was happening up there. Witnesses. Perfect.

'It's over,' Arnau said. 'The islands remain under the emir's control. Your play for power has failed. Your men fight like wild animals, but they cannot win now, and when you die in front of them, that fight will go out of them.'

'Overconfidence is a flaw I have noted in Christians,' the Lion replied, and brought up his sword into a ready stance.

Arnau remained where he was, preparing, lifting his own blade. Standing so close to the parapet was, of course, asking for trouble, but here they were visible to soldiers, courtiers and the ordinary folk of the palace, and that was paramount to what had to happen.

He remembered those times standing in the dust outside the walls of Rourell with the German knight trying to teach him. Arnau had been confident that his skills were adequate, that he could face any man with a reasonable chance of victory. Then he had met Lütolf, and been swiftly disabused of that notion, as the

German put him down in the dust repeatedly with remarkably little effort. He had learned hard that such a fight was more about readiness, control and reaction than about strength and speed. And he had discovered that while he was strong and fast, he had been unprepared and lacked control.

His gaze strayed over the Lion of Alarcos, seeking a clue. Like Lütolf in his time, the Almohad lord seemed to be devoid of any tells. Arnau couldn't anticipate what the man would do. He felt the tension rising once more, and forced himself to relax. He needed to be calm, prepared, to clear his mind of the many worries and thoughts crowding in on him and concentrate solely on the man before him.

'Blessed be my Lord God, that teacheth mine hands to war and my fingers to battle,' he said in a calm, clear voice.

The attack came without warning. The Lion suddenly swung his blade wide at Arnau's left side. The young Templar bore no shield, his left hand empty, but his reaction came swiftly and instinctively, given speed by his calm mind and observation of his foe. He dropped to a crouch as the Moor's blade whispered over his head, but by the time he rose, advancing as he did so, sword lancing out in a riposte, the Lion had already dropped his weapon into a guard and he turned that blow aside easily.

The Lion of Alarcos stepped back.

'You are faster than I anticipated. Rare skill for a man of so few years.'

'And you are just as fast as I anticipated.'

Without warning, Arnau thrust his blade forward, leaping into a lunge, knowing that his chances of penetrating the man's mail shirt were small, but that great damage could be done without even breaking an iron link. He had thought it a good attack. He had moved without warning, and had been as careful as possible to give no indication of what was to come, but the Lion was still somehow ready for him, slapping his sword aside as he ducked to his left. In a continuation of that same move, the Almohad spun, his sword rising from a parry into a slash. As it came round in a deadly arc, Arnau thrust his own blade into the way, feeling the shockwave of the two weapons meeting with impressive force reverberate all the way up his arms and into his shoulders. Damn it, but that hurt. His backside was causing him little trouble now, and apart from a little hoarseness, his throat was fine, but his shoulders still ached whenever he was not distracted by something else, and swinging the sword and meeting blade to blade was causing enough pain to make him wince and gasp.

As the two men separated again, the Almohad lord gestured at him with his free hand.

'You cannot hope to win. Perhaps if I were tired and you in full health you might best me. But I am well rested, and your shoulders still pain you from the cellar, if I am not mistaken. Every blow we trade makes me a little more weary, but every blow robs you of your strength at a much greater pace. Soon your shoulders will seize and you will find that you no longer have the strength to raise your sword from the ground. Then I shall have to take your head. I had hoped to extract from you the names and locations of everyone for whom the *Qātil wari'a* cares, but I shall simply have to bend more effort to that quest, and start by making you an example. I shall hack off that smirking face and drop it to the cobbles for your master to look upon.'

Arnau narrowed his eyes. From a man like della Cadeneta this would have struck Arnau as a boast or a threat, delivered with malice and intent to shake him, to push him into making a mistake. From the Lion of Alarcos, it came over as an emotionless statement of fact. Abd al-Azīz was making no boast; he was simply informing Arnau of his intentions. And the horrible thing was that Arnau could see just such a sequence of events coming to pass. The Almohad was right. While the Lion might tire a little with each exchange, Arnau was still suffering the ill effects of what had been done to him in the cellar. He had told himself that he was sufficiently recovered for this, but the truth was entirely otherwise, and the Lion had recognised that instantly. Arnau would weaken fast and be unable to finish this. His only hope was a swift resolution to the fight. He had to take the Lion down, and he had to do it now.

Steadying himself, he sized up his opponent once more. The Lion wore a chain shirt with sleeves that continued to the wrist. Like Arnau his hands were bare, and also like Arnau he wore no helmet or coif, his head covered with just a hat that would save him from nothing. His chain shirt hung down to his knees, and beneath that he wore some sort of colourful trousers, and no mail. Arnau stood precious little chance of punching through the mail, and delivering enough of a blow to the chain to damage the body beneath took an awful lot of strength. The weak spots, then, were the head, the hands and the lower legs. Of course, the Lion knew that too.

It had to be unexpected.

He struck swiftly and decisively. Dropping as he leaped forward, he swung the sword in an arc at the Lion's left knee, which would shatter under the blow, especially with no chain protection. Predictably, the Almohad's own sword came down in a block, the man deftly stepping to his right to allow space for Arnau's blow to miss.

But the knee was a feint, and one that was outlandish, relying upon just such a response. As Arnau's blade swept through the air, the angle of attack changed and it rose, coming up to meet the Lion's arm as it descended to put the block in place. Arnau felt the thrill of victory coursing through him. He had done it. He had tricked the Lion into exposing a weakness. He would win, and all would be right.

His shock and dismay as the Lion's arm seemed to fold out of the path of his blade like a closing hand fan were absolute. He had been certain he had got the best of the man, but the Lion of Alarcos had simply managed to pull himself out of the way in time, and Arnau's sword cut up through empty air, carrying much of the young Templar's remaining strength with it. In the blink of an eye, Arnau realised just how good this man was, and with that epiphany came the knowledge that he couldn't win. He had used almost everything he had in that one attack and yet it had still been so easy to avert. He could see no way he could manage anything better, while the Lion seemed to have barely broken a sweat.

Worst of all, as Arnau's sword flew up harmlessly, cleaving only air, the Lion reacted with astonishing speed, his own blade coming down unexpectedly from somewhere. Arnau had no choice. It was an inelegant response, but the only one available. He threw himself to the side, slamming into the parapet of the tower, and teetered there for a perilous moment, almost tipping over it and plummeting to his death.

He gasped, and shivered. He had almost died there. He was shaking and leaning on the battlements, his shoulders screaming at him, his strength ebbing, and unable to think of a way out. By comparison, the Lion of Alarcos returned to a calm stance, sword gripped tight, a light sheen to his forehead the only real sign of exertion. The man was too good. Arnau couldn't beat him.

Therefore take ye the armour of God...

Arnau slowly lifted himself from the battlements and straightened. He took several deep breaths, keeping his gaze locked on the man before him. Faith, Balthesar always told him. *Have faith, Vallbona.*

'Therefore take ye the armour of God,' he said suddenly in a clear, if slightly scratchy, voice, 'that ye may stand in the evil day, and in all things stand perfect. Therefore stand ye, and be girded about your loins in soothfastness, and clothed with the habergeon of rightwiseness, and your feet shod in the making ready of the gospel of peace. In all things take ye the shield of faith, in which ye may quench all the fiery darts of him that is the most wicked, and take ye the helmet of health, and the sword of the Ghost, that is, the word of God.'

'Your heathen prattlings are nonsensical,' sneered the Lion.

'These words are like arrows in my quiver,' Arnau responded. 'They are links in my chain shirt. They are strength in my muscles and hope in my heart.'

'You are a fool. A blind fool.'

And Arnau made his final attack. His shoulders were so painful and his strength failing, and he knew for certain that after this he would be lucky to lift the tip of the blade from the ground. But he had summoned up every ounce of spirit and strength in his being, wrapping them in the words of the Holy Scriptures, and forcing them into his arm and the blade it held.

He swung.

The Lion at first smiled a horrible smile, but the corners of his mouth came back down and his brow creased in concern and surprise as Arnau's last effort came. The blade in the young sergeant's hands swung round in a powerful back-handed slash, and the Almohad managed to drop his own sword into a parrying position once more with relative ease, but Arnau's blow was infused with the power of desperation, of need, of righteousness, and of God. Despite his own strength and energy, the Lion stared in shock as his sword was knocked aside, his hands going numb from the strike, and the Templar's blade slammed into his left arm. Both men heard the limb snap beneath the mail.

Arnau fell back. He was spent. He knew he had used up everything in that last blow, and his sword fell now, his fingers throbbing, his shoulders afire. He collapsed against the parapet and began to slide down to his knees.

The Lion of Alarcos stared in shock. He managed to retain his sword in tingling fingers, and he was upright, but somehow this pup who was sorely injured, weak and tired had managed to deliver a blow substantial enough to pass through his guard and snap his arm like a twig.

Fury and determination flooded into the Almohad's face now.

Arnau knew it was over. He had done all he could. He had at least wounded the man and with luck the bastard would contract a sickness in the wound and die of it, soaked in sweat and pus and agony. It was a nice thought, but the Lion would probably survive this and escape to find one of the many excellent Moorish doctors, who would likely be able to help him.

Arnau heaved in a breath, and then another.

The Lion was recovering. Arnau could see the man gritting his teeth against the pain in his arm, but it was not his sword arm and he still had plenty of strength. The Almohad lord took a step towards him. In desperation, Arnau shuffled backwards, using the wall for support. The Lion swung, and it was only by a miracle that the young Templar managed to scramble back swiftly enough to avoid death. The Almohad sword rent the empty air and came back up, readying for a second blow. Arnau continued to hurry backwards along the wall, but knew the game was up as his painful shoulders bumped into the other wall and he knew he was cornered, quite literally.

The Lion advanced on him implacably, a Satanic figure in red and silver, his sword rising for a final blow. Arnau almost choked with shock and panic as a shadow suddenly fell across him and the *wazir* stepped between him and the advancing Almohad.

He had no idea what it was that the emir's man said to the enemy lord, but all it seemed to do was anger the Lion of Alarcos. It was with an almost dismissive, careless swipe that the Almohad lord cut the old man's throat with the edge of his blade and pushed him out of the way.

The last droplets of the *wazir*'s falling blood spattered onto Arnau as he leaned back against the stone parapet, cold and miserable, awaiting the descent of death upon him. So many good men had died, and now it seemed more were fated to do so.

A new voice suddenly cut across the scene, and the Lion of Alarcos stopped dead in his tracks. The words were Arabic, but even with his complete lack of comprehension, Arnau could feel the fire and the hatred within them. He turned his weary, beleaguered head to see Balthesar emerging from the doorway onto the tower top, sword in hand, eyes cold and full of determination.

The Almohad lord turned and paced away from the exhausted sergeant towards this new arrival, replying in equally intemperate Arabic. Arnau stared. Death had been so close there that he could almost taste it, and it was little comfort that it had so suddenly been averted, for in saving him, Balthesar would be placing his own life in the gravest of danger.

Behind the Templar came other men, courtiers and guards. Witnesses to the event that had to transpire here. Balthesar had come to finish what he had started on the plains below Valencia more than twenty years ago.

He had come to kill the Lion of Alarcos.

CHAPTER TWENTY

FRIDAY, 11 JUNE 1199

11.55 A.M.

Arnau, having seemingly been given an unexpected and sudden stay of execution, exhaled his terror as he watched the Lion of Alarcos pacing back towards the wall's centre, where he had been when the young Templar had first emerged. Arnau's eyes strayed to the huddled shape of the *wazir*, lying in a pool of his own blood, and the wave of regret hit him. This brave, wise and peaceful man had given up his life in an effort to save Arnau's: a Moor sacrificing himself for a Christian. These were the times that blurred the common view for the young Templar.

But Moor or no Moor, there was no denying the evil of the man currently facing Balthesar with a face like a demon mask. The Lion of Alarcos could be accused of evil – and *would* be by any churchman to be found in Aragon – purely in being a proponent and architect of the harsh Almohad caliphate, but Arnau knew now just how far the man's wickedness went, in torturing the young Templar purely as a means to find a way to torture the older knight. Of course, Balthesar had done things in his past that had clearly verged on the wicked, or perhaps crossed well over that line, but the old knight had sought peace and atonement in the arms of the order. Perhaps now, with this long-postponed confrontation, absolution and true peace could be his.

If he survived it.

Balthesar looked weary and shaky as he stepped forth, sword in hand. Whatever had happened down at the gate had involved a blade, for the old knight was sporting a cut above his left eye that kept him blinking away crimson, and his green *burnous* was black in places with spatters and washes of blood, most of which at least was not his. But Arnau could see the wide dark patch beneath the knight's arm, where the wound he had taken in the street fight a few days ago had once more opened up with his fresh exertions and soaked through the bandages. Moreover, the old man had finished securing the gate for the emir and immediately pelted through the palace once more, climbing so many stairs at speed to reach Arnau and the Lion. He would be tired and achy. He had never looked older to Arnau's eyes, but then he had also never looked more determined, nor more dangerous, either.

Of course, Abd al-Azīz was also wounded and, despite having the appearance of just a middle-aged man, Arnau reminded himself that this Moor had already had a grown son more than two decades ago when he fought Balthesar at Valencia. The Lion of Alarcos was also far from a young man, and he too would be tired from the minutes of swordplay with Arnau.

Two Titans, then. Two men with a lifetime of experience and enmity behind them, both skilled beyond measure, both sure of themselves and fired with belief. Both weary and both wounded. Abruptly, Arnau realised that he would not be comfortable placing a wager on the outcome of this contest either way. Aware that there was every bit as much chance of the Lion walking away from this as Balthesar, Arnau gripped his blade and hauled himself up to lean against the wall, standing straight and trying to will life and energy back into his tired limbs and the deep bone-ache from his shoulders. If Balthesar fell, Arnau would need to finish this.

The slaves that had accompanied Arnau and the *wazir* onto the roof were now shuffling past the other figures and disappearing back through the door and into the palace, wary of what was unfolding atop the tower. Their absence left only Arnau with the bodies of a courtier and the *wazir* in one corner of the tower, half a dozen other courtiers and green-clad guards standing close to the door, and the two old enemies facing one another with smouldering eyes.

'I do not want to kill you,' the Lion of Alarcos said to Balthesar, ending the strained silence.

The old knight simply nodded. 'That's lucky, since I have no intention of letting you.'

'Death is too good for the *Qātil wari'a*. Three caliphs I have served since the day Valencia fell to the Faithful, and each one has supported a fatwa demanding your head. I have shamed myself for three decades by failing to deliver it, and even now I would rather you lived to suffer as I systematically destroy and ravage everything for which you care, and it pains me that you force me into a position where I must simply butcher you and give you peace.'

'Presumptuous,' Balthesar replied calmly. 'Do not be too overconfident, Abd al-Azīz, for I have not spent those three decades sitting by the fire telling tales.'

'Perhaps you should have done, and then we would not be here.'

Balthesar nodded. 'I came to Mayūrqa to find a relic, with no knowledge of your presence here, and no intent to become involved in your plots. But as the young sergeant over there led me to realise, the Lord did not bring me to these islands to find a pile of old bones, no matter how sacred, but to put an end to your attempt to destroy the last true *taifa* and make Mayūrqa part of your malevolent empire. I was carried here by faith, but I realise now that it was misplaced. I had faith in the hollow thing I sought, while the faith I needed was in the Lord's plan that truly brought me to you.'

'You Christians and your *great plan*. Allah's plan is for the caliphate to encompass your world, to grow ever stronger as once the caliphs of Baghdad were. To bring order and true belief to those sons of the Prophet who have strayed from the word, and to teach the whole world the truth, that they may finally reach heaven and not be damned by their infidel ways.'

Balthesar sighed. 'This is not about God, Abd al-Azīz. I know that God brought me here, but this is about understanding and freedom. I will not watch you and your caliph do to Mayūrqa what you did to Valencia. The emir will stand yet. Now cease your talk.'

The Lion of Alarcos did just that. Eyes burning with hate, he stepped forward from the wall, sword wavering only slightly in his right hand, broken arm hanging limp at his side. Balthesar also took a step forth, limping as the part-healed wound in his side bled fresh and the remaining stitches pulled painfully.

The two wounded men closed and, at sword reach, began to circle like gladiators of old, eyeing one another warily. The first attack, when it came, was so fast and unexpected that Arnau missed it in a blink, catching only the aftermath.

The Lion had lanced out with his sword and Balthesar had danced aside to avoid the blow. Arnau realised just how sharp the attack must have been to catch the wary Templar by surprise, and it had been strong and accurate enough that he had forced Balthesar to bend in such a way that it caused him a great deal of pain, likely popping the rest of his stitches.

Though he'd missed the first blow, the young sergeant caught Balthesar's response. Despite the pain, and gritting his teeth, the old Templar turned his stagger to the right, away from the Lion's thrust, into a three-step dance that brought him onto the Almohad's left side, where he swung with a speed and power that surprised Arnau, given his condition.

The Lion struggled to deal with the blow. He had spent precious moments recovering his sword from his own lunge and had not quite enough time to turn with the knight's advance, so that as Balthesar swung, the Almohad was forced to spin on the spot and slam his sword into the path of the oncoming blade.

For a heartbeat, Arnau felt frustration that the knight's attack had failed when so clearly it had almost succeeded, but while the two swords clanged together and then rasped apart as the men separated, the young sergeant realised that Balthesar had never expected to cut into his opponent. Just as the Lion had attacked in such a manner as to make the old man suffer from his existing wound, so Balthesar had done the same in turn.

As the Lion had spun, managing to parry the attack, his broken arm had swung free, flailing loose, and the agony of that was clear in the Almohad's face, for tears welled up in his eyes unbidden, and he bit hard into his lip, drawing blood which ran down into that neat, pointed beard.

Arnau was impressed. Both men were aware of the skill of their opponent and were using whatever they could find to cause damage.

The Lion of Alarcos danced back away from Balthesar, edging closer to Arnau as he did so, buying himself a little space to recover. Arnau watched in fascinated horror as the Almohad used his sword hand, blade still gripped in it, to help lift his broken arm, and with a supreme effort of will and no doubt more pain than the man had ever experienced, thrust the hand of the ruined limb down into his belt, anchoring the broken arm into place and preventing the Templar repeating such an awful move.

In a further attempt to keep Balthesar from doing so, the Lion now kept his right side facing his enemy, rather than his left. Arnau momentarily considered leaping forward and trying to kill the man from behind, since they were tantalisingly close now, but he swiftly shoved the idea aside. Doing so would rob Arnau of whatever strength he had left, and if he missed and then Balthesar failed, there would be no one to finish it. Well, there would be the green-clad guards near the door, of course, but if the Lion came out triumphant, what certainty did Arnau have that those same men would not bow to the Almohad lord? That very possibility was the whole reason for this public display of swordsmanship. And that was the other reason: the Lion of Alarcos had to die honourably, from a noble strike, and not a stab in the back. It had to prove that God – or Allah in the case of those watching by the door – sanctioned the Lion's death and therefore the emir's rule.

The Lion stepped out of Arnau's reach anyway now, as he breathed deeply, suppressing his pain and concentrating on the ageing Templar, who remained still, blood dripping from his side and dotting the floor beneath him.

Arnau half expected words then, with the two men facing off and unmoving; half expected chiding and the slinging of barbed insults. Instead all that happened was a tense and nervous silence as the two men sized one another up.

This time Balthesar struck first, but only by a fraction of a heartbeat, as the Lion also attacked hard. The old knight's sword had swung back slightly, held low, so gently and slowly that Arnau had not noticed him doing it, and it therefore came as something of a shock when the Templar's arm picked up speed exponentially as it swung back and over while he took two sharp steps forward, sword coming down now in an overarm swing. The Lion had begun to move even before the knight's first step, dipping to his right to keep his good side to Balthesar, blade coming out in a swipe to the side as he went.

The two men clashed, trading those blows so swiftly and so fiercely that the young sergeant almost missed them again. Balthesar's overarm chop cleaved only air as the Lion had danced aside, and the Almohad's swipe did connect with the back of the Templar's mail shirt as he passed, but robbed of so much speed and power that it barely rippled the rings, let alone caused any damage.

This time there was no silent perusal as the two men eyed each other. As the Moor and the knight both spun to face one another again they reacted in a trice, attacking savagely. Arnau watched, his heart in his throat as two men of advanced years fought with more speed and ferocity than the young sergeant had seen even in the youngest of warriors.

The two men's swords clanged and clashed again and again as they swung and thrust, hacked and sliced, dancing this way and that, turning a slow, deadly circle, sometimes coming close to one parapet with the Lion keeping a wary eye on the drop behind him, sometimes Balthesar noting the closeness of the edge as he retreated along it. All the time, the Lion took advantage of the Templar's side wound, forcing him to bend this way and that with each strike so that the old knight suffered as much pain and discomfort as possible as the blood continued to leak from the reopened wound, soaking the green *burnous*. And with every attack, the old Templar used the Almohad's broken arm to the best effect, keeping to his left side as much as possible and forcing the Moor into positions where he would knock his shattered arm on the stonework, causing him to whimper in pain.

It was not a pleasant contest of arms, both men suffering endlessly, yet on and on it went, strike after strike, so fast and furious that Arnau found himself constantly expecting the combatants to collapse to the floor, exhausted.

Suddenly, as the Lion swung once more in the press – a slash that rose as it swung, threatening to cut up beneath the mail shirt's hem in a fatal blow – Balthesar responded with a downward blow, diverting the attack, and the two blades grated and scraped along one another until the cross guards of both swords met and locked, their wielders so close now that their breath steamed in one another's face. The combatants grimaced and snarled at each other across the locked weapons. The old Templar took his advantage then, his other hand coming up to add its grip to his sword, forcing the Almohad's blade back, the strength of two hands against one. But just as Arnau was anticipating a final blow with the Templar's sword cleaving his enemy's face, the Lion lashed out with a booted foot, catching Balthesar below the knee.

Knocked off balance, the old knight fell back, his sword scraping free, and the Lion was on the offensive now, his blade swinging hard, coming down with such power that the observing sergeant imagined it cleaving even the flagged floor in half. Despite the fact that Balthesar was almost on his knees now, staggering to stay upright after the almost crippling blow to his leg, he managed to lift his sword, one hand on the hilt, the other near the tip, and catch the enemy chop a foot above his head. Expertly, the old knight, as soon as the blades met, tipped his own point down and removed his left hand so that the Lion's sword skittered away harmlessly.

The Almohad had put such momentum into what he had clearly hoped to be a killing blow that he could not quite arrest his movement, and he staggered forward and down as his sword smashed into the floor and scraped across the stone. Balthesar almost finished it there, as his sword came round swiftly in a hard slash and slammed into the Lion's mailed back. It had to be an agonising blow and likely broke several ribs, but the Almohad was not done, for even as he fell, he was turning. As he cried out in pain at the knight's blow, so his own sword came up and over in a powerful arc, slamming down into Balthesar's mailed arm. It was a miracle that the attack did not break the old knight's sword arm, for the Templar by pure good fortune had his arm at just such an angle that the Lion's blade glanced off the mail and bounced down the chain sleeve, bruising and causing pain and numbness, but robbed of the strength to shatter bone.

The two men staggered away from one another. They were almost spent now, and Arnau could see it. Both men were exhausted beyond reason, and both were suffering. As the Lion of Alarcos straightened, he bellowed in pain and shook for a moment, his ribs causing him agony. Balthesar rose and tried to lift his sword, but his arm was too badly beaten. With a grunt of pain, the old knight swapped his sword to his left hand and lifted it to face the raised blade of the Moor. Arnau noted nervously that the tip of the old knight's sword dipped several times, and swayed even when raised. Not only was Balthesar weary, but his left hand simply did not have the strength of his right. He would be slower, weaker, and much less effective with that arm.

Yet as he two struck once more, it was clear that he was still on even terms with his enemy, for the Lion could not lunge or chop without crying out in agony, his broken ribs sending sharp pain coursing through him with every strong movement. The Almohad was failing, perhaps faster than Balthesar now, and Arnau felt a surge of hope at that realisation. Even as the young sergeant realised this, the Lion also knew he had little time and strength and must finish it fast. With a roar, the Almohad launched a deadly attack. His cry of *Allāhu akbar* echoed out from the rooftop as the Lion swung his blade this way and that: left to right, right to left, left to right, wincing with each swipe as he advanced, Balthesar backing away from the vicious assault, trying to parry the blows, but with a weak and exhausted off-hand so that his sword was simply batted aside with ease at each sweep.

Arnau watched in shock, his momentary elation shattered at the very real probability that Balthesar was about to die, for he was giving ground, unable to stop the attack, and almost back against the parapet with its huge drop.

When the next thing happened, Arnau stared in astonishment. He only realised as the final conflict unfolded that Balthesar had been *giving* the Lion this struggle. He had not fought to stop the attack, simply slipping his blade weakly in the way in order to save what strength he had left, giving ground deliberately in order to gain just the right position.

Snarling, the Lion of Alarcos, Abu Rāshid Abd al-Azīz ibn al-Ḥasan, had his Templar opponent at the parapet and swung down in a killing blow.

But Balthesar was not there. As soon as the Templar's heel had touched the stone of the surrounding battlements, he'd dropped and ducked forward. The Almohad lord, unable to stop his momentum, fell against the parapet. For a brief moment it looked as though he would keep going, toppling out into the air, but his centre of gravity was just low enough to keep him on the rooftop. He was spent, though, and had nowhere to go, face down over the battlements.

Arnau watched Balthesar rise from his crouch like the wrath of God, sword coming up, held in both hands like an executioner. The Lion turned, face white, desperate, and lifted his own blade weakly in a last effort to save himself.

Balthesar's blade struck the Lion's sword arm midway between wrist and elbow. Had the arm been held low the mail might have stopped it, but with the arm raised as it was, the mail sleeve had fallen back and the old Templar's sword struck only light cotton and flesh. Arnau watched, wide eyed, as the Lion's hand and forearm fell away, still clutching the sword, blood jetting from the severed arm.

The Almohad lord let out a cry then of such pain that Arnau almost felt a pang of sympathy. The Lion of Alarcos stared at his ruined arm, his other one also broken and useless, still tucked into his belt. He was done for, and everyone now knew it. The old Moor's eyes narrowed, filled still with hate and violent intent despite his predicament.

Balthesar let his sword fall to the stone floor and staggered for a moment, threatening to collapse in exhaustion. Then, summoning a reserve of energy from somewhere, he simply walked forward and lifted his arms, pushing the glaring Almohad, tipping him back over the battlements to fall out into the air, where he plummeted without a cry three storeys down to the stone flags of the courtyard. Arnau did not see him land, but he heard the wet crunch, and then the mixed din of moaning and relief from the men of both forces down below.

Balthesar dropped to his knees, and Arnau wondered for a moment whether the knight was so weak and tired that he might faint, but noted with pride and respect that the old man was, in fact, praying. Odd words drifted back to him; it surprised him that the old Templar was speaking Arabic. Praying for the soul of the Lion of Alarcos, Arnau realised. Just as Ramon had administered the *viaticum* to the men he shot from the tower during the siege of Rourell, so Balthesar gave his fallen foe the respect of praying for his soul in his own custom and language. Pious as he was, and despite his months of becoming used to the ways of the Temple, Arnau wondered then if he would ever be as noble in spirit as the three old knights of Rourell.

New sounds insisted themselves upon him now, and he turned to see that the courtiers and guards had stepped aside and footsteps were echoing up the stairs beyond the door. Despite his lack of command of the Arabic tongue, Arnau could still tell voices apart in it, and he recognised with relief the silken steel tone of the emir.

A thought occurred to him, and he scrambled across to the site of the Lion's demise just as the emir appeared in the doorway behind them, his *taifa* safe once more, and his throne secure.

EPILOGUE

SUNDAY, 13 JUNE 1199

10 A.M.

Balthesar frowned sceptically at the object in Arnau's hands. 'A falsehood is a falsehood, no matter how you frame it, Vallbona.'

Arnau shook his head as he lifted the ornate silver box. The cross upon the lid had been a nice touch, and he could imagine how the Moorish craftsman had felt being asked to fashion it, but it was as good a reliquary as Arnau had seen in his limited years. The forearm inside might not be from the blessed Stephen, the first martyr of the Church, but only he, Balthesar, the emir and half a dozen Moorish lackeys and craftsmen knew that.

'Faith is the thing,' he said. 'Having faith is what's important, remember, not necessarily the physical focus of it. We have faith in the Lord God, but we cannot see or touch him. Besides, I would not be at all surprised to learn that the relics of Saint Stephen which are kept in Rome contain both arms.'

Balthesar shot him a fierce look, but Arnau weathered it with aplomb. 'I say here is the arm of Saint Stephen, a thing of miracles, which was brought to the islands by Bishop Orosius half a millennium ago, which survived centuries of Moorish rule because they respected the relic, and kept it from harm. And now we return it to Christian lands at Rourell, where it will make the house important and will draw funds and manpower that we sorely need. That is what I say and only one man in all of Aragon and Catalunya will be able to truly deny it. *Will* you deny it, Brother?'

Balthesar remained silent for some time, looking at the fake relic uneasily. Finally, he straightened and sighed. 'I suppose it is fitting that Abd al-Azīz do something good, even if it is in death. We shall call it payment for the fact that I prayed for him.'

They turned at a ligneous scraping to see the ramp being pulled aboard. The Moorish trader was preparing to put to sea on the short voyage to Tarragona, where he would sell his goods and deliver the two Templars back to their own lands. Arnau's eyes rose from the deck, past the walls of Madina Mayūrqa to the towers of the Al-Mudaina beyond. He could see small, gleaming figures upon them, and it felt good to know that they were the emir's men, for the last of the Almohad soldiers had been released to depart the previous day.

It had surprised Arnau at first that the emir was letting them leave and not simply doing away with the force that had sought to depose and replace him, but the emir had explained that the death of one lord of the Almohads might be too small a matter to start a full-scale war, while the imprisonment or execution of an entire Almohad force would be another thing entirely. And so the black-and-white-clad soldiers of the Lion's army had been escorted back to their ships in the harbour and ordered to depart the island and not to return.

'Do you think it will last?' he asked.

'Hmm?' Balthesar turned to him. 'What?'

'The emir. The *taifa*. The independence of this place. I was extremely nervous of coming here, and I've been quite nervous while we've been here, but now that we're leaving I find that I've become unexpectedly and oddly fond of the place. But clouds are gathering, aren't they? Will it last?'

'Nothing made by man lasts, Vallbona,' sighed the older knight. 'But this place? No. Sadly not. The emir has bought himself time, but without a strong military ally, that is all he can do: put off the inevitable. This place has been too out of the way to be a focus for the wars that rage in Iberia, but it is becoming more central now, and with the last *taifa* and the last emir, it is becoming a prize for everyone.'

'That saddens me.'

'Me also. But the caliph will not rest. The Almohads will come again, and next time in greater force, for now they know that only a full invasion will deliver Mayūrqa to them. And when they do it will be the end of the era of *taifas*, and the end of the world in which I grew up. And if the Almohads do not come soon, then Pedro of Aragon, or Alfonso of Provence, or even a force gathered by the Pope, will do so, seeking to add the islands to the Christian world as part of their ongoing war with the Moors. No, I fear the emir's time is almost up.'

The ship lurched for a moment as it jerked away from the jetty and prepared to make for the mouth of the port and the open sea beyond. Arnau felt in some ways sad to be leaving this place, but in other, and more important, ways relieved to be returning home, where he could once more don the black robe and the red cross of the Temple.

'What next?' he asked idly, tearing his gaze from the towers of the palace and turning to look ahead, out to sea.

'Next? Back to the preceptory. To finish the rebuilding and to return it to strength, for the time of peace is passing. The aftermath of Alarcos brought a lull in the wars, but things are building once more, Vallbona. The great powers manoeuvre and prepare. Soon the order will be called to war, and your training is far from complete. But for now, we go home.'

Historical Note

ith *Daughter of War* I sought to find a new angle to the story of the Knights Templar, and did so purely through chance. In my research, Wtrying to find an angle, I happened across two women who are recorded in historical texts as female Templars. Not just associates either, but full sisters, even a preceptrix running a house. I sought to build a story that explored more than just the martial arm of the order and the supposed heresies that were cited in their downfall. In essence I wanted to use the fascinating story of the Templar sisters, as well as spinning a great yarn, to explore more of the nature of the Templars, who they were (particularly in Spain) and what they did. And the more I read, the more I realised that Templar history in Iberia went far deeper than the Reconquista – Christian against Muslim. In fact, that was to some extent peripheral to the order's time in Iberia. And so, in fact, the Moors played a very small part in the book, with the good guys and the bad all being Christian.

As that book neared a close, I already knew what I wanted to look into in the second book. I wanted the reader to experience Moorish Iberia. As such I sowed the seed at the end of the first book that would send intrepid Templars behind enemy lines in the search for one of the many relics that must have been lost when the Moors swarmed across Iberia from the eighth century onwards. Again, my story fell together quite by chance. I did some research into the relics of pre-Muslim Iberia, and stumbled across a fairly obscure reference that formed the basis of the plot for me. I won't go over it again in much detail as you've just read it in the book, but essentially there are references to Bishop Orosius delivering the relics of Saint Stephen, protomartyr, to Menorca and not then on to Braga, whence they were meant to be bound. There are several vague and conflicting stories about this, including the forced conversion of Jews on the island using the relic's power. I might cite Elizabeth A. Clark and Peter Van Nuffelen as two of my principal sources there.

Of course, there is always the irritating fact that the relics are also supposed to then appear in Africa at El Alia, and that recognised relics of that same man are kept in his church in Rome. Some might find uncomfortable conflicts in this. I know I do. In the medieval era this does not seem to have been the case, with all acknowledged relics being worshipped, even if a saint somehow appeared to have two skulls. In fact, claims of the validity of such relics seems to have sparked some competition. My perhaps inelegant solution was to have the Menorca relic be simply a forearm of the saint, allowing for the rest of him to be elsewhere, which also played well to my plot. *Mea culpa.*

But I digress. The fact was that, for me, I had a relic appearing on an island that then became Moorish territory, and which never left, disappearing from the record. This was perfect for my tale. Better still was the realisation that in 1199, Mallorca (Moorish Mayūrqa) was the very last independent *taifa* kingdom in Iberia, and this was a particularly fraught time in its history, where its ruler actually had more in common with the Christian kings of Aragon and Castile than with the Islamic caliphate of Cordoba under the Almohads. Just the briefest glance told me how much material I had to work with here. I will hold my hands up. I try not to rely on Google or Wikipedia at any level of research, but my poor Spanish and complete lack of Arabic made delving into records of the era and location somewhat troublesome. To quote the (translated) Catalan Wikipedia site, though, with reference to that last emir: 'In 1199 he launched an attack on Ibiza, which, defended by Abd al-Wahid and Abu-Abd-allāh ibn Maymun, failed. During his rule the Almohads tried again to conquer the *taifa* until finally, in 1203 under the caliphate of Muhàmmad an-Nàssir, [he] was defeated and executed.'

Initially this second book was planned as a tale of the retrieval of the relic and an exploration of what Moorish Iberia was like for a Christian, but that simple line that the Almohads tried to conquer the place changed things for me. Suddenly I also had political and military elements involved. Thus were the Almohads introduced to the plot. And with their introduction, I had the opportunity to tell Balthesar's tale (hinted at in book one). A chance discussion about Palma city (Madina Mayūrqa) with the amazing Isabel Picornell Garcia of the Alderney Literary Trust led to the discovery that her ancestor Guillem had been involved in the conquest of the island in 1229 and received lands there from the Count of Roussillon for his part. Knowing now that I had local independent Moors, Almohad zealots and two undercover Templars on the island, I simply could not help adding an Aragonese party to the mix, including a young Guillem, some thirty years before he would be back, conquering the island.

Essentially, politically, Mallorca was a mess, or at least is to look back on. Simply pinning down which ruler of the island was in power and by whose leave at any given time is difficult. But in a world where I knew that the emir was nominally independent, yet was reaching out to Christian monarchs for aid against the growing power of the caliphate, finding out that there was an attempt at seizing control by the Almohads was enough to build my plot. Thus what began as a quest for bones, single-minded and driven by Balthesar, gradually twisted to become a struggle of faith and reason against blind zealotry and hate.

This is, as anyone who knows me will attest, quite close to my heart. Such unthinking ire is at the heart of much of the world's evil, and could be overcome if people only thought and reasoned more. And that is something that I have tried very hard to put over in the book. This is not a case of 'Christians good, Muslims bad'. It never was. There were good and bad Christians (as we saw in book one) and also good and bad Muslims (as I showed here). The Almohads seem to have been almost universally despised, and not only by their enemies, but also by their subjugated lands, which were largely Muslim. These were the Da'esh, or ISIS, of their time. As such, I cannot find it in myself to portray them as anything but villains. And where the Almohads are Da'esh, the Emir of Mayūrqa and his people are those beleaguered Islamic populations who have been systematically brutalised by ISIS. I hope here that I have been able to show that the Moors of Mayūrqa, just as the Muslims of today's societies, are often quite pleasant, peaceable and reasonable people, and that we cannot judge a whole religion and way of life because of a band of zealots. I condemn men such as ISIS and the Almohads. And similarly I laud the Muslim lands who defy them as I do the *taifa* of Mayūrqa.

The language barrier in the story could have been insurmountable, but I have found ways around it, not least in having Balthesar, raised within the Muslim world, speak Arabic fluently. I had trouble locating information on the languages of the time, but it seemed to me likely that religious minorities like the Christians and Jews would have probably adopted Arabic for day-to-day speech. They lived among the Moors and had to buy food from them, trade, work, pay taxes, etc. They must have spoken the Moorish tongue. Indeed, in the most informative thesis by Martin Sebastian Goffriller, he quotes archaeological evidence that supports a gradual 'Islamicisation' of non-Christian Iberians, in that they seem to have gradually adopted the ways of their rulers probably through simple expedience, even when they retained their own religious beliefs. A man had to be able to understand his tax official, even if he was a Christian, after all. I have probably downplayed the number of these people living under Moorish rule on the island, since such religious minorities do not play a large role in the tale. Perhaps there were many more large neighbourhoods, but I have kept their appearance in the tale minimal for two reasons.

Firstly, the history of Moorish Mallorca is very poorly recorded, even in Arabic texts, some of which I have dipped into in translation. The physical evidence is minimal, the written more so. Thus details about the Moorish era on the island are scant compared with records after the Christian conquest, and so I did not want to explore too much detail without any real grounding in it. Secondly, less than half a century before this there had been Christian revolts against the new Almoravid ruler Muhàmmad. In fact, Ramón Rosselló notes one of only two mentions of the Al-Mudaina in medieval sources being the *Kitab Takmila* which tells of Christian slaves besieging the palace in 1184. As such it seems likely that many Christians would have fled, ostensibly converted, or hidden from potential danger in the following years of the same dynasty, and our tale takes place only fifteen years after that insurrection. This, by the way, is something to note: there is a tendency among students of the region and era to think of the time of the *taifa* as halcyon days of togetherness and understanding. At some times and in part, that was certainly the case, but at other times it was far from true. Like all changing political and religious landscapes, from one decade to the next attitudes changed. That being said, under the *taifa* at least there was room for that attitude to change. The caliphate would not allow for such deviation. Da'esh again.

Balthesar's history might seem outlandish, but there are parallels to be seen in medieval Iberia. The great Rodrigo Diaz (El Cid) himself actually spent more time fighting for Moors as a mercenary than he did for Christians. And with the fluid situation on the peninsula men such as he could fight with Christian against Moor or vice versa, but also for Moor against Moor or Christian against Christian. This is one aspect of this time and place that draws me, rather than the zealous focus of the Holy Land. Balthesar is in fact highly plausible as a character of that time. To have him involved in the fall of the *taifa* of Valencia, a land that had once been in El Cid's grasp, and which would become a foreshadow of Mayūrqa was too tempting to avoid.

Arnau you'll know if you've read book one, so I won't go into his history. And I've mentioned Picornell, who would eventually be involved in the island falling to the Christians. That leaves only two characters to discuss. The emir himself is largely my own creation, based upon the simple shape of a historical figure. Abd al-Azīz, however, is *entirely* my own creation. I did toy with using in his role one of the more dangerous and brutal warlords of the time, but none fitted into the timeline the way I needed it, and so I created someone from scratch. He is, however, partially based on a number of characters of the era, including Abu Yahya, who was one of the main contenders for the role and who would become the Almohad governor of Mayūrqa after the emir's demise and until the Christian conquest.

Locations are hard to pin down in Moorish Mallorca. On the Christian reconquest the obliteration of all things Moorish was so thorough that all that now remains to be seen in Palma are:

An arch over a street that had been a gate in the Moorish walls.
Part of a bathhouse that had been used as garden sheds for centuries.
The 'emir's Arch' over the palace's private dock.
Fragments of the Al-Mudaina palace, visible amid later Christian work.
The gatehouse of the Gumāra fortress, which later became a Templar preceptory.

The rest of the island fared little better. Of the house and garden at Al-Fabia, which was indeed the emir's country retreat, little remains from Moorish days other than a coffered ceiling, two inscriptions, and gardens that have been liberally replanted and redesigned by later owners. Al-Bulānsa (Pollença) remains, including its Roman bridge over which our heroes fled, but the town was rebuilt and redesigned after the reconquest when it had, ironically, been gifted to the Templars in its entirety. In my story I needed the bones of the saint to disappear and I had that happen on a mountain road across which I journeyed when researching on the island, and which impressed me with its bleak and rocky glory. Halfway along it is the monastery of Lluc, the island's most sacred site. In my tale the priest carrying the bones ends up here. It seemed a fitting continuity to name him Father Lucas and have him in some way become the progenitor of Lluc. The half-built sanctuary is fictional, but the nod to the wooden statue of the Madonna that would in coming years be the miraculous find that led to the settling of Lluc was self-indulgence. My understanding and portrayal of such ancient Romano-Christian shrines and reliquaries was partially informed by a visit to the ruins of the basilica of Son Pereto near Manacor, and to the museum in that latter town, where a relic-containing altar can be found.

I will also hold up my hands to my exploration of Palma (Madina) under the emirs. I have based my geography and descriptions of the city on maps, a model and description of the city to be found in the museum at Bellver castle, and personal wanderings, but the Al-Mudaina palace I have played with. My depiction of it will probably be far from the truth.

There have been studies of the history of the complex, which is still a summer palace of the Spanish royalty, but the existing form of the place will be far removed from what stood in 1199. My depiction is largely fictional, including a few elements I visited and saw, and partially drawn from the later structures on the spot. I do have to say that exploring the corridors and twisting ways of parts of the palace gave rise to my description of Arnau's journey through the place. For a historical investigation of the Al-Mudaina, along with the Gumāra and other Moorish fortifications and the world in which they sat, I would recommend Goffriller's thesis for the University of Exeter, 'The Castles of Mallorca'. There come points in every novelist's planning and execution where he or she has to weigh the balance between invention and historiography. Sometimes the balance has to tip one way or the other in order to make a book into a story rather than a factual treatise.

And one tiny and interesting aside: I relate the old notion that cats have multiple lives in my final scenes, coming from the mouth of the Lion himself. I looked into this, and the notion that a cat has not nine, but six lives, is an Arabic one.

As you'll have noted from this short explanation, independent Mallorca was not to last long. Abd-allāh ibn Ishāq took control of the *taifa* as the last of the Almoravid line in 1187. He lasted until 1203 when, despite all efforts at defence and diplomacy, and at least one failed Almohad attempt at control, the caliphate finally succeeded in taking control of Mallorca. It remained nominally a *taifa* – the last *taifa* – but its ruler was a governor on behalf of the Almohad caliph and not an emir himself. The last emir died in 1203. The rabid Almohads would rule the islands less than three decades before the Christians came to conquer. I wonder, in light of my research, how many Moors might have considered this a blessing at the time. Later, things would change, of course. In the centuries to come, Christian Spain under rulers like Ferdinand and Isabella was far from a tolerant paradise. In fact there are echoes, in post-conquest Christian attitudes, of the zealotry of the Almohads. But what you have witnessed in this book is the very last flowering of tolerant Muslim rule in Iberia. Without wanting to present spoilers of what is to come for the series, I will explore a little of what followed. The disastrous Christian loss at Alarcos in 1195 set the Christians back many years and almost halted the reconquest. It was appalling. And its loss gave the Almohads the upper hand, putting lands like Aragon in a position where they could not afford to ally with Mallorca. In 1212 there would be another battle (to which I will come in due course). Las Navas de Tolosa is the flip side. It is where fortunes would be reversed. From that day on, amid the myriad Almohad corpses, Moorish Iberia was on the run. It would take almost half a millennium yet, but after 1212, the decline had begun.

Again, I will come to this in future books, though in the meantime there are new challenges for Arnau and his compatriots. Book three – *City of God* – will see our favourite young Templar heading east, to that great sandy crucible where legends were made, on crusade. The future of Rourell hangs in the balance as always, with enemies surrounding it, as unpopular as a religious house could be.

Before I sign off, I am not putting together a separate acknowledgements section for this book, but I feel the distinct need to shout to the heavens my thanks to the excellent نوار لأ ســـليلة (Salilat Lanwar), a brilliant Moroccan teacher whose help honed the Arabic in this book, given my own vast gulf in understanding of the tongue. And also my heartiest thanks to Chris Verwijmeren, whose knowledge of medieval archery is unsurpassed, to the point where rather than correcting me on individual points in a scene, he just helped me rewrite the scene entire. Thirdly a thank you to the fabulous Isabel Picornell Garcia on Alderney, whose fascinating insights into Mallorca and Palma led me to including her ancestor in the book. Finally of course, to Michael Bhaskar at Canelo for some cracking suggestions in the content edit.

These are really the best of people.

Simon Turney, September 2018

Made in the USA
Coppell, TX
02 September 2020

36090092R00184